THE BID

THE BID

JAX

APHRODISIA
KENSINGTON BOOKS
http://www.kensingtonbooks.com

APHRODISIA BOOKS are published by

Kensington Publishing Corp.
119 West 40th Street
New York, NY 10018

All Kensington Titles, Imprints, and Distributed Lines are available at special quantity discounts for bulk purchases for sales promotions, premiums, fund-raising, and educational or institutional use.

Special book excerpts or customized printings can also be created to fit specific needs. For details, write or phone the office of the Kensington special sales manager: Kensington Publishing Corp., 119 West 40th Street, New York, NY 10018, attn: Special Sales Department, Phone: 1-800-221-2647.

Aphrodisia and the A logo Reg. U.S. Pat and TM Off.

ISBN-13: 978-0-7582-4178-8
ISBN-10: 0-7582-4178-X

First Kensington Trade Paperback Printing: October 2010

10   9   8   7   6   5   4   3   2   1

Printed in the United States of America

THE BID

1

"3,000 jewels!"

The offer snapped out above the din of the auction patrons' drinking and conversing, immediately earning an appreciative murmur of response. The bid was high and a large jump from the previous offer. The sense of excitement in the room spiked palpably.

"A fine offer, sir!" Rhou Mas Hin chortled as he paced the length of the stage in broad, showman's strides. The long, hide-wrapped crop in his hand zipped sharply, like the high note of a song, as it cut through the air and pointed to the object up for auction. "But not nearly fine enough for so prized a specimen! A slave of such amazing form and health, such fine lines and coloring! Guaranteed to be clean, disease free, and utterly perfect breeding stock if that's your need. Why, this versatility alone makes this one worth so much more. A house servant, perhaps? Clearly strong enough for fieldwork. Or, as I would much prefer for myself, a trained sexual servant."

"3,100 jewels!"

The counteroffer made Rhou grin slightly. He'd known in-

stantly how valuable this captive would be, and he was prepared to push the reasons why in order to drive up the price.
He also knew his market very, very well. He knew what the in-
habitants of this planet needed, and he knew even more what
they craved.

"A wise woman you are, mistress," he complimented the
bidder. "Have you ever seen this coloring before in your life?
Hair so fair it is white, like the virgin snow of the Yemm mountaintops. How prized and lucky a child born to a noble House
would be considered if they bore this fascinating coloring! Or
think of how envious your peers will be when they come to a
party and are served by such a gorgeous tidbit. They might
trade valuable favors with you if they could coax you into
sending the slave to their rooms after they retire. This alone
will repay whatever cost you extend to acquire such an asset."

"3,200!"

"3,500!"

"I say a good 4,000 jewels ought to do!"

Rhou laid his palm against his chest and bowed to the High
City official making the offer, knowing he'd just broken into a
whole new territory of bidders. Once one of *them* coveted
something, then they all began to covet it. Now it was time for
the hard sell. Rhou stepped closer to his product, touching the
crop to the slave's chin.

"The stasis field keeps this male docile, but I promise you
there is great prowess and power packed into this physique.
Take note that the broad shoulders and chest are thickly muscled, and here we have a lean waist with lovely definition and
no visible fat. Long, powerful legs. Just look at those thigh
muscles! This will allow for speed and flexibility. Undeniably
he is a powerhouse, my good friends. He's been outfitted with
the latest in micro-translators and tagged with a tracker/loca-
tor. All the standards, including pestilent homeworld deterrent.
There are a few scars"—Rhou glossed over quickly—"but they

are merely proof of his fighting skills and his ability to take injury and survive. I guarantee there is no lameness or defect to be found from the visible to the cellular levels." Rhou studied the nude body of his inventory carefully for a moment. He clicked the small remote in his hand and the platform began to turn slowly. The stylized display also ran an enhancing light over the contours of the slave's warrior build, highlighting his fitness. "Now, I make no promises of docility or even the beginnings of being broken in. He is fresh from the wild places, a barbarian at heart. My supplier says he captured this one from Jheru Afrat, the wildlands of a planet called 'Wite.' I don't need to tell you of the lusty and bloodthirsty ways of the planets along the outer rim, now do I? But don't let his wildness put you off. The breaking in of a slave is the very best part, is it not?"

The remark elicited a fury of bids, covetous laughter, and envious excitement from those in the rear of the room who had long ago found the bidding to be out of their means. Rhou hardly paid attention to the amount of the rising bid anyway. All he knew was that it could and *would* go higher. He was best served by focusing on his next selling point. His slave was positioned in stasis with his hands cuffed wide apart at the wrists, and his feet braced and cuffed similarly at the ankles. The added safety measure of a torso restraint had been added for this one because he was known to fight free of his stasis if it wasn't balanced just right. Still, in spite of the extra restraint, the position made for a perfect showcase even when Rhou stopped the revolution of the stand.

"And did I mention . . . ?" He paused for effect as he used his remote to send a stimulant pulsing through the stasis field, causing muscles to bunch and flex, and his commodity's eyes to flicker open. "He has eyes as green-yellow as a bellcat!"

White hair and green-yellow eyes. Rhou didn't blame his audience for their exclamatory reactions. He had hardly believed it himself, not even when he had first seen it with his own eyes. Bids were flying now, coming closer and closer to the stage. The nearer the stage, the wealthier and more powerful the patron. Only the highest-paying patrons, those with special invitations usually extended by the auctioneer himself, would sit in these expensive seats just for the privilege of viewing prime goods close up.

For his last trick, Rhou added an aphrodisiacal stimulant to the mix, allowing it to flood the tissues of the unconscious male. Predictably, the slave's penis began to fatten and fill with his now adrenalized blood, becoming quickly and impressively erect. Rhou took his crop and ran it up along the underside of the thrust-out cock, assuring all attention was on the awesome piece of flesh. Slaves and sex most always went hand in hand in some fashion or another. It wouldn't be a proper sell if he ignored displaying this slave's finest asset.

"Now here," he practically purred, "we see this slave's best aspect." The lurid remark made his enraptured audience titter, men and women alike pretending they weren't thinking their most deviant of thoughts in that instant. "A grand cock and sac. He has been tested for fertility already, and I have the paperwork to prove these testicles are full of ripened seed and capable of manufacturing much, much more over the years . . . if that's your focus. But you must confess, this rod would be worth its weight in jewels even if he were barren! I have rarely seen so mighty a tool on a slave. Thick in circumference . . . long enough to send its seed to root deep in even the most stubborn of wombs. The foreskin was removed some time ago, perhaps in a tribal ritual when he came of age. I would allow the stimulant to continue until he ejaculates, but the slave has proven himself very potent and it might bring him out of stasis."

The disappointed moan of the audience lasted only as long as it took for him to discontinue the stimulant. Then bids flew like birds up to him. Rhou managed them with smooth expertise.

"Damn me, I say 6,000 jewels and be done with it!" the Baron Majum burst out, slamming his fist on his table as he outstripped the last bid by 1,000 jewels. The handsome baron's predilection for gorgeous males had made him the perfect invite to the auction, and Rhou had known he would be unable to resist so tantalizing a treat. It was all over now. Once Majum decided he wanted something, no one dared gainsay him. The Baron might have the beauty of vitality and looks all in his favor, but necessary doses of tolerance and sanity had been sorely neglected.

Still, crazy or not, the man's jewels shone just like they should. Also, the Baron liked to tip Rhou an added surcharge whenever he brought "special" auctions to his attention.

"Excellent taste, Baron," Rhou praised him, watching the avarice that swept over the man's face as he stared up at his prize. "Six thousand jewels going once . . . going twice . . . ?"

"The House Drakoulous bids 2 gems, milord auctioneer."

Rhou almost fell off the edge of the stage. Two gems?! Surely he hadn't heard right! No slave in history had ever sold for 2 gems! But he watched the shock rippling through the other buyers and the red fury exploding over the Baron's face and he knew it was a legitimate bid.

Rhou's eyes quickly sought out the representative of House Drakoulous. In a mélange of classes and a crowd of races, he still stood out in relief against the rest of the room. His height alone was impressive, and there was no way to discount the fact that he was an outstandingly beautiful male. However, it was his coloring, just like the merchandise at Rhou's back, that truly astounded. Only, he was as blond as gold, rather than white. The curtain of his long, golden hair was left to settle freely about his huge shoulders, the length ending just between the blades. A long string of priceless jewel beads had been strung onto a slim rope of the gleaming hair from the top of his left temple all the way to the ends. He stood back casually against a rear wall, not up front where the prestigious House Drakoulous would have been expected to sit, his thick arms crossing a massive chest and a slave band connected around his biceps. The rich garments he wore, the sparkle of exotic embroidery, all lent voice to the wealth of his Master and his House.

Rhou would have gotten a pretty penny for that slave as well, were he up on his block tonight. His fair hair and handsome visage alone would have done. But alas, he was already owned and protected, according to that thick band around his arm, and now he would be coupled with the slave his House was about to purchase. They would make a nearly matched set and would be the envy of every House in the city. Two fine stallions in the Drakoulous stables. At such a price! This would be talked about for ages, and it would solidify Rhou's reputation on this planet as a merchant of the finest slaves for the rest of his life.

"Sold!" Rhou blurted out, not even bothering with the formality of offering for more. Everyone there knew the bid was beyond exorbitant, and even with the High City's notorious House rivalries, no one would counteroffer such a price. Not even the furious Baron, who went apoplectic before dumping over his chair and storming out of the auction house. Rhou quickly waved forward his assistants to prepare the slave for transport as the room broke up into a buzz of excited whispers. The Drakoulous slave pushed his way forward through the crowd, ignoring all questions and wheedling for gossip as the Rhou hurried off the stage to meet him.

"Master Drakoulous will want the promised paperwork proving fertility," he demanded instantly as the Rhou scanned the slave's band and downloaded the payment in full. He was shocked the slave would have access to so much wealth, but it only proved how high he was held in his Master's esteem.

"But of course," Rhou said, reaching into his documents bag and extending an insert chip to the slave. "You have a good eye for flesh, and your Master will be pleased."

"Of course," the blond male murmured as he accepted the gems for the documentation. "Have him delivered to House Drakoulous immediately. He has not been abused in any way, I take it?"

"No!" Rhou sputtered, aghast that a slave would be so bold as to question him in such a way, question his reputation!

"Very well. See that it remains that way. My Master is very particular about the treatment of slaves."

"Yes, yes, so I see. You're kept in a fine style."

Rhou knew he was sneering simply because his pride was bent at this slave's audacity, but there was something that flashed dangerously in the blond's eyes that told him it would be best not to push his luck. Besides, it was always best to stay friendly for the sake of future sales, if he was the one who routinely did the selecting for the House slaves. It was never wise for a merchant to alienate anyone, no matter what their station.

"Tell them at the gate that Najir has sent you and they will accept the delivery if I am not there myself," the slave instructed. "I expect you no later than sunset."

Rhou kept silent and simply bowed his head in acknowledgement. This Najir may be a slave, but he was a powerful slave and it was clear that he knew it. So long as he lived under the protection of the mighty House Drakoulous, he was to be shown respect and all courtesy. The intricate metallic band around his upper arm with its ruby encrusted symbol announced it to all who encountered him.

As Rhou turned away, though, he secretly got pleasure from the idea that House Drakoulous might have taken on more than they were bargaining for. The new slave had been difficult to maintain. He balked against his captivity with a fury, threatening to kill his captors if ever he became free. Luckily, today's technology could prevent that so long as one was careful. But as he had mentioned, in spite of technological superiority, the slave had fought his way out of stasis sleep more than once on the power of sheer force of will.

Anyone who fought like that was going to be quite a challenge to train.

Najir made only a quick stop at the bazaar before hurrying home. He was on foot, as he preferred whenever given the chance, so he lengthened his stride to improve his speed. He shot past all manner of pedestrians that shared the walkways with him—slaves, servants, and other commoners. Nobles and aristocracy out shopping for the high touch merchandise in the merchant shops. Clothing told the tale of their origins and their position on the rungs of society's ladder. Jeweled adornments told a different story. One of wealth. Nobility and wealth did not always go hand in hand, but it was a fact that those with money earned far more respect than those without.

Najir was no fool. He was aware how lucky he was to be from a House with both wealth and class behind its name. When he had been sold into House Drakoulous ten years earlier, he hadn't known a single thing about this society he now called his own. He had come from a completely different planet and a different culture altogether. Now he knew everything about this beautiful but deceptively dangerous planet and he still shuddered to think of all the other fates that might have befallen him. The worst, he believed, was to be bought and used by a man like Baron Majum. Slaves had died under his cruel hand. So had others. Free men and women. The stories of his notorious penchants for violence and humiliation were the stuff of nightmares, especially for those who could be bought and sold at the whim of their owners.

It had given Najir great satisfaction to buy the new slave out from under the Baron. Normally, he didn't like to draw attention to himself, his reasons good and many, but he'd known the instant he had seen the white-haired male on the auction platform that the Master of House Drakoulous must have him. If for no other reason than that he was by far too superbly savage to tolerate any other master in the city. Certainly not the Baron. The price was high, but he wasn't concerned with that. His Master would have paid twice as much and better.

Najir reached the gates of the grand estate of Drakoulous and they were already opening for him, the guards recognizing him on sight. Najir broke into a loping run as he hit the main drive, following it up the hill for a good distance before finally reaching the mansion itself. The pneumatic gates were automatic here, scanning his retinas without his even stopping. Access was instantaneous as he crossed the front gardens and lawn, entering the main doorway after yet another scan. The technology was standard, every home and shop capturing the identity of its patrons automatically.

Najir cut directly through the grand foyer, exchanging a brief greeting or two with staff and servants as he passed them. He hit the main stairwell, taking the sweeping mosaic steps all the way to the top floor where he knew his Master would be hard at work, earning the money that kept the household in such comfort and esteem. He finally came to a halt at the wide double doors leading to the main offices.

"Enter, Najir."

Najir smiled and did exactly that, throwing open both doors and advancing. Hearing his entrance, the Master of House Drakoulous rose from her table and faced him as he dropped to a single knee and bowed his head.

"My Lady."

"Najir," she greeted him, rounding her worktable and reaching out to stroke fingers through his hair. "You are bursting with news, I see."

"Yes, my Lady. I have found what you have needed for so long."

It took her a moment of thought and a lightly crinkled brow as she considered his meaning. Najir couldn't resist a chuckle, and he knew it was the cause of her instant understanding. She drew in a soft, shocked breath and took his face between her hands. Searching his eyes, she demanded, "Tell me! Tell me everything!"

Najir did so quickly, leaving out no detail of the auction and its central commodity. He watched with great pleasure as his description of the new slave made her pupils dilate with excitement. To his surprise, she also dropped to her knees and threw her arms around his neck, hugging him so tightly he couldn't resist wrapping his arms around her supple body and hugging her in equal measure.

"You brilliant boy!" she praised in a whisper against his ear. "And better still that you set Majum back on his ass in the process. He must have been livid!"

"Positively," he assured with a chuckle.

She quickly stood, drawing him up to his feet as well. "That alone makes our new addition worth each and every precious stone. When does he come to me?"

"Any minute now, my Lady."

"Oh, Najir," she whispered fast and hot, her dark eyes dancing with delight. "What a wonderful time this will be! I can tell you are looking forward to it as well. You will enjoy having a companion, I think."

"I enjoy seeing you take great pleasure in things," he countered, reaching out to stroke thick fingers down the length of her throat. She smiled, purring softly in pleasure at the familiar and favorite touch.

"Hold on to that idea," she told him with a promising wink. "I have much to do if I am going to work on our new friend immediately. I wasn't expecting this wonderful fortune and I am completely unprepared!"

"I'll go to the living quarters and see to preparations there," Najir said before she needed to instruct him. He knew what needed to be done and she would easily trust him to do it. "Shall I arrange for anything special?"

"No. Just see that he is situated with great care and left in total stasis until I'm ready. I will prepare the rest myself. Now go. Hurry!" She laughed in delight, clapping her hands together as she turned back to her workstation. Najir paused for only a minute, grinning as he watched her run both hands over her gloriously curved hips, whispering softly to herself of her plans.

Then he hurried off to do her bidding.

2

"That fucking *bitch*!"

The resonant roar was punctuated with a mighty crash as the Baron Wheyn Majum grabbed up the nearest piece of furniture and flung it into a wall clear across the room. The table shattered into splinters and glass, spraying a kickback of debris for several feet.

The Baron's guard, Captain Hyde Sozo, watched his employer pitch his fit with darkly amused eyes, though he knew better than to show any other outward signs of his humor.

"What bitch would that be, sir?" he asked, although he already supposed he had a pretty good idea.

The Baron turned on Sozo in fury, jerking an indicative finger toward the guard. "That highborn whore is going to regret the day she thought to send a slave to spit in my face on her behalf!"

"I assume the auction didn't go well?" Sozo ventured as he hitched a hip onto the corner of a nearby writing table. He swung his leg absently, the hilt of the *frizzon* blade tucked into his boot catching and refracting light again and again.

"She sent that blond, muscled confection of hers to the auction house so she could buy a new toy for herself, while publicly cutting me in the process," Majum growled as he marched angrily to his desk and broke open a smoking blot, taking a deep draw on the hand-rolled combination of herbs and narcotic. "Damn but he was a prize, Hyde! Never have I seen anything like it. Drakoulous's confection comes damn close, but he doesn't have the bellcat eyes this one had. And this new one was bigger. Rougher."

"Impossible to bring to heel?" Sozo queried archly, knowing very well what it was that pleased his boss.

"He would have cut his own throat before obeying me," Majum agreed with dark avarice in his black eyes. "I knew it the minute the auctioneer said he'd fought free of the stasis field more than once."

The captain laughed out in sharp disbelief. "That's impossible. Unless the Rhou has been buying substandard equipment or forgetting to calibrate before using it." Sozo shrugged a shoulder grudgingly. "Still, even then it's an impressive trick."

"So you see why I was willing to pay a pretty price for him," the Baron remarked as he watched the guard captain reach for the decanter resting on the table he was using, filling glasses for them both. "And now *she* has him! Gods, what a matched set they will make if she breaks him alongside Najir. I'd like to punch a fist through her conniving skull." Majum's leather glove creaked as he fisted a hand violently for emphasis.

Sozo caught up both glasses and crossed to hand one to the Baron. "I always wondered how she got that first barbarian under her control. Remember his auction? He'd already killed one of the assistant handlers. You wanted him bad, too."

"Don't think I don't remember that," Majum spat after tossing back half of the drink in a single swallow. "That was the first time she fucked with me over a slave. I should never have let her get away with it. Now she thinks she can do it again? She's going to pay prettily for this, I promise you that."

"All right, barring that opportunity at the moment, I have a question for you," Sozo posed, giving Wheyn a crooked grin. "Rhou has peddled flesh to you for years. He knows damn well what you like and that you will pay those pretty prices he so enjoys. All he has to do is send you an invitation to the auction when he knows the right tidbit has come along."

"You said there was a question," Majum grumbled irritably.

"He's made a great deal of gem off of you over the years, Wheyn. Inviting you guarantees him a sale. He knew you'd come and you'd buy. So why would he extend an invitation to your bitterest enemy?"

The Baron frowned as he pondered that for a moment. "It was a public auction. She needed no invite."

"Fair enough," Sozo agreed, "but Drakoulous hasn't been seen at an auction since she bought her last confection. Now, how do you suppose she knew she would want exactly what was at this auction at this precise time?"

"Because she's a spying little whore who needs to have her head hung from the High City walls!" the Baron hissed. "Gods! What I wouldn't give to get that woman in my dungeons!"

"She isn't your type," Sozo reminded him dryly.

"Oh, she's exactly my type. She can feel pain, can't she? After that, the rest is details."

Captain Sozo watched the Baron's aristocratic features very carefully as the acting Master of House Majum took a seat in his chair, stretching out his athletic frame a moment before kicking up his feet. Sozo had been protector and companion to the Baron for the better part of fifteen summers now, and he knew just about every expression the man had and knew exactly what it meant. Right now, it meant Majum was plotting something. That was the only time he ever looked so smugly thoughtful.

"Careful, Wheyn. The Chamber has sanctioned feuds between the Houses. They still go on, everyone knows that, but you have to make sure anything you do can't be proven back to you or you'll pay the price of exile."

"I know. I have a few ideas nonetheless. And I know you're always willing to help me out."

"That's my job," Sozo chuckled. "Besides, it's fun to watch you work. You are a true artist."

"Thank you, Hyde. It's so good to have one's skills appreciated." The Baron grinned at his companion as he toyed with his glass. "But it's your skills I'm looking forward to utilizing. Tell me, old friend . . . you wouldn't happen to know anyone exploitable in the Drakoulous House, would you?"

"Are we talking exterior guard or internal servant? Any slave will turn on their Master given the right motivation. Commoner servants are always buyable. But her House is notorious for being tough to sway. Loyal bunch of bastards. Luckily, you and I both know no amount of loyalty is foolproof." Hyde's expression turned deeply thoughtful. "Give me a couple of days. I'll find some cracks and see where we can stick a wedge. What do you have in mind?"

"Just find me that wedge and we'll go from there."

Vejhon tried to draw open his eyes for the billionth time, and to his shock they actually began to obey the command. Feeling heavy, as though he were working against an intense gravitational force, he blinked open his eyes and tried to focus on anything he could. At the same time, he attempted to assess himself for any new damage or any further undesirable circumstances.

It was easy enough to remember the situation he'd found

himself living in ever since he had been drugged, taken captive, and spirited away from his home planet so many months ago. Back before all of this, he'd been Vejhon Mach; Colonel Mach of the esteemed Valiant Forces, to all those who knew anything about the war ravaging his homeworld of Wite. The Valiants were the glory of Wite's global armed forces. They were the lead victors in some of the most decisive battles fought against the Creet alien invasion. Vejhon was a warrior born and bred, a notorious hero and leader who had very few equals in both his prowess and the cunning of command needed to outsmart the unwelcome Creet bastards.

He had become a target because of it.

It would've been better had the motherless Creet simply assassinated him, but he supposed that was the point. The Creet knew the fate they'd consigned him to would cause him far more suffering; payback for all the Creet lives he'd taken and destroyed with such relish as a patriot of Wite, while at the same time robbing his homeworld of a much needed commander.

He had been on his way home, actually, for the first time in months, when he'd been ambushed. He took pride in the fact that despite being pumped full of tranquilizing narcotics, he hadn't gone down easily. He had fought his attackers hard, breaking a few necks in the process, searing faces and descriptors into his memory for later use when he would exact his revenge for this atrocity against him.

When he'd awakened in a holding cell aboard the first in a series of cargo transports, to say he went a little bit crazy was an understatement. He had known the minute he'd woken up in that cell, staring down at a long line of cells filled with other captives, exactly what was happening. The slave trade in other quadrants of the galaxy was lucrative and rampant, enough so that kidnappings and pirating were a realistic fear for anyone traveling the spaceways. The idea that he, the colonel of the

Valiants, was now reduced to being enslaved and on his way to be sold in some distant market, was horrifying and absolutely untenable.

He had fought it every step of the way.

So much so that they had been forcing him into stasis now for long periods of time to keep him tame. During these times he was aware of very little and recalled almost nothing, but he still fought for consciousness at the very least. It was not in his nature to relinquish control of himself, and anyone who thought to teach him otherwise was in for a damn nasty surprise.

But Vejhon wasn't all brawn and bluster, so he was extremely cautious as he came awake slowly this time. He felt as though he had been sleeping for ages, the hangover effect from being in stasis longer than recommended. When he'd last been brought awake, he'd been in yet another cell and on display for yet another trader. The trader had demanded consciousness as proof of Vejhon's senses being fully intact. The flesh peddler had almost lost a limb when he had tried to touch the merchandise and the merchandise had taken a good gnash at his arm.

But who knew how long ago that had been, and how many trades had taken place since then? Fury broiled up beneath Vejhon's skin, pumping adrenaline into his rousing systems and speeding up the waking process. He knew full well the things that could be done to him while in stasis, against his will and desire and he none the wiser for it. It sickened him to think of all the possibilities, and it fueled his outrage as he opened his eyes to view his latest prison.

It was so opposite of what he had expected, Vejhon began to doubt he was even awake. After months being trapped in small seven-by-seven-by-seven cubicles, stark but for the warped reflections of himself in the metal plating, the vast expanse of a well-appointed and outrageously large room was completely opposite in scale. Wary of the luxurious trappings, his belly tightening as his mind began to deduce the meaning of the change, Vejhon slowly took in the room, its obvious exits, and anything he could use as a potential weapon, should he find opportunity to escape.

The central piece of furniture in the cell—and it was a cell, he realized, as he flexed his hands and wrists in the manacles binding him tightly to the wall—was an enormous bed, covered in rich, dark furs that looked lustrous and soft even from his distance. The bed was at least nine feet long and twice as wide, laden with a multitude of colorful and unusual looking pillows. Banners of colored fabric streamed down casually from the ceiling, wrapping softly around the frame in various places.

Besides the bed there were long, cushioned sofas, lounges, and chairs all arranged in a cozy conversation corner. A pair of cushioned tables were set up a short distance from there, and behind them was a bathing area with a very large oval tub set down into the stone of the floor with steps leading into it. Otherwise, a few paintings and rugs were the only additions to the delicate moss green stone that lined both the walls and the floor of the entire room. The ceiling was a mosaic of a million small tiles placed perfectly together to create a swirling, graceful design that seemed to meander aimlessly and have absolute purpose all at the same time.

It was a room of wealth and comfort, something that translated no matter what culture or planet he was going to find himself in. It stood to reason that he had just become the latest toy in someone's personal playroom. Someone who could afford to buy rare and expensive flesh. And considering the time it had taken for him to travel to this destination, he'd be safe in assuming he was a rare creature indeed to these people.

Vejhon looked down at his own body, grimacing at his nudity. He was far from surprised. Slaves, he had been told, were not allowed clothing until their master bought some for them. Since he had no master as yet, he would remain nude. It was meant to be devaluing, he supposed, but it didn't quite work that way for him. He'd worn better and he'd worn worse than his own skin before, and he had no problem at all with being naked. What he did have a problem with was this interminable confinement. He was lashed so securely to the wall, spread-eagle and perfectly flush to it, that he had no range of motion except with his head. His muscles and joints were stiff and more than a little sore, but he was also pleased to see that the impulse programs in the stasis fields had been put to use, keeping him at close to his usual bulk in muscle. Still, it was a lazy reward and did nothing to keep his flexibility and reflexes in practice.

He quickly grew bored and started looking around the room again, searching for advantages in the details. This time he took better note of the immediate area around himself. There was a closet of some kind. And a strange stand shaped from metal that bore many heavy hooks. Odd devices of all shapes and sizes hung from these hooks. Some were made of metal, others of some kind of hide. Still others were studded with valuable gemstones and glittered under the recessed lighting that ran along all the edges of the room. Just looking at the strange paraphernalia made his entire body go tense, his imagination filling in the blanks with dread and disgust.

It was easy to surmise what he had been bought for. All he had to do was look at the bed. A gripping anger clutched at his chest as though it would suffocate him. It would be bad enough if some female alien came strutting in there thinking she was going to own him and tame him, but he could think of a worse option yet. If he'd been bought by a male of some species with homosexual tendencies, Vejhon would either be free or dead by nightfall. Perhaps so in both scenarios. But if a male thought to touch him, to make use of him in such a way, blood would fly before Vejhon would ever allow it.

His keen hearing picked up the approach of footsteps from

somewhere outside of the room, but it wasn't until then that he realized that while there were many windows, there were no obvious doors. Even the closet was more of a wardrobe, a large piece of furniture exclusive of the walls around it. But the footsteps gave him an idea of which direction to pay attention to. He tensed tighter and tighter, every muscle in his body winding up in preparation for . . . anything.

When the wall to his left gave off a soft pneumatic hiss, drew back an inch, and then slid open about four feet to the right, it revealed something a little different than he had been expecting, but no less contemptible.

A couple. One a male, a large fair-haired man built like a soldier . . . built like Vejhon himself. His skin was a smooth tan, dark enough to indicate a great deal of time spent out-of-doors, the tone just uneven enough to show that it wasn't a racial coloration. His stride was confident, his eyes immediately fixing on Vejhon in watch of whatever potential threat he might pose. It was a look Vejhon was quite familiar with, having trained it into soldier after soldier over time. He couldn't help but be a little impressed by that wariness. After all, here he was tethered hand and foot to a stone wall, naked and weaponless, where most people would dismiss him as non-threatening. But he could see quite clearly that this other warrior was taking nothing for granted and he wasn't about to trust his captive in the slightest.

As for the woman . . .

She closed the door with a brisk wave of a hand over a hidden sensor and crossed over to him without any hesitation or fear. She made a subtle gesture and her giant companion stopped where he was, taking a watchful stance as she moved to stand before Vejhon at a minimum of arm's length. Had his hands been free, he could have reached out and grabbed her around her delicate little neck.

After months of having strangers assess his flesh in a careless and dismissive manner, it was actually very noticeable a difference when he realized she looked nowhere but into his eyes. She was just a few inches shy of about six feet tall, he guessed, but since he was nearly seven feet tall himself it still made her seem small to him. She wore an arresting crimson-colored gown that was very close to being sheer as it clung to a noticeably generous shape. She was slender without being too slim, the fabric of her dress swaddling round hips and ass, and high, proud breasts that would easily fill a large man's hands.

Perhaps he assessed her body first because of a subconscious need to bring her down to his level of exposure, but it didn't take him long to become intrigued by the other things about her that were so markedly different. First, there was the long cord of her hair. It came over her shoulder and was banded with gemmed clasps once every six inches or so for nearly the entire length of her height. It was also the most amazingly pure black he had ever seen. Like a sleek Surrey eel, it caught light and gleamed, equal to the adornments that confined its length. The women of Vejhon's homeworld, just like the men, were all fair. Blond to white, at most red to the lightest of browns. He had never seen a woman with black hair before.

Nor had he ever seen one with skin the color of the noonday sky. Her coloring was shades of sky and powder blue, a fascinating fairness of an entirely different sort. Her complexion was flawless, even luminescent if he had to give a descriptor, but it was most definitely blue. Soft, delicate shades that only darkened around the edges of her clothing, leading him to think her racial coloring deepened as it flowed over her breasts and other private areas. Her lips were dark, a mix between a deep violet and a midnight red, and he suspected a match to the large, dark nipples tipping her breasts, which he could see against the fabric of her dress.

Her eyes, which had never once moved from his as he had made his assessment of her, were dark and sultry, a blend between midnight blue and black. They were like the night sky on his homeworld. They were set in the face of a beautiful woman, framed by thick, boot-black lashes and delicate arching brows. Her cheekbones were an elegant, aristocratic sweep beneath otherwise soft curves of a lush and pretty face. She looked young, and had he been another type of man he might have believed her air of innocence, but he had lived through too much war to ever assume anyone was capable of innocence.

He flicked one more assessing glance over to the male standing guard behind her. The two were clearly not of the same race, probably not even similar species. Not that such couplings were unusual, what with space open to anyone and everyone who could afford to travel it, but it wasn't lost on him that the other male could easily have come from his own homeworld.

Vejhon had too many questions and despised being in a position that afforded him little leverage in demanding answers. The realization was burning furiously in his eyes as he crashed gazes with the woman he could only assume considered herself his owner. The very idea made his hands curl into defiant fists, instigating a step forward from her wary and watchful bodyguard behind her. Again, a single soft gesture with her hand brought him to a halt. She hadn't even turned to look at him, nor had she spoken a word. Her bodyguard simply resumed his watchful stance, the muscles in his body tensed tightly as he anticipated any possible trouble. The subtle communication made it very clear to Vejhon who was the dominant between them.

He suddenly wanted to laugh in her face. If she thought that she could get him to behave like a well-trained pet, like she had with this other male, she was going to be sorely surprised.

"Welcome to your new home," she said at last, her voice a low, sultry rasp that caught him by surprise. It made her speech feel intimate and decadent; and while it suited the courtesan's body she boasted, it was out of place coming from the backdrop of her angelic countenance. "I can only imagine what you are thinking and feeling after what was, no doubt, a long ordeal. I was promised you were not abused, and I hope that is the truth."

"This entire atrocity has been an abuse, lady," he snapped irritably.

" 'My Lady,' " she corrected him gently. "I know there is much for you to adjust to in the coming days, but it is important that you address me with respect. A slave can be put to death if he is observed being disrespectful of nobility, and whatever you may be feeling now, you do not strike me as the sort of man who would relish a death of that type of shame."

Vejhon had been ready to shoot back one of his best barracks retorts, but now he hesitated. There was logic to her request. Logic that centered on the benefit to his life and safety, rather than her desire to have him kowtow to her. He narrowed his eyes on her, wondering if he was being artfully played.

"I am no slave," he gritted out between tight teeth.

"Your present circumstances say otherwise," she noted. "But I realize that you were slave to no one before you were brought to this part of the galaxy. You were, no doubt, a powerful and independent man where you come from." She took a single step closer to him, bringing her close enough to elicit a sharply indrawn breath from her guardian. "However, on a planet full of people who look exactly like me, you will be known as nothing but a slave. You will stand out in every crowd, you will be coveted, and you will no doubt be captured or killed if you try to travel this world without the protection of the House that owns you."

"No one owns me," he hissed, outrage making him jerk at his manacles. To her credit, the serene beauty did not even flinch.

"Perhaps not your spirit," she acquiesced softly, "but so long as you are on this world, I own you. Your body is my property and your fate is mine for the choosing. Believe me when I tell you, your circumstances could have been far more horrific than even your worst imaginings, and very almost were. One day, you will realize you owe Najir a great debt of thanks."

Vejhon looked back at the big blond male when she nodded toward him and mentioned his name. Najir. He looked back to his "owner" and abruptly wondered if she had a name or if she would insist on "my Lady" and nothing else.

She took a couple of steps back, her movement an effortless glide over the smooth stone. Now she began to assess and contemplate him as a whole, her blue-black eyes making it easy to follow where she was studying him from one moment to the next. Vejhon was overcome by a mixture of confusing emotions as her gaze moved liked a warm, physical touch over his skin. Impotent fury, total bafflement, and now an unexpected response of pride and stimulation as he watched the contented pleasure that altered her expression. She was vastly satisfied with his body, according to that look, and for some reason he was glad of it. So much so that, as her eyes stroked toward his groin, his cock began to respond to her inspection. Vejhon cursed himself for the hot-blooded reaction, not understanding how he could betray himself by growing hard before someone who had *bought* him. He most certainly was not going to perform for this woman like the good little slave boy behind her. Gods only knew what all of Najir's duties entailed. He probably fucked her pretty brains out twice daily, getting hard on command just as he had been trained to do.

Like a pet. Sit. Stay. Fuck.

His disgust and anger at the thought helped him get his body back under his control. For the moment. She was looking dead into his eyes again now and he knew she was fully aware of his momentary response. After all, he was chained naked to the damn wall; it was pretty hard to hide. What he didn't understand is why she didn't gloat or take obvious pleasure in the small victory over him. This was a war. They were going to be battling one another for some time to come, didn't she see that?

"Very well," she said at last. "Let's start with the basics. What is your name?"

"Colonel Vejhon Mach, commander of the Valiant Forces in the army of Wite."

"Here you are only Vejhon," she said, actually sounding regretful. "Perhaps Jhon for short, if you like it."

"Why do you bother asking me my opinion on things after you remind me that I have no choice to begin with!" Vejhon rattled his bonds, shuddering with outrage and straining toward his captor as though force of will alone would free him. "You'll call me what you want to call me and you won't give a damn what I think of it!"

Her dark eyes watched him, looking almost a little sad, until suddenly she moved forward and came right up to him. She reached out, her hands graceful and elegantly manicured, her slightly pointed nails painted to match her gown. Vejhon was completely taken off guard, not only that she went to touch him in spite of his rage, but because her light blue skin gave him the false illusion that she would be cold to the touch.

Instead, as her fingertips skimmed his temples and her palms moved to cup his face, he found her to be incredibly warm. She smelled of a rich perfume, something probably blended solely for her that enhanced both scent and pheromones. It reminded him of the aromas of chocolate and sex, a deadly sweet combination both sultry and inviting.

She moved close, her body near enough to radiate warmth against him. She angled his head to assure he was looking down into her eyes. "Things"—she breathed softly against him—"are not always what we assume. I would think as a trained warrior you would know this." He felt her thumb stroke over his lower lip, the caress so oddly disturbing to him in its intimacy. She felt as though she were radiating into him, like a sun he must soak in for warmth and life. His rage, so pure and powerful only a moment ago, dissipated like an out-washing tide.

"Vejhon, I'm sorry your life was taken from you. I regret so deeply what you have lost in the process of ending up here. However, if you can bring yourself to accept that you can have a new life here with us, I promise you it will be just as fulfilling if not more so than that which you have left behind."

"If you regret it so badly," he countered roughly, "then why not simply send me back? Why do you do this? You perpetuate this misery when you buy flesh off of peddlers like some bauble or a new dress! You make the market that encourages them to steal people from their worlds and lives! From their families!"

"I did not make this market, Jhon, and even if I never bought another slave, it would not impact a trade spanning thousands of cultures on dozens of worlds."

"One less culture on one less world can be a beginning to an end," he rasped in frustration.

"Oh, I have no doubt of that," she agreed. "But we are discussing one slave, in one household, in one room at the moment. When you were taken from your world, your captors injected you with a pestilent deterrent. A dormant genetic virus that, once it is released, cannot be recalled. This virus will only become active when brought into contact with something common and uniquely indigenous to *your* homeworld. If you ever step foot on your planet again, you will die within hours of doing so. So when I say you cannot go back, I am not speaking with my personal gain in mind."

He had known this. He had been told this again and again, from captor to captor, as they encouraged him to give up his fight to be free and return to the world he loved and defended. But he had never believed them.

He believed *her*.

It struck him like a physical blow, sucking all the oxygen out of his body.

"It is a cruel practice, as is a great deal of what slave traders do to others like you. I do not deny that." Vejhon felt her stroking him along his temples, the caress soothing the shock from his system. She leaned in and gently touched her mouth to his, kissing him softly. It was completely non-sexual, like a sister or a mother might do to comfort a loved one. It only made his head ring with more confusion, even though it eased him physically. "I will make you this promise, Vejhon," she murmured. "If you invest your trust in me, I will help you to become a part of your new world. I will help you replace what you have lost as best I am able."

"I have lost my freedom, my Lady," he growled, stressing the title with contempt. "Will you replace that?"

"As best as I am able," she agreed with a nod, amazing him with the sincerity she managed to put behind the vague remark.

"How stupid do you think I am?" he bit out, jerking his head out of her hands since it was the only thing he was truly free enough to do. "Your approach is sweet as sugar, but your promises are as bitter and incomplete as a wine turned to vinegar."

She stepped away from him the instant he began to balk against her touch, and Vejhon tried not to miss the warmth of her closeness to his bare skin. The ambient temperature of the room kept him from being chilled, but her absence made him want to shiver nonetheless. Yet another reaction he couldn't understand any more than he could control it.

"Very well," she said with resignation and a sigh. "We shall have to come about this by a more difficult route."

"Lady, if you thought this was going to be easy, then you aren't near as smart as I thought you were."

The insult did not affect her, but it certainly didn't sit well with her boy toy behind her. The other slave was clearly so inured and enamored of his mistress that he took offense whenever she was insulted and threatened. How had she taken a man of such obvious power and managed to mold him into this disgusting display of obedient loyalty? Vejhon couldn't escape the tendril of dread working through him that told him that if he didn't entrench himself against this woman with every last cell of resistance and strength in his body, looking at Najir was as good as looking at himself in the future.

"Najir, you are dismissed."

3

The directive was soft spoken and almost matter of fact. Yet, Vejhon watched with surprise as Najir hesitated to obey his mistress as instantly as he had been doing up until then. Clearly he feared for her safety and disliked the idea of leaving her alone with a barbarian warrior who insulted her, with one who would not care anything about her health or safety should the opportunity to escape arise.

"Najir?"

A simple name spoken, but the layers of tone and intent within it radiated from the single word. It was a scold and a reassurance all at once. There was even a hint of secrets that flashed between them as she exchanged a long look with him. Finally, he bowed his head in acquiescence and obeyed his Master. He left the room, sealing the door in his wake.

"You haven't asked me who I am," she noted as she walked a short distance away and opened a small chest made of wood standing close to the hooks and their strange occupants. As she opened the chest it displayed trays of what looked like jewels and jewelry. The contents of that box could buy him passage and freedom anywhere a dozen times over. "Not my name, or where you are, or anything about the woman who owns you."

"The only thing I'm interested in is what your neck will sound like when I snap it like a twig."

She ignored him. "My name is Hanna Drakoulous, Master of House of Drakoulous, one of the most powerful Houses in the political structure of this society. To belong to this House," she pointed out, "is to be protected by a great and powerful name."

"Owned, sweetheart," he bit back caustically. "Call it what it is. 'To be owned by this House.' Don't think for a minute I'm going to let you whitewash that fact from my mind with euphemisms and other delicately put bullshit."

"I did nothing of the kind. Free or *owned*, those who live here *belong* here," she said with conviction. "This House is a covenant, Vejhon Mach. One that cannot be broken. One that, once you enter it, you will not want to abandon. You stand on the threshold of a new life. All you need to do is accept it, and it will be yours."

She withdrew something from the jeweled collection and made her way back to him. He stiffened instinctively at her approach. This time she did smile at the reaction, the expression just a little too wicked for Vejhon's peace of mind. He let his eyes dart to her hands and the thing that she carried. It was a thick band of platinum or white gold, he couldn't immediately tell which, and it had the figure of some kind of catlike creature carved into it. Set in the creature's eyes were two lone gemstones, amethysts of a deep and unusual violet . . . or a stone very much like them. Jewels and precious metals were the only common currency between the worlds that were part of the spaceways, but no two planets bore all of the same type, making the value of the gems rise and fall between locations. There were a few universals, though, something that could be found most anywhere, and those maintained a steady value. The purple gems in the band appeared rare enough to hold great worth.

She stopped near his left side and reached out to touch his clenched biceps. Her fingers gently ran over the veins and contours of his arm until she reached the manacle at his wrist. Vejhon ought to have protested violently, rattling his bonds with all of his strength and anger, but he knew it was a waste of energy at this point and decided to save it for a more effective opportunity. This woman was going to find her lush backside on the shit side of his list right along with all the others who had brought him to this point. He would satisfy himself with that knowledge and his surety in his ability to eventually escape this nightmare.

She snapped open the band, making him realize it was hinged so cleverly he hadn't even noticed the utilitarian accent. Reaching for his arm again, she moved to snap the band in place.

"If you put that thing on me, I swear to all the gods I will rip your fucking head off."

The threat didn't even make her hesitate.

"No, you will not," she answered matter-of-factly. "In fact, once this band is in place, you will never be able to hurt me without hurting yourself. It is a safety measure, so you will forgive me if I find it wise to use it, since you take such comfort in threats and in your own wrath."

She snapped the band on easily, Vejhon helpless to do anything but growl at her with ferocity. Then she pressed both of the gems simultaneously and he felt a series of sharp, needlelike stings zipping into his skin around the entire circumference of the band.

"Gods! You bitch! What did you do?!" he roared, his voice echoing with resonance off of the stone walls.

"I told you. It is to assure that you cannot cause me harm. It does not subvert your will in any other way," she reassured him. "You can be as angry and violent as you like, so long as you don't combine it with laying hands on me with the intent to hurt me."

"I can't *touch* you, period! You have me chained to the wall like an animal! What more reassurance can you possibly need? Are you truly that afraid of me that you need to manipulate an already helpless man?"

"Actually, I am not afraid of you at all, Jhon."

He would have laughed in her face at that obvious lie, only her eyes were so serene and seemed so believably honest. She gave off no clue that she harbored any fear of him, and that was simply something he wasn't used to. Everyone feared him. His enemies, his troops—every one of those bastards who had traded him from ship to ship until they had brought him to this end. Even though he'd been caged and bound, he had seen the fear behind the greedy excitement in their eyes. He had seen how they had stood back from the force fields separating him from them even though there was no way he could possibly approach.

But she did not fear him.

Hanna reached to touch him again, this time laying a gentle hand against his chest.

"I am going to give you an opportunity, Jhon, to appreciate the difference between what you will find in this House and what you would have found in another. Unfortunately, this means I must play both roles, so that you may come to this understanding. But we will keep this between only you and me if you allow it. If you give me too much trouble, then I will have to include Najir, and I wish to save you that humiliation. Do you understand?"

Hanna watched his jaw tighten until he had developed a furious tic in the muscle of his cheek. He was guaranteed to hate this. To hate her. At least at first. But it couldn't be helped. He had been so gloriously powerful in his former life, and though he had been in captivity for months, he still clung to that former idea of himself. Hanna would happily cultivate his warrior half in the future, but first he must come to accept the truth of his situation.

And while she disliked the idea of bludgeoning his proudly stubborn will, the end to her means made her heart race with excited anticipation. He was everything she needed, everything Najir had promised her he would be. She stood back to look him over once again, her amazed eyes still trying to accept the fabulous concept of the perfect treasure that he was. Najir was going to be vastly rewarded for this. Besides the perfection of his white platinum hair and those cat-green eyes, Vejhon was a masterpiece of flesh and muscle. His skin was tanned dark, especially above his waistline, no doubt because he had spent time working his body while shirtless in the sun of his homeworld. She could feel the strength in him radiating in great waves, thrumming into her like a sonic boom whenever his fury spiked. His energy was a flawless symphony, such utter perfection. Strength, stamina, will . . . and gorgeous looks besides.

Oh yes. He was perfect.

But he was defiant and wild as well, his stubbornness making him dense to the dangers around him in his new life. He saw her as a threat just because he felt his pride was at stake? There were worse dangers in this place and more precious commodities than pride that needed protecting.

"Jhon, do you know what most women of this world buy a slave like you for?"

"Clearly whatever you damn well please," he snapped.

"That's true. However, you are special. You see"—she gave him a suggestive little smile as her fingers ran down over the well-defined muscles of his chest, heading to the rocklike hills of his taut stomach—"when you were up for bid on that auction stand, your best assets were put on display so everyone would be very certain of your value." Hanna lightly scraped her nails past his navel, slowly stroking her way toward his pubic region. She didn't need to look to know he was stimulated despite his will. His brief reaction to her earlier had notified her that he was attracted to her, regardless of his desire to be otherwise. But that wasn't the way she wanted to manipulate him. It wasn't the point she wanted to make.

She drew back from him and returned to her chest of jeweled objects. She withdrew the ring she was looking for and held it up for him to see as she returned.

"Female Masters of High Houses wear these everywhere. They never go anywhere without them." She slid the ring with its gemstone of clear crystal facets onto her right ring finger. She turned the gem inward, so it was in line with her palm, and reached to touch her fingertips to his chest. "You were in stasis at the time, so I am going to show you what you were so blissfully unaware of, Vejhon, during that common little auction."

She pressed her palm against him and instantly the sting of injection burned through his muscles. This time he did roar with fury, bucking against his restraints, trying to force her touch away from him. All she did was lean back slightly, keeping away from his gnashing teeth. Then she simply stood back and watched as the stimulant flooded his system.

Vejhon felt the sudden upsurge of adrenaline in his blood almost instantly, the feel of it very familiar to him as a warrior used to seeking its highs. He thought about using it to truly test the strength of his metal bonds, but he'd already injured himself, the tight manacles cutting up his skin and now chafing it raw whenever he moved. It was his own fault. He knew better than to fight metal, but she had pushed him too far beyond reason.

Then, an abrupt heated sensation began to rush through his blood, fluttering along his skin like fast-flying birds skimming insects off of water. The heat quickly became a burn and he became very aware of where that burn was headed. It scorched down his body, down every sensitive nerve in his tissues until it felt like his entire pelvis was in an overdrive of sensation. He watched with a combination of horror and dismay as his penis began to flood with pulsing blood, the sensation perpetuating itself like the stroke of an artful hand as he grew more fully erect. There was nothing he could do. His body, in this respect, was completely out of his control. No thoughts, no amount of anger or disgusting imagery he tried to conjure in his mind could change what was happening to him.

In no time at all he was heavily erect, his cock so hard it was fully parallel to the floor and aching with the fierce throb of his stimulant-laden blood. Humiliated and horrified by the drug she had administered, Vejhon wished an agonizing death on her with his savage eyes and his poisonous thoughts. Again, she seemed unaffected by his glare, but neither was she gloating over her triumphant puppeteering of his sex.

Hanna stepped forward in a way that forced him to focus fully on her eyes. It was close enough that Jhon felt the fabric of her dress against the head of his distended phallus, the rubbing sensation of its silken texture sending feedback up along the shaft in a screaming message of pleasure. Vejhon tried to draw in air to breathe, but all commands to his brain fried under the massive drug-heightened wave of bliss.

"Imagine yourself before a crowd of avaricious women *and men*," she made certain to remind him, "and your handler is now going to prove how excellent a prospect you are for being put to stud on a planet where a superior percentage of the populace is infertile. He injects you with stimulants to display your fine equipment, and in your case, to show how easily the stim works on you even while in stasis." Now she reached between them and slowly touched her soft fingertips to the sensitive skin and nerves along the length of his shaft. A sensation of pure electrocution bolted along every sensory pathway in his body, making him seize with the shocking pleasure, tense muscles distending even farther under the force he used to try and control his reaction.

As though she was stroking a precious thing, she ran her fingers up and down the length of his swollen rod, locking him into being buffeted by sensations too outstanding to be real. She continued her narration. " 'Look, ladies and gentlemen,' he says, 'at the fine, thick cock I offer you. Hours of fun for yourself as a private concubine. Certainly fit to fill a room in your brothel where he will be in high demand as a whore. And for those who farm out studs, here is a tool ready to breed. No need to tame him if he proves too contrary; merely lash him down and let the stim do the work.'

" 'Of course,' " she continued relentlessly, " 'he could make a wonderful house slave, where he could service any guests you invite to stay, both in and out of bed, once you have grown bored with him for yourself.' " Hanna knew how sensitive he had to be right then, and she took advantage of it by closing her fist slowly around him. She found herself distracted for an instant as she realized he was so thick that even her long fingers could not wrap fully closed around him. The realization made her a little bit breathless, and she had to force herself back on task. "Perhaps he had a few potential buyers come up to test the feel of the merchandise," she speculated. "They do that often. Let them touch, stroke . . . feel for themselves the hardness and sensitivity of their prospective toy."

Vejhon was rasping for breath in a combination of fury, the hyper-stimulation of drugs, and her obliterating touch. Her stroke felt like a magical relief and torture all at once against his bursting flesh. *Blood of the gods be damned*, he had played with sexual stims before . . . what man hadn't? But never with a reaction so frenetic as what he felt under Hanna's touch. Warm and soft, but sure and firm in a manner that did everything to make a conflagration out of already burning nerves. He hadn't rushed to the crest of needing to orgasm so quickly in all of his life, not even when he'd been a hypersexed youth first trying to figure it all out.

It had to be the stim, he argued with himself, shaking sweat out of his eyes, the ends of his hair flicking around the crown of his head. It was stronger than those of his world. That had to be why. There was no way in hell otherwise that he would so ferociously crave what she was giving him. Yet, even as he blamed the drugs, a sinister whisper in his subconscious was trying to make him admit there was more to it than that.

"Some will even drop to their knees and take a taste of you," she whispered in a vivid purr. She licked her dark lips absently as she rubbed her thumb over the purpled head of his erection. She probably didn't even realize she'd done it, but watching the contrast of her blush-pink tongue licking wetly over deep violet red was like touching a flame to fumes for Vejhon. It became horrifyingly easy for him to imagine her mouth opening over his cock and the stroke of her tongue as she swallowed him down. All the while, in reality, she was flicking her thumb over him, swirling it in a deadly imitation of that very act, until he felt the hard twinge of readiness tightening his balls.

He swore nastily in her face, cursing her and his own fate. His own weakness. Still, she stroked him down his length and up again, her fingers milking pre-cum from him and slicking up the stroke she handled him with until he began to vibrate with the tremors of nerves screaming for release.

"Your seller no doubt let you be toyed with for some time to prove endurance. And then, he proudly announces that you are so fertile your ejaculate could populate a planet! Right before he injects you a second time."

Her artful hand instantly released his penis as the opposite palm slapped against his chest and, as promised, her ring spurred another injection into his bloodstream. "Now," she breathed, "your body is overwhelmed with the aphrodisiac you've been fed. It disconnects your mind from your body, re-moving all of your will from the equation, overriding any resis-tance. There is nothing you can do but feel. Feel the burning of your body, the pump of blood into your already engorged cock." She stepped aside, making certain she did not touch him anymore. "No one has to touch you. No stroke is necessary. Nothing can stop the release that is boiling up out of your con-trol."

But he was clearly going to try his best, Hanna noted. His entire body was coated in sweat, a shuddering of resistance trembling through every flexed muscle he could force under his command. His efforts truly were futile, but she had known he would fight. She wanted him to fight with everything he had. This way, he would really know what might have awaited him had Najir not attended that sale.

"As you are nothing but a slave, you could be laid out and tethered just as you are now," she mused, allowing her rousing sexuality to filter strongly into her voice now. It was the pure beauty of the man before her and the outstanding ferocity he used to fight that stirred her, though, not his helplessness and defeat. "In your present state a woman could climb on top of you and ride you until she is ready for the climax she is manip-ulating from you. Or better yet, if a man had liked you . . ." She trailed off meaningfully, her stare hard on him as he shot dag-gers through her heart from his eyes. The arteries on his thick neck were distended with effort, and anticipatory fluid dripped down the length of his glistening phallus. "Or perhaps you pre-fer men anyway," she said with a shrug of a shoulder, even though she knew full well it was women who aroused him. He had looked at her body enough times and in enough ways since she entered the room to assure her of that. "Of course, in that case a man might ride you, or you might find yourself on your hands and knees preparing to—"

"Shut up, you sick bitch!"

He roared the insulting command just as his body burst the confines of his control. Orgasm ripped through him like razor wire, tearing him apart from pride to penis. He came so hard that his semen jetted across the floor several feet, long viscous streams at first and then harsh spitting globs as his glands tried to obey the irrational demands of the stimulant he'd been fed. Vejhon's vocal outrage as he climaxed growled off the high ceilings of the room, and then came the inevitable low groans of agonizing pain as his cock tried to spit out fluids that were no longer available. It stood out from his body, still rock hard and jerking torturously, remnants of cum dripping from the open slit at the head.

Had he not been tied hand and foot, he would have fallen to his knees by now. None could stand up under this kind of painful bodily betrayal. Even Hanna could not remain stoic, giving herself away by biting her lip and curling her brows in sympathy. When it finally ended for him, he gasped hard for breath, pulling his head up and catching her in the compassionate expression for a second before she recovered herself. He was bleeding at every single manacle point, a testament to how he'd fought against himself. His failure, she knew, was utter humiliation for a man of his type.

It had been the same for Najir. He had been the first rare bird she had found captured, and now she had another. Najir had found another. He had looked at this man and seen himself all those years ago. Seen him as Hanna had seen Najir the day he had been auctioned off like a prized thoroughbred pet. What she had described to Jhon had been what she had seen Najir suffer through that day. Hand after hand touching and stroking him, mouth after mouth sucking at him and licking him. Some seeing how far they dared to go in public. Only, Najir had not been in stasis. He had been awake and aware as the stimulant and a dozen men and women buyers raped him of his will and control. Then the flesh peddler had injected the second stimulant and the crowd had delighted in the ferocious explosion of his ejaculation and his outcry of anger that accompanied it. Hanna knew her neighbors, her fellow nobles, and she knew that some of them thrived on that kind of pain from others . . . that terrible kind of suffering.

She was not one of them.

4

Najir watched through the transparent wall as Hanna quietly went about dampening a towel and cleaning the floor herself. He knew she would never allow a servant to come into that room to witness any part of what she was being forced to do. Just as he knew she wouldn't touch Jhon just then, even to clean his body or wounds, because the stimulant that had ravaged him would make him scream if he were touched too soon.

Najir's handler at his auction had not been so thoughtful.

The memory made the muscles between his shoulders bunch and tense and he fought off the chill it left behind. Najir knew why Hanna must take the new male through these paces, because he understood Vejhon about as well as he did himself. Oh, there were sure to be differences between them, and in truth he was hoping there were broad differences in their makeup, but the inured basics of pride and denial were very much the same. He realized that a wall of pure fury had been blocking all reason and logic in the warrior's mind. The betrayal of his freedom would have kept him balking, deaf to all attempts to gain his trust. Hanna had been forced to inject him harshly into reality, and Najir understood that better than anyone.

He watched Hanna replace the hateful ring in its box. Jhon was fully occupied with catching his breath and coping with the relief that was coming as the stim wore off. There was no longer room for anger within him after such an ordeal. Najir knew his Hanna would take no pleasure in Vejhon's defeat. When she spoke, though her voice seemed steady to her captive, Najir—who knew her so well—heard the sadness underlying her tone.

"This is what you would have known every single day, as often in the day as your owner pleased, had you been bought by another. I haven't the heart to play evil to the extreme of the Baron who nearly walked away with you before Najir intervened and bought you out from under him. The Baron's predilections are . . . monstrous. Few survive his ideas of intimacy." She took a deep breath, sighing soft and long on her exhale. "Sleep. Eat. Bathe. And think over everything you have learned today, my proud one."

She turned on her heel and left the room. A moment after the outer door closed tight behind her, a second pneumatic hiss let her into the private observation room where Najir stood. Their eyes met and an instant expression of compassion rippled across her features. She must have seen something in his features that revealed the pain he'd felt when reliving his past experiences through Vejhon. She hurried up to him, enfolding him in her soft, reassuring embrace, drawing his head down to her graceful shoulder.

"Shh, dearest," she soothed him, her magical calming fingers stroking through his hair. "It is over now."

"He will hate you now. As I hated everything after that."

"But he is just as sharp as you. I can feel it in him. It is part of his beautiful power. He will slowly put the clues together as his emotions ebb from their high of hatred." She nuzzled

Najir's cheek and he felt her smile. "He won't understand what comes next. He will be baffled at first, but it will all come eventually."

Hanna released him so she could turn back to the wall looking into the room. Vejhon would never know he was being observed through solid stone. No one but Hanna and Najir had the code to activate the technology it used, or to get into the private room itself. Hanna moved to the control panel set into the stone and her fingers quickly tapped out a command. Inside the room, the metal bands binding Jhon to the stone wall sprang open and, finding himself suddenly and unexpectedly released, he fell forward onto his knees and hands.

Hanna had no desire to watch what would follow, so she deactivated the viewing wall. It was as though she and Najir had suddenly been sealed off alone together in the long room. The dismal little place had been built by an unsavory relative long ago, so he could spy on his guests and whomever else he wanted to in a measure of comfort. It ran the entire length of the back wall to the large suite, with several portals available for best viewing perspective. Back then it had been kept in great comfort with many amenities close at hand, including lounges set before each window so one could recline as they took in their sport.

Now the old, age-worn lounges were all that was left, the walls and floors stripped bare of everything else. The environmental systems kept dust away, but the room still echoed of neglect. Hanna had not used it before or since the first week of Najir's residence in her home, all those years ago.

The room had darkened considerably as the light from the other room was cut off from them. Najir felt Hanna touch him through the material of his shirt, her fingertips stroking over his pectoral muscle as she sidled up close to him. His heartbeat jumped up in speed as her lush figure snuggled up along his side and her mouth reached to brush his neck.

"Weren't you holding a thought for me?" she asked, her whisper sultry sweet against his skin.

Najir smiled into the dimness above her head.

"Tart," he taunted her. "You're just horny because you got a good feel of that impressive cock of his."

"So?" she asked, shamelessly shrugging a shoulder. "Are you telling me you didn't get hard just watching me stroke that impressive cock?"

She had him there, and she knew it. Unlike Vejhon, Najir knew her intimate touch had been meant as a lesson and not a violation. Watching her bestow her caresses had triggered a flurry of sensory memory and longing. Hanna followed up her speculation with a foray of fingertips down along the front of his pants, easily encountering his quickly developing erection. She chuckled wickedly when he snapped his tongue at her in a silent scold for her audacious manipulations.

"You are shameless and insatiable," he accused in a growl against her ear that sent shivers of delight down her body.

"And horny," she reminded him huskily. "My pussy is soaked just from the feel of him."

"Not because he came so hard for you?"

"No!" She jerked back harshly, seeking his dark eyes with an expression of disbelief. "Do you honestly think I would get any pleasure from degrading another human being like that?"

"No. Of course not," he soothed her gently, his fingers reaching to smooth the creases of fury from her forehead. "I don't know why I said that."

"And he didn't come for me," she continued bitterly. "He ejaculated because a drug forced it on him. It could've been anyone in that room."

"Shh, I know. I know," he said, his regret and sorrow radiating through the gentle touch of his hands. "I'm sorry, Hanna. It just touched so close to my memories. I must have gone through every single emotion he was feeling, right along with him. It was like stepping back in time and . . . I-I'm still not thinking clearly."

"I knew you shouldn't watch," she whispered painfully, turning away from him to press her forehead against the cold stone they could no longer see through. "I don't know why I let you talk me into it."

"Because you didn't want to do it alone, Hanna. You borrowed from me to make your point, bringing him in to that experience you and I shared so long ago. It was key in bringing us together, and it is crucial to keeping all of us safe. Now, he will forever be part of a terrible knowledge, but he will need it if he is to join us on our journey into the future. I don't think I would ever have trusted him otherwise."

"Neither would I, Najir." She picked up the tail of her hair, toying with the end of it in a familiar nervous habit she had. She brushed the thick bottom of it back and forth over her palm a dozen times or more as she thought. "I feel evil," she confessed suddenly.

"No! Never!"

"Well, selfish then! To do this just because we need him so badly . . ."

"Stop!" he commanded her harshly. "That is not the reason why and you need to remember that. At least, not the only reason why. Yes, he is perfect for us. The first in a decade to come along who could come this much closer to perfect. But you were right when you told him what would have become of him had you not intervened."

"Had *you* not," she corrected.

"Had *we* not, then," he acquiesced. "Had we not intervened he would be in Majum's household this very instant, Hanna, being mauled and raped and worse."

"So much worse," she murmured.

"Yes. This is all a means to an end. Remember that. You have never quailed when handling unpleasant tasks before, so why this time?"

She turned to look up into his eyes, her hands reaching to grasp his wide shoulders. "Because I see so much of you in him. I saw your pain and fury from that night all over again."

"And you will show him the way away from it just as you did me, my Lady," he whispered softly to her as he brought his lips to her soft cheek. "You will show him how easy it is to love you. You will teach him all the reasons why you've earned my undying loyalty and commitment. And one day, I have no doubt, you will even make him come for you, harder and with far more pleasure than any stimulant ever could manage."

That made her chuckle softly, her body relaxing as his hands gathered her against him. She felt his large palms sliding down her back and cupping over her bottom briefly as he hugged her tightly to his huge frame. The embrace brought her pelvis to pelvis with him, reminding her instantly of the uncomfortable dissatisfaction of both their unfulfilled bodies. She had been running on an excited high ever since Najir had hurried in and told her of his discovery. She had turned him away then, knowing she would need that frustrated energy to take her through the next few hours . . . including the interlude she had just left. But as much as she would love to avail herself of Najir's sexual prowess, she knew that this part of their relationship had drawn to a definitive close the moment he had bought Vejhon for her . . . and he knew it, too.

"So tell me, my Lady," he murmured softly into her ear. "What is your next move with our new companion?" Najir continued to cuddle her close, already knowing that, while sex must no longer be a part of their life together, they both refused to change their other intimacies in any other way.

"Mmm . . . to let him get used to his new limited freedom

for a while. Let him digest and deduct from what he has seen and learned."

"Let him get comfortable before dropping the next bomb on him?"

"No. Not too comfortable." She hesitated a moment. "I think I will send you in to him as well."

That made Najir go still for several long beats. "Really?" he questioned her. "You think that's wise?"

"Are you questioning your Master, you naughty slave?" she asked, her pretty blue eyes sparkling with the tease. "I think I shall have to punish you for that."

"Mmm, promises promises," he taunted her. Tempted her. "I only meant . . ." Najir broke off. "He resents me. He holds me in contempt for what he perceives as my relinquishing all of my independence to you. He sees his nightmare version of his future when he looks at me."

"Ahh, but you and I know better," she observed.

"We definitely do. But it will take a lot of time before he comes to understand that."

"Trust me, dearest." She hugged him with all of her strength.

"Always, my Lady," he breathed. "Always."

5

Vejhon staggered to his feet entirely on principle.

He fell back against the wall that had just spit him out and continued to gasp for breath. His body still quaked with shock and exhaustion, so he gave himself the luxury of a minute to pull himself together.

He had to admit . . . he had no idea what to think or what to feel. He'd run through every extreme emotion there was in the past hour or so, not to mention being on a nonstop high of hatred and wrath whenever he'd been given the luxury of consciousness these past months. His body felt as though it had been pushed through every military endurance test of his lifetime, except it was as though he'd tackled them back to back to back. He looked down at his wrists first. Oddly enough, he hadn't seen them bare in months, so there was something extremely surreal about the absence of the imprisoning cuffs. He also hadn't realized he'd developed both scars and callouses on both of them. Probably his ankles as well. The thigh, chest, and biceps restraints had been used much less frequently once he'd been submerged in stasis, so the damage from them was minimal.

At the moment, however, each of those contact points were bleeding, except there had been no biceps restraints in place here. No doubt so that blue-skinned bitch could collar his arm as if he were a prized pet.

Vejhon reached for the band and examined it, tugging at it even though he already knew it was anchored firmly in place. If there was a trick to it, he'd have to figure it out later. Right then, he needed to wrap his head around a few other things first.

For example, why had he been set free? The room was loaded with windows along one side, some of the glass appearing to be plate. Granted, it was likely to be "unbreakable," but in his experience, if it had a seam, it had a weakness. Fortified by this prospect, Vejhon tried a few steps across the room. Again, that surreal sensation. Like stepping on solid land after sailing or riding space, it felt queer to move his weight forward without having it instantly restrained.

He made his way to the first window, laying a hand on the smooth surface and looking out at the planet that was trying to claim him. What he saw was a vast sweep of well-tended grounds that led to a fortified wall. Sentries walked the top of the wall and along the lawns, and were stationed at the one gate he could see. Vejhon's brow furrowed as he tried to figure out if all of that was to keep people in, keep people out, or both. For the time being, he voted on both. After all, it was a slave-driven economy from what he had gathered, and you couldn't have your assets escaping.

He also could see that House Drakoulous was situated high enough on a hill to afford a spectacular view of the enormous and densely populated city all around it. From what he could see, there were a few big houses up high like this and the size and manner of housing decreased the lower into the city you went.

It never ceased to amaze him how standard things could be from culture to culture, even with vast amounts of stars and black space lying between them. Vejhon had actually never traveled away from Wite until the wars. Into those years he had been forced to concentrate a good deal of experience in xeno-culture. It hadn't been so hard once he had figured out the constants. Most cultures had a class or caste system, most had an economy, and many were populated by humanoids. Upright walking bipedals were a recurring theme no matter how strange the stage.

Though he had to admit, this was the first time he'd been to a culture where everyone was blue. Most of the guards were blue skinned, and from what he could see of the pedestrians walking the city pathways, his captor had been telling the truth when she'd warned him how easily he would stand out.

As Vejhon ran his hand over the glass of the window, inspecting it for a weakness, he tried not to think about Hanna Drakoulous. The things she had said and the things she had done only jumbled up his brain and his emotions, and he needed to focus on basic survival at the moment. Beauty, lust, and treachery could wait for a while.

There was no actual window, he quickly realized. All of the "windows" were made of stone. It was a fascinating piece of engineering and clearly of optical technology. What better way to see the world outside, yet maintain total privacy? Perhaps cameras outside of the windows reflected back the view, because as he moved from window to window the vista was flawless in depth and perspective. He'd never seen anything like it.

Vejhon's travels along the wall of windows had brought him to the section of the room dedicated to grooming and bathing. The deep oval tub suddenly looked appealing, his wrist and ankle joints whining for some heat and clean water to ease their woes. After all, it had been next to forever since he'd bathed; since he'd done much of anything really. Eat. Sleep a real sleep. See the out-of-doors. Be *in* the out-of-doors. And since he doubted that last one was going to occur anytime soon, maybe he was best off taking advantage of the opportunity to rest and gather his strength and wits. Gods knew he had to figure out what kind of game it was that Hanna was trying to play on him. Then he had to figure out how to suffocate the life out of the manipulative piece of xenotrash. Once he covered all of that, he'd haul ass off of this planet as fast as possible.

He walked toward the tub, examining it in order to figure out how it worked. Wite had used ultraviolet cleansing technology for a while now, but he'd experienced the luxury of water baths before. Vejhon took a step down to get a better look and instantly the sound of sliding stone sounded as two portals opened in the far side of the tub and water surged out of them at incredible speed. Before he knew it, the tub was full and hot and he was experiencing the first act of civilization he'd been allowed since this had all started. The simplistic right to take a bath. It galled him that he recalled Hanna ordering him to do exactly that before she had left, but not enough to be stubborn about it.

In truth, the woman was right about one thing: he wasn't the man he had been when he'd last had a foot on Wite. Nothing would change the fact that at heart he was a soldier . . . and a stone-cold killer when he had to be, but that man would never have paused to bathe and think before all of this. The diehard soldier would have been throwing himself around like a trapped animal trying to escape.

But if he'd learned anything from this experience, it was that anyone could be brought down in value to absolute nothingness, and it was humbling to know he wasn't as invincible as he'd always thought he was. So now he would think. Rest, build strength, bide time and information, and work it all out right. It had to be right. He'd never make it out of the city alive if it wasn't, never mind off the planet. The truth was he knew next to nothing about where he was and how things worked. It was vital he learned, even if it meant playing nice with his enemy for a while.

The very idea of cozying up to the woman who had violated and humiliated him left a taste like acid in his mouth and sparked his banked anger. He rubbed his temple as pain lanced through his head in response. He forced himself to resist the urge to spend time wishing seven kinds of death on her. It would be a waste of time and energy, and it certainly wouldn't make him feel any better about what had happened. He focused instead on washing away all remaining evidence of her crime against him, as well as the haunting echo of her touch on his flesh.

Female Masters of High Houses wear these everywhere. They never go anywhere without them.

That is what she had said about that thrice-damned ring she'd used.

Except . . . she hadn't been wearing it. Not when she had arrived and not when she had left. Still, if this was her playroom, why would she need to wear it anywhere else? It made sense that she could keep it here to be used only with her latest toys.

Vejhon exited the bath feeling a bit more grounded and truly refreshed. The aches in his muscles had been eased away by the heat of the water and his wounds were cleansed. He found some medic patches on the countertop with the towels. He dried himself and tended his wounds. Best of all, the towel became the first thing like clothing he had worn in a hell of a long time.

He ignored the bed for the moment, deciding to explore everything more thoroughly. The room wasn't obviously bugged or monitored from what he could find, but he didn't take it for granted. There was technology here that he'd never seen before and anything was possible. He peeked in the small cabinets and drawers of the furnishings scattered about, and then made his way to the large wardrobe near her chest of jewelry and trickery. Honestly, between the rack of hooks and that chest of subversive baubles, he was expecting the worst when he found the doors to the wardrobe unlocked and pulled them open.

What he found was clothing. A lot of it. Rich fabrics, top to bottom, inside and out, everything he could need and amazingly all in his size. Clearly, Hanna had gone to great trouble to be prepared for him. Vejhon shut the doors and turned his back on the finery. Oh, he'd need it eventually if he was going to get out of there, but at the moment he didn't feel like dressing up for the bitch like some pretty, well-behaved doll.

Like Najir. The clothes were similar to what he'd seen on the other slave.

Man. Other man. Vejhon was no slave and refused to refer to himself that way. She said it was inevitable and that he'd have to accept it? Well, fine. Let the inevitable find him. He wasn't going to make it easy. So he decided to head over to the bed and, after pulling everything back and inspecting it sternly, he chose to lie down. Or to be more honest, his body decided for him. Between his draining ordeal and the drawing heat of his bath, he was asleep before his head hit the pillows.

"Good morning, Master Drakoulous."

Hanna drew to a halt and turned with perfect poise and posture to face her greeter. She felt Najir come to a stop behind her, the tension rippling through his body a force of energy she could almost taste. However, she trusted Najir not to show any outward signs of his hostile emotions as the Baron of Majum House approached them.

"Good morning, Baron," she returned, smiling pleasantly as she exchanged politeness with the enemy of her House. The Feuds were ended, and she would obey the law, but she knew

Majum would not. The man had murdered her parents and countless others. He had a taste for it and a talent for it and people like that didn't just stop. Neither did they let go of life-long grudges and feelings of vendetta.

"How do you find your new toy, my dear? I must say, I hope he was worth the bid. As envious as I am, no mere flesh is worth such a price." The Baron walked up so that he was close enough for her senses to absorb the smaller details about him. It might not deceive her, but it always amazed her that such hand-someness and appearance of refinement could be grown over so foul a soil.

"Oh, he was worth the price," she assured him, meeting his dark eyes with all her honest pleasure pouring out of her. "He was worth the price and so much more. Najir has been amply rewarded for his keen eye and quick bidding on my behalf."

"I'll bet he was," the Baron said, his air unsuccessful in hiding his sudden stiffening. "Perhaps now that you have a new confection, you will consider selling the old. He's getting a bit long in years, isn't he?"

"Najir?" She laughed as though it were the most ridiculous concept on the planet. "Najir is as fit and fine as the day I bought him."

"Out from under me as well, if I recall," he said with a chuckle that sounded as forced as it was.

"The perils of an open auction I am afraid, Baron," was her sweetly polite reply. "No, Baron, Najir will make a fine match to the new slave. I plan them to be the finest pair of studs ever seen, the envy of every woman in High City."

The Baron's false smile faded as he stepped a little closer and lowered his voice for her ears alone. "Tell me, Hanna, why do you persist in baiting me? You know I will find a way to wound you." He raised his voice again. "I am curious why I have not seen your brother Kaino around in so many months. He is sorely missed at all the clubs."

Hanna felt the strike go through her chest, her heart pounding hard from the pain of it as she narrowed eyes on the Baron. She wondered if he realized how very hard she resisted the instinctual urge she had to rip his throat out. The Baron knew very well that Kaino had gone off on a journey to "find himself." The idea had been that he would travel the world and see how others lived and thrived. Other cultures had always fascinated him. However, despite his promises to keep in touch, Kaino's communications had abruptly ceased only two months after he had left. Ever since then, Majum had persisted in dropping these poisonous hints that he'd had something to do with that . . . and that she wasn't likely to hear from Kaino ever again.

"I believe I mentioned before that he is traveling. He is a grown man with a taste for adventure, and I doubt I will be able to lure him back here anytime soon when there is a world to be explored. Of course, he is only third in line to inherit, so he even has the option of going offworld." Hanna did not lower her voice as she delivered her counterstrike. In fact, she raised it. "I thank you for asking after my family, Baron. Tell me, how does your nephew fare? You must be so delighted that in only two years he will reach majority and no longer be in need of your guardianship. He will finally be able to take all of your burdens as acting Master to House Majum away from you as he claims his rightful inheritance. Is he well?" Again her quick, cunning smile of perfect pleasantness. "I would hate for some mysterious illness to affect him as it did his poor sister. What a tragedy for you to lose the girl while she was in your care! I know you must be striving with all effort to see your nephew arrives healthy and happy at his waiting seat in the Chamber of Masters."

"He's quite healthy I assure you." The Baron made his assurance through tight teeth as he glanced around at the other Masters who stood nearby on the steps to the Chamber of Masters. They were observing the exchange with interest . . . some even with unconcealed amusement. "When he takes his seat, it will be as though I am right there beside him. I'm training him well."

"I'm sure you are teaching him everything you possibly can."

To anyone who knew the Baron, the implication was clear. Since everyone at hand was a peer, few felt the remark slip past them without understanding.

"My Lady," Najir interrupted softly at her back. "The Chamber convenes in five minutes."

"So it does. Well, we shouldn't be late, Majum. I will take my seat, and you will take your nephew's for now. Business as usual, then."

She nodded a farewell and went to leave, but she had barely moved a step when the Baron's hand clamped like a vice around her arm. He found her ear as he jerked her shoulder hard against his chest.

"Beware that clever tongue, Hanna, or I will cut it out and lay it beside your brother's. Or perhaps I will take your heir's first and leave your House without succession. I hear your sister Ashanna is impossible for you to control these days, and I would hate to cut apart one Drakoulous bitch only to have her replaced with another. I already made that mistake with your mother."

Hanna turned her head slowly and met the Baron's black eyes with cold contempt and fury in hers. This time she joined him in his whispers.

"Now let me warn you, Wheyn," she hissed, his name dripping from her lips like spit-out poison, "that unlike my mother, my nature is not so peaceful. Pray your taunts about my brother are never proven, because if I discover you touched even the air around him, I will eviscerate you. I will bathe my face in your blood and then lick away every drop with ultimate pleasure afterwards."

Her threat was so unexpectedly vivid and vicious that the Baron released her arm and took a step back. The believability Vejhon had discovered in her eyes was not exclusive to him. Majum could see the coldness of her truth and the honesty of her threat. He had never realized that the daughter of so temperate a woman as her mother could ever be so ruthless. Where had she learned it from? And where did she hide it? Even he couldn't help exposing his less savory side in public now and then. In her eight years as Master of her House, she had given no clue at all to her bloodthirsty nature. Should he believe her? It was more than likely a bluff . . .

Wheyn flicked his eyes to Najir. The slave had stood passive the entire time, although he had been close enough to catch some of the exchange. The slave would pay with his life if he attacked a free man of any rank without permission to protect his Master's life, but the big bastard looked as though he didn't much care. Najir clearly wanted to rip Wheyn's head from his body.

Impressive. If Majum hadn't hated the bitch with such a passion, he'd ask her how she managed to control the brute, even when it was obvious he did not wish to be in control of himself. Whatever her technique, he was beginning to think that she might even be able to break in her new confection as well one day. As he watched her walk off, Najir in tow, he forced himself to master the furious scream of jealousy the idea sent ripping through him.

6

Sunshine on this planet had a distinctive rose-colored hue.

It was Vejhon's first thought as he woke only to wince at the brilliance of the sun reflecting from the imaging windows. His next realization was that he wasn't alone.

He was damn slow, in his opinion, as he rocketed to his feet and struck the target lurking beside his bed with full impact. Apparently not all that slow, because Najir took the hit without so much as an attempt to block. Jhon had rammed a knee and shin into the other man's chest as he had come out of bed on a single pivoting foot, but Najir was a big, solid bastard, and he only staggered back a step or two before digging his balance back in. Still, it gave Jhon time to reapproach.

Yeah, he thought grimly, *I'm slower than sludge*. Too many days in stasis had taken their toll. The result was Najir's smooth ability to strike him right underneath his next attack. Both men moved with full power and total commitment, Jhon's strike only glancing off Najir as the slave countered with a fast, mean maneuver that hauled Jhon off his feet and sent him tumbling off his opponent's back. Jhon discovered the burn of friction against his skin as he hit the stone floor sliding.

Using the momentum for advantage out of pure habit, Jhon rolled right back up onto his feet, and he tried to regain his balance as Najir approached looking mightily pissed off.

"Don't be an idiot!" Najir snapped, coming to an unexpected halt and discontinuing the altercation, something Vejhon would never have expected or done himself if he'd been attacked "I know how you feel and what you are thinking, Colonel, but your temper and outrage at others does not belong in *this* House! This House is your salvation. My Lady is your precious savior, your guide into a life of unimaginable wonder, and all you want to do is fight it?"

"I'm a warrior," Vejhon sneered. "It's in the job description. And I highly doubt that your leash holder is anybody's savior. If I hadn't promised my mother not to use certain words in reference to a female, I'd tell you exactly what she is."

It was actually amusing to watch the color of fury that climbed the other man's neck. Najir curled his hands into fists and used what appeared to be extraordinary restraint to keep his feet firmly in place and his fists out of Jhon's face. Vejhon had to give the man his due. In his top shape, it was likely that he would have wiped the floor up with Najir, but he had never had that kind of control over his emotions and impulses. He had adapted to the weakness, using it to make himself a better fighter and leader in the long run, but he'd always been notorious for his temper.

"I know everything you're feeling right now," Najir announced. "Ten years ago, had I been faced with a man of our power and strength behaving docilely and respecting to someone of this society, I would also have been as disgusted by him as you are by me. We are not so different, you and I, and yet . . . we are just different enough to make you the luckier man."

Najir obviously had no plans to explain that remark as he continued, "When Hanna bought me ten years ago, I had suffered my time on the auction stage fully awake and aware, bound from tearing the hearts out of those who abused me against my will. It was Hanna's first and her last auction. She was so horrified over my treatment that she couldn't ever attend another, no matter what her needs. One day you will realize what a sacrifice that has meant for her."

"So what? She couldn't stomach it, so she sends you in her stead. She thinks she can pretend she isn't a part of perpetuating slavery because she doesn't do the actual buying of those who draw her bath and cook her food?"

"Hanna has only two slaves, Vejhon," Najir informed coldly. "Me and now you. This House is run by paid commoners, servants earning wages. It is the only House in the city to do so fully."

The information gave Jhon pause. He narrowed suspicious eyes on Najir, trying to read whether or not he was being honest. Then again, it was completely counterproductive to the training of a slave to say things like this. What he said amounted to a woman who actually couldn't tolerate slavery. But then why . . . ?

Jhon asked the question with only his expression, and Najir nodded in understanding as he relaxed just a little. "She has her reasons for the exceptions she has made with you and me, and it is not my place to speak of them. She will reveal herself in her own time and way. What I will discuss with you is how Hanna spent her time with you earlier."

Najir saw the rushing clouds of fury that ran over the other man's expression, and he didn't blame him in the least for it. But that response was why he had come there in the first place.

"What do you know of it?" Vejhon asked furiously, a sheen of red coating his vision.

"Because I've lived it! Hanna reached into that nightmare

and plucked me out of it. But at the time, like you, I didn't know she was different from the others and I didn't trust her either. For you, it is worse, because she was forced to submerge you into the ice of her culture herself, and she damaged the path to trust with you for the sake of your life and comprehension."

"Do you get that vague way of saying shit from her, or is this common around here?" Jhon snorted contemptuously.

"Fine." Najir took a step closer and both men tensed. "She drugged you. She touched you. She forced your body into orgasm against your will. And I am here to tell you how lucky you are that it was her doing all of it. Yes, it felt like a violation, and it was. But she only did it to show you a little of what you will suffer if you try to leave the safety of this House. If you run away, in this society, you become fair game for the hunt. Anyone who can recapture you will own you. Do you understand?"

"What's your point?" Vejhon asked gruffly, although he had a terrible sinking feeling that he already knew what it was.

"Run, if you want. Go. Try to do what no slave has ever done. You are powerful and resourceful, you might make it farther than any of them. But be warned," Najir said, his voice dropping to an ominous tone that Vejhon realized came from a terrible place of knowledge within the man, and not just theatrics. "What she did to you today is bliss and delight compared to what you will face once captured by another. Hanna is singular, I assure you. No one else will weep in their heart with guilt after they have violated you. No. They will revel and celebrate, delight in your manhood, your will, and all the monstrous ways they can create to tear it out of you. Hanna feared for you if she failed to make you see this fact. What she did, she did to save and protect you."

"Why couldn't she just tell me all of this? Just like you are telling it to me now! Why the—?"

"She tried. You were too busy threatening to kill her to hear her. Besides, I guarantee it is a lesson you won't ever forget, and Hanna needed you to have that burned in you so you would never be careless or blasé. You don't yet want to realize it, but what she did has saved your life. Or better yet, saved you from a fate worse than death."

Najir finally stepped back and with a nod toward the conversation area he indicated a tray of bread goods and what looked like cheeses.

"It is late and past dinner, but my Lady knew you would crave something when you woke."

"Past dinner? With all of this sun?"

"Night will come tomorrow. You will see. Many things are unique here."

With that understatement, the other slave exited through the door, leaving Vejhon with a head full of conflicting input and thoughts. He tried to weed emotion out of it, but hell . . . becoming a slave on an alien planet was emotional business.

"He didn't eat."

Hanna looked up from her workstation, a ready frown on her lips as Najir reported the fact to her. She stood up and stretched a long arch of her back, trying to move her kinked-up muscles enough to relieve their knots.

"Not even a little? He must be starved after being in stasis so long."

"At his size and muscle mass? I imagine he is. But I think he doesn't trust us not to drug him."

"Would you, after what I did?"

"Well, he's being thickheaded, then, because I already re-explained that to him." Najir frowned this time. "I suppose only time and visible proof and action will convince him."

"And I suppose that is my job," Hanna agreed with a sigh. "What is he doing now?"

"Sleeping. I believe he was displeased with his performance during our little scuffle, so he spent time exercising and working through fight stances and maneuvers. He also refuses to get dressed. He's not modest, I'll give him that."

"Don't criticize," she chuckled. "You wouldn't wear clothes for three days. You said you'd rather be dead than dress like a woman. I had not realized that in your culture only women wore trousers. The men wore kilts."

"Yes." Najir's grin was pure mischief. "Trousers were meant to keep the men out, and kilts made it easy to do just the opposite."

"Najir! Naughty man," she teased, sidling up to him and brushing a hand down his hair.

"Just how you like me," he countered.

The tease brought her up a little short, her body language instantly becoming aloof. He immediately knew why, and he couldn't help the sting of hurt that raced the edges of his skin.

"Najir," she began a little awkwardly, "you realize . . ."

"Don't." He cut her off. "I am perfectly aware of the situation. I have always been aware of what would happen. I am no adolescent and I can accept what I myself have set in motion, Hanna."

"Dearest," she soothed, instantly moving into his embrace, all coolness vanishing as she hugged herself around him. "I only meant that I need the line to be clear. We enjoyed each other our last time together, did we not?"

"Immensely," he assured her, unable to help the return of his wicked smile.

"So we did. And now that I am certain we understand each other, I want everything to be just as it always was. All our free and easy ways together should stay exactly the same. I won't change anything else between us. You are my best friend. I would be lost without you."

"You exaggerate as usual," he retorted gruffly, clearing his throat before lowering his head to whisper in her ear. "I will grieve, Hanna. I won't kid you about that. It's been ten years between us. But if, as you promise, nothing else changes, then I can bear it. I can bear anything that makes you happy. If I couldn't . . . if I were that selfish . . . I would have walked away from that auction, left him there for Majum and never looked back. Never said a word."

"It wouldn't have occurred to you," she swore with soft vehemence. "You are incapable of such deception."

"Only with those I love." Najir took her by her chin, tilting her head back and finding her soft and sweet lips. The kiss deepened, crossed the line into bittersweet passion for just a moment, but then he pulled back and stepped away from her. The tears filling her eyes were more than he could bear. Fighting the tightness in his throat, he said, "I have some training with the guards in a little while. I'd better be headed to the yard."

He turned and left the room, refusing to look back and forcing himself to look only forward.

Vejhon awoke with a start when he smelled food. There wasn't a single thing about it that smelled familiar, but he knew it was food because the aromatic scent made his stomach twist into a painful knot of want. Gods, he hadn't eaten in so long he wasn't even sure his stomach would keep anything he ate. Although, he thought with a grimace as a loud rumble of demand ground out of him, it was willing to try in spite of his own reluctance.

Rolling over, he took a moment to adjust to the changed light in the room. Daylight had disappeared, but the recessed lighting along all the seams of the walls and ceiling had taken over the job. The room was very well lit, almost like daylight itself. Most worlds, in his experience, ran on cycles or days ranging from twenty to thirty hours in length. From what he had surmised watching the slow course of the sun for the past day, this world spent an entire cycle in daylight and the next in total darkness. It was unusual, but not unheard of. The planet rotated so slowly on its axis that schedules had had to be adapted to provide a healthy balance between waking and sleeping time, whether it was dark out or not.

"Did you enjoy your rest?"

Vejhon jerked upright in bed at the sound of her voice. She was setting a tray onto the table acting as center point of the conversation area, the same location Najir had used for the previous plate of food. The platter was the source of those amazing smells, he realized quickly, but he tried to school himself so she wouldn't be able to read how strongly he desired what she had brought. She'd proven herself an accomplished torturer, he thought bitterly, and the control of a prisoner's food was a classic manipulative tool.

"Come, Jhon," she invited with a sympathetic little smile. "I'm not here to harm you in any way. That unpleasantness is over with. It will never be repeated so long as you are within the protection of this House, and I am hoping that will be for a long, long time."

"I'll bet you are," he bit out sharply. He swung up onto his feet and paused when he realized there was no one there to protect her from him. He was free to approach her, to touch her . . .

. . . *so long as you don't combine it with laying hands on me with the intent to hurt me.*

Vejhon reached to rub at the metal around his arm that she had called her safety measure. A neurotransmitter, perhaps, engineered to cause pain as a deterrent so a slave wouldn't harm his master. But . . . Vejhon had bucked incredible pain before and managed to kill enemies by the handful in spite of it. And it wouldn't take much to disconnect her spine from her brain. Only a few seconds.

He approached where she was and watched with amazement as she actually turned her back on him to begin setting out the covered dishes she'd brought. It was too prime an opportunity to waste, and he was too well trained a warrior. His brain was already calculating how to use her hand to activate the door across the way even after she was dead. Guards could be dealt with, and in the darkness he could find a million places to hide in a city. Vejhon's entire body shifted into automation. The quick length of his stride covered the distance in a heartbeat and his hands reached out to grab her by her head.

He barely saw her move, her speed was so remarkably unexpected. She swung her arm back, capturing his wrist and squeezing the painful wound on it mercilessly as she came around with her second hand and flat-palmed him in the ribs so hard he felt his body jolt up off the floor. He automatically countered, the warrior in him taking over and certainly not caring about anything but his goal. She'd taken him by surprise because he'd underestimated her. He wouldn't double the error.

He grabbed her by her hair and jerked her cleanly off her feet by it. The power he used to drag her back against himself sent her spine crashing into his breastbone.

And that was the end of it.

Vejhon learned the instant he touched her in violence the power of the deterrent she had affixed around his arm. The pain that launched through every molecule of his body was so extraordinary, it was almost fascinating. It lasted only a few seconds, probably because that was all it needed to render him completely unconscious.

Hanna was held captive by her hair as the Goliath behind her seized from the feedback of pain and then fell backward onto the floor. She landed with a grunt on top of him, her back to his chest, and took a moment to gasp for breath before cursing loudly to the empty room.

"You stubborn son of a bitch!" she growled in frustration.

She'd known that, though. And she'd expected this, too.

Hanna rolled around on top of him, straddling his belly on her knees as she leaned over him and smacked him lightly in the face. He jerked at the slight stimulation and she braced her hand on the floor by his head as she waited for him to come out of the stun. It acted harshly and quickly, but it also didn't last long. It was meant to give just enough time to bind the slave safely, but she wasn't going to do that. She didn't even want to use the damn deterrent, but Najir had insisted and she realized he was right.

Case in point: one unconscious, pigheaded alien male.

"Come on, wake up," she coaxed in a singsong voice as she smacked her fingers lightly against his cheek again.

His eyes flickered open, revealing that beautiful green-yellow coloring and, as close as she was, the fact that his pupils were more ovoid than round. She was distracted by that just long enough to be taken by surprise when she felt his hands clamp around her rib cage.

"Get off!"

He threw her off of him, sending her tumbling on knees and elbows over the carpet. To her credit, she ended up in a spry roll and rounded up into a crouch. Not a bad trick in a dress, he had to say. She also got honorable mention for the fact that his ribs were on fire from her strike earlier.

Vejhon got up and, letting his frustrated anger propel him, he crossed to the wardrobe and jerked out a pair of pants to replace his inadequate towel. If he was in for a battle with her, he was damn well sick of fighting naked. Especially when she insisted on climbing all over him! It was damn dirty pool for her to sit over him like that when she knew she wasn't wearing a single damn thing under that dress. It was a short wrap of silky blue fabric that almost matched the powder-soft tone of her skin, and reached no farther than mid-thigh on her. Needless to say, he'd gotten a good feel of the warmth and softness of her bare sex as she'd sat astride him. He forgave himself for the instant push of heat in his blood because of it. Like bathing, food, and all the rest, it had been a long time since he'd had a woman, something else he'd been used to having with a measure of regularity before his incarceration.

Besides all of that, he was growing increasingly confused. He felt no remnants of the pain used to knock him unconscious, and a glance at the steam coming off the food she'd brought told him he hadn't been out for very long at all. What kind of a deterrent was that? Effective for a minute or two, perhaps, probably long enough to drug or shackle a violent slave, but she had done neither.

He watched her warily as she rose to her full height, finally taking time to look beyond the curvaceous swells of her body and the femininity of her wardrobe. He quickly began to see more. Long, powerful major muscle groups that flexed into definition as she walked. The grace and reflex of someone who had trained a very long time, perhaps her entire lifetime as he had, to defend herself.

And that meant she had either a cause or a need to do so. Very few could make the type of commitment it took to be a lifetime warrior just because they craved it. Often it was need, like self-protection . . . or cause, like revenge against aliens who were destroying your home, that drove them to the top of perfection.

But she was the powerful head of a respected House in this culture, surrounded by guards and others who would protect her. Why would she feel the need to train herself to such an extreme? And protect her from what? The only danger he could see was himself, and he'd only just recently become an issue.

"Are you going to sit and eat with me or would you prefer to roll around on the floor some more first?"

The way she arced a single, slim black brow as she squared off with him with one hand on a curved hip, a smile he could only label taunting toying over her dark lips, was just shy of a challenge. She wasn't afraid of him, and it was just dawning on him that it had nothing to do with the band around his arm.

"Do you own even an ounce of self-preservation?" he asked her gruffly. "How do you know this thing isn't beatable?" he asked, flicking a finger at the band.

"Oh, everything is beatable," she agreed, "and if anyone can defeat that band it will probably be you."

"Why aren't you afraid of me?" The demand was out before he could check it, and he gripped his teeth together when he heard the frustration in his tone. She didn't mock him as expected, though. She'd walked to the table and finished her task of removing trays and arranging them like a buffet.

"Who says I'm not afraid?" she countered.

"You don't radiate fear. I have a sense for it and you don't give it off, not even when fighting."

"People fear different things, Jhon. You're talking about fear of pain and fear of death. I don't fear those things for myself, it's true. My fears are quite powerful in other areas, though, I assure you." She ran her jewel blue eyes over him briefly. "Perhaps that knowledge will please you enough to sit and eat with me."

She took a seat, smoothing her dress along her body first, and indicated the seat across from her over the table. He had to admit he was surprised she offered him the distance. He had almost expected her to have the audacity to pat the chair nearest her in invitation.

Not wanting to stand around looking indecisive, Vejhon quickly took the offered seat. He ran his eyes over the alien foods, searching for familiarity. Before he had even finished his survey, she was drawing up a curved plate and serving generous portions of meats and what looked like root vegetables smothered in glazes and sauces. Then she leaned over the table to offer him the serving. She met his eyes as he hesitated, then reached onto the plate for a round something and popped it into her mouth. She chewed and cocked a brow, again a silent challenge.

"Not poisoned. No aphrodisiacal or stimulant drugs. Just borta, odji, and grigi meat, as well as some huss, frita, and porta roots. I chose these because . . . they tend to be favorites of nonindigenous people on this planet." She grimaced. "Slaves," she corrected herself, tilting her head and sighing. "Please, try some."

Vejhon took the offered plate and picked up a utensil for eating. He dug into the food as quickly as he thought his stomach could tolerate, casting increasingly curious glances at Hanna. She served him something to drink, folded a linen, and handed it to him. Then she sat down and began to serve herself.

If he had been confused before, now he was completely mystified. What sort of master waits on her own slave? And it didn't even look as though she'd given the act much thought. It was as comfortable on her as though she were serving an honored guest. This alien female never seemed to stop changing. She altered in aspects more often than a tumbling gemstone and he had no idea what to make of her multiple personas. If she was playing a game with him, the infrastructure of it was completely lost on him. She had laid an irrefutable roadwork of dominance earlier, and then slammed the door shut on it in the next breath.

This is what you would have known every single day, as often in the day as your owner pleased, had you been bought by another, she'd told him.

Which implied she would not be inclined to repeat the act often. Or at all. Vejhon was finally beginning to understand the gist of the message she and Najir had been trying to pound into his head. She would never force him to perform for her again. She would never demand his humiliation in that way again. He would not have been so lucky elsewhere, and she had made very certain he would appreciate the difference. Or so she would have him believe.

But he was still a slave to her, damn it! If she wasn't going to toy with him in her bed, then she had something else planned out. Vejhon forced down the twang of disappointment he felt when he realized she wasn't interested in him as stud material for whatever reason.

Insult, he corrected himself hastily, not disappointment. It was strictly his flawed male ego at play. He should be grateful he faced a fate other than becoming a whore. If there were levels of slavery, whoring was low on the ladder.

"Why am I here?" he asked at last, setting his plate aside. "You say I'm a slave. What will my purpose be?"

Hanna laid aside her utensil slowly, keeping her eyes lowered as she formulated a response that would be honest without revealing too much. "You are here because I need you. This household needs you."

"So you want to make me a house servant?" he bit out.

"No, Jhon, no . . ." She sighed long and slowly before finally meeting his eyes. She had no idea how the frank clarity and color of her eyes impacted him. It's why he had come to believe the things she said to him when normally he trusted no one else. "Your talents would be wasted as a house servant, Jhon. I'm not like some of these foolish women in these Houses"— she motioned toward the darkened city vaguely—"who hunt slave markets for warriors just so they have beautiful muscle waiting on them hand and foot. Your muscle has a purpose other than the way it catches my eye."

The statement was extremely revealing. Not just the realization that she probably wanted to use him as a warrior, but she had complimented him and admitted an appreciation for his body. It was the first proof he'd had of her interest other than what he had surmised from the stroke of her eyes.

And that was when he realized he had begun detaching her from her actions upon his arrival in this room. She'd completed the entire performance speaking in a narrative, as if it would all take place separate and apart from her. Except, he hadn't been listening at the time. He hadn't been able to get past the concept of being a slave and the rage that had come with it for months, to the point where he had been self-conditioned to react with it.

Regardless of that, he reminded himself, no matter what her intentions, it had been *her* orchestrating his humiliation. It had been her uninvited touch on his body. It was she who'd injected him until . . .

Vejhon's hands curled into tight fists and a storm shadowed his eyes.

"Don't think you can play nice with me and it will make what you did better," he snapped abruptly. "Nothing can. And nothing can change the fact that you bought me as a slave and it is something I will detest and protest with every fiber of my being."

"Sweet unbelievable mercy!" she exploded in temper, surging to her feet as she paced sharply away from the table and then back again before facing him. "What will it take? Hmm? Breaking my neck as you just tried to do? Will that make you feel balanced? Will it restore your manhood against me? Tell me, what do I have to do to counter the evil I have done to you? Because believe me, I already know I owe you something for it."

Vejhon blinked, too stunned to do much more than stare up at her and try to absorb her tirade. Every word out of her mouth gave him power over her, and she was throwing it down before him and almost begging him to pick it up and use it against her. If she was trying to hold her position of mastery over him, she well and truly sucked at it.

There was a kind of amusement to that, but it faded quickly

when he clearly saw the light of inspiration enter her eyes. Fascinated, he watched as she marched across the room with obvious purpose.

"Door, locked." She announced the command aloud, and sure enough, Jhon heard bolts shoot home in the door across the way. Instantly on alert, he surged to his feet and hurried into her wake as she began detaching her hair circlets and tossing them onto the bed. Her hair unwound into a thick black cape that covered her shoulder to shoulder and brushed in sensuous little ripples down the whole of her back, thighs, and calves.

Then she reached into that cursed chest and withdrew something quickly. She threw it at him and he fumbled to catch it as she turned her back to the wall that had held him captive.

"What are you—?"

He choked off his query when she reached for the hem of her dress and shucked it off in a swift motion, letting the garment fall carelessly down the sheet of her hair behind her where it hit the floor. She kicked it away from herself without hesitation. She reached for the lower length of her hair, draping that half of it over her shoulder like a fur stole, resting her back against the wall, stretching out her arms and bracing her legs.

"Restraints, please. For a female."

Sure enough, restraints snapped out of the wall and locked around her wrists, her biceps, her ankles, and her thighs. They tightened, drawing her securely upright against the wall.

Vejhon looked down at the stimulant ring she'd thrown to him, the vile thing sitting in his palm like a sleeping scorpion, just waiting to be woken so it could sting.

"There. Now. Will this do? Measure for measure? You can do exactly what I did to you . . . more even, if you think it will help."

"Except you can give the command to release yourself

whenever you like," he said automatically, although his voice was a bit numb with continuing disbelief over what she was trying to offer him.

"Voiceprint restraint release, Vejhon Mach." There was a responding beep. She cocked that brow again, the challenge ringing so clear now. "Speak your name and you will have control over the restraint release."

"Vejhon Mach," he said, unable to help the impetus of the moment and the opportunity for payback it was offering.

There was an answering beep, and without missing a beat she gave another command. "Delete restraint access for Hanna Drakoulous."

"Warning," a disembodied voice replied. "Access deletion is for primary authority. Restoration of access can only be restored at central workstation. Are you sure you wish to delete primary authority access for restraints?"

"Correct. Delete primary authority access to restraints."

"Deleted." The response was punctuated with a last beep. Hanna turned her sharp blue eyes onto Vejhon.

"The central workstation is upstairs. You now have total control over the restraints. There is nothing I can do. You have the ring as well."

"I also have a band around my arm, if you recall," Vejhon retorted.

"That prevents you doing violence to me. This isn't violence. Do nothing with the intent to cause me dangerous harm and you will suffer no feedback. Fortunately for you, this is only a violation. Would you care to continue?"

Jhon couldn't believe she had done this. It was certainly too good to be true. The ruthless militant in him seethed with exultation at the commanding advantage and the opportunity to counterstrike. On the other hand, the part of him that had so recently been a victim sent a twinge of distaste running through him.

He stood there, taking the time to absorb everything. He looked at her and really saw her for the first time since she'd stripped herself bare. She was, in a word, stunning. He had been convinced that bodies that incredibly fit and sexy existed only in a man's imagination. She was tall and lean, her muscles accented by her outstretched position and the tension she no doubt felt for her subservient position. As he had thought, her skin was a slightly darker shade of blue as it ran down over her full, healthy breasts. And like her wickedly dark lips, her nipples were deep purple and scarlet berries, pulled into fat peaks by the chill of the wall at her back. Her belly was taut and flat, abdominal muscles etched ever so lightly under her skin. Her navel made him smile for some reason as it stood out a cobalt blue from the rest of her.

Below that . . .

The killer legs and fabulous hips he'd already known about. Not that they were easy to dismiss, because they weren't. Like before, he had to acknowledge that it had been a long time since . . .

Dark. And darker. That was the only way to describe the way her skin colored as it traveled from the bottom of her navel to the curve of her genitals. He could see the violet shadows of her labia even from where he stood. Unexpectedly, his entire throat and mouth went dry, even while his heart began to drum a resonant beat, as though it were keeping time for the whole planet.

"Why are you doing this?" he asked, walking up to her as their eyes finally met.

"Because you need me to. Because, Jhon," she said with soft intensity, "I will do anything to get you to trust me."

"And what if I said that it's impossible? I trust no one. I never have. I likely never will."

"It doesn't change the fact that I have to try. Or that I owe you this. This is as much for me as it is for you. I hated doing what I did to you. And the only way you will come to understand that is by doing it yourself. Just understand, as much as I hated what I had to become to distribute that lesson to you, that is how very important the lesson was. Do you understand?"

"Not yet," he said with clear and quiet purpose, "but I will."

7

She wasn't afraid.

Hanna hadn't been lying when she had said that. Oh, she was taking a great risk stripping herself before him, but she only needed to maneuver with care to pull it off. What she truly hid was the rush of excitement that had her skin bubbling with gooseflesh. Her advantage in this scenario was that she knew what would be coming, and she wasn't resistant to it.

Vejhon knew this, too. He toyed with the ring he held for a long minute as he thought about how to best take advantage of the situation without hurting her, and thereby himself, in the process. He had to give her credit . . . either for guts or stupidity. The jury was still out on that one. She had handed herself into total helplessness, and this only minutes after he had made an attempt on her life. Since he already knew how shrewd and calculating she was, it forced him to reconsider all of her motives. That she was willing to go so far to earn his forgiveness and his trust either made her desperate or extremely considerate of his feelings about all of this. For that, he was going to opt for a little bit of both. Only, what was it that could make so powerful a woman desperate for help from what was, from her perspective, a bought slave?

He moved up closer to her, as close as she had been to him when she had begun touching him. Their gazes held, that clarity in hers so frank and so damn honest. Unable to curb the impulse, he reached out and traced a finger over one of those mocking little brows of hers. His fingertip slid until the tail of her eyebrow ended in a point, leaving him with a choice to stop or continue on to her skin. The lure was incredibly tempting, the curves of blue so fair and fascinating. Fighting the urge, he stepped back and raked his eyes down her body, forcing himself back to the familiarity of lust and sex appeal, rather than the unnerving sense of . . . of something else. Something he couldn't and wouldn't immediately define.

It was so intriguing to see her dressed only in the drape of her hair. The way she watched him so steadily, so fearlessly, while naked and vulnerable to his desires. He'd never imagined how powerful a feeling it could be, to be in this position. Yet, it carried enormous weight. He was used to being responsible for the well-being of others, but this was total dependence, wasn't it? Like a child who survives only by your care of it, or someone who is ill or wounded who has no recourse but to trust you to aid them.

"You left knives and other stabbing implements on the table," he remarked, testing her trust, although the comment was disembodied from his actual thoughts. "I can hurt you without ever touching you. I can throw every weapon I've ever held with deadly accuracy."

"I told you, I am not afraid of pain or death, if that is what you truly must do to draw equal with me."

But she knew he wouldn't. He was a warrior and a killer, but Hanna could see in him that he needed lawful justification to merit the murdering he did. Did what she had done justify murder? She could tell even he did not think so. Very casually, she flicked lazy eyes to the wall behind him. Najir was not observing. She had purposely chosen to come while he was in the training yards. Not that he wouldn't obey her wishes had she asked him not to watch, but she had wanted the time alone with Jhon without having to follow up with an allocution of what had transpired afterward. She didn't want to share everything with Najir. Not until she knew it wouldn't be like throwing citrus juice on a deep wound. She despised the idea of causing him any pain. He didn't deserve that.

But should he return and decide to check up on her, there could be trouble. Najir would never tolerate the scene that was unfolding. He didn't trust Vejhon yet. Hanna had no choice but to invest trust . . . because everything hinged on her gaining it in return.

Vejhon realized there was a wealth of possibilities before him. He slid the ring onto his smallest finger, turning it so he could inspect it.

"I could inject you with the stim, I suppose. But only once. Leave you needing more." He looked at her and dropped his touch onto her mouth, the contrast of his skin against her lips reminding him too easily how she'd already stirred him up once just by licking her lips. Just when had she become so damn attractive to him? he wondered with surprise.

Probably about five minutes ago, he answered himself, when she'd thrown herself on his mercy just to gain a good opinion from him.

Curiosity defeated him, and he moved forward until he was replacing his fingers with his mouth, kissing her just softly enough to feel her. Jhon knew it was a mistake the moment he felt the unexpected intimacy of it, the warmth and softness of the damp connection striking up a strange and fearful sense of fitting perfectly with her. She was holding her breath, eyes wide open and surprised at his gesture of gentility. So damn ingenuous. So unbelievably unique.

He reached to touch a thumb to her chin, pulling down gently to guide her mouth open beneath his. She drew breath, held it deep, again in expectation, and made it too damn hard to pull away and leave her unfulfilled. Besides, he had a craving to know what she tasted like. Jhon's tongue darted into her mouth to relay that information back to himself, but an instant flashed past and it no longer seemed to matter. Or rather, it seemed to be all that mattered.

Her kiss struck him like lightning, jagged and hot, a bolt of pure power coming from nowhere to singe and electrify. That was how he went from a light caress to sealing himself to her and diving for her tongue with hunger and intensity. Hanna might be restrained, but it didn't stop her from matching his sudden aggression. She opened to him, drew him in deep with a sound of appetite and the slink of her talented tongue. Her powerful confidence and the sheer skill she used to engage him and draw him in was astounding. As worldly as he was, or thought he was, he'd never encountered a woman who could kiss with such . . . power. He couldn't explain it, but it was as though she were bleeding raw need into him. Hunger. He felt her torso straining toward him, pulling against the stiff restraints, her soft breasts touching his bare chest lightly, so that he felt the firmness of their erect tips drawing against him.

Jhon reached up suddenly, wrapping his hand around her throat and tearing back away from her as he pushed her flat to the wall. He pulled for breath in deep, disbelieving draws and licked the flavor of her from his lips. She relaxed into his will, although she, too, was breathing hard as she studied him with sensually hooded eyes.

"Too bad you're standing," he rasped. "With a mouth like that, I can think of excellent ways of employing it." The crudeness was unwarranted and purposeful, a knee-jerk reaction to force distance because distance was so badly needed.

"You could always free me," she suggested.

Vejhon went suddenly still at that. She didn't want her freedom. He knew instantly that wasn't what she wanted by making the request. She wanted . . .

"Thinking about it?" she coaxed, tilting her head and licking her lips slowly.

"You would do that?" he asked, unable to completely hide his confusion and shock. "You would get down on your knees for a total stranger?"

"You would allow a total stranger to take you into her mouth?" she countered.

Well, hell, if she was going to be all logical about it . . . Yeah, if the stranger had lips like that and a tongue as carnal as hers, he most likely wouldn't hesitate. "So, I free you," he speculated, "you take me into your mouth and suck and stroke me until I climax . . . then what?"

"You mean besides swallowing, I take it?"

Vejhon choked out a laugh, her quirky brow teasing it out of him. She smiled slyly.

"Ask a stupid question . . ."

"I didn't say it was stupid," she argued lightly. "But the 'then what' is really up to you. You are looking for a way to humiliate me? It will take more than treating me like a whore, honestly. I think I'm too naturally inclined toward sex for you to shock me with it. So are you, for that matter. You're a soldier. Typically people in life-threatening, on-the-edge careers express their sexual needs with frequency and tend to do it without remorse."

"Yeah," he agreed absently. He reached out to run the tips of his fingernails down her side, no longer even trying to curb his impulses. He started beneath her armpit and slid down to her hip, riding every contour of every rib and curve along the way. She barely squirmed, but he watched with satisfied fascination as chills raced along her skin in sheets of little blue bumps that were chasing each other in waves. She had responded openly to his kiss, yes, but this reaction was far more telling to him, even a little equalizing.

Jhon was hooked and he knew it. He already knew, deep inside of his own mind, that he had no cause for vengeance anymore. He hadn't since the moment she'd deflated his every preconceived notion about her by throwing herself down like a gauntlet. Still, that didn't mean he wasn't beyond considering an alternate challenge. It was like seeing a wild creature tethered but not tamed. Men had wanted to tame the wild things since all the worlds were young. It was probably in their blood, their very genes, to be lured by such deadly, beautiful passion. So proud and powerful in her own right, who could earn the right to keep her? How did one take possession of a woman who owned everything . . . including him? This was what he thought as he let his hand slide over her hip, stroking toward the soft swell of her backside.

"Don't forget—!" She gasped, cutting herself off and jerking slightly in the manacles. He watched her eyes widen, her lips parting in slight surprise. Jhon froze the instant he realized the mistake he had just made.

"Oh, damn," he swore softly, pulling his hand away to glare at the ring around his finger. He hadn't meant to do it. He'd forgotten about the damn thing completely. Jerking it from his finger, he threw it across the room so it rang and skipped over distant stone. He reached to cup her face in between his hands, pulling her gaze up to his. "Hanna, I didn't mean to do that!"

"It's okay," she said on a breathless exhale.

"No. You don't understand." He drew back and slapped a furious hand against the wall near her head. "It's enough that you offered this! Don't you see? I can't think of a way to exact revenge because the minute you did this I knew you never meant me any harm. How can I claim vengeance on someone who meant no harm?"

"Harm was done," she said softly, her chest rising and

falling quickly as a soft lavender hue tinged her cheeks. "Intention doesn't matter if *you* feel harm was done." For the first time, she put her head back and closed her eyes, visibly trying to ride the upsurge the stimulant was pummeling her body with. "Jhon . . ."

"How do I stop this, Hanna?"

She shook her head silently.

"Bullshit! You have an antidote. I don't want this, Hanna!"

When her eyes flew open, Jhon caught hold of his breath. Her pupils were so wide that there was barely a trace of blue to be found around the black voids. A low sound rumbled up out of her throat, a small cry or groan that sounded much like a purr.

"Touch me."

He couldn't react. For the first time in his life he couldn't make himself take action. He just stared at her as he stood tensely before her, watching the flush of color rising along her skin, seeing the soft sheen of perspiration breaking all over her. She was lashed down tight, but her body managed to arch and squirm provocatively all the same. He knew that feeling, knew how hot her blood was at this very moment. Knew exactly where it was all rushing to.

"Step away, then!" she cried out suddenly. "If this is the torture you choose, then step away and let me suffer it! I can't bear the scent of you. . . ." She groaned, knowing such a statement was playing right into his hands, if indeed he was doing this on purpose. How would he ever have known how easy it was for her to smell the tantalizing potion that was his pheromones? Testosterone and soap . . . and the scent that was his and only his. Together they all blended and teased her mercilessly. And that was *before* the stimulant. Would he ever realize what agony he was about to dish up to her?

Hanna's body locked up in a fit of need, the signals beneath her skin all screaming at her at once. It robbed her of sense and breath in a way she had never experienced before. Everything burned! Why? It shouldn't be this way. This unbearable! Not with only one injection!

She had made a critical misjudgment, she realized with dismay. In her haste to level the playing field between them, she had forgotten to take her biochemistry into account . . . not to mention the fact that the ring was meant to dose a male. A large male.

"No, no . . ." she panted softly as her muscles seized, a hysterical panic lacing her voice as she laughed at how beautifully she had set herself up for him. Whether he wanted it or not, he was about to have all the vengeance he could possibly stomach.

"Release the restraints!"

Like a charm, the manacles retracted, and Hanna fell forward against him. She tried to draw back, crying out as his rough hands swept her too-sensitive skin and her naked torso connected with his.

Divinity!

The feel of his flesh, hot and vital against her own was like living in joy with gods. She couldn't hope to show restraint as she threw her arms around his neck and hauled herself completely flush to his body, her leg snaking around his hip and thigh. Her mouth sought his and found it with perfection. Tears of relief leapt into her eyes when he allowed her the kiss she demanded, his hands grasping her shoulders to steady her squirming body as he thrust for her starving tongue.

He had to be out of his mind. Gods! It was like being wrapped up in a dream to have this flawless creature clinging to him with every ounce of enthusiasm she possessed. Her nails bit at his shoulders as she struggled to get inside his skin or better. She sucked and toyed with his mouth as though she were starved, and he the only sustenance. She tore away from his mouth and suddenly her lips were on his skin, his throat, his shoulders, and his chest. She overwhelmed with her uncanny ability to arouse and seduce, his entire body pulsing hard with abrupt need, and his half-dormant penis responding to the on-rush of heat that flooded it.

As they'd discussed, it wasn't long at all before she had her tongue gliding down the center line of his belly, her hands scouting ahead for him as she slipped like a sinuous python down his legs, her hair gathering in a pool on the floor behind her. Vejhon's useless hands could only cling to her hair as his head fell back with blind sensation. Her hands touched him, stroking his erection through the material of his pants, her caresses as voracious as her mouth had been . . . as it promised to be. Her fingers were deft and quick as she undid the fastenings across the front, releasing him into her waiting hand.

It was when her touch closed around him that he was jolted into a tormented awareness. He suddenly recalled the last time she had touched him, as well as the reason she was behaving the way she was in that moment. He stiffened in shock at his own behavior, at how incredibly dishonorable it was to do this to her. It was a thought that almost leaped overboard and swam away when her tongue darted out to lick across the head of his cock, making her groan with ecstatic delight. He echoed the sound, his body shuddering as he sucked in air through his teeth.

No! NO! In so many ways, *no!*

He would never know how he broke free from her without falling on his ass in the process, but he staggered back and bore the painful, protesting cry of a body in fierce demand. Not to mention her agonized scream of frustration. To her, he was torturing her as she had done to him. To him, he was striving to do just the opposite. How humiliated would she be if she did this under the influence of a drug? It was, at last, a level playing field. She was as out of control of her actions as he had been of

his. And he hated it. He despised being the one who had orchestrated this agony for her.

Vejhon quickly got back into his trousers and hurried to her
kneeling, bent-over figure. He kneeled, too, and she screamed
again, hitting him hard and shoving him with both hands in
anger and frustration.

"Stop it! Don't tease me if you won't let me have you! You
bastard! Don't!"

He ignored the tantrum, scooping her from the floor effort-
lessly and moving to the bed where he laid her across its middle. She sobbed in real pain, her limbs moving in constant,
restless sensuality, her hands caressing her own skin as it howled
for stimulation of any kind. The image gave him a jolt of inspiration, and he carefully stretched out beside her on the bed,
making sure not to touch her. He reached for her hand and
took hold, even that simple contact making her gasp and jerk.
Unable to help the impulse, his lips touched the tears running
down her temple.

"Shh, Hanna . . ." he soothed softly. "I will help you."

Jhon drew her hand down her torso, guiding her straight
down the center of her body. He could only hope her physiology was similar to what he was familiar with as he brought her
fingers to rest on the baby soft skin of her pubic mound. She
grew no hair, the entire area smooth and perfect. He backed his
center finger along hers and together they eased past her outer
labia.

He had to bite back a groan, his brain screaming curses at
him, when he felt how hot and how awesomely wet with readiness she was from the stim. It made little difference that it hadn't
been produced by his own skill, except to his conscience. It
made the sensations no less divine, no less tempting. Her thighs
instinctively fell wide open, and his torture was completed
when his sensitive sense of smell drew in the appetizing per-

fume of her sex. Vejhon turned his face into the bedding as he bit down on the inside of his lip, forcing himself to ignore the pounding pulse of his highly interested cock, and coaxing her to finish what he had so cruelly started.

Hanna touched the clit at the top of her kitty and she gasped out hard at the feedback it sent through her hyperstimulated body. Nerves screeched with relief and then yowled for more. More! More touch, more scent . . . more Vejhon. But then she felt him drawing away and she jerked to grab for him, to pull him back to her.

"No. No," he whispered, turning against her ear as his voice ground out the word as though passing it between millstones. "Touch yourself, Hanna. Give yourself relief."

"You!" It was a protest and a demand all at once.

"I . . ." He swallowed noisily and closed his eyes as he threw himself on his sword. "I want to watch," he rasped, barely hearing himself over the chorus of his heart and his breath. He hadn't meant to be any part of it, but he was just realizing that she was no good at taking for herself without somehow giving in return. It was a painful way to learn how increasingly mistaken he had been about her, but he grimly accepted the punishment he deserved. "Show me. Show me how you come, honey."

She opened her eyes and turned to seek his. He watched tears roll out of them and into her hairline and prayed she accepted his offer. He was only a man, after all, and he was reaching his limits as he watched her wriggle in need beside him. She nodded just once, but it was enough to free him. He got up from the bed because he knew he couldn't be lying beside her as she reached orgasm. He'd never survive it with his honor and conscience intact. He'd end up using her to the hilt and beyond, and he couldn't even begin to imagine the consequences for them both if he did. He moved to retrieve a chair from nearby and settled it just offside of her spread thighs. This way, he could focus on her face and not on her sex, which was splayed like an offering before him.

Gods, if you get me through this, I swear I will try to be a better man, he prayed. He had to have become one already, to a degree. Gods knew, before he'd been through this ordeal of debasement, he never would have thought twice about taking advantage of a woman who was, for all intents and purposes, in heat. He would have been happy to oblige her and damn the consequences to her feelings. Now he was forced to wonder about the brothels he'd attended over the years both on and off his home planet. How many of those women had been, in essence, slaves? How many had used stims and other drugs to get them through their nightly encounters? He'd never cared to ask the question before. It had never made such a difference to him before.

But now he had to focus on the present and let the past take care of itself. Now he knew what the answer to the question was and here and now he had to struggle with himself to make all of the right choices. Ignorance was one thing, but purposefulness something entirely different.

He wasn't a stranger to watching a woman bring herself to climax. The unfamiliar part would come later; when he denied himself the pleasure of showing her he could use her body to top her own performance.

"Tell me," she begged him softly from the bed. "Tell me what you want and I'll do it. I'll do anything."

Jhon sat back in the chair and decided he must have been an evil bastard at some point in a previous incarnation. Maybe he had beaten old women and stewed babies and pups for supper. Whatever it was, it had to be truly and purely malevolent, and *this* was payback. What else could account for the past few months of his life? Not to mention the next minutes to come.

For want of a better word, he thought with a grimace.

"Just touch yourself. Everywhere it feels good. I want to watch you feel good."

She didn't do him the favor of closing her eyes. Instead she fixated on him, holding his gaze steadily as she did as instructed. Her free hand drifted lightly by the fingertips down her throat and then up the slope of a firmly rounded breast. Jhon knew the feel of her skin now, so it was all too easy to imagine what she was feeling as she did this. What he didn't know was how those thick, gorgeous nipples would feel. Unique, he thought as her nails flicked over one. Satisfying. On the tongue, against his palm. Heat flushed his face and neck, and he knew it was visible because she smiled for the first time since she had entered this crisis. The smile was too damn self-satisfied and wicked for his peace of mind. She'd grin like an idiot and shout from mountaintops if she could just feel how hard he was right then. He already had a moist stain of pre-cum saturating the thin fabric of his pants, and he was strangling within their confines.

Her opposite hand wasn't being coy either. She hadn't waited even a second before sliding her fingers down along the wet slit it was nestled in. She was so primed that she gasped the instant she touched herself. Her lashes fluttered as a tense sort of bliss skipped over her features. Had he thought she had the features of an innocent? No. This was a siren, sex and temptation etched into every sweeping curve and underlying bone. The true intensity was in her unwavering eyes as she held onto him, seeking approval, guidance . . . response.

He hardly disappointed. Watching her breasts bounce lightly as she reached for herself, hearing her breath catch and her fingers slide through juicy flesh, it was absolutely incredible, and he knew his expression said so. Her lips parted to accommodate her breathing and the low moan she exhaled. That starkly pink tongue popped out and reminded him of the all-too-brief taste she had taken of him. His cock throbbed angrily, demanding release from its prison and release from its hell.

"You have nice long fingers," he heard himself saying. "They should reach pretty far inside of you."

Hanna couldn't breathe as the suggestion danced through her already sparkling brain. She had to focus on him or she was certain she would blow apart like dust and cease to exist. Her heart was tapping in rapid staccato, working too hard to manage the stimulant that was Vejhon as well as the one in her bloodstream. Other than that, it was all about her own touch on her own body and the way it screamed over her crying nerves. It didn't take much to bring her to the edge. All it took was his last instruction and her desire to obey it. She slipped first one . . . then two fingers into her vaginal opening, her nails sharply arousing as they tripped over her second clit. Everything went a shade of gray as the pleasure rode through her, and when it cleared he was still there and watching her more intently than ever.

"You need to touch yourself, too," she said, demanding rather than requesting. She watched as he clutched his hand around the arm of the chair briefly, the other running over his mouth. His mouth that tasted like heat, a touch of salt, and something just out of range of definition, she recalled.

"I thought this was about what I wanted," he said, his voice catching hoarsely.

"It is what you want," she breathed. "I can see it in your mind. I can see your body begging for it." Her gaze dropped to his lap and her proof positive of that.

He shook his head mutely. She didn't know what that meant exactly, but she didn't like it. Hanna quickly dropped her legs and stood up. Jhon jerked in his seat and watched her warily as she stood in front of him. Then she slowly sank to her knees, her limber joints setting them wide apart as she sat back on her heels and feet. She cocked her head in silent challenge and shifted the rules of the battlefield as she sat like that, barely a couple of feet away from him, and held up two fingers, both of which were glistening with the dew of her own body. Snaring his eyes yet again, she slowly drew her fingers across her lips, as if she were painting them with herself. She paused only to lick them clean right before she set one finger against her tongue and closed her mouth around it, sucking it deep within.

Apparently, Jhon wasn't meant to be a better man. He wasn't even meant to survive this ordeal, he was convinced of it. His heart felt like it was going to rip out of his own chest, and his erect phallus was ten seconds from sliding into his palm.

Wrong. *Five* seconds. That was exactly how long it took for that fit, nimble body to bend back over her heels, her back arcing until her hair pooled into a pillow for her shoulders right before they touched the floor. She now lay kneeled back, her thighs wide apart and her pelvis upthrust against the hill her heels made under her backside. This afforded Vejhon the view he had tried to avoid, only much closer and in a much more provocative and subservient position. She topped off this acrobatic taunt with the return of her fingers to her pussy.

"Here kitty, kitty," she teased in a throaty, singsong voice meant to be the total temptation it was.

"Bad kitty, kitty," he growled dangerously back at her. But he was a lost cause and he knew it. He didn't even take offense when she laughed as his engorged cock sprang eagerly into his waiting palm once he'd allowed it freedom.

In the long run it might be the better choice. It would greatly reduce the chances of what could happen next after he watched her do this. As he encircled himself, he tried to think how long it had been since he had done *this*. He dismissed the question as unimportant next to the vision of the black-haired beauty finger-fucking herself into rising excitement, her other hand coasting from breast to breast, pulling and pinching each nipple so hard that after a while Jhon and Hanna both began to gasp for breath in time to each tug. His palm and fingers had become lubricated by his own fluids after his first stroke, so every single one after that was a sensory wash that felt like nails scratching down his back in ecstasy.

Again their eyes locked, only this time they could both read the coming crisis building in each other's gaze. She was on stim overload so she was far ahead of him, but she wasn't above using any trick in her book.

"When you come," Hanna breathed, "I want you to come on me. I want you on my skin, Vejhon Mach. I want to see you burst all over me."

"Oh dear gods," he gasped, the hearing of her proposal driving him out of his mind with pleasure. "Are you—?"

"Yes! I'm sure!" She cried out the affirmation like anger, only it was compounded ecstasy climbing through her like upsurging waves. Jhon watched, sliding forward to the edge of his seat, as she blushed with increasingly darkening shades of lavender. She gasped hard for every breath, her thigh muscles clenched tight enough to show him perfection of definition. She was vibrating with the tension of the coming explosion and he was doing a fair imitation himself.

Jhon saw her orgasm like the ephemeral possession of a wild animal. She arched up, hips seeking and fingers swirling and she screamed like an untamed thing, the pitch like the cry of a cat. *Here, kitty, kitty.* It was his last coherent thought as he dropped to a kneel between her knees, his own orgasm an internal match to her primal scream. It felt as though the other day had never happened. As though he hadn't had release in years. He wouldn't close his eyes for all the freedom in the worlds at that moment as he watched himself ejaculate in great staccato bursts across her belly and breasts. He ground his teeth together to hold back his own primal cry, releasing it in low, masculine grunts of pleasure personified instead.

If that weren't enough to drive a man insane, she ran her free hand up her wet body and spread his essence into her skin and onto her lips and tongue. The sight kept him coming far longer than was natural for him, but long enough to hear her chase her first climax with a second. This one was painful for her, her body raw and oversensitive, the stim playing its angry tricks. She cried out, jerking her hand away from herself as if she'd been burned. Vejhon sat back hard on his heels, shaking head to toe as droplets from his sweat-drenched hair skipped onto and down his body.

For a long time, the only sound was of their labored breathing.

8

Najir stood on the other side of the wall, looking down on Hanna and the man with her.

When he had returned from the yards to find Hanna missing, he had instantly known she was with him and had felt a full-blown fright unlike anything he'd known in his life. He had run all the way to Vejhon's room and, disregarding any thought of privacy, he had not even hesitated to go to the viewing room. He'd activated every portal, racing down the corridor in a frantic search for her. He hadn't seen them beside the bed at first because it hadn't occurred to him to look along the floor. Now he did see them and he stood frozen as he watched the unbelievable tableau playing out before him.

Hanna had always been indescribably gorgeous in the throes of orgasm. It felt like such a waste to turn her back to you sometimes, where you couldn't watch her face as easily, but sometimes it was so worth it. . . .

He understood. Despite the agony screaming through him on a distant level he was in too much shock to access, he couldn't possibly blame Vejhon for the act of coming across Hanna's pretty skin and body. He knew what it felt like, knew what it looked like . . . he just knew.

And now he knew what it looked like from a whole new perspective. He laughed a little, the sound tremulous at best as he laid a hand against the wall and closed his eyes. Strange, how he still had the taste of terror in his mouth. It seemed so obscene now.

How had she done it? How had she taken Jhon from plotting their deaths to *this* in just a matter of hours? Oh, if anyone could, it was Hanna, he made no mistake about that. But he had expected time. Just a little time to prepare for it. A day. Maybe two. And he had never wanted to see it.

He had only himself to blame. Anyone knew Hanna could take care of herself. Who did he think he was, trying to play her protector? The reality was, she protected him. Without her . . .

Without her.

He was without her.

But nothing else would change. He had sworn it. And he never, ever broke his word. He just wished he'd promised not to break the bastard's neck as well, because if Mach so much as bruised Hanna's feelings, Najir was going to be in a hell of a mess.

And then Hanna made a pitiful mewling sound that struck through both men with a horrible sense of impending trouble. Vejhon forced himself to attentiveness, leaning over her to see her face. She rolled onto her side, her back to Najir, her hair sliding away from her shoulders.

Najir bolted, running for the other room.

Jhon caught Hanna before she made it to her side and rolled her back, scooping her into his arms just as her skin drained of color until even her lips looked pale.

Hanna screamed as he clutched her tightly to his chest and rose to his feet. She tried to shove him away from touching her, the overload of feedback from the stim like torture of a whole new variety, but Jhon resisted without realizing the harm it was doing.

"Let her go!"

Jhon stumbled at the unexpected voice resonating with fury at his back. He jerked to look at Najir as the other man closed on them with purpose blazing in his dark eyes.

"I'm not trying to hurt her!" Jhon barked, too impatient to explain his goal was to help. Why waste time speaking of it when action was so desperately needed?

"I know that, fool! If you were, you'd be unconscious by now." Najir crossed past Jhon and jumped down into the tub. It immediately began to fill with its remarkable speed as Najir looked to Jhon. "You gave her a stimulant?" he demanded to know.

"It was an accident. . . ."

"I'm not placing blame! I'm trying to tell you, you can't touch her now. The stimulant is a nightmare after orgasm when given in two doses. Even the simplest of touches—"

"I didn't give her two doses! It wouldn't have been an accident then if I had, now would it?" Regardless of the argument, Jhon responded when Najir beckoned to him to hand Hanna into the tub. He passed her to the other man and watched as he sank to his knees with her, settling her into the water.

"Then this doesn't make sense." Najir cast about for an explanation as Vejhon dropped down into the bath as well. "One dose shouldn't do this. Hush, Hanna, hush," the slave soothed softly. Jhon watched him stretch her out and immediately understood what he was doing. Keeping his touch limited to her ankles, and Najir keeping his only on her shoulders, they kept her almost entirely submerged except her face. Like a sensory deprivation tank. Their voices dropped to whispers.

"An overdose?" Jhon suggested.

Najir looked up at him. "How would that happen?"

Jhon heard the suspicion in the other man's voice and hardly blamed him. Coming into the room because his mistress was screaming must have aged him a millennium. "How the hell would I know? It's her damn ring." Jhon saw her flinch at his raised voice and he instantly regretted his temper. "Shh, Hanna, it's okay. . . ."

"The ring. The one she used on you?"

"She gave it to me . . . said she wanted to level the playing field." Vejhon grimaced. "I swear, I had no intention of using it. Not after knowing it firsthand. I just forgot I had the thing on."

"And it sounds like Hanna forgot to dial down the dose," Najir said grimly. "She must have gotten one meant for a man our size and race. The PAN are notoriously more sensitive than we are and Hanna in particular has a . . . unique chemistry. On the plus side, she will process it out quicker than we would."

"Good." Jhon paused to study the other man for a moment. "Our race?"

Najir looked up in surprise and rapidly reviewed what he had said. Damn. A slipup he couldn't afford. Worse, one Hanna couldn't afford.

"I mean aliens in general."

Vejhon had interrogated enough prisoners in his time to know when someone was lying to him, and Najir was lying big-time. Why? If Najir was from Wite, why lie about it? He would think the man would celebrate seeing a fellow patriot after a decade of living in this alien culture.

"I see," Jhon said nonchalantly. "How long will we have to keep her in here?"

"Until she stops crying at least," Najir said softly, his large fingers reaching to lightly touch her forehead. It was a touch of such simplicity, but it also reflected a depth of affection Vejhon instantly recognized, simply by virtue of never having known it. Not to receive, and certainly not to give. He watched carefully as Najir frowned when she shook him off. "Still very raw," the other man murmured, completely oblivious to how much he was giving away.

Love. Najir loved her. Not the adoration of slave to master, as Jhon had thought, but as a man loves a woman. Did Hanna return the feeling? If so, what was her purpose in having Jhon there? She'd locked herself in those restraints fully expecting him to use her body however he liked. She'd eagerly made the offer, so she must have felt free to do so. He made no mistake about her wanting him. She had kissed him with pure need and desire, had devoured him like she was starving for him . . . all this before the accidental stimulant. It may not be her only desire for him, but it was a central one.

If it was for the sake of variety, why select a male nearly twin to that which she already had conquered and was devoted to? Or maybe, he thought with a sick sensation in his belly, he was to play stallion for her, providing fertility Najir could not.

No. She had had the opportunity to use him as such without needing to bother with how he felt about it. Regardless of the goal he couldn't see, he didn't understand Najir. If he loved this woman, why would he purchase his own rival? He had to have known the risk he was taking bringing a second male into her sphere; why had he purposely done so? As Vejhon looked down at Hanna, he couldn't help but become angry with Najir. What kind of man would give away, or even so intimately share, a crucially prized possession so easily? Jhon felt a furious sensation of surety that if he were ever to finally know love for a woman, for anyone really, he would never be so cavalier about it. He would never risk the loss of that love and he would do what he did best to keep it secure. He would fight. Any way he could.

After a few minutes, Jhon managed to calm his overworking thoughts. He seemed to feel better as Hanna relaxed, easing away from the worst of her pain as they gently turned her between them, trading her weight. Hanna stirred, reaching out of the water to close her hand around Vejhon's forearm.

"A good sign," Najir informed softly. He moved to rest her feet against his thigh as he reached to get soap and a bathing cloth. He built a lather in the cloth, then held it out to Jhon. Their eyes met across her body and the other man nodded down at Hanna. "She needs to be cleansed."

Vejhon suddenly recalled what had happened only minutes before Najir had entered. How had the other man known . . . ? Understanding dawned even before the question could be completed. Taking the cloth, Jhon submerged it in the water.

"I take it there is an observation window into the room."

It was a statement, spoken low and carefully, but in no way in doubt of itself. Najir cursed himself for a fool, but he didn't lie this time. He gave the man that much respect.

"I was out training with the security forces. When I found Hanna missing, I overreacted. If you recall, you have threatened to kill her several times. Not to mention making the attempt on me."

"I recall," Jhon agreed.

"I shouldn't have invaded your privacy. Hanna will be unhappy with me if she knows I had done so while you were together . . . more so when she realizes I have given this detail away before she had the opportunity to tell you herself. Rest assured, Hanna and I are the only ones with access to that room . . . and I will never use it again. You have my word."

There was a bitterness to the oath, and Jhon instantly forgave Najir the trespass, as well as accepted his word as bond. It was clear that the slave had gotten a good enough lesson in respecting privacy without Vejhon losing his temper over the matter. It must have been like a knife in Najir's gut to watch the woman he cared for so deeply play palette to another man's sexual art.

"This won't bother her?" Jhon asked as he began to wash the canvas of her body clean of any remaining traces of their encounter.

"Not anymore. She's stopped weeping and she initiated contact with you."

"But she is still in some form of shock," Jhon noted as he drew her back against his chest gently to better balance her.

"Exhaustion is more like it."

Najir let her legs rest freely in the water and rose to his feet. Jhon watched the other man get out of the tub, water streaming from his clothing as he crossed to the wardrobe and pulled out one of the embroidered shirts from within. He returned to the tub just as Jhon finished his task. Together they raised her up to Najir's hold, her wet hair plastered to her back and body everywhere. To Vejhon's surprise, Najir didn't bother with drying her before quickly pulling the shirt over her, hair and all, and buttoning her up. Was he now, suddenly, trying to shield her from Vejhon? It made no more sense than anything else, considering recent events, but Vejhon knew that somehow all these odd actions and discrepancies added up to a singular thing. A single secret between Najir and Hanna that he wasn't privy to . . . but was somehow going to become a part of.

"I'm going to take her to her room," Najir said. "She will sleep for a while, so don't be disturbed if you don't see her for some time."

Jhon could only nod, not seeing how he had much choice in the matter. This time he was very certain of the emotion he felt because he *had* felt it before. The twinge of jealousy rode through him like a whip, the hardest snap of it coming as the door sealed behind Najir's exit with her.

But jealous of what? Of their freedom to come and go? Of their knowledge and understanding of things he was in the dark about?

Jhon couldn't escape the feeling that although those were excellent reasons, they didn't quite touch on the truth.

Najir walked the short way down the hall to Hanna's room. Once within, he brought her to her bed and stripped her of the sodden shirt. He retrieved towels to dry her with, patiently patting dry the length of her hair. Then, holding it aside, he gently dried her back and the silver rosettes that spotted her between her shoulders, all the way down the length of her spine.

The man he had purchased for Hanna was too shrewd by half. It wouldn't have taken him long at all to realize that none of Hanna's race had these marks . . . and certainly not much longer than that to figure out why.

Hanna awoke with a startled gasp, sitting up quickly. There was no describing her relief when she realized she was in her own bedroom. That relief lasted all of two seconds; then she saw Najir sitting beside her bed, his dark eyes glittering in the sunlight of what she hoped was only one day later than when she'd last been awake. He didn't look very happy. Or angry. In fact, his expression was like stone, something she wasn't used to seeing on him at all. Not since he'd first arrived in her home.

"How much damage have I done?"

Najir broke his tableau of stoicism to give her a brief smile. He rubbed the back of his neck, telling her he probably hadn't left her side for a minute.

"I can't say for certain. I don't know everything. I came in . . . later."

Hanna narrowed her eyes to slits of suspicion.

"When later?"

"Later than the stim, sooner than I wanted to."

Najir had become too used to showing his emotions to her over the years. His voice stumbled over the sentence just enough to tell her she had done exactly what she hadn't wished to do. Hanna quickly left the comfort of her bed and drew up the lengthy skirt of her nightdress so she could climb into his lap like a young girl, wrapping her arms around him in comfort.

"I never meant to cause you hurt," she said softly beneath his ear. "You shouldn't have gone in the observation room while I was alone with him. You knew what you might find."

"I wasn't thinking of that, was I?" he snapped, his words harsh and mean. "I was too busy being scared to death the barbarian would hurt you as he'd promised! It was too soon for you to go in there without some sort of security. And it was utterly insane for you to let him have that ring!" Najir grabbed hold of her hair and pulled her back by it so he could let her see the fury in his eyes. "I don't even want to know how else you tried to 'level the playing field' for him," he hissed softly, "because knowing you I can only guess too well!"

Hanna freed herself from him, scrambling off his lap when her affection was so angrily rejected. She wasn't used to it and it stung, but she supposed she deserved it. She couldn't have everything as perfect as she prayed for. She couldn't make this transition without hurting Najir. She couldn't keep Vejhon without keeping him a slave, and she couldn't free him without the result of enslaving others she loved more than even her own life.

"It worked, didn't it?" she countered softly, keeping her back to him as she wrapped her arms around her suddenly chilled body. "How could I get his total trust unless I offered it first? Especially after what I did?"

Najir watched her cross to her dressing area. She chose something to wear and quickly changed into it. Then she sat down to run a brush through her hair, grooming herself meticulously as he watched. He had done this often, sat and watched her do these simple things. They had been moments of great pleasure and contentment for him; now it simply made him grieve.

Hanna looked up and met his gaze in her reflection glass, his expression choking a sound of dismay out of her. She threw down her brush and ran over to him, dropping to her knees between his feet and resting her damp face on his chest as he welcomed her hug this time.

"Tell me what to do," she begged him. "I will do anything for you, Najir, if it will bring you peace. Tell me to free you, and I will find a way. Tell me to find you a mate worthy of you, and I will search the universe tirelessly. Do you want to be rid of this House, rid of me? I will send you to live in the country places. No one will bother you if they think you keep the residence for me. Tell me!"

"I want . . ." He sighed long and low. "I want what I have always wanted. I want you to be happy. I want you safe and secure. I want to give you what you were cheated out of when you made the mistake of buying me."

"Najir!" she gasped, utterly horrified. "I never thought, never once, that I made a mistake! I would have bought you had you been a woman, for mercy's sake! Anything to put an end to that nightmare of an auction. Please! Don't treat the last ten years so cavalierly. You will break my heart. Or is that what you want? To break my heart like I have broken yours?"

"No," he said hoarsely. "I wouldn't wish this feeling on my worst enemy, never mind a woman I love so dearly. And you are not responsible for the state of my heart, Hanna. You made it very clear that nothing could come of us. And I have accepted that. I will be fine. Yesterday just . . . caught me off guard. I don't know why," he said with a grimace. "I knew you would win him over quickly. How could he not find you as irresistible as I do?"

"Mmm, now you are flattering me to make up for yelling at me."

"True, and yet it is a truth, too. There is chemistry between you. You have him thinking . . . feeling in ways I doubt he is used to. I'm not certain he has had much use for emotions other than those of anger. Probably because he lacked opportunity. He is capable of them, though; I could see it in the way he handled you when we were bringing you out of the stim. Guilt, concern, care . . . but it squeaks on him like rusty hinges on old gates. And Hanna"—he took her head between his big hands and looked dead into her eyes—"don't wait any longer than you have to. He is shrewd. Too much so. You must catch him between the point of trust and too much knowledge. On him, it will go by much too fast if you aren't careful. It was not wise to be nude with him."

"I thought my back was going to be to the wall the whole time. I didn't expect . . . but you're right, I cannot afford to be careless now. Not when I am so close."

"And Hanna . . . I am not leaving. I can't, you know. I have invested too much time in this House to abandon it when it is about to undergo a rebirth such as this." He brushed back her hair and kissed her forehead. "And as much as it might hurt to love you, it will utterly destroy me to leave you. One I can get over, the other I cannot."

Hanna nodded gravely, turning her head to kiss his palm. "So you stay."

"And I stay out of the observation room from now on. Vejhon knows of it, by the way. I let something slip. Stupid of me. But I gave him my word I wouldn't invade his privacy again."

"It's all right," she said. "I don't care if he knows. Not now." She stood up, adopting a brisk attitude. "Anyway, I have a day's work to catch up on. See Jhon has all of his needs met . . . unless . . ." She trailed off awkwardly. Hanna simply didn't know how to avoid including her right arm in everything she did. "I can get someone else. . . ."

"No. He mustn't have any unnecessary exposure, you know that. I will handle it. I am better now that we have talked."

"And we will talk again whenever you need to." She swore softly, reaching to squeeze his hand. "I swear it. Whenever you need."

"Just as I am here to do whatever you need, whenever you need."

"A guard."

"A guard? Damn me, Hyde, you have to do better than that!" the Baron barked.

"All right, then," Sozo acquiesced with a huge grin as he propped a hip onto the desk Majum was sitting at. "How about a guard at House Drakoulous with a very big family of young brothers and sisters?"

"I hope you're getting to a point very soon," the Baron groused, slouching in his chair to reflect how unimpressed he was so far. After his encounter with Hanna on the steps of the Chamber, after what she had said to him, he wanted the smug bitch to bleed from her eyeballs.

The captain knew his friend so well. He even began to chuckle, braving the deadly glare it elicited.

"Very well, then," he said quickly, holding up both hands in gracious surrender. "How about a guard at House Drakoulous with a big family of young brothers and sisters . . . all of whom are in your dungeons at this very moment?"

Majum jerked upright in his chair so fast that he almost sent it shooting out from under him. Sozo gave in and rollicked with laughter as the other man shot to his feet, and grabbed him by both arms.

"Great ghosts! I know you know better than to fuck with me about something like that!"

"Never," he assured.

"How many? How many are boys? How young? What did you tell the guard?"

"There are six altogether, and four are boys. They range in age from nineteen summers to twelve summers. And before you ask, the boys are nineteen, seventeen, fourteen, and twelve. The girls are sixteen and thirteen."

"Damn me, thank the gods for commoner proliferation! That slut whelped them out hot on each other's tails, didn't she? What of the guard? I suppose you lied and told him we wouldn't hurt his little family if he did what you asked him to?"

"Not at all," Hyde chuckled. "I told him we'd *stop* hurting his family as soon as he did what I asked him to."

Majum threw back his head and laughed at that. "That is priceless! All the better if you told him who has them. My reputation does proceed me."

"As you so proudly like to remind me. And yes, though I didn't give a specified name, the implication was quite clear." The captain shrugged. "On the off chance he's stupid enough to tattle to his Master, he can't testify as to who I was, as I was in disguise, and who you are, because your name was never mentioned. We merely bury the bodies and the evidence and like magic . . . instant immunity from harm."

"Genius! Pure genius. But I do hope you haven't already figured out your plan for breaching the Drakoulous House. And I haven't decided yet if I will assassinate the bitch herself, or her two confections. I will need time to choose."

"Oh, not to fear, my good Baron. You have plenty of time to think. And to play with your new guests. I would never deprive you of that so quickly. Where's the fun in it?"

"Let me guess, Hyde," the Baron chuckled. "You want the girls."

"Well, sixteen is a mite long in the tooth for me . . . but I could find it in my cock to make the exception."

The quip made Majum laugh all the harder.

"And the thirteen-year-old?"

"She's a fine, round little thing and she stinks of virginity. Aye, I'll take her for certain."

"Done! Perhaps we can do one of the eldest brothers side by side as you take a girl. We'll see first who is most protective of whom. Then we can see the look in their eyes as their best-loved sibling is done beside them, eh? Damn, I'm hard just thinking of it," Majum pointed out, rubbing a fierce palm down along his obvious erection.

"Why think when we can do?"

"So true."

9

Hanna was nervous. She paced back and forth outside of Jhon's room, rubbing her hands together as she thought herself in a circle about the next step she needed to take with him.

Oh, but he wouldn't understand! How could anyone? It was so hard for her to understand and she was the one who lived with this curse. This blessing.

She paced for so long that Najir found her there. He came up to her and immediately wrapped her up into the comfort of his huge embrace.

"Hanna," he soothed her gently.

"Najir, I don't know what to do. I don't have the right to do what I know I must do if I am going to save this family. I want to be up front and ask him to do this thing with honor, but . . ."

"But you and I both know that no one is going to volunteer to die. No one ever has in the entire history of this family. None can understand that in order for there to be great reward there must first come great sacrifice."

"You would have done it," she noted. "Had you been more

like him, you would have done it gladly. You love me and this family now."

"After a full decade, yes. But Hanna, you no longer have that kind of time. Your family will never know full life unless someone like Jhon first dies. And time grows short. He is becoming keen to the understanding that there is something he has that I do not. I am afraid I have made it none too obvious that I would do anything for you, and that my love for you runs very deep indeed."

"I know it does," she whispered softly, renewing the tightness of her hug around him. "And I know you are right."

"The fate of six others rests in your hands, Hanna," he reminded her gently.

"Seven," she corrected, turning her head to look at the door. "Seven others."

"True," he agreed grimly. "But death will bring a new birth to this family. It will become stronger and fuller for it. It is a sacrifice that must be made. Do not waver now, Hanna. Please, I beg of you. If I have the strength to bring him here so he might replace me in your affections, then you must have the strength to take the next step. Otherwise all of this is for nothing."

"Yes," she whispered. "I know." The understanding forced her to find strength. She stood up straight, leaving his arms. "I need you to go in first. See he is well fed and answer the questions I know he will have. I will come in shortly after you leave. Then this will draw to a close."

"And bring a new beginning," he reminded her. "For all of us."

"Pray that you are right."

"I will pray. It is all I can do," Najir said softly.

"I need you to tell me some things."

Najir paused briefly in his stride across the room to set

down Vejhon's tray. He nodded shortly. "I will answer as well as I am able."

"And I will love the day I hear that phrase for the last time." Jhon chuckled as he rose from the bed he'd been lounging on, taking note of Najir's surprised curiosity at his laughter. "Yes, he has a sense of humor. Somewhere." He laughed at himself again. "Either that or I'm a little stir crazy."

"You had questions?"

"Sort of. Hanna mentioned a rule. A slave can be put to death for not addressing someone with respect."

"Yes. My Lady. Or my Lord. Depending on the sex, you see."

"Yeah. What else? I want to know what else can get me killed around here. I've made a habit of staying alive and I think I'd like to keep it that way for a bit."

"Hanna will be delighted to hear that."

"No doubt."

"Very well." Najir sat down in the conversation area and for the first time, Jhon saw him actually lean back and relax. The man always walked around like he was at full attention. Vejhon was the first to appreciate military discipline, but there was such a thing as overkill even in his book. Sometimes, relaxation was the difference between death and life just as much as vigilance was.

Jhon sat down as well, looking forward to something to ease his boredom. Since he doubted Najir would bring in a couple of fighting staffs and a few men for the beating, this would have to do. He selected from the food, beginning to recognize favorites already. He nodded an offer to Najir and, to his continuing surprise, the slave accepted and took a plate of meat for himself.

"Your best rule, of course, is to be as low profile as possible," Najir said. "There are those who are not above foul play to obtain a slave."

"I see. Kidnap them, wait till they are declared runaways, and then 'find' them?"

"Exactly."

"Pricks."

"Yes," Najir chuckled. "But stay visible and in public places and all will be well. Hanna does not desire slave behavior, she only wishes us to do it so we can remain unharmed. For instance, to walk behind her in silence unless addressed directly."

"Lovely," Jhon said dryly, grimacing.

"You may not lay aggressive hands on anyone who is free, unless they imminently threaten your life or the life of your Master. Even then you had best be able to prove it. Not an easy thing. And it becomes less and less easy to prove the higher in rank your accuser goes. Of course, there are ways, and Hanna's rank speaks for much as well, but you need to have charge of your temper. Recklessness does not go well with this position in life."

"I may have a temper, Najir," Jhon countered, "but I have an art for concealing and controlling it when I must. I am not known for being a commander who acts rashly. I could hardly have become Colonel of the Valiants otherwise."

"I don't doubt it," Najir agreed grimly. "And that is a good thing because this is a society that fights with stealth and cowardice. They threaten with words in whispers while smiling with amicability for others to see. Knives find hearts in dark alleys and a moment's lack of vigilance will mean death. And there are those who realize that, for you and I, our own deaths are something we have reconciled long ago, so they will not hesitate to strike where our hearts lie in others."

"Effective. I have used it myself when necessary," Jhon said. "But you speak of using innocents, and I do not. My enemy may love his brother more than himself, but unless his brother has done ill himself, he doesn't belong in the fight. If the brother is as evil as his kin, then I feel no guilt in using him."

"Spoken like a true man of war. You have truly been in the worst of its evils, I think." Najir looked as though he wanted to ask him about it, but Jhon watched him dismiss the impulse. "Furthermore," he continued as though his original lecture had never come to a pause, "slaves are always banded. Unbanded slaves are considered runaways."

"Uh-huh. Figured that much out myself."

"Slaves may carry no coin. Your currency is your band. The mark of the bellcat is the emblem of House Drakoulous." He indicated his own armband. The stones set in it were different, but otherwise the etched catlike shape in the gold was obvious. "It tells merchants that anything you purchase is to be charged there. And of course, if a slave purchases large amounts of items that can be considered rations or travel supplies, it is messaged back to the owner immediately."

"To thwart the clever runaway."

"Basically. You will find a lot of checks like that around you. Slaves are treated like barely tamed thieves. Most merchants will insist on delivering the goods directly to the House until you become better known and trusted to be . . . controlled." Najir sat forward a little. "But you must look on it differently than that. I consider my behavior a long-term deception. A crucial act of undercover immersion in an enemy state, if you will."

Najir had Jhon's full attention. The tension coiling up through the soldier was quite clear. "Hanna," the veteran slave continued, "is constantly in threat. You have taken note of the guards? This city, the High City, stretches for miles in all directions before it ends and officially becomes the Low City. In all of that acreage, this uppermost crest of the mountain we are on is where the High Houses sit. There are forty in all still standing after war, famine, and more through the long centuries. Each House has a Master, and that Master holds equal political power as all the others in the Chamber of Masters, our body of lawmakers."

"Ah, but we both know nothing is equal when it comes to power and desire," Vejhon countered, his expression sardonic. "There are innumerable underhanded ways to try and manipulate a vote if you do or do not wish to pass a law."

"Which brings us to the Feuds. The House Feuds have gone on so long that no one recalls when or how they began. For the longest time Houses freely murdered and kidnapped heirs and members in a mass of guerilla politics. The net of hatred was destroying the PAN, that is certain. But sanctions were finally brought into place against the Houses. Anyone caught in the act of Feud will be exiled from the Chamber and from the Cities."

"So let me guess: the trick became not to get caught and not to leave a trail . . . but the Feuds are very much alive?"

"Some, at least. There are families that have made peace and you can see we are the better for it. But there are some who will never reconcile. The jealousy and hatred runs too deep. Hanna has tried to extricate herself from her part, but there is more than one House that focuses contempt on House Drakoulous, either because of issues long past, or because of the unshakeable power Hanna and her mother before her exhibited when it came to voting their consciences. This House has always been a marker of great change, a leader in reform in issues that those inured in their sins and spoiled by their privilege did not want to see reformed.

"Luckily, this House has its friends as well. They are difficult acquaintances to keep at times, and none I know of own Hanna's total trust and faith at this time, but she holds hope for the future of her people."

"It sounds like she is hoping for miracles." Jhon shook his head. "By what you describe, what you both have described in great detail, this is a very corrupt society. Morally, for certain. Likely economically. Positively socially."

"Economics and our diplomacies with others on the outside are actually quite sound, considering. We are isolated from the rest of PAN . . . the country we are called," Najir explained apologetically, realizing he had neglected to do so. "PAN is isolated from the rest of Vitale—our planet—because it is a continent free of borders with others. We are surrounded by oceans. The High and Low cities rest on a lush mountainscape, even running into the valley below a little where the farmlands lie and the country places are. But beyond that, you see, are the Yemm Mountains and the Goran Desert. Their intemperate conditions make them hostile places to live even with today's technologies, so people prefer to live beyond them along the coasts and near the easy access of the large spaceports.

"To prevent smuggling and other problems, travel to and from Vitale is limited to those ports on the coasts of the continents. All goods going inland from continental borders are offloaded from their delivery ship, put through an inspection process, and then allowed to be loaded onto short flyers for the trek inland. Anyone caught landing spacecraft inland without express permission to land in an inland port is subject to be shot down on sight or destroyed on landing. It would be suicide to try, really. Our neo-orbital satellites blanket this world with a sensor net too sensitive to toy with. This world," Najir said with a low intensity, "will never fall prey to those alien races who try to insidiously inject forces for invasion."

Like the Cree had done on Wite. Vejhon knew that was the reference, and he boiled with the need to confront the other man, but controlled the urge fiercely. Had he wanted to speak in specifics, Najir was the type to speak plainly enough. The other man was confirming Jhon's suspicions about his origins, but for his own reasons would not come to say so directly just yet.

"So the economics are sound, and the planet secure. All Hanna has to do is clean up the moral fiber of her people and it's a done deal," Jhon said, his liberal use of sarcasm matching his wry smile.

"Was it not you who said 'One less culture on one less world can be a beginning to an end'? Hanna believes each little step she takes will lead toward that. When she heard you say that, she was no doubt elated to find you felt the same way. I would hate for you to disappoint her."

Not a scold, not a threat, simply an honest observation with a great deal of heart in it, Vejhon thought. Had circumstances been different, had he met Najir on Wite, it was his kind of heart and loyalty that he had always recruited with fervor into the Valiants. The only type of trust and companionship he had known had been amongst his men. Never too close, because that risked flawed thinking and other things unhealthy for command, and never totally trusting because even the best of men could be turned for the right price. But Najir's absolute love and loyalty for Hanna was like Vejhon's absolute love and loyalty for Wite. In his time, Najir must have been a damn good warrior for Wite's cause. That would have been back at the beginning of the war. Now, he had accepted he couldn't return to his home, and he had found a new cause to invest himself in.

Hanna.

"Have I answered your queries for now?" Najir asked, watching the other man think with the same enthusiasm he had seen him use to exercise.

"And as a result, created more."

"It will be that way for a while. But Hanna will arrive in a short while and you can ask her what you will." Najir rose and gathered the tray and plates they had done justice to. "I thank you for sharing your meal with me."

Jhon nodded at the politeness, a little amused by it because really it was not his meal to begin with. After Najir had taken his leave and he had washed up a little, Vejhon had little else to occupy himself with than the circuit of his thoughts.

From all the pieces he had been gathering, the entire country of PAN was run from this single city. The exact representation of other classes was a bit shadowed, but the Masters of the forty High Houses decided on what was law . . . no doubt among other duties. To be a voice of such political power, and obviously one that often dissented, was a heavy burden. Yet, Hanna gave no outward signs of the weight so far, or the responsibility she had to the rest of her family. She hadn't even mentioned her family.

That, he supposed, was probably clever on her part. She would risk herself, but she wouldn't even speak of those she loved . . . just in case Jhon got any ideas she wouldn't care for. Trust, but not total trust. Ahh . . .

Fear. She had said her fear lay elsewhere.

It lay with her family.

How did she become the charge of her entire family when she was so young herself? Her age escaped him, but her youth was obvious in both her looks and her health, not to mention the fact that she was still idealistic in the way only the young could manage. He was not old, far from it, but he was old enough to feel the shortening of time as far as the extent to which he worked his body. Old enough to be isolated and embittered about a great many things. Enough to envy and crave the youth and optimism he saw in a black-haired beauty.

Gods, how she had gotten under his skin already! Intentional on her part or not, it didn't matter. She occupied his thoughts, worked his brain at solving tiny bits of the puzzle that she was, an endlessly fascinating cryptology. He realized that there was little else for him to do in the boring little room; he even acknowledged that it all could be ingenious tactics meant to brainwash him into obedience, but somehow it didn't really matter.

He couldn't return to Wite. He realized that. Others outside of Najir and Hanna had told him so, and he had accepted that as fact. After all, the only way to get proof was to step foot on the planet and drop dead. He would opt out of empirical evidence in that instance.

Slavery he would not accept, but there was something hidden beneath the surfaces here, and Hanna was orchestrating it with a clear plan in mind. Rebellion? He could get into that. Covert deception? Hmm, a challenge for him to be sure. Jhon had been much better at out-and-out firefights than sneak and peek undercover bullshit that required a great deal of patience and inaction in the name of maintaining a cover. It had been a while since he'd had a challenge for himself he was actually afraid he couldn't meet. It could be a blast.

So, as far as substituting one life for another was concerned, as was pointed out to him most thoroughly, it could have been much, much worse. Besides, it came with fringe benefits. Black-haired, blue-eyed, blue-skinned, curved benefits.

"I would pay a good price to know what thought has you smiling like that."

Vejhon jolted in surprise. The woman walked on air, he swore it. He hadn't heard her make a sound. He moved to face her, his smile lingering a little longer as he let his gaze slide down her long, lithe form. She was wearing a body-hugging suit with legs reaching to her ankles and sleeves rolled just above her elbows. It was the first time he could recall her not wearing a dress of some kind, but the way the black fabric rested snugly to her skin made it a welcome change.

She looked fit and well, far better than when he had last seen her. Jhon had to resist the urge to cross over to her and inspect her for himself with better care than he could from a distance. Najir had said she was fully recovered; she looked fully recovered, and he would make himself accept that.

"Do you own shoes? Does Najir? I don't believe I have seen you wear any."

"All Houses in the High City have the custom of removing all footwear in the foyer. The feet are cleansed there and then you are welcome to walk about knowing the floors are clean. It is healthful for when young children come to visit, because they spend much time on the floors. The custom also serves as a sign of peace. That you are relaxed and plan to stay a while is reflected by taking the time to unshoe yourself. You respect my home and everyone in it when you cleanse your feet here."

"An interesting idea. A good detail to know." Vejhon walked up to her, reaching out to smooth back a stray hair from her cheek. "I enjoy the things I learn from you."

Hanna smiled softly at the flirtation of his touch and his words of double entendre. His closeness warmed her, as did the fact that he was trying to be charming for a change, and actually succeeding at it, in her opinion. The question was . . . would there be a question? Would he use this charm to further a cause of his own, like escape, for instance? What did he want from her?

"I am glad you are well. You aged me a decade the other night," he murmured quietly, close to her cheek. "Have I mentioned how sorry I am for causing you such agony?"

Hanna's eyes widened with surprise and she pulled back to find sincere regret in his green-yellow gaze. "You never meant to do it. It was an accident."

"I know, but I have to apologize for it," he explained, his voice remaining low and hypnotic, "because although I would take back every instant of pain you suffered if I could, I wouldn't trade away the rest of it for any price."

Hanna made a soft sound in her throat as his hand slid around her waist and up her spine, drawing her into his body with a snug pull. Jhon ground out a low response as she curved flush against him, her skin and shape making full contact with him. His eyes traced the low dip of her neckline for a moment before returning to her stunned blue eyes.

"You were unbelievably beautiful, Hanna," he whispered against her ear. "To watch, to feel . . . but was that you, I wonder? Or was it just a drug?"

"It was a drug," she replied breathlessly, "releasing me to you before I was ready. And you could have taken me, but you didn't. Why? What did you owe me? Nothing. What did you feel for me? Nothing. So why wouldn't you take what was so hard for you to resist? None would have blamed you for it."

"I would have," he confessed tightly. "And maybe you would have. Or do you blame me for not fucking you, Hanna? Is this your goal? You made it clear you have hunger for me." Vejhon punctuated the remark with the brief drop of his mouth against hers, holding himself there in a teasing stroke only until she gasped and tried to reach for more, then he pulled away out of her reach. "But you are too complex for lust to be your only use for me. Fertility? Are you looking to breed?"

"I am not using you for stud!" She snapped out the denial, stiffening in his hold.

He simply held tighter, his hand sliding to her curved rear end and dragging her in tight to his responding body. The resistance of her squirming was erotic as hell and damn distracting, but he needed more from her than the response of his own body. However, the responses of his body had obvious effects on her. She was an incredibly sexual woman, and he was realizing quickly that it was almost as good as torture to tease her with the vulnerability of her own nature.

"Then what are you using me for, Hanna? I need to know! My patience is not my best virtue, and after seeing you like I saw you . . ." He braced against the vivid recall of his memory as it replayed the image of her laying bent back before him, her body and voice begging him to join her . . . and he shuddered head to toe with the burn rushing through him. He knew

Hanna felt it, too, and he heard her throaty little whimper. "But I won't move a single inch closer to you until you tell me what you want from me," he said through gritted teeth. "No matter how insane it drives me, I swear . . . Hanna . . ."

"Don't," she gasped, her eyes liquid with emotion as she stared into his. "Don't tease me if that is how you feel. You can't know how it hurts!"

The word was like dynamite to him, and he released her explosively, stepping back hard. Hurts? He might have laughed, had he not seen the truth of it in her eyes. "I don't understand! Is this held over from the stimulant? I thought you were better!" Guilt and fury chased over him.

"I am!" she gasped back, trying to recover her spinning head as she was thrust from the heat of a potent male she wanted so badly and into the empty chill of the room. She knew he didn't understand, and she knew she couldn't explain, and it was untenable. It was a horrible impasse that, to him, must look like a cruel game.

"Then explain! Explain it all, Hanna! What do you want me for? Why am I here? Is it because I would rather die than do what it is you wish of me? I am feeling like I am being fattened for the feast in here, Hanna, and you come in to play with me like a toy so you get your use of me before you send me to fry at supper!"

"No! I told you, no!"

"You always tell me no! Never a yes! 'Yes, this is why I need you here, Jhon.' 'Yes, I am treating you as equal as promised, Jhon, instead of just paying lip service to it.' 'Yes, let me show you why your trust is worth it!' Come, Hanna, tell me yes." Unable to help himself he came close to her again and caught her head between his hands so he could brush his lips across her forehead in a coaxing caress. "Tell me now, what am I here for?"

Hanna had reached up to grip hold of his wrists, her eyes

sliding closed as his mouth stroked warm and dry against her. Then she broke away abruptly, stepping back quickly. Their gazes held for a long minute, and then finally, she exhaled in a short bursting sigh and walked away from him. Vejhon watched her go until he realized with surprise that she planned on leaving the room.

"Hanna!"

She stopped short, turning to look over at him. "You asked me a question, Jhon," she said in that low tone that sounded so much like an invitation. "Would you like an answer or not?"

It hadn't even occurred to him that she was trying to respond to him. He had thought he was being dismissed. He'd misjudged her yet again, and was beginning to seriously dislike the habit.

"I would like an answer."

"Then we must leave this room. Or did you want to stay here for a few days longer?"

Leave the room? Oh yeah, he wanted to leave the room all right. But he'd never even contemplated the possibility that she would let him go anywhere so early on. Certainly not without a couple of guards or Najir nearby to assure he wouldn't attempt to run. Yes, he had come to understand the dangers they had described, and while it was unwise to trust a single source, especially one in control of everything you do, it was unwise to disregard the source completely as well.

Hanna raised an expectant brow, waiting for a response from him as she crossed her arms beneath her breasts. Vejhon beat a hasty path to the wardrobe, grabbing the first thing that looked like a shirt out of it. It turned out to be a tunic made of a simple, light, woven fabric, with extraordinary geometric embroidery lining the hem, the V-neck, and edges of the sleeves. The color was a fair shade of olive, and he realized it was one of the colors that would accentuate his eyes and hair. He didn't know how to feel about that. It had that "dressed-up pet" feel to it. However, in the face of escaping the boredom of these four walls, he'd wear whatever it took.

He followed her as she passed her hand over a sensor and opened the door. "It will work for you, too, now," she pointed out casually. "It has been so ever since you made a voiceprint. The first time you do it, the system will voice-identify you and copy your palm print and retina scan. You will be free to walk the house and gardens."

How much of an ass was he? He hadn't even realized he'd had freedom just the wave of his hand away ever since she'd given him control over the restraints! The really funny thing was that until yesterday he had tried to mess with the door quite a few times, trying to get out. But after his experiences with Hanna, he'd been so focused on the internal, on the raging of his own thoughts, it hadn't even crossed his mind.

10

Vejhon realized as he went to step out of the room behind her that his captivity had become an ingrained state of mind over the past months. There was a silent pull of shock within him that nothing held him back from crossing the threshold of the door, and adrenaline exploded into his bloodstream when he stepped into the free space.

"The only doors that won't work for you are secured for privacy reasons, sometimes due to the nature of my work, and the gates along the property perimeter are still out of your access. I realize that just makes this all seem like a bigger and better cage, but I can't let you loose in the city until you have learned more about the society you have become a part of. It just wouldn't be safe. Plus, outsiders will expect it to take time for you to be trained to obey like a proper slave. We must keep up that appearance."

Outsiders? She made it sound as though she wasn't a part of the world beyond her gates. Fascinated, Vejhon scanned the hallway. There were no guards, there was no Najir. He had assumed she wouldn't take him out of his room without at least having some kind of backup guardianship in the halls. Then again, he now knew that she had every reason to trust in her own ability to guard herself.

The hallway was made of the same glossy stone that lined his entire room. Apparently, the entire house was built of the stuff. It did range in color dramatically, he noticed as they made their way past open parlors and down a set of stairs lined with mosaic tiles. The pattern depicted something different on each step, like the stages of a story unfolding in reverse order. If one had come from the bottom upward, he would have seen it open up in its intended sequence. This tale seemed to be about the cycle of a man's life. It started with a dark image representing death, guiding the man to a distant beyond. By the time they reached the landing, the last step was of a serene mother about to give birth to the life that had crossed all its stages step by step.

"It's wonderful, isn't it?" Hanna said when she noted his interest over the artistry. "It took the artist an entire year to lay the tiles and seal them. It was well worth it. You can even see the shadows of each fold in the mother's dress. The detail is just breathtaking."

"Very impressive," he agreed gruffly. "I would never have the patience."

"I think you would be surprised at your own capabilities, Jhon. It is perhaps only a matter of what you haven't had the opportunity to explore."

She didn't wait for a response to that speculation, turning to head away from him. Again, how easily she turned her back on him. She didn't seem to worry that he would make an attempt to get away from her. And perhaps it was because she didn't act like she needed to tighten the leash that he followed her so easily. Even obediently. The word in his own head made him tense. Was this all some sort of clever training method, he wondered again, and was he falling for it so quickly?

On guard a little more sharply because of the pattern of his own thoughts, Vejhon followed her across a wide foyer with an enormous full-colored chandelier hanging above a center medallion inlaid in stone on the floor. The medallion looked like a sun with multicolored stone rays, and the light cast by the chandelier sprayed a shower of colors over it.

The house was incredible. Huge, but easy to map in his head. There were markers of unique forms of art everywhere, like the stairs and the chandelier, and while they served to make it easy to navigate the huge mansion, it also spoke of the Mistress of the house. She clearly liked to keep herself surrounded by original and beautiful things. It was also a great deal of house for only one person, so again he was forced to wonder about her family, its size, and where they might be.

Hanna reached to put her hand over the sensor that would open a set of double doors she was approaching, but abruptly she pulled back and curled her fingers into her palm in hesitation. She paused to glance over her shoulder at him, her delicate black brows swooped down in concern. Thinking better of entering the room, and likewise making Vejhon incredibly curious, she turned to face him.

"Vejhon Mach, your life is going to change drastically once you enter this room." Just the graveness of her tone convinced him of that. "Do you think being kidnapped and sold into slavery was a severe change of life? It is nothing compared to this. The difference is, I believe this will suit you far better than that did. But . . ." She took a deep breath as she held his gaze using all of the connection and intimacy they had developed so far to communicate with him. "But I also believe that this time you deserve a choice. Something no one has given you in some time.

It isn't much of a choice, but it will be yours to make just the same."

She rested her hands nervously against her hips as she smoothed over them in what he realized was an anxious habit. She had talked of fear before, and for the first time he could truly sense she was afraid of something. His sense for it caught it radiating off of her in waves of energy, and the scent of chemical spikes in her bloodstream that accompanied it. What was she so afraid of? Of what choice he would make? Was she afraid of what was in the room beyond? Or did she fear his reaction to the room behind the doors?

To say he was completely captivated was an understatement. He had never been so amazingly curious in his life. He wasn't usually the curious type. He'd always been more interested in following directives, orders, and mission plans, straightforward actions with straightforward goals. It was odd, but she was uncannily on the mark when she said he hadn't been used to having choices. In the military there was no choice. Not really. You obeyed commands and that was it. At least, for the most part. He'd never been a maverick, but neither had he ever been afraid to improvise when necessary.

"Your choice is this," she said in her rich, solemn alto. "You can either enter this room with an open mind and a total commitment to what you will find, even though you will be completely blind to what is inside, or . . ." Hanna picked up the tail of her hair, probably without even realizing it, and began to sweep the broom of the ends over her palm. Another nervous habit. ". . . or I will allow you to be sold to another household where you can try your luck at a bid for freedom or whatever else it is you think you want. However, once you leave here, your actions and your well-being will no longer be my responsibility."

Her tone fascinated Jhon. She was being cold. Methodical

even. She had drained her voice and expression of all emotion, something so dramatic on her it was impossible to miss the difference. It was as though she were trying to completely detach herself from the moment.

"And before you ask it," she continued flatly, "I cannot give you freedom. I have power in this city, but not to break those laws. Not yet, anyway. Your value to me, though very high, is not worth the damage that particular kind of lawlessness would bring to my House."

Hanna watched Jhon carefully as she exploded the bomb of impossible choice on him. She knew it was unfair, and at least she had said as much. It was a choice between potential horrors for him, at least from his current perspective. This was why Hanna had wanted him to fully appreciate the possible ramifications of the choice to be resold. Had she not made his potential fate clear to him, he might have been cavalier in a bid to be rid of her. She prayed he had come to realize that what was beyond her gates was far worse than what was possibly behind the doors before him.

"So, I either trust you that the world outside your gates is as brutal and impossible to navigate as you and Najir have represented it to be," he said shrewdly, watching her carefully for her reactions, "or I don't."

"Trust is everything, Vejhon," she said, her voice rising in intensity just a little. "Without it, you and I can go no farther. If you cannot invest complete trust in me, this becomes an insurmountable situation and the only thing we can do is dissolve our relationship. You cannot know this, but believe me when I tell you that there are so many people who would love to see this House destroyed. I need you to understand one simple fact. Please. Realize that I am risking everything on you at this moment, Jhon, *that* is how badly I want you."

An intriguing turn of phrase, he thought as he watched her

breathing hitch up faster and harder, like a woman becoming increasingly afraid . . . or aroused. It was at the point where he wasn't sure of the difference on her. It was fear, excitement, and pheromones he scented on the air, the combination heady and intriguing in so very many ways.

Vejhon moved toward her abruptly, his hands reaching to hold her captive around her sides as he roughly backed her up against the door in question. She gasped, the sharp indrawn breath accentuating her neckline as her breasts rose against it. To his surprise, she turned her head and looked away from him, not meeting his eyes. She held her hands up against the door and curled them into fists as if to touch him would burn her. It was as though she were refusing to acknowledge the way his body was crowding hers. He meant her no harm, the bracelet around his biceps remained dormant, so what was she afraid of then, if not him hurting her? Why turn away?

Unable to resist, Vejhon lowered his head until his nose touched the side of her neck. He inhaled against her skin. That concentrated scent of sweetness and sensuality was so wildly churned up with the adrenaline in her blood, it was like bathing his sense of smell in an aphrodisiac. Vejhon didn't actually know what he was doing or why he was doing it, just that it was such a strange and demanding response, the urge he suddenly had to take a deep taste of her and a great deal more.

Maybe it was because she was being suddenly so submissive, where before she had been nothing but dominant and self assured. There was something about seeing her and feeling her quake gently in suppressed emotion that made him long to take command of her. It was probably just his conquering nature or his instincts in exploiting his enemy's weaknesses, but whatever it was, it was powerful stuff.

"Jhon, you have to choose," she whispered, her head turned so far her cheek touched the chilled door.

What Jhon didn't realize was that Hanna was trying hard to remain neutral. She didn't want to be accused of trying to sway him by nefarious or feminine means later on. It was crucial that he say yes for his own reasons, not for hers. She had already manipulated him far too much for her peace of mind. Najir's assurances aside, she knew she had been selfish with him.

Because if she let herself go the way she wanted to just then, she would already have hold of him and be wrapping herself around him as tightly as she could manage. Just his nearness set her blood on fire. She had known the instant she had seen him that she would feel this way one day. Najir had known it, too, the moment he'd seen Vejhon on that auction stage. Everything else aside, why wouldn't she find him to be worth craving, really? He was handsome and powerful, his will all but indomitable. Even now, the instant he had seen her hesitate and withdraw, it was in his blood to take advantage of it—to regain footing and position and stake an aggressive stance. It was exhilarating to feel him revel in his own power, and her body burned with responses she forced into repression.

"Do you mind if I ask a few questions first?" he asked, his whispered words brushing his lips against the skin of her neck along with the heat of his breath. Hanna shivered, unable to help herself as gooseflesh rippled down the front of her chest, tautening her nipples against the teasing brush of his body.

"I can't answer everything, but I will . . ."

". . . answer as best as you are able?"

Hanna tried not to moan softly when he moved his mouth to her ear as he spoke. "Yes," she acknowledged breathily.

"You don't want me to be your slave, do you?" he asked, the answer having already slowly become clear as he had pieced together all that she had been saying to him, although without ever saying it directly.

"I can't tell you any more about that than I already have. Not until . . ."

". . . I make my choice. I think I am beginning to see a pattern here." Vejhon drew back so he could look down into her face, those startling blue eyes still managing to stand out starkly despite the soft blues of her skin tone. "If I were a thinking man, I would think that you want exactly that, but you can't say so until you are certain I won't run off and spill the beans to someone else. Anyone else. Yet, you won't force me onward when you very well could. You own me, as you said. My physical body is yours to do with what you please. You went through so much trouble to make certain I had firsthand experience with the evils of your world . . . my guess is you traded a little part of your soul away in the process. Why back down now?"

"I am just doing what I have to do to protect my House. But it isn't worth much if I have to become like those . . . like those who . . ."

Vejhon watched her run into walls of conflict like hovercraft crashing full bore into buildings. She wanted to say things but her conscience was working overtime now, forcing her to edit herself so that she didn't give away any influencing information. However, she didn't have to say anything more for him to get the gist of the point. She wouldn't enslave him against his will, and she would gladly enslave him if he volunteered for it.

He found himself dropping his eyes to the dark lips that had caught his fascination early on. "Clearly you are going to get things you want and need if I follow you into that room," he remarked, looking back into her eyes, "but what will I get? What possible advantages are there for me? And I mean besides what evils I won't have to face on the other side of your gates."

"Isn't that enough?" she asked, her pupils wide and troubled.

It was, and he knew she was counting on that to be enough. Thus her actions so far. "Perhaps. Humor me and tell me more."

"I can't," she insisted. "I can't tell you more. I have nothing else to entice you with. Not now."

"But you will later?"

"Perhaps," she echoed. "It will be entirely up to you."

Now that, Vejhon thought, sounded all too intriguing. What was more, the color along the cheekbones of her face darkened to a shade of lilac that, if he wasn't mistaken, was the equivalent of a blush. He reached out with a thumb, tracing over the warm shading slowly as he thought about the significance of the reaction. He decided then that since she couldn't satisfy him with specifics, he would keep his questions to the basics.

"Will this cause me harm?" he asked, barking out the question like he would have done in an interrogation.

"I believe . . . in the long run, no."

Hmm. Not a promising wording.

"Will it go against the basic principles I hold?"

"I don't know you well enough to make that judgment, but if you are who I feel you are, then it will suit you more than you can ever realize."

"Will I be a slave or will I be free, Hanna?"

She blinked, but didn't hesitate as she reached up and touched gentle fingers to his face. "In truth, you will be both, Vejhon. And neither one of them will be easy for you. But I can promise that you will learn to manage a balance and you will see the value in living both ways."

Cryptic as ever, but probably a far better offer than he would find anywhere else on this planet. And in the end, there lay the gist of his dilemma. This planet. Was this where he wanted to spend the rest of his life? There had to be other places. Better places. He wasn't sure he believed her when she said there was no other way for him to leave, though he did think *she* believed that.

"Have you lied to me about anything? About the retrovirus? Any of it?"

"I wouldn't do that." She looked offended enough to be believed. Then there were also those nakedly honest eyes of hers.

"Okay, then, I have just one more question."

Vejhon didn't miss a beat. He lowered his mouth to hers, catching her surprised little cry between his lips as his hands tilted her head to match her to him. He felt her hands come up to catch him at the backs of his arms, her nail tips clutching at him. It was as though he had cut through an invisible tether she had been using to hold herself in place. The tremulous caution of an instant ago disappeared and she surged up into the kiss and his body as though she were starving for him. Now *this* was what he'd always expected from her. The aggression of a woman who commanded her own fate. She opened her mouth, stroking her tongue along the seam of his lips, and it was as though she had painted him with fire. When he opened to taste her, it was like swallowing the flames whole. She burned over his senses, her taste as sweet as her scent and just as sultry.

Hanna moaned softly when he swapped aggression with her, his entire body shoving her back into the door that already hugged close. His tongue sought hers, tangling erotically in a trade for taste and sensation. Why? she wondered. Why had he done this? Initiated this? What was his query? What was he trying to learn from her?

He could feel her thinking, the wild questions and confusion running through her. He found it satisfying, really, that the shoe was finally on the other foot. Let her wonder, he thought with an inner smile as he drank deeply from her lush mouth.

Vejhon left her mouth at last, drawing for breath as hard and quickly as she did, acknowledging the way his entire body had lit against her like dry tinder. It would be damn hard to keep control with her, he realized as he shifted his hips and body against her, knowing she was aware of the blossoming erection she'd inspired just with a kiss. It was impossible not to want her that drastically. His thoughts flashed with violent speed through the details he'd captured in his mind, images of her and the moments she had most tormented him with her breathtaking sensuality. She had drawn him in just a little bit each time, each event almost simplistic on its own, but when layered together they had an incredible impact.

For Hanna, her body felt starved, her sexual nature roaring with its extreme needs. She knew very well what her appetites were like, but this wild hunger for him felt so insatiable. It frightened her in as much as it excited her. She knew what he would choose. Either by instinct or desperation of need, she came to understand that he would come into her world. The very idea of it sent rivers of liquid heat rushing down the length of her body.

Jhon didn't want to leave the intense warmth of her, but he was aware that a task awaited him, and he sensed he would need his wits intact for it. She dazzled his mind and body far too easily, and he could see the appetite lurking hungrily in her eyes. Hanna was also trying to rein in that need, the struggle represented in her gasps for breath and the damp perspiration on her skin. Not to mention the powerful grip of her hands on his arms.

Then, she suddenly caught her breath and stiffened. He watched her cock her head to the side so she could see around him, making him aware that they were not alone any longer. Vejhon turned slightly away from her to find Najir standing behind him. He was a respectable distance away, but Jhon still tensed. He took the other man's measure quickly, trying to decipher his stony expression and the tautness of his body language.

Jealousy.

"My Lady." Najir greeted Hanna with a stiff nod. "Are you certain this is wise?"

Hanna gently extricated herself from Vejhon, stepping clear of him with great poise as she came around one giant to face off with another. She reached out to rub a hand down Najir's forearm in comfort, smiling at him compassionately.

"It won't matter in a few moments, Najir." Hanna turned to look back at Jhon. "I believe he has decided to join us."

Najir frowned as he bit out the statement, "Just yesterday he made threats against your life."

"So would you, if I had done to you what I had done to him." Hanna didn't understand why he was suddenly challenging her like this. Hadn't he been the one urging her forward not too long ago? What was behind his sudden interference?

Hanna reached to take Vejhon's wrist in her other hand so she became strung between the two warriors. "If you recall," she said, "it only took you two days to begin to ease into my world, and I think you would have come around sooner than that even if you had not suffered so much on the auction block."

The two men traded looks over the dark head of the woman between them. "Don't take this lightly, Colonel," Najir spoke up abruptly, the warning in his voice ringing clear. "You cannot have regrets later on. There is no changing what you are about to do. Trust me when I tell you, doubt cannot and will not be tolerated. Neither will betrayal."

"No more so than it was in the military I used to serve," Vejhon countered.

"But there you had a cause. Something close to your heart that made it easy to be loyal. Here you have nothing but your own survival motivating you. What she is about to give you is a gift beyond your wildest imagination. I won't have you casting it back into her face because you desire revenge against her."

"Najir!"

"No, Hanna," Najir barked back sharply. "He needs to understand."

"I think he does," she argued.

"Do you?" Najir bit out, looking back to Vejhon. "Do you comprehend even the littlest bit what is happening? The gift she is giving? The gift *I* am giving?"

"Najir," Hanna said, this time softly and with no little pain as she visibly squeezed the hand she held. "Dearest, please . . ."

"Hanna," Vejhon interrupted her, "I think his question is fair. And my answer is no . . . not really. She's been vague and cautious, unable or unwilling to say anything with any detail. Just as you have been. But if I didn't appreciate the impact of my choices before, speaking with you has made the difference, Najir. My life has been a nightmare for months, and you're right, it's self-preservation that motivates me to a degree. However, while you strove to show me what potential there is lying beneath the surfaces of this House, I believe it is your loyalty and your steadfast faith that has convinced me that there is value in the idea of making a life for myself here. If I am mistaken, Najir, I hope you have the honor to tell me so."

Hanna's head turned back sharply to Najir, her breath holding still as Najir was handed one last chance to be selfish, to think only for himself. She knew he wouldn't, knew he would rather die than do the dishonorable, but what she feared was that it was a cruel temptation, and that it would come with pain he didn't deserve.

"Very well," Najir spoke up at last. "That is all I needed to know."

Like everything else, the statement was perplexing and cryptic. Jhon didn't know what to make of any of it, but he was ready to get it all over and done with . . . whatever it was.

Najir stepped around his mistress, standing beside Vejhon at the door and waving his hand over the sensor. As the entrance began to open, he turned to the newcomer, placed a hand on his back, and said calmly:

"This is going to hurt."

11

The statement was accompanied with a powerful shove forward into the room from the center of Jhon's back. The warrior stumbled forward at the unexpected tactic, but recovered quickly enough to round on Najir with fury.

But Vejhon froze in mid-movement as the occupants of the room caught his attention from the corner of his eye. His entire body rippled tightly with tension and out-and-out fear response as he turned his head to find himself staring into the glistening green-yellow eyes of a dozen or so enormous cats. Jungle cats. The breed was alien to him, but there were feline familiarities from his own planet that identified them easily, like paws and claws, long carnivorous teeth, massive sleek bodies built for speed and power, cunning and hungry eyes that could nail any prey in place. Only never had he seen a breed so big. Their golden and spotted coats shimmered sleekly over bunches of pure, incredible muscle unlike anything he'd ever seen before.

Jhon whipped around to look for Hanna, confusion roiling inside of him. She was there, but he noted that Najir was not and the door was closed behind them. There also was no visible sensor for opening the door from this side. There were other doors leading out into a lush hothouse and then potentially gardens beyond, but there were a great many teeth and claws between here and there.

The cats had been sprawled lazily around the enormous room, some on lounges, some on tables or up high in the empty bookcases, but most on the floor in a pile of tails, ears, and fur, either sleeping or busily bathing each other with large pink tongues.

However, the instant he had stepped into the room, they began to stir. The first to rise was a big spotted bastard, its shoulder width and boxy musculature indicative of a male even before its sex became obvious when he stood up.

Once the male rose, the rest followed. Leaping down from perches, drawing up onto massive paws, they all became completely focused on Vejhon and Hanna.

"Hanna, what the *fuck* is this?" he demanded through his teeth, afraid a shout would startle something he didn't want to startle.

She seemed to ignore him as she stepped around him and walked into the midst of the big cats. Jhon watched with disbelief as she trilled to the animals as if they were pets and began to stroke each one on their heads between large ears or over spiky whiskers. The room filled with low roars of appreciation, huge sinewy bodies crowding around her to rub against her, nearly knocking her down in their crush to show her affection.

"Yes, my loves, I'm here," she cooed softly to them. "I missed you, too. I'm sorry I've been so busy. You see, I have brought you a new plaything."

Vejhon stiffened in shock when she looked up at him and a full dozen heads turned to take his measure with enough uncanny intelligence in their eyes to make him believe they understood her perfectly. He watched with horror as the group began to move toward him as one, those growls, huffs of deep breath, and now the punctuating roar vibrating louder and louder against him.

"Try to remain calm, Jhon. Remember, this won't hurt for very long."

Vejhon had a hysterical urge to laugh.

"You conniving, deceitful little bitch," he choked out.

As if they understood him, the pride of cats roared angrily at him, swiping near him with massive paws. He backed up, but the wall was fast behind him, forcing him to look into eyes that looked so eerily like his own.

"Relax," she coaxed him as she moved forward among them. "They only want to know you better. If you insult me, they will become violent. You made a choice, remember? You have to trust your own choice and trust me."

"I didn't agree to die!"

"Actually, in a sense you did. You agreed to put your old life to death and make way for a new one. They are merely the instrument of that death and rebirth. Don't fight them. If you hurt them, it will end badly. Please. Please, trust me and try to stay calm."

Vejhon made the incredible mistake of looking into those uncannily believable blue eyes. Like some kind of hypnosis, the effect they had on him was instantaneous. It was surreal and ridiculous, but she made him believe her. So long as he held on to her eyes, the crystalline blue so pure and honest, he had faith.

When the first paw grabbed him, he hardly felt a thing.

Jhon's eyes opened with a light flutter of lashes.

The universe screamed.

He grabbed for his head, slamming his blinded eyes shut and blocking his ears from the scream of noise blaring madly around him. The sharp movement wrenched open his skin in long tears along his side and hip, the slingshot of pain making him roar out loud.

"Shh, Jhon, I'm here now," a low, familiar voice soothed him with soft concern and tenderness as careful, delicate hands fell onto his bare skin, feeling cool against the burning of it. "Easy, Jhon. Try to relax. It will calm in a few minutes, I promise you."

Hanna. He knew instantly it was her, though not because of her voice. The smell of her was everywhere, as though he were awash in it. He remembered it clearly, recognized it even at this intensity. Sweet sex and sensual chocolate, and deeper than that a bewitching musk that lured and tempted, spearing him with a memory of her lying splayed open on a bed, hot, wet . . . waiting.

All the noise and light faded as he focused the only sense he owned that wasn't rebelling violently, focused it on that intoxicating combination of aromas, turning his head toward it. His cheek touched skin and he shifted just a little farther so he could open his mouth and taste her with a long, slow lick of his tongue over the warm, silken softness of her.

He heard her gasp in surprise, and then hitch up a breath as his sampling of her skin began to climb toward the deepest concentration of that unbelievable scent. He skimmed and laved delightful warmth and soaked in the little sounds she made, until he hit fabric. He couldn't help his rough sound of frustration, nor the instinctive rooting for access that had him abandoning his covered ears to the onslaught of noise just so he could use his hands on her.

"Vejhon!" She rasped his name as her hands tried to countermand his actions with firm, staying movements. "I know it's all overwhelming, but take some time to adjust before you—Jhon!"

Jackpot. He yanked aside fabric, hearing it tear and not much caring. He tore at it again, feeling her entire body jerk under the force of it, a low, grumbling sound of satisfaction rushing out of him when it gave way to him. His thoughts were simple and clear. All he wanted was to drown in the smell of her. The richer the better. And, although he was blind and all but deaf, he found himself licking his way unerringly into the depths of her beckoning pussy.

His tongue touched concentrated aphrodisiac, or so it seemed to him, because the whiplash of pleasure that raced through him far outstripped her mewl of delight. His entire body rippled with excitement, all of his senses now blocking out anything that wasn't centered against his mouth. Eyes still closed, he slowed to a detailed, tracing draw of his tongue along the outer lips of her sex. Her skin was perfectly smooth, radiating intense heat and fragrance as he glided over it.

Jhon moved his body, now feeling the backs of her thighs with both hands and dragging her harshly beneath himself so he could better bury himself between her legs. He felt her fingers enter his hair in reflex, a pull and push of protest that he quelled by sticking his tongue deep into the flesh his hands were spreading open to him.

"Oh, damn," she hiccupped on a staggered breath. "Jhon," she moaned, "you don't understand what you're doing!"

He begged to differ. And did it matter? He had never tasted anything so delicious in all of his life. He was no stranger to women, but he knew without a doubt that there was no experiencing anything like this anywhere else in the universe. His body was wracked with pain, but he didn't care. He couldn't see, but he didn't care. All he could focus on was the incredible aroma of heated musk, and now the feel and flavor as well. All of it raced through his senses and into his brain, screaming wavelengths of near ecstasy down the entirety of his body. He had to raise his hips to make way for the pulse-pounding tumescence he quickly developed as his woman finally stopped struggling and instinctively shifted her hips to raise herself into his foraging mouth. Now her hands were holding him to her; soft, low trills of pleasure rolling out of her.

He used searching fingers to spread her fully apart, and immediately he found the tight knot of flesh and nerves that was her clit. He confirmed the find by swirling his tongue around her in slow, torturous circles, lapping up her hypnotic flavor and hearing her outcries of response.

"Vejhon! Mercy, don't stop! Don't!" She canted up into his mouth as he sucked on her clitoris, rolling and tugging her against his teeth until he could feel her entire body bending back like an overstrung bow. "Jhon, please . . ." she begged in a sob as he repeated the sequence again and again. Her feet climbed his back mindlessly, her fingers clutching his hair and her thighs stroking against his ears.

Scent. She suddenly was soaked in it, an even more intense concentration than before. He felt the fluid running down over his fingers and quickly moved to chase it to the source. Her entire body jolted as he tongued her from her perineum to the opening of her vagina. He left a lazy finger against her clit like a book marker and thrust his insatiable tongue inside of her. He licked and swallowed down every drop of her essence he could get, and then strummed her clit for more. Again and again he did this to her, never quite letting her reach peak, and not much caring. All he wanted was that scent and savory sweetness to go on forever while he feasted. Then, after deciding to use his tongue on her clit once more, he licked his way up toward it . . .

. . . and found it unoccupied by his working finger.

Puzzled for a minute, he recaptured his bearings with the touch of fingers, lips, and tongue all around her wet pussy. When comprehension dawned, it dawned with a hard rush of blood in his cock and a wrenching tightness to his balls. Two clits. One to play with an inch or so above the one tilted toward the top of the opening of her vagina. That meant if he were to stroke into her from above, he would hit across her second clit on each movement in and out of her. Amazed, he tested his theory to see if he was right. He fluttered his tongue over the finding just as he worked a finger into her. Neither did he neglect the higher set circle of nerves, his thumb flicking over it just as before.

"OH!" she cried out. "Oh, fuck . . . no . . . no . . ."

She said no, but her body felt like it was on super vibrate. He felt inner muscles clamping around his finger, making his impatient cock twitch and drip eagerly. Gods, he needed to fuck. He needed it so badly he couldn't even keep still. Pain, sound, light . . . none of it affected him. His focus was all on the sweet little bitch beneath him getting ready to come. He should be inside of her. Riding her to the outer rim and back. But another part of him, the part that wanted to eat her pussy forever, wanted to make her come so he could smear the resulting juices all over his face and body. He wanted her scent. He needed her scent on him. Everywhere. Forever.

When a tiny voice of logic intervened to remind him he could easily have both, Jhon chuckled wickedly against her, and began to work a second thick finger into her body as he lapped up over one clit straight to the other, then back again. He played, drawing a figure eight around them again and again with his tongue, loving the feel of her nails scoring his scalp as she lost her senses, thriving on the way she mewled and cried in higher and higher pitches as she built up for release. It was so much fun, so much to play with, he couldn't decide how to finish her best. Then he just decided to skip between the two nubs, sucking one then the other again and again against the twirling massage of his tongue.

"Jhon . . . Jhon, it's too much," she rasped, her nails taking little nips of him again. "Oh! No! I can't!"

She could. And she did. She exploded like a sun flare, bursting with fire meant to affect the entire universe. She locked up tight around his fingers, squeezing in a vice that felt like it could snap his knuckles. Just imagining that vice around his heavily swollen cock made his pulse roar in his head. Then he felt the rush of hot, viscous juices running over his fingers and hand, allowing him to slip free of her so he could set his tongue to the chore of savoring every last drop. Her limbs were shaking against him, and she was crying out his name. When he touched his tongue to that clit so near her vaginal opening, he felt her ricochet like she'd hit a springboard, her orgasm double backing on itself and turning her downswing into a second screaming peak. The response was absolutely fascinating, not to mention productive for his appetite for her essence.

Unable to bear it any longer, he blindly climbed her shivering body, setting his inflamed prick against her drenched and sensitive sex. Her hands streaked down his back as he rubbed against her, lubing his penis in her juicy pussy before notching the swollen head to her entrance. Oh yeah, he needed to fuck her into oblivion. The way he was feeling right then, he could come all night long and it wouldn't be enough.

"Wait!" she croaked, her throat dry from the rasping speed of her breathing and the screams of pleasure he'd wrenched out of her.

He didn't want to wait. He started to stuff himself into her, little increments so he could feel it all again and again. She whimpered, instinctively tilting her hips to accommodate him yet again. Feeling sadistic, he pulled back after only an inch and took himself quickly back and forth across that tempting little clit. He did it again when he felt her react with a full-body shudder.

"Mercy, baby, please," she begged in his ear, her nails biting into his shoulders. "Wait."

"No," he said adamantly. "I need to fuck you. Hard. Deep. Come inside you."

"Who am I?" She gasped the question when he started to slide inside of her again. "My name! Oh . . . Jhon!"

"Hanna," he rasped. "Hanna. I wanted you the minute I saw you, Hanna. Beautiful blue skin like nothing I've seen before. Curves that can kill. And that mouth so dark I can't look at it without seeing it sucking my cock dry in my mind. Bad, bad Hanna who stroked my cock and didn't need that second stim to make me come that hard." He punctuated the observation with a heavy thrust. He needed to be inside of her deep and hard so suddenly that he put all of his power into the movement.

The clutch of muscles seizing around him was so unexpected and so powerful that Vejhon gasped out in shocked delight. Of course, he didn't know better, so he tried to withdraw for a better stroke. The sucking draw of a muscular vice that refused to release him sent his blood pressure skyrocketing. The sensation was incredible, striking every key nerve at the head of his already overanxious erection, and rippling along the thick shaft only partially submerged in her body. Desperate to move, to stroke, to fuck, he tried to move again and again, only making her clutch all the tighter and quickly jerking him to the edge of orgasm.

"No. No no no no no," he groaned. "Hanna, gods, don't . . . I need . . . why?"

"Still," she instructed breathlessly for the second time. He was so overwhelmed he hadn't heard her the first time. "Keep still a moment. Just for a few seconds. Don't struggle . . . oh baby please, don't move."

He wanted to listen, but he couldn't seem to make himself keep still. In fact, the draw of her body had him completely enthralled. There was a kind of rhythmic sucking to it reminiscent of being drawn on by an eager mouth and hand. He was being pumped and he couldn't break out of the pattern. Again . . . and again . . . he fought against her, yet moved in tempo to her at the same time. She was whispering, panting something to him.

But his head was humming with the crescendo crashing up into him.

He came like a rocket, the orgasm ripping up through the pathways of his body with a burn that made him feel like he was shooting pure acid into her. But not really into her. He was seizing with pleasure, gripping at fabric beneath his hands violently as he bucked and ground out grunts of obvious satisfaction. He shuddered with the effort it took to handle the impact.

Then he finally drew a full breath and let all his weight drop over her. He felt the bath of his own cum drenching him as it ran out of her resisting body. Vejhon finally opened his eyes, fighting the screaming sensitivity to the light so he could look down into her face. Her expression was unreadable, as though she were being cautious to react, and he was suddenly embarrassed for his lack of control and selfish behavior.

"No. Don't think that way," she said, her voice so breathily sexy it made the hairs on the back of his neck prickle. "We have a lot to learn about one another. That takes practice." She smiled in a way that knotted up his nervous system all over again. "I like practice." She grinned and nudged up a brow lecherously. He laughed, unable to help himself.

For about five seconds.

Then everything came rushing back over him. Like a second orgasm, only not nearly as much fun and nowhere near as welcome. Pain. He was sliced up along his skin in a dozen or more places and in his furor and haste to have her he had pulled open every single wound. The hurt was intense and sharp and he couldn't imagine how he'd been able to ignore it. Even for the sake of sex.

The smell of sex was definitely all over both of them now. He was breathing it in with every breath, the musk and sweetness of her body hotly combined with the testosterone and spice of his. He'd marked her thoroughly and everyone would know she was his.

The possessive and distracted thought was so unlike him that it snapped him out of the tangent and sent his attention back to other details. His demanding senses were settling, although they still seemed to blare at him in a too-loud cacophony of information. He noticed Hanna was simply watching him, as if she expected something from him. He lifted his weight onto his palms, groaning a bit when the movement jarred his injuries, and looked down at their connected bodies.

He was naked, she was not. Well, mostly not. He'd torn her dress up to her navel, the fascinating cobalt blue indentation of it making made him smile when he saw it. They were in his bed. The bedding . . .

. . . was saturated in blood.

He knew it by its smell, shocked he hadn't noticed it before. He jerked away from her, scrambling back to see her in her entirety, searching for injuries.

"It's yours, Jhon."

His. Of course. The wounds. From what? He stared at the slashes across his sides and thighs, over his back, hips, and buttocks. His skin was smeared with blood everywhere, and so was hers.

Clean her. The instinct to clean and care for her was instantaneous and unquestionable. Uncaring of his own wounds, he swung himself out of the bed and scooped her up after him. One step into the tub later, and he was stripping away her ruined dress and waiting for the soothing heat of the water to cover them. It stung as much as it eased, but it was for the best, he knew.

Gently, after arming himself with soap, he began his task of bathing her. He was meticulous, cleaning every spot he could find, even making her giggle softly as she patiently withstood his obsessive need to see her skin spotlessly free of his blood. Handling her with far more care than he had a few minutes ago in bed, he turned her around so he could see to her back, moving the thick braid of her hair forward over her shoulder. He drew in air quickly when he saw, to his unending fascination, that she had stunning spots of silver blue running along her shoulders and tapering down her spine all the way into the crease dividing her gorgeous backside. He traced the rosettes' pattern, seeking texture differences and finding none.

"My turn," she murmured over her shoulder before she turned back to face him. She made him sit back in the water, soothing him softly when he cursed at the stinging of his wounds. She found a bathing linen and chose a soap very carefully. Once she had soaped up the linen she slowly began to cleanse his every wound and all of his skin. The soap must have been medicated, because about halfway through he noticed a numbing effect and the scent reminded him of a kind of antiseptic.

"I don't remember how I got hurt," he mused absently.

"Do you remember meeting my family?"

Family? He would remember that, wouldn't he? He'd been damn curious about them. Yet he had no recall. There wasn't much making sense to him at the moment, besides the fact that she was starting to smell really appetizing again.

"Do you remember the special room? The one with the bell-cats?"

"Oh hell yes," he said, his body startling with surprise. "You said I was going to die. I thought you were feeding me to your pets." He pulled back to stare at her, confusion furrowing his brow. "That's how I got hurt."

"That's how you died," she corrected. "Once my family approved of you, as I knew they would, they began to take you across to our world. You've come over to the Otherside now, Vejhon. You've become part of the family. Look . . ."

She touched his head and turned it until he was looking in the reflecting glass behind him. In amongst the scratches . . . the claw marks . . . was a pattern of spots just like hers, only his were a muted gold that almost matched his hair. He knew damn well he hadn't had spots on his back before, and those sure as hell *were* claw marks all over his body. He'd been mauled by her cats. It looked like every single one had gotten a lick in. He whipped his head around and narrowed dangerously angry eyes on her.

"I'm a few chapters behind, cupcake. You want to explain all of this?"

"Yes. I wanted to explain it when you woke up but . . ." She trailed off, not needing to finish. He seemed to recall her asking him to wait. He also recalled the drive inside of him that had made him refuse to listen. Even now her draw on him was dynamic and really damned distracting.

Taking initiative, Hanna laid gentle, coaxing hands on his shoulders and made him rest back in the water. Her touch soothed, even as it stirred, but Jhon forced himself to focus on his need for information as opposed to the needs of his unusually hungry body. As she calmed him and continued to bathe him, Hanna spoke with full disclosure for the first time in a very long time with someone outside of Najir and the family.

12

"Call it a blessing or call it a curse, but my family has carried it for hundreds of years. In fact, there was a time when many families were able to travel to the Otherside. The Otherside meaning the world of the beasts. A special world where we could live between here and there, as people or as beasts, trading from one to the other on command. Because of this skill, many people looked on my ancestors as gods. In time, that would change. A religious war targeted us as infidels and pretender gods. Though we are powerful, these fanatics hunted us to near extinction. This House is the only one to have survived with the ability mostly intact. When we go to the Otherside, we become the great and powerful bellcat."

"Wait! Are you telling me that when you refer to meeting your family, you mean those *cats*?" Jhon was so aghast he hardly knew how to react. The concept she was proposing was preposterous . . . and not a little insane. "And 'cats' is too mild a term, Hanna, because they're massive, lethal predators!"

Hanna didn't blame him for his disbelief and took no insult

in his descriptors. She realized she had such a long way to bring him yet. "After this genocide," she continued, "in order to preserve our survivors, we left the jungles we once called home and became pretenders in the society of our destroyers. We hid in the safety of normalcy. If we use care, there are no outward signs of our heritage, except for the spotting down our backs which can be hidden under clothing or cosmetics if need be. In this way we began protecting ourselves; by gaining social status, power, and, unfortunately, with a great deal of inbreeding.

"Then the great apocalypse came and all but the strongest families of this nation were destroyed. Our ability to shift into the Otherside helped to protect some of us from that horrible time of cataclysm. Forty-four Houses survived in all, including ours, and each would earn a seat in what would become the Chamber of Masters and the beginning of a new world.

"Unfortunately, this meant our genetic pool became severely limited. Our need to stay hidden remained paramount, lest we be hunted again and destroyed, so breeding with outsiders was out of the question. Our numbers dwindled, and the ability to shift from the Otherside became limited.

"An example would be during breeding. Due to multiple fetuses, the risk forces females to spend all of their late pregnancy in the Otherside, living as our cat selves. When we give birth, we birth a litter of kits. In the past, even as little as a century ago, a few months after birth the kits would learn to shift out of the Otherside, becoming babies. These children would then have the power to become the cat at will for the rest of their lives.

"It's believed that inbreeding is why our kits stopped becoming babies. It was a curse. They became trapped in the Otherside. Only the firstborn kit in a litter retained the ability to shift. The rest remained cats, with the intelligence of people, all their lives. There was only one exception. If the eldest of a litter met with death, it released the nextborn from the Other-side, and they would alter into the form of a person for the first time. Oh, it is a horrid curse, Jhon. The younger kits never know life out of the Otherside unless their sibling before them dies."

The detail of her story was amazing to Jhon, and if it weren't so wild it would be easy to believe those honest eyes of hers. "So you're saying all those cats are your brothers and sisters, and you've never seen them?"

"I see them every day, Jhon," she laughed softly. "I know and love them with all of my heart. They're bright and funny, cranky and stubborn and all the things you expect your siblings to be. The only thing they cannot be is people. I spend a lot of time with them in both of my forms."

"You mean you travel to the Otherside. As a bellcat." He stated it, verbally searching it in a way that would help him to grasp it. Her nod of affirmation was unnecessary. Things, little details, started to filter out of his memory. The feline way she moved, the sounds she made, her speed and strength, her pointed nails, the spots along her back . . . it all fell into place. "That must be something to see," he mused, the speculation a soft challenge.

"The feel of it is even more amazing," she remarked with a small smile. "But Jhon, I need to explain your place in this story." Hanna wanted to strangle him in a hug as he sat forward, his body language radiating full attentiveness even though she knew he felt doubt. "There seemed to be no cure for our genetic dysfunctions, although many in my family have pursued science and medicine in search of a solution. Mean-while, cousins continued to wed cousins, and firstborns only knew their siblings as cats.

"Then, only a single generation ago, my mother, who was a firstborn kit, fell in love with an alien slave. He was tall and powerful, a warrior in his soul and by his trade." Unable to help herself, Hanna began to touch the distinctive trademarks she numbered. "He was fair of hair and had eyes like a bellcat." She settled her hand on his chest and frowned. "My family was infuriated and appalled at the idea of an outsider becoming a part of our covenant. It wasn't even possible to breed with alien slaves, they thought. Not to mention the horrors of public disgrace and the illegalities of such a class crossing. You see, though we may breed with slaves here on PAN, we may not marry them or in any way elevate their status. My mother wanted to run away with her lover, to find a way to wed him. My grandfather, Master of this House and responsible for everyone's well-being, saw no choice. He knew that the rash act she was plotting would expose the House to a public scrutiny it couldn't afford. If she did this thing, their secret could be exposed, threatening them all to yet another act of genocide. The notorious narrow-mindedness of the PAN insured that.

"So, one night he tricked her slave into the room downstairs, setting all the members of the family on him. The slave knew my mother's secrets, knew the creatures attacking him were his beloved's sisters, brothers, and cousins, so he didn't fight. He couldn't bear the idea of hurting her by hurting them. So, he gave himself over to their will. They took mercy on him when they saw his nobility, each cat running a single paw through his flesh deep enough to allow him to bleed to death as quickly as possible.

"He died and my mother found him the following morning under watch of her family who'd committed the crime. Grief-stricken, she kept his body sealed away with her in her room, letting no one come near her for three days." Here Hanna took a deep breath and made certain he would see the truth in her eyes by holding his gaze firmly. "On the third day, the slave opened his eyes and awoke, as if he'd only been sleeping the entire time. It couldn't be explained. Everything was the same for him, and everything was different. He seemed to live, breathe, and bleed just as before, but he had also grown the spots of the family on his back. His senses became the high-powered senses of the bellcat. Eventually, he would even master the ability to shift to the Otherside.

"And as much of a miracle as that was? The day my mother and father consummated their mating while in the Otherside, my mother's sister, the secondborn of her litter, suddenly shifted out of the Otherside for her first time. Don't you see? They had found a new path to setting a kit free from the Otherside! It was a blessing no one could have anticipated. No one knew why or how it had happened, but it *had* happened!

"But, when they tried to repeat the act for my aunt using slaves from other worlds, they failed. Time and again, they failed. The slave would enter the room and once it died it remained dead. The magic would not repeat itself. It reached a point where my aunt refused to sacrifice any more lives, and the family agreed. My father's shift to the Otherside, they felt, must have been a freak occurrence. Something was special about him that couldn't be duplicated. Or perhaps . . . the sheer power of their love had been the cause.

"My aunt was murdered in the Feuds a few years later," Hanna said, the contempt in her voice a very familiar song to Jhon. "The instant of her death, my uncle came out of the Otherside and into this one. By the time the Chamber of Masters passed down a moratorium on all feuding, the damage was done. Now there were no more cousins to marry. You see, while we can copulate in both forms, we can only conceive as people. The family trapped in the Otherside cannot reproduce. Only those who could shift could conceive. My father and mother had become the final breeding pair.

"Until the day my uncle attended a slave auction. Our family never cared for the practice of flesh peddling after my father became my mother's mate. It just happened that my uncle was with friends and he attended with them. There he saw a beautiful blonde warrior dragged out onto the stage. She was proud and powerful, fair of skin and hair, and had the eyes of a bell-cat." Hanna smiled whimsically, affection filling the retelling of a story she had no doubt been told many times as she'd grown up. "He claims he fell in love that very instant. He didn't even have the patience to haggle over her. He stood up, offered an exorbitant sum no one would counter, and took her home. He gained her trust and affection, but he was forbidden to tell her his family secret. Yet, he had to convince her to put her life in his hands. He also had to convince *himself* to risk the life of the woman he had grown to love. He could have her, but she would be barren because she was not one of us, and he would be consigning his brother, the last kit, to a life locked in the Otherside.

"So, like before, he brought her to the family and she gave herself trustingly as the cats each made their mark. She died for three days, and when she awoke, she was part of the Otherside. And again, the instant they consummated their love on the Otherside, his brother was finally able to cross, living as a person for the first time.

"My parents are dead now, but my uncles are both mated. They spend time between here and our House in the country places. The isolation of the country allows them to live more freely as families. It allows them to forget their wives are slaves. To wed a slave is considered an abomination, Vejhon, but this family will break those laws for the sake of our loved ones, although it must be done in private only. Slaves do not exist in this House, except in the minds of others looking in. Appearances only. Otherwise, we are all equals. I told you I could give you freedom. . . ."

"As well as you were able," he finished for her. He sat there silently and thinking for a moment, studying her. "There were at least nine cats in that room. That can't possibly all be from a single litter."

"No," she chuckled softly. "I was my parents' firstborn kit from her first litter. My mother had two other litters besides mine. Four kits in each. I have a firstborn sister and brother who shift freely between worlds. We had hoped that kits from a better mixed genetic pool would be free to walk between the worlds, but I'm afraid it may take a few generations to undo the damage done. At the moment, the only way to free this family is through aliens like you, Jhon."

"Like me . . ." Vejhon's eyes, so much more like a cat's than ever now, narrowed as he considered her words. It only took a moment for his entire countenance to shift into a dark wall of fury, and Hanna felt her heart seize with dismay. She tasted fear as she faced the possibility of his rejection, of his contempt for what she had led him into. It had been a part of the risk, but she'd had little choice. She'd needed him so very badly, for so many reasons.

Vejhon seized hold of her upper arms and surged to his feet. The violence was leashed, but it was like containing a deadly storm inside of a spider's web. Any minute it would burst free to destroy her.

"Like me . . ." he hissed, drawing her up until they were face to face. "And like Najir?" he demanded roughly. "Is he yours? Am I intended for someone else? If so, why would you let me think . . . ? *Why would you let me touch you*?" Vejhon was in a physical agony that had nothing to do with his wounds. Everything inside the center of his body was contorting with horrible pain. She'd asked him to stop and wait, over and over, and he hadn't heeded her. Was he meant for her sister? A cousin maybe? "No. No! I won't give you up! You're mine, do you hear me? I made you mine!"

In an instant Hanna found herself out of the tub and on her back, water pouring off her body and into the thick carpet beneath her. Before she could draw breath, he was over her, his body covering her completely as he pushed her knees apart and settled himself intimately between her thighs.

"I did it wrong, didn't I?" he asked in a coarse and frantic whisper, brushing the words across her ear. "I didn't know your body, and I wasn't prepared for that sweet trap you set for me. I can make it different. I can make it better. I can make you mine."

Hanna knew he didn't realize it, but he had begun to growl beneath his words. He felt threatened, felt his spoils were in danger of being stolen from him. His instinct now was to mark her again, deeper and more thoroughly than before. The idea gave her a little thrill and made her shiver, but she couldn't let him upset himself due to a misconception.

"I am yours, Jhon," she assured him against his ear to be certain he heard her through the haze of his new animal instincts. "No one else's. Najir is not one of us. He's not from the Otherside."

Vejhon stilled, his thundering heartbeat rushing in his ears. He stared down at her and said numbly, "You bought him. He's a slave. You said you don't keep slaves. And he knows. I can see that he knows of the Otherside."

"I bought him," she acknowledged. "It was my first auction and I couldn't stomach what they did to him . . . and what I knew his future would hold. I admit, I thought he was perfect for the transformation, but there were flaws and we never attempted transition."

"Flaws?"

"His eyes, for one. The auctioneer had doctored the color using an injection, but they altered back within days. It turns out we make better companions than we would mates anyway.

We love each other a great deal, but we both feel something is missing."

Vejhon already knew that the statement was only a half-truth. At least from Najir's perspective. "Have you been lovers?" Jhon queried gruffly, already knowing it was the worst thing in the world he could possibly ask.

"Yes. On and off over the years when the fancy struck us. We're isolated by these secrets," she pointed out quietly. "Besides a few servants and guards, it's just Najir and the family in this House, and I'm very much a cat with all the appetites that come with it. As you are finding out, our taste for lust is powerful. But Najir has always known that once I took my true mate, our interludes would end. He knew when he bought you that you would be that mate, and that he was resigning his access to me. I belong to you and no one else."

"No one else," Jhon murmured, staring down hard into her eyes. "Why do I feel this way? Why do I suddenly need to own you like a prize, the scent of your body enticing me like a starving man is lured to a feast? I'm overrun with impulse after impulse." As he spoke, he was rubbing himself against her, rocking gently above her as his hardening cock drew a path up and down between her labia. Every time he stroked over her clits she drew in soft, excited little breaths.

"Because," she hiccupped with a little moan of pleasure. "I am in heat. I have been since the moment I saw you, Vejhon. I have craved you so much. Feeling you in my hand burned you onto my memory and my chemistry, but I couldn't . . . Oh! I can't think when you do that!" she groaned.

"And when the female bellcat is in heat, she sends the males into heat as well, is that right?" Jhon mused with a smile of understanding as he teased her vaginal portal with little prods of his fattened cock.

"Yes," she laughed breathily.

"I noticed," he retorted, remembering how uncannily irresistible he had found her even before this change that overwhelmed him now with nothing but pure craving. "So have I been a victim of chemical manipulation all of this time? Is any of this real?"

"The choice you made was real. I struggled to keep sex out of it. I didn't want you to accuse me . . . like this."

"I'm asking, not accusing. And you are right. I made a very clear choice. And now I'm making another one. Tell me how to love you. I need to fuck you good and proper and I mean right now."

She giggled for a second, and then lifted her bottom to coax him a little farther into her. "It's only a matter of control, Jhon. You invade, I resist. You wait until the muscles relax and then . . . you are free to fuck me as hard as you like, as long as you like, as often as you like. Better yet," she purred, "as often as *I* like."

"Why do you resist?"

"I don't know. Perhaps a reflex to assure fittest survival. Only a bellcat with power and strength of control will persevere to spread his seed. Mmm." Hanna rumbled low in her throat, a sultry and beckoning sound that sought out Jhon's spine and shook the tree of nerves awake. "I thought you wanted to fuck me, Jhon," she taunted softly, pulling him down to the lick of her tongue. "Or if you like, we could just take time to taste one another. I long to rub the taste of your cock all over my tongue."

Clearly the thought appealed to him. She felt the rush of excitement that ran through him in his grip, his breathing, and the amazing hardness invading her. She also saw it in the wildfire intensity of his eyes as he raked them over her body and face.

"Later," he rumbled roughly. "I haven't the patience to watch you do that to me right now. Not when all I want is to make you mine the way I ought to have already." Jhon slid farther into her on the back of the observation, his musculature tensing tighter and tighter in anticipation of that trap that sought to undermine his needs. He braced a hand by her head, the other on her hip and holding her how he wanted her. His mind was already working on ways he could potentially defeat her body's natural defenses. He was a soldier after all. Defeating all kinds of fortifications was in his job description.

Hanna could hardly catch her breath as he moved so torturously slowly into her, as if that would prevent the inevitable. She knew it wouldn't, but she wasn't about to criticize. Every nerve ending lining her vaginal sheath was screaming with sensation as he teased past them. Not to mention he was purposely slipping back and forth against her nearest clit.

In surrender, Hanna let her arms fall away from his body, her hands lying in abandon above her head as if invisible restraints held her. She closed her eyes and turned all of her focus onto the flesh he touched and prodded. Right about the time he rediscovered that trap he sought, he also found the hard point of her left nipple and its dark areola. He sucked her into his mouth on a sort of sudden gasp, the shock of pleasure riding through him as her muscles fisted around him, reminding him of why it had been so hard to keep in control last time.

Hanna cried out as his teeth tugged hard on her sensitive breast. He hadn't yet learned how many nerve endings she had in her breasts, nor that they were nerves shared on the pathways of her clits and vagina.

"Wait," she gasped, the encouragement punctuating the way her chest rose again and again in her breathlessness. Vejhon smiled inwardly because she was rhythmically thrusting her breast up to his voracious mouth. Still, he listened to her advice, holding himself perfectly calm even though her muscles tried to con him once again.

And just as she had said, her body relaxed after a long

minute or two. The release was so liberating and exciting that he drove into her fast and hard, as if he were afraid she'd resist again. But as promised he sank into her perfectly, their pubic bones connecting.

"Okay, now we're making progress," he muttered a bit savagely as he nipped and bit at her fat, juicy nipple. He traded sides, hearing her squeal as he withdrew in search of an energetic rhythm at the same time his tongue wrapped around the berry-dark tip of her tit.

When she screamed out so sharply, his name bolting out of her as her body stiffened, he worried at first that he'd hurt her unintentionally. However, as he raised his head and saw her face contorted in bliss and felt her shuddering around him, he realized she was coming with unexpected impact and suddenness. Jhon braced his knees and dove into her seizing body in long, tight strokes, riding her orgasm like pushing through an extreme storm. In both cases, everything was wet and wild, sending his adrenaline spiking as he strained to go as deep as he possibly could. He had been deprived of her true depth, cheated of his right to spread himself inside of her. Jhon reached out to wrap a powerful hand around her head and face on the right side, gripping her in a silent, commanding little shake. Her eyes flew open, midnight blue sparkling up at him from around black oval pools shot wide with ecstasy.

"Gods have mercy, you're a memory I've needed for so long," he rasped as he watched her shiver and cry out with every forward thrust he gave her. It was like a never-ending peak for her, not to mention sexual torment for him. He was wondering if he'd ever be able to breathe again as her legs suddenly curled around his hips. It resulted in a shift of her hips and his pitch, abruptly tautening something inside of her that teased the underside of the head of his cock every time he swept across it. The overload was electric.

Vejhon felt the end rushing up on him quickly, but he wasn't letting her conduct this particular orgasm. This was his time, his mark, and he was leaving it his way. He jerked her up from the floor, yanking her onto his thighs as he knelt with them braced hard apart. The wet boa of her hair whipped against his back with the momentum and she coughed out a purr of pleasure as she sank down hard onto his shaft, the thickness of it stuffing her more than full. But what he was doing by shifting position was forcing the sensitive nerve center at the lip of her vagina to stroke along the length of his cock every time they mutually lifted and resettled her onto him.

"There we go," he said to her when she dropped her head forward and jerked in a long, high-pitched gasp of response. He sought an ear to whisper into as he used all the power in his body to pump her onto him again and again. "Tighten up . . . yes . . . grab my cock like you're never going to let me go. I'm so deep now . . . keep me. Keep me deep inside you." Vejhon paused to groan with his own ecstasy as she joined his cause with the sleek power of her own body. She rode him, her pelvis canting over him with faster and faster gripping need. She was grabbing breath and holding it now, forcing vigor into her ride.

Jhon dug brutal fingers into her hips and buttocks as they mutually worked for release. The entire world faded away for them both and Hanna felt herself shimmering apart an instant before her entire awareness narrowed to a single tiny spot of light. She felt it detonate like a collapsing star, an explosion of power and light and energy, but a collapse inward into a weaker, smaller being.

Vejhon felt her ignite around him, her clutch on his cock violently perfect. Instinctively his hands grabbed her around her back as that tingle in the seat of his testicles turned into a scream of rushing sensation. Everything inside of him seized, nothing working, nothing focusing . . . nothing but that single point of action in his body as he sprayed his cum forcefully inside of her again and again.

For the longest time it felt as though it would never stop. It was when he reached the point of pain that she suddenly lost all strength in his hold, her entire body collapsing forward against him and her head dropping with a lolling roll. Her sudden unconsciousness also released him from her milking grip on his penis. Sliding out of her body had to be the most agonizingly poignant thing he'd ever felt. As though it could help replace his loss, he gathered her close and tight, bare skin to bare skin, resting her head on his shoulder. But though it felt good to hold her that closely, it was bereft of her energy and personality. And when she didn't rouse for him after a minute or two, he felt an automatic panic settle over him, chilling him across his chest and down his spine.

Not knowing what else to do, he scooped her up and carried her to one of the lounges. He laid her out, her blue limbs so flawless against the white fabric. Once she was safely settled he sat beside her and tried to rouse her from the faint. She looked unbelievably peaceful and content, like she was sleeping, but she wouldn't awaken and it was beginning to make him worry.

Rising to his feet, his hand still holding hers, he looked around the room quickly. He decided to find Najir, knowing the slave was far more familiar with her physiology. He drew on clothes quickly, not caring that he had freely bleeding wounds still. After jerking a soft, clean fur from the bed and covering Hanna with it, he rushed to the sensor across the room. He had mapped the halls in his mind and some of the open rooms, but he had no idea where Najir's quarters might be, or where he would be right then.

But as he stood in the smooth stone hallway, the dull roar of his senses that, until then, had strictly focused on Hanna, began to rustle to attention. The house, he realized, was full of people. A great many people.

Servants. Security. Family. He knew all of this because he could smell heavy traces of them all, and each scent identified itself in a different way. Family seemed to smell faintly reminiscent of Hanna. Security smelled of the same fabric used repetitively for their uniforms, and they were armed. He could smell the ozone from weapons that had been through practice fires. Servants also wore uniforms, but of lighter materials, and they smelled of cleansing products in one fashion or another. Since Najir fell into none of these categories, Jhon figured his best shot was to seek a frequent scent that fell outside of these other regular ones.

It was confusing at first, how to separate and then follow a single trail, but after a minute or two it was almost as though he were following a light-colored string that had been left for him as a guide. He realized he could even tell in which direction things had moved strictly by the deterioration rate of a scent in one direction as opposed to another. This also told him which of many trails was most recent and wisest to follow.

Vejhon's race had always had sharp senses, so he adjusted to the magnification very quickly. He realized he was following a male, increasing the odds of having picked up the right trail. The path took him right to the family room Jhon had been introduced to with such shocking submersion. He didn't hesitate, swiping his hand past the sensor.

It didn't surprise him that it wouldn't open for him. This room held her most dearly prized secrets in the world. She wouldn't let anyone else have access except those most trusted. It didn't faze him in the least that he wasn't one of those people . . . yet.

"Najir!"

He bellowed out the call, hoping somehow he would be heard. He doubted it, though. A roomful of jungle beasts and he couldn't hear a single sound from them? That meant it was soundproofed.

"Can I help you?"

Vejhon turned sharply to face the person who spoke. He was presented with the only other blue-skinned person he'd seen since awakening from stasis. She was a petite and almost miniature thing. Her black hair was kept short and close to her head, sticking out in messy spikes that made her look like she'd just tumbled out of bed. Judging by the sheer sheath gown she was wearing, a white that showed him just about every detail of her body beneath, she might have just come from bed after all. Her eyes were a soft sloe shape, long black lashes blinking sleepily over amethyst irises.

As his eyes coasted over her, hers did the same to him. She seemed to smile wider the more she looked. "My, my, look what the cat dragged in," she joked tartly as she took in his wounds.

Vejhon wasn't amused.

"I'm going to guess either a sister or a cousin," Jhon said dryly, that common trace of scent that hinted of Hanna making it obvious to him.

"Oh, I'm a sister. Firstborn, second litter. My brother, firstborn, third litter, has gone off in search of . . . who knows what. Been gone for a year. All the rest of the family is in the country . . . or in that room. But I suppose you know that already," she mused, absently sucking on a fingernail. Unlike Hanna's sexy red, she had hers painted a bold, dangerous black. "Now me . . . I just came back last night. And low and behold, Sissy has a new beau. How clever of her."

The compact woman came closer to him, making sure he could see she was just as curvaceous as her sister, if on a shorter scale. She couldn't be more than two inches over five feet. Even then Jhon thought he was being generous. But apparently her lack of height did nothing to phase her confidence. She radiated it *and* her energetic sexuality like a beacon, and she obviously expected anyone and everyone to answer it.

She reached out to touch him, her hand falling just below his slave band on his arm. "My, the family did a number on you." She traced a long, furrowed claw mark over his forearm. "You know, my sister is supposed to be caring for these. How inconsiderate and thoughtless of her to let you bleed and suffer like this. It must be so painful."

"Hanna isn't thoughtless . . . nor is she inconsiderate. She's unconscious and I cannot rouse her."

That news made the little woman stiffen with immediate interest. Jhon couldn't tell if there was concern as well.

"Hanna?" she asked in disbelief. "What happened?"

"She fainted," he responded shortly.

"Faint—!" The black-haired creature threw back her head and laughed. "You artful little devil!" She seemed completely amused and delighted and Jhon was starting to feel his temper. When she saw his expression she chuckled again. She boldly linked her arm through his and turned him back toward the stairs. "Not to worry," she assured him with a grin. "She will rouse on her own in a little while. You see, Drakoulous women are designed for sex like . . . the latest and best of technology. Every part of our body can be erogenous in some fashion and it never takes much to arouse us. However, because we're wired to be so sensitive, with dual clits and hypersensitive G-spots, sometimes we can have dual or even triple orgasms at once. As delightful as they are, they're also like overloading a computer with a massive program it can't process. Under that kind of duress, the system will shut down . . . and so will we."

They reached the landing where Vejhon's quarters were located and she stopped to look him over in a manner he could only describe as covetous. "Apparently," she purred, "you're blessed with all the best of talents and did everything just right." She grinned wickedly as her eyes brushed longingly past the obviousness of his dormant penis in the close-fitting pants he wore. "Believe me, when she wakes in a few minutes, she will be gushing with delight and praises."

"You're certain?"

"Yes. Quite. But if she doesn't wake within the next fifteen minutes, you can come find me. My room is not far from yours, actually. It's just around the corner. Right across from Hanna's. We are such a close family and . . . well, we like to be within easy reach of each other when we're home together."

Jhon thought it was far more likely that Hanna preferred to keep a close eye on her sister. This one had trouble and mayhem etched all over her flirtatious little body.

"What's your name?" he asked with a fabricated smile as she surreptitiously fondled the contour of his biceps.

"Ashanna. But call me Asha or Ash."

"Ashanna?" Vejhon smiled for real at that. "That wouldn't mean 'as Hanna,' would it? Sounds like your parents were so taken with Hanna that they hoped you'd be just like her."

Ashanna's eyes darkened and narrowed until the sloe shape looked positively ferocious. She jerked her hand away from him. "Well, as you can see I'm nothing like Hanna! Not in looks or in attitude. In fact, we are polar opposites and I'm glad of it."

"Don't you like your sister?"

Jhon could immediately tell when she realized her temper and touchiness over her name had revealed a little too much. She laughed a little uncomfortably, touching her hair as if to groom it casually into place.

"I adore my sister," she said, possibly meaning it and possibly not. "It's just difficult to grow up when everyone is expecting you to be exactly like such a paragon of perfection like Hanna." There was a touch of bitterness that Ashanna couldn't hide within the remark. Deciding to cut her losses for the moment, she manufactured a smile for him and a little wave. "I am off to snooze. Tell my sister to care for those scratches when she awakens. We wouldn't want them to get infected, now would we?"

"No, I don't suppose so. Thanks for the help."

"You are welcome."

13

Hanna opened her eyes and found herself looking into the cat's eye pupils of her new lover. A sensation of ridiculous happiness rushed over her as she remembered the obliterating ride of pleasure he had sent her on just before she had lost touch with the waking world. Her smile must have looked a little goofy because Vejhon began to chuckle softly.

"You okay?" he asked, reaching out to touch the back of his finger to her still-lavender cheek. "You know, you might have warned me about this. It's hard on the coronary system when you unexpectedly make a woman pass out for twenty minutes."

"Is this how you express worry?" she asked him with a teasing smile. "And I would have told you had I thought about it. However, it's never happened to me before so it wasn't something I expected. Anyway, I was more concerned with your adaptation to your new . . . your new life."

Jhon was sitting beside her on the lounge, leaning down over her and staring down into her eyes. When she remarked on the changes he was going through, he simply shrugged a shoulder, as if it weren't in the least significant.

"I took a little inventory while you slept. Sharpened senses, fast reflexes, and extraordinary strength . . . there's nothing so different about that for me really. Though I know that is likely to be only scratching the surface."

She cocked her head, studying him as she lifted her touch to the line of his jaw. "To say the least," she agreed. "You do seem to be better adjusted."

"Well, submersion in panic tends to force a man to get his act together pretty quickly."

"I'm sorry."

"We've been over that. I was fine once your sister told me it wasn't unusual for women of your—"

"My sister!" Hanna jolted upright, pushing him back from her as she tried to find her feet. Vejhon moved back to give her room, watching carefully as she reacted strongly. She walked away from him, the fur dropping disregarded to the floor.

"Is there a problem?" He hardly had to ask. He'd already gotten his own impressions of her sister that might explain her reaction.

"I'm about to find out."

Without much other choice, Jhon followed her as she activated the doorlock and walked without hesitation into the hallway. He bristled at her moving into a more public position while she was completely nude, but she pushed her way into another room only a few yards away.

It was her room, he surmised quickly. Everything about it instantly reflected the knowledge to him. The smell, the coloring, and even the small cat snoozing in the center of the large bed. It was a fat thing, much smaller than the beasts he had seen before, with black and white speckled fur sticking up in odd tufts here and there. Its eyes opened just far enough to check out who had disturbed the room, then closed again with complete unconcern.

Hanna went to an area of the room that held displays of clothing at the ready and she quickly drew on a chocolate-colored dress that hung loosely and shimmeringly over her figure in a boxy sort of style. The charm of the outfit was in its natural cling. Despite its vague cut, the fabric was attracted to her body beneath.

Vejhon remained silent and unquestioning as she briefly paused to straighten her hair, and then moved back out of the room with a brisk step. She crossed the wide hall and slid her hand past the sensor to her sister's door. A chime sounded, letting them know she had been notified of their presence.

Hanna was impatient. She paced away from the door, leaving Jhon standing before it. He watched her make a wide circuit and then begin another, just as the door slid open to reveal Ashanna. Since Hanna was several steps away, Asha saw only Jhon standing there at first and she lit up with a smile and a flirtatious lean against the frame of the doorway.

"Back so soon, lover?" she asked cheekily.

"I could ask you the same thing, Ash."

Ashanna jolted at the sound of her sister's voice and a blush of lavender ghosted briefly up her neck as she stood sharply straight. She painted on a smile and beamed at her sister.

"Hanna, dearest, so good to see you."

She reached with outstretched arms to take Hanna by her shoulders and touched cheeks with her briefly. If it was meant to be a sign of affection, it was sorely lacking on the parts of both women.

"You as well, Ash," Hanna returned, her usual truth and intensity not present in her completely blank expression. "But you'll forgive my surprise. You are supposed to be in the country place with our uncles and their families."

"I was bored out of my mind." Asha waved the matter off. "I'm afraid I am a city girl through and through."

"Asha, we had an agreement," Hanna said sternly.

"Must we discuss this now?" Asha asked, giving Vejhon a pointed glance. "This is a family matter, Hanna," she said, laughing uncomfortably as she fluffed her fingers through her hair.

"If you hadn't noticed, Vejhon is family now."

"Barely," the petite woman sniped in a sharp little snap. Then she shrugged at Jhon. "No offense, lover."

"Call him that again, little sister, and you'll be pulling my claws out of your throat," Hanna hissed suddenly, a low tremulous growl lacing the threat as she stepped up hard into her sister's face. "You disobey me. I am Master of this House and you will learn that fact the hard way if you must, Ashanna."

"Hanna, please," Asha said, her entire demeanor shifting to one of frustrated pleading, the most honest emotion Jhon had seen on her to date. "I miss my siblings. I miss my things! All of my friends are here!"

"You should have thought about that before you put this House at risk with your selfish behaviors!" Hanna snapped. "*You* forced me to banish you to the country place, Asha; I did not want to send you there. We agreed you would stay there for a year or until you could prove you could control your impulses."

"But I have! I swear I have!"

"In only three months? I doubt it. You couldn't even wait long enough to contact me before coming here. If you had I would have asked you to wait until Jhon's transition was farther along at the very least. But as usual, you considered only your own needs. Don't get comfortable, Asha. You're going back." Hanna exhaled in a release of temper. "And get Kuriken off my bed. He is your companion and should be in your damn bed."

With that parting directive, Hanna turned away and marched off down the hallway. Jhon paused only to cock a brow at Ashanna, a simple way of expressing his amusement over the exchange. Then he followed in Hanna's wake as she led him away in a flutter of silky brown fabric. For the first time he found himself going up the mosaic stairs to an upper level of the House. She passed many doors, all of which had old-fashioned hand grasps for opening them, as opposed to the technological alternatives. At the end of the hall, Hanna pushed open a set of double doors that opened into a room flooded with rosy sunlight. Every wall except the one on the side they had entered from had been made to view the out-of-doors seamlessly. It appeared as though the room was at the end of a wing and the walls on three sides faced out onto the landscaping of the property.

Here Jhon could see so much more than he had from his rooms. The sheer enormity of the city around them alone had been completely ill-conceived in his mind. He swore softly under his breath as the panorama around him showed miles and miles of densely packed but tidily rowed buildings. The most startling aspect was how clean and white everything was. With a few exceptions, every building had a white exterior; only the trim on them seeming to vary. The result was a brilliance that dazzled the eyes and boggled the mind. It also made it easy to pick out the green-blue foliage of the parks, the red clay–colored roads mapped everywhere throughout, and the fact that there was an enormous area circling around the center of city that was nothing but colorful tents and banners of cloth.

"The main bazaar," Hanna said quietly from her place before a wall several steps away from him. Her back was to him, so he wondered briefly how she knew what had caught his attention. Then he became more focused on her tightly indrawn body language, the way her arms hugged tensely across her chest.

"I am guessing Ashanna is a bit of a trial?"

Hanna snorted, marking the observation as an understatement. "Asha doesn't understand the difference between necessary risk and unnecessary risk." She looked over her shoulder at him. "I hope you do."

He bristled at the implied insult. "Now what's that supposed to mean?"

"It means it's very hard to have power and restrict yourself from using it no matter how justified you might think it is! You are a freedom fighter by trade, Jhon. How easy do you really think it is going to be for you to walk the streets acting the part of a slave, unable to stand up for yourself or others?"

"Just when did this foul temper of yours become about me?" Vejhon demanded. "For your future reference, Hanna, my entire existence on Wite was about holding back my impulses to fight my way through each and every one of the Cree. I lead the most powerful force of freedom fighters, yes, but we're also the most effective because we don't go off half loaded and with our pants around our knees!"

"Led."

"What?" he snapped.

"You said you lead them." Hanna turned to show him the distress etched over her features. "Don't you mean led? Past tense?"

Damn. Shit.

"Yeah, I guess I do," he sighed. "You have to give me a break here, Hanna. It's a lot of change in a short time."

"And not much of it is for the better," she noted bitterly, turning back away from him.

Feeling like a jerk for his slipup that implied he would rather be somewhere else, Vejhon walked up behind her and cupped his hands around her shoulders gently. He rubbed his thumbs over the taut muscles along the back of her lower neck.

"I doubt my choice to stay with you less and less with every passing second, Hanna," he said softly against her hair. "Any misgivings I could conceive of are fading quickly. And it's true, I haven't been out in your world yet and it will probably really piss me off when I do face it, but it's part of the trade-off, isn't it? Here's a warrior's analogy: You can have incredible muscle mass, or you can have amazing agility and flexibility. There's only one delicate point of balance where you can reach the best of both worlds, and it takes a lot of work to maintain it just right once you do achieve it."

He tugged her, turning her in his hands until she was meeting his eyes. "I've never been afraid of hard work, Hanna. I'll do what it takes to find balance. Don't lose faith in me before I even have a chance to try."

"Asha has had this power all of her life, and yet she has never found balance."

"I am not Ashanna," he felt compelled to point out. "She is young and spoiled; I am a man of experience and discipline. I already know what my weaknesses are and have worked hard to manage them. And Hanna," he said quietly, leaning forward to press warm lips to the rise of her cheek, "knowing how important this is to you makes it equally important to me."

The sentiment was so unexpected, so rife with a feeling of tenderness and respect that Hanna felt shock rippling through her mind. She had not thought to earn such things from him so quickly, if at all. She had all but forced this new life on him, her desperation moving her to manipulate him with every tactic she could conceive of. To her, this was no different than an arranged marriage. There would always be chemistry, their cat natures making it an integral part of what was between them, but she had not fooled herself into thinking this would ever be a love match. She might have hoped for it, but she had already sensed Vejhon had little experience in such emotions, and even less desire to try them.

Friendship, companionship, lovers . . . these she hoped for.

All other hopes she kept quieted down and resigned to the place in her mind where foolish girlhood fancies belonged. There had never been any guarantee that just because a slave would suit physically and come to trust her, it would lead to the deep, abiding love her mother and uncles had so luckily discovered. She was just lucky to have found him at all. Blessed. Blessed to have the chance to free her next brother from his captivity in the Otherside once Jhon learned how to shift for himself, allowing them to come together in animal form.

Hanna drew back and beamed at him, the smile heavy praise for his thoughtfulness and his efforts to appease her worries. He smiled back, the grin so full and unexpectedly charming on him. It was probably ill practiced, considering his life growing up on Wite, but perhaps that was part of its enchantment. It was honest. An irresistible flash born of his genuine pleasure. It made her heart melt warmly in her chest. If she made him happy, if she could only make him content, perhaps he would find a measure of peace living on her world.

Unable to resist such a charismatic lure, Hanna reached up for his mouth. At first she just nipped and sipped at his lips, the fine shape of his mouth coming together as his smile faded to better accommodate her teasing, brushing kisses. His thick masculine hands came up to engulf her around the sides of her face and head, cradling her between rough, lifelong callouses and the strength of sudden intensity. She smelled the aroma of his skin and body, the tangy sharpness of blood that still seeped pungently from reopened wounds. She recalled that it was her duty to tend those wounds, to see that he healed properly. Unfortunately she lost the recollection the instant his mouth asserted itself against hers, his tongue probing with sly confidence between her lips.

His kisses always seemed to obliterate her. She had always delighted in the ways of a man who knew how to take command of a kiss, but Vejhon was an aspect she had never quite encountered. There was something, an essence of intensity in his confidence perhaps, that always seemed to add so much depth and dimension to the ways he took her mouth. She was used to being aggressive and even a bit demanding, and she still was, but when Jhon kissed her as he was then, she could easily just sink against his body and let him make his own way across her senses.

Jhon felt the boneless slide of her body against his and he slid his hand down the length of her back to get a good hold of her. Supple silk slid between his hands and her skin, a sensuous echo of his molding caress. Gods, how he loved the shape of her! The sleek underlayer of muscles and the soft padding of femininity accentuating the hypercurvaceous dip of her lower spine; the tuck of her taut waistline that flared as his hands moved upward until the weight of her divine breasts was filling his palms, her chubby nipples already protruding between his fingers teasingly.

Hanna gasped good and loud when her back connected with the icy cold stone wall behind her. The difference between it and the hot flesh of the man along her front sent chills of contrast bursting wildly over her. Her reaction made him chuckle low in his throat, the deep timbre of his voice making him sound almost devious. The taunting toying of his fingers around her sensitive areolas only added to the perception.

"Have I told you how much delight I take in these plump and pretty nipples you have?" He drew away just long enough to scoop up the hem of her dress, pushing it quickly up to her shoulders and exposing the assets he so admired. He stared at her breasts for a long minute, his fingers drawing along their outer sides until his hands were acting like a frame for her chest. "The perfect finish to perfectly lush breasts. See how you fill my hands, Hanna?" Jhon demonstrated, cupping her and molding her with gentle thoroughness.

"See how you fill mine?" she countered wickedly, her unnoticed fingers suddenly announcing themselves as she cupped him through the fabric of his pants. Hanna ran a strong finger down the obvious length of his shaft, her thumb teasing at the head while her entire palm sought to nuzzle him. She even slid low so she could cup the malleable sac beneath the erect rod.

"Gods, what you do!" he hissed, unable to help reaching to back his hand to hers, pressing her into him while his teeth clenched tightly together. "I swear I haven't felt this randy since I was first in the service."

"Just how old *are* you?" she asked impishly, the mischief in her eyes purposely baiting.

"Old enough to take my hand to your ass, princess."

"That's 'my Lady princess' to you, slave," she taunted him.

"Why, you little . . ." As though he would make good on his threat, he grabbed her shoulders and whipped her around in an about-face, pressing her against an only slightly warmer slab of stone. She yelped as her heated nipples and breasts contacted the chill surface, and then again when she felt him scoop up her gown in back and expose her bottom to the priming smack of his hand against her. Hanna instantly went to turn back around but he affixed a powerful palm between her shoulders and held her pinned to the wall. "Uh-uh," he scolded in a hushed voice near her ear as his body crowded into her from behind. "Might as well enjoy the view, sweetheart. You're going to be facing it for a while."

"Jhon!"

He ignored her, instead concentrating on fitting her finely rounded ass against the swollen length of his cock even as he started to free himself from the bind of his clothing. Keeping her firmly in place, he took a long moment to caress each soft blue cheek individually, reaching as far down the backs of her legs as he could each time without giving her the opportunity to escape his superior leverage. Then he rubbed himself against her again, his cock settling right along the niche between both of those luscious curves. She was so damn warm, and unbelievably soft. Nothing could possibly be as soft as Hanna's skin.

Hanna felt the heavy weight of his erection lying against her, and her heart was pounding hard in anticipation and the excitement of her vulnerability. She knew he couldn't . . . wouldn't hurt her, but there was a lot he could do that *could* escape the borderline of violence and avoid setting off the slave band he wore. A band she was supposed to have replaced by then. She had already had a special mimic made up for him. Just like Najir, the band would appear like any other, but it would no longer serve the purpose of a deterrent to violence.

"I wonder how deep a shade of lavender we could achieve on this pretty bottom of yours?" he mused, smiling when the muscles of her buttocks and thighs tensed against his. But before he took his own query to heart, he took a moment to pull her hands above her head, laying her palms loosely against the stone, to keep her from giving in to the urge to push against the wall. "Don't push away," he warned her, just enough deadly intent lacing his tone to make her swallow hard.

Arm cuff or no, she knew better than to take him less than seriously. To prove the point, Jhon slid his hand over the front of her hip, following the V of her leg and hip crease into the valley between her legs. Hanna felt his knee nudging hers farther apart, the intrusion of his muscular thigh forcing her legs wider and wider. She wanted to comply because she knew his fingers were seeking sexual treasures, but at the same time it was opening her up to vulnerability where he was nuzzling up behind her.

His fingers did dip into the heated, moist flesh he'd exposed, but it was only the lightest and seeking of touches. "Hmm, hardly wet at all," he tsked softly in her ear as he jolted her with a sudden cupping of her pubic bone in his palm. He took a single step back and pulled her right along with him. The action severely accentuated the bend of her waist, thrusting her bot tom out and resetting her wide stance with even less leverage than before against the wall. Now she had to brace her hands just to keep her sense of balance. "Oh yeah, that's damn pretty," he breathed roughly after leaning back a little to inspect his handiwork.

He took another step back, sacrificing the warmth of her body against his aching sex so he could take a good look at her. Now he could see the soft blue tinge of the skin of her bottom as it shaded darker and darker until it became the intimate darkness of her pussy. He could even see that precious second clitoris she had in its place at the edge of her vaginal opening. He wasn't sure if giving her a good smack on her irresistible backside was going to result in him taking a floor nap, and that she hadn't offered the answer didn't mean anything, but he was definitely willing to take a chance.

Vejhon rubbed his hand soothingly over his target area thoughtfully, smiling a little wickedly.

Old, eh?

The sharp popping sound in the air actually seemed to come before she felt the smack. She had been tensely anticipating him pulling away from her to make his play against her flesh, but he'd done the entire recoil so fast, and so hard, that she had no idea it was coming until it was over. She cried out in delayed surprise and sensation as fire burned over her flesh, running up her back, down her leg, and straight across the vibrating lips between her thighs.

"It was"—she gasped for breath—"just a question!" She panted softly after the powerful sting began to fade. "You're the one always talking about your youth like it was eons ago!"

Well, she should have expected the second smack after that, she thought with a long, breathless cry caught in her throat in the wake of it. Mercy, the man was strong! And the way he spanked his hand against her she felt the print of his palm long after the actual strike, right down to the location of his pinky finger. He drew his hand away from her and she tensed, but to her shocked senses he placed his finger at the very base of her spine and drew it straight down through the sensitive valley between her bottom, over the tight cobalt bud he came to first and then on over her perineum to the lip of her vaginal entryway. The caress had her in shivers of unexpected pleasure, as did the realization that he had discovered a much more satisfactory appearance of her sex's secretions. He dipped his fingers into the slick honey and then reversed his erotic path up to her spine, wetting her with her own fluids the entire way.

Vejhon stepped back up tight against her, the throb of his aching cock ferociously demanding the contact. He slid both hands down to her hips, his thumbs reaching to pull her cheeks farther apart until his tumescent flesh was lying in the slippery little river he himself had painted over her. He could hear her sexy little panting and saw the edges of the flush on her face. Jhon was not generally a selfish lover, although he could remember a lot of times when he had been selfish, a hazard of his career and, very likely, his sex. But this was probably the only time he could recall the high color on his woman's face meaning so damn much to him. In fact, the more she reacted, the more stellar his own reactions. Still being selfish in the end, he supposed, but at least with worthwhile motivations for a change. What better motive than to make Hanna feel good? To make her come for him?

Hanna moaned noisily when he shifted against her and stroked his throbbing penis through the path between her labia, soaking himself in her while at the same time stimulating more of the heated liquid from her excited body. Once he was entirely lubed by her he could hardly find it in himself to remain very patient. Especially when she kept tilting her hips trying to catch him with her fitted body.

"I shouldn't make it this easy," he growled at her as his fingers slipped through the dampness lightly coating her skin.

"Neither should I."

With that, she dropped forward onto her knees, the slipper-iness of her body freeing her from his grasp instantly. She had already turned around by the time he went to fish after her, but he stopped still when she reached to grab his pants by the waistband, easing them down over his abused skin. She helped him step out of them and then sat back on her heels to look him over thoroughly, a small frown marring her expression.

"I should be tending to these," she murmured softly, mov-ing forward to touch a particularly deep furrow at his right quadriceps. She leaned over, displaying the long line of her spotted spine to him as she gently kissed the wound. Slowly then, her tongue snaked out and ran over it, the contact alone soothing the soreness away for him. Then the lick became a kiss, then a flicker, and another slow kiss that climbed up the skin of his thigh. Her breath tickled and stimulated the gold dusting of hair on his leg, this time making *him* the victim of an erotic chill that raced straight to his excited cock.

When her hands bracketed his lean hips, she paused to watch the rippling flex of tension that made the muscles of his legs jump out into definition. Then she focused fully on the im-pressive rod bulging eagerly only a few inches away. He was of a fine length, but it was his thickness that fascinated and thrilled. The gradation of color on his skin, from the translu-cent tan along the shaft that showcased fat, pulsing veins in dis-tension, to the deep flushed purpling all along the smooth round head: this made for a virile display that seemed pur-posely set for attracting a woman. The right woman. This woman.

Hanna took a breath and then exhaled in a soft, hot stream across the head of his cock, making it bounce in an eager twitch of anticipation. He stared down at her, completely transfixed as she purposely licked her dark lips. She now knew what her mouth did for him visually, and she wasn't holding back a single trick of temptation. Not while her bottom still burned with the feel of his hand. There was more than one way to make someone burn.

Hanna was close enough that he could imagine the lightest brush of her lips against him, except he knew she wasn't quite close enough because when he oozed a heavy drop of pre-ejaculate it landed on her chin instead of her lips. She laughed soft and sultry, her pink tongue flicking out to nab the salty fluid below her lip. Vejhon groaned as if he were being tortured, especially when she hummed her approval at his taste and swiped at her chin with a finger so she could suck on it to obtain every last bit.

"Gods, Hanna! You're killing me," he gasped roughly.

"But it's such a sweet death," she countered, finally reaching forward to touch her tongue to the head of his cock. His blood roared in his ears, not to mention everywhere else, making him pulse hard against her lips as she used her tongue to draw him between them. When she fully closed her mouth around him it was as though a haze had fallen over his vision. He tried to blink it away quickly, unwilling to miss even an instant of the sight of her sucking him inch by inch into her hungry mouth.

Dark, dark lips closed over him, and within her mouth her tongue flicked and teased along the ridge demarcating the head. Then she reached to close a hand around his shaft, helping to guide him deeper into that warm, wet, sucking haven. True bliss. True blinding bliss, Jhon thought as his new senses seemed to suddenly abandon him. Sight, sound . . . all he could do was feel. His fingers dove deep into her hair, grasping it up into tight fists until one of her jeweled catches popped off and pinged onto the floor somewhere. His hips surged forward into the growing rhythm of her mouth and the guiding slide of her hand. The rasp of his breathing echoed everywhere, along with the sound of his own pulsating blood.

Vejhon felt ready to burst out of his own skin, his cock

aching with how incredibly hard he was. The mad urge to sob screamed over him when she sucked him deeply down the back of her throat just as she raked her nails gently along his scrotum.

"Hanna! Stop or finish! Now!"

His bellow of command penetrated her haze of delight just long enough to make her comprehend his point. She realized by the curt way he said it that she didn't have time to dally over her choice. She set him free with one last draw and a little pop of sound. The instant she did, he turned her so hard and so fast the floor burned her knees. He pushed her onto her hands, then lower as he raised her bottom high before him. He was going to forget. She knew it instantly. But she had no time to remind him as he plunged deep inside of her, searching for a seat in a single thrust. It failed, of course, and she could hear the grind of his teeth right before he blew out a violent breath and growled a chain of curses.

The lockdown of the muscles inside her nearly caused his head to explode. He had trained for a lot of endurance markers in his time, but what he went through to keep his act together for that next minute beat them all hands down. By the time he had the access to her depths that he had wanted all along, he was drenched in sweat and shaking from the effort. He reached forward and clamped a hand down on the back of her neck and jerked her the rest of the way onto his stone-hard cock. If she made a single sound, he was oblivious. He let his hand rake down her spine on his way to grasping both her hips for counterforce.

"Hard. Fast!"

He heard her demand somehow, but it didn't matter because he was already way ahead of her. He withdrew and began a plunging cadence into her that immediately took on a force of its own. She braced against him, but eventually her knees came up off the floor with each connecting crash of their bodies. He was so thick and full inside of her and she felt like she was going to burst apart. The position neglected both of her sensitive clits, but as he neared climax he reached for her. He needn't have bothered. She felt his orgasm rushing up on him and the pitch he took into her body combined with his frenetic pace set her shaking.

She came because he did, because they were connected like that now. She moaned in deep, long coughs of pleasure as fire raced through his body and jetted into hers. She heard him roar, the primitive sound all cat as it echoed off the walls of the empty room. She wanted to answer, but she could hardly keep a breath or stay steady. At least she stayed conscious. At least this way she could feel him gathering her close and rolling over until she was sprawled over him as he lay back along the floor. Her dress shimmied halfway down her body and he smoothed it over her backside in assistance.

"The damn door is open," he groused when she queried him with a lifted brow of amusement.

"*Now* you're worried about that?"

"*Now* I realize it," he countered with a chuckle. "I was distracted right up 'til then."

"Mmm," she agreed with a pleased sigh as she nestled her cheek against his chest. "People rarely come up here. My offices are here and the storerooms. I come to this room to think or calm down when I am peeved. It helps to see the size of the city, to see what I am partly responsible for."

"Why put that pressure on yourself?"

"Because it's true. The votes I cast in the Chamber of Masters change people's lives, sometimes for generations. Hopefully for the better, but I have seen what badly conceived laws can do, and how hard it is to get them reversed after the fact. Every last one of the Masters should feel that pressure, but I know they don't. So many look on it as a boring duty of their station they are forced to attend to. Between them and the ones who would abuse the power given them, those who take these matters most seriously are double burdened. When I look out there, I have to be certain I see everything."

"The big picture."

"Yes."

"Tell me something?"

"Sure."

"What did Asha do specifically that has you so upset with her?"

Hanna sighed the weary sigh of a much-put-upon guardian. "She instigated a fight. She was out with friends, crossed paths with a rival House, and broke the laws of the Feud moratorium. Frankly, she is lucky I am the one who banished her. An act of feuding can get the entire House banished from the cities for fifty years. However, in this case, she was a lone female facing down six males. She beat the hell out of them, so you can imagine they didn't want to press charges and announce the fact to the world."

"Of course not," he chuckled, very familiar with the male ego.

"But the worst part about what she did was that she showed off her speed and agility. She accessed her cat to draw out the savagery she needed and the extraordinary strength she used. Jhon, she might as well have shifted into the Otherside right there in public."

"I can see why that would upset you."

"The only saving grace sometimes is that we in this House remember the massacre of our people far easier than anyone else does. The Apocalypse took care of that, really. We are now just a vague reference in the history books, not even worth a lesson in the city schools."

"Then why so much fear, Hanna? Why would anyone ever connect a young woman who fights like a demon with a race of beings long thought extinct, if they are even thought of at all? It is far more likely they think your House trains for all eventualities, especially when the Feuds are, from what I am gathering, so recently ended."

"Eight years past," she agreed. "And I know you are right, Jhon. But so am I. Erring on the side of caution cannot hurt, but carelessness can."

"I realize that." But Jhon couldn't help but think of all that her family had given up in the process. They no longer lived in the jungle homes that protected them, no longer lived with the wild things, and were forced to live side by side with a society they feared every minute instead of living and running free. Even their right to live in the world of people had, in essence, been taken from them, because of their fear of being hunted. Perhaps if they had remained hidden in their original homes after the massacres, they would not have lost the ability to shift out of the Otherside.

Fear had its place, but what she spoke of was paralysis. Any warrior who froze in fear was as good as dead in the end.

"I think," he said instead, "it's time you showed me what you look like as you change to the Otherside."

She lifted her head and laughed. "I think it's high time I tended these wounds. Then we can go play with my brothers and sisters."

Jhon made a face. "I'm not sure I want to. Playing with them is how I got like this in the first place. And might I say they don't exactly play fair. Some of those cats are almost twice as big as I am. Nine to one was extremely unfair."

"Come on," she laughed as she climbed off of him and offered her hand down to him. "Get dressed before I start to ravish you again."

Vejhon paused in rising to his feet, seeming to think about that possibility.

"Forget it. Not until after you get bandaged up," she laughed.

"You had three days to do it," he groused. "You could have done it then."

"We do nothing different than the way it happened the first time for fear of altering the process. You came awake and for that I am very glad."

"That makes two of us."

14

Jhon had no idea what he had been expecting really, but it wasn't what he saw. He stood in the rear gardens, the area Hanna liked to call "the enclosure." There wasn't very much enclosed about it. It was a run that started in the enormous family room in the House, passed through a large conservatory with a perfect replication of a humid, tropical atmosphere, and then opened up into acres of free-growing gardens. The grasses, shallows, and brush in this area grew thickly and without rule, since no gardeners were allowed to tame it in any way. This was where Hanna's family ran free, or as free as they could with eventual walls to cage them.

To the guards and the neighbors, Hanna had the most exotic collection of wild bellcats anyone had ever dared to gather as pets. It was considered one of those fashionable eccentricities of the rich. Hanna had amused Jhon with stories of other Houses trying to imitate her collection, only to find themselves in over their heads and asking Hanna to take the creatures off their hands. In those instances she would ship the animals back to the wild. She was saddened enough by her family's captivity. She would hardly wish to perpetuate it against wild things.

Jhon enjoyed the open air and wildness of these gardens. He stood with two large cats on either side of him, both females and both leaning their heavily heated bodies against his legs. Felina and Sylvi. Hanna's sisters. Felina had a darker gold coat, the shaggy length of it spotted with streaks of beige and rosettes of tan. The texture was as soft as clouds. Sylvi was covered in gold and white fur, but hers was short and close to her lithe, light skeletal structure and felt like the dense bristles of a good brush. Sylvi was a light and spry smaller cat, made for the chase and the ability to run her prey to the ground, unlike Felina, who was muscular and heavy, made for the hunt and battle.

But as unique as all that was in its own right, none of it compared to the amazing sight of Hanna shifting into the Otherside. She had come out amongst her crowding family, speaking to them as if they had actual points to make to her. When he questioned that she laughed at him.

"Of course I can," she had laughed, patting him on the shoulder as if it were a silly concept that she couldn't talk to her own family . . . and he supposed it was. "Soon you will figure out how to do it as well. We can sense thoughts with power behind them. It's easier among family and animals, but with people, too. A highly emotional thought will radiate like . . . like a marquee. It announces itself."

"You can read my mind?"

"Better now than before, but not like a book or conversation tool. Only things you focus and project, or project with emotions like shock, delight, or fury. You act like a burst transmitter, and if I'm awake and focused, I should catch it."

"Good to know, really. I think we need to go over all of these new details a little more thoroughly."

"Ideally, that was exactly my plan. However, you are the

one who keeps injecting sex and lust into the whole thing, messing up my good intentions." She'd grinned when he had growled softly in agreement.

After hearing how hard it was for her family to move freely through the shift, he had expected Hanna's shift to be difficult and maybe even traumatic. Instead, she had simply found an open space in the family room, taken a power step or two for a push off, and then leaped forward with arms outstretched through the air. As if she was trying to launch herself into flight, actually. But as she hit the arc of her jump a golden line of light appeared at the tips of her fingers and widened rapidly to accept the size of her body as it passed through.

Except when she came out on the other side of the light just as fast as she went into it, she wasn't Hanna the woman any longer. Appearing front paws first, finishing her leap, was a sleek gold and black coated cat with stunning outset eyes of bellcat green. Left behind to fall to the floor, as if it had all suddenly fallen from her body, was her silky brown gown and the jeweled clasps she used to bind her hair.

Astounded by how fast and easy the change appeared to be, and by the nature of the rift she had seemed to pass instantly in and out of, Vejhon had crouched to touch the dress for a moment. Hanna grew quickly bored with his examination, though, and she'd let him know with a head butt in his side powerful enough to knock him over. She was changed now and she wanted to romp and show off. And frankly, he had wanted to watch.

So they were in the gardens. Hanna was playing with her brothers and sisters in some sort of game of bellcat tag that involved a lot of chasing and sudden tackles. They ran full bore after each other, and then into each other, tumbling over the ground. He noticed the males would get into scuffles sometimes, asserting dominance.

Hanna was truly beautiful as a cat. That gold-black fur coat accentuated her muscular body with gleams of light and shadow. Then, if she rolled over, golden rosettes spotted her underside and were just blended enough into the black that you couldn't see them unless she went belly up. Jhon had no doubt it was Hanna. Her eyes were exactly the same, sharp and honest and full of that thoughtful intelligence. Her claws were tipped with her favored polish, a detail that made him chuckle. What really fascinated was the long sweep of her tail and the way it always found a place tucked or curled around her when she sat, an act of refined elegance . . . and how much it reminded him of how neatly she kept her hair against her body.

He figured he now understood why they called it the Otherside. They entered into some sort of dimensional gateway and came out on the other side transformed. The concept intrigued him and he looked forward to learning how to make that passage himself. He wanted to know what it felt like, what it looked like, from the perspective of one who changed. Again, his curiosity reared up voraciously as he tried to think of what could possibly allow this family to make that passage, and why some of them could not. Hanna claimed it was an issue of inbreeding and genetics, and maybe it was, but it almost seemed too select, too purposeful to Vejhon. It was as though they were being denied permission to use the shift until a certain condition was satisfied. Like the taking of a mate outside of the family who could be brought over to the Otherside.

And what made his type able to be transformed and no other? Was it the physical details, or was it because he came from Wite? Was there something genetic within him that allowed his body to make this drastic change? Hanna said he had died, and he had no doubt he'd come close to it with those wounds, but what if it were more like . . . a coma? Or a metamorphosis state? It was clear by the functions of his body and the fact that he bled that he wasn't dead. If nothing else, he thought with a grin, his sexual appetite alone proved he wasn't dead.

All this intrigued him. He'd never had a penchant for anything but soldiering, and he'd loved what he did for a living, but what he was seeing here was enough to make him want to devote total time and energy into learning everything he could about it. There had to be explanations. He knew others in her family—maybe even Hanna herself—had probably tried to learn them, but he also felt his was a unique perspective. He was practical and partial to logical points that didn't have fear or the dire love of a family attached. Nor did he have the reverence of over a millennium of heritage when he watched the change Hanna had made. She did. They all did. No doubt they all knew every story, every ounce of awed history attached to their long-lived line. Their fight for survival had imbedded it in them.

He would have no such partiality, no such prejudice. And while he was no scientist, he was a tactician. He knew purposeful maneuvering when he saw it, and the Otherside was being very purposeful in its manipulation of her family . . . as though it in itself were a consciousness in control of them.

Hanna ran toward him, the muscles of her fierce and powerful physique rippling all along her big body. When she opened her mouth he saw the pink of her tongue settled behind enormous canines and rows of equally intimidating teeth. One bite into someone's neck and those long, ivory teeth would puncture all major arteries on both sides. One strong shake of powerful neck and body muscles and the cat could disconnect a victim's head right from its spine.

Jhon could appreciate why control and discipline were necessary.

Hanna leaped at him through the air and, just when he thought he was going to end up with a few new scratches, she hit the top of her arc and the golden white light flashed blind-ingly, spitting her out in the form he was more used to. She landed against him and toppled him to the ground, but he was little worse for wear. So Jhon found his arms full of a naked blue-limbed beauty, her loose hair tumbling all over him and her bright eyes laughing down at him.

"Isn't it wonderful?" she declared with delight. She scram-bled up onto her knees and, straddling the width of his chest, threw her arms up toward the bright sky and breathed deep. "It's so freeing to be the whole cat," she confided. "I go through every day with half the cat inside me, seeing and feel-ing and listening to everything, even reacting a little with those instincts, but when you become the bellcat . . . oh, I can't wait for you to see for yourself!"

"Neither can I," he agreed.

Najir stood back and watched as his beautiful Master moved with steady ease through the Chamber of Masters, selecting whom she wanted to speak with very carefully and with obvi-ous sincerity of emotion and objective. He always liked watch-ing her work. She was so passionate about her causes and used her power and influence with the greatest of care and skill.

But Najir also kept his eyes in a few other places.

Leaning slightly to his right and keeping his voice low, he imparted information to Vejhon, who was attending with them for the first time. "There is the Baron," he pointed out softly, knowing Jhon would follow his eyes easily.

"The one who almost bought me," Jhon mused.

"The worst enemy our House has," Najir corrected. "This man killed my Lady's parents with his own hands. What's more, he did it the eve before the passing of the Feud morato-rium. He had several Masters assassinated who were going to vote for the sanctions, but he took personal pleasure in slaugh-tering my Lady's mother and her favorite slave . . . my Lady's father. The vote passed anyway because those like my Lady took up their parents' mantles immediately, putting aside their mourning to see it get done."

"She is a courageous woman," Vejhon agreed softly, consciously uncurling his fists as he thought of the pain she must have suffered at the Baron's hands. "Her enemy is my enemy," he murmured. "Why has no one punished him for his crimes if you all know of them?"

"It was part of the moratorium law. All acts before the moment of that law's passing were to be pardoned by all people. It only put in place punishments for future transgressions. The Baron knew that he would win either way the vote went, in a sense, so he simply enjoyed himself trying to swing it his way."

"Sick bastard."

"Exactly. And that merely scratches the surface. But he is not the only one to have a care for. Master Deyadou, there in pink, is infamous for his tantrums if he loses a vote that is important to him. Master Curro, with the russet hair, likes to buy votes, favors, and illegal things like the services of slipknives . . . assassins . . . and anything that will improve the wealth in his coffers. Master Gernat has a penchant for kidnapping slaves for either his own uses or ransoming. He's not the only one, but he is the best at it."

"Thus your advice to always watch my back," Jhon recalled grimly.

"Your newness makes you a target because you are most likely to want to 'run away,' but your size will discourage as well. You wouldn't be easy to take and transport without witnesses."

"It's like watching her walk through a damn minefield," Vejhon said with gruff concern as his eyes swept the room and tried to follow Hanna at the same time. "That one, in yellow with the strange hair and darker blue skin: I don't like the looks of him."

"Mmm." Najir tried to press the smile from his lips for a moment. "That is Master Fardes, and he craves my Lady greatly. Since she is unmarried, he thinks he might get her to become his wife one day. So he plots and plans and watches her with covetous eyes. And he isn't the only one. Our Lady is considered quite beautiful among her people. Her wealth is an attractive asset. And then there is her power."

"Tough luck for them. She's taken." Vejhon growled low through his teeth. Then Jhon recalled whom he was speaking with and he stiffened in discomfort. He wasn't the sort to gloat in the face of another man, and he and Najir had developed a careful sort of friendship as the more experienced slave taught Jhon how to be a slave without being a slave.

Najir saw his discomfort and raised a hand to dismiss the matter. "You should be proud. And you must be protective of her. Take your glory in the prize you have earned, Jhon. She is one of a kind and needs someone who treasures that with voracity. The insult would be to take her for granted."

"To be truthful, I do not feel that I have earned anything. Fate and fortune played strange hands and luck alone landed me here. I do very little for her, and she provides everything for me. I am kept without earning my keep."

"An idea that chafes at men like us," Najir agreed understandingly. "But give it time. My Lady leans on others a great deal in times of trial and we are all that supports her. Our strength and advice move her to make the daring strides she takes. Your value goes well beyond playing courtesan and stud. Believe me."

"You know, if we weren't in public right now I think I'd belt you for that remark."

Najir chuckled. "I'm certain you would. I meant no insult. I merely know how you feel, is all." He leaned closer. "Jhon, pray she never has serious use of your other talents. That would mean she was in danger, and with her brother missing . . . that will mean Ashanna becomes Master. Asha is spoiled and selfish, like many of these others. She is not ready to be here."

Jhon knew it was very true. Over the past days he had encountered Asha far more often than he had wanted to. The young woman was shameless in her behaviors and her appetites. When she wasn't out catting around, she was constantly trying to catch Jhon and, he suspected, Najir alone so she could try out her charms on them. Najir was free to do what he liked as Jhon understood it, although he didn't think he'd quite gone so far as to bed the chit yet. However, *he* was not free and she knew it. She was purposely trying to bait him to provoke her sister's jealousies, though to what purpose he couldn't quite figure out. Was it a heavy-duty case of sibling rivalry? What was fascinating about it was that Vejhon couldn't be less interested in the minx if he tried. Now, he'd never been a one-woman guy before, never even having had a real relationship, but with Hanna . . .

With Hanna everything was different.

She wasn't like any other woman he had known. She was hard-working, confident, strident when she needed to be, and she indulged in all of her appetites with relish—that last part a particular favorite of his. Food, sex, and play were her top three favorites once her responsibilities were met for the day. She also seemed to like the bazaar a great deal. She often went and returned empty-handed, but it was obvious she had enjoyed herself regardless.

Hanna enjoyed her life in general. Unlike her whiny and conniving little sister, she took nothing for granted. Vejhon had started to develop a powerful core of respect for her. He understood now why Najir was so loyal and protective, and he even understood that it wasn't all because of his emotional attachment to her. But Najir had kept withdrawn and quiet since Vejhon had woken from his three-day transition, keeping his feelings locked away from even the shrewdest eyes. He was dealing with them on his own, and again, Vejhon respected that.

"Is Han—uh, my Lady going to the bazaar today?" Jhon winced when Najir turned a critical eye on him for the mistake. It was taking some adjustment for him to remember to address her properly in casual conversation that didn't include her personally. When Hanna was there in person, he actually took great pleasure in titling her "my Lady."

"That is her plan. But today you will accompany her."

Jhon couldn't conceal his surprise. For the last few days he had been sent to the house after the COM session was over while Hanna took care of her other chores.

"Is that wise? I'm only just getting the hang of navigating the city and the people in it."

"Your instincts are all you need once you master the issues of respect. You are there to serve her in everyone else's eyes, but your true purpose is to protect her life."

"I don't need you to tell me that," Jhon said. "I am always prepared to protect her life."

"The trick, Vejhon, is to know the point when she cannot protect herself. Don't ever forget that she is as much predator as you or I. Her rights to defend herself are clear. Yours are not. Only her word will save your life if you commit violence. No one else knows your slave band is inactive, allowing you to commit acts of bloodshed."

"How is it I was able to attack you when I had the true band on, Najir? If it's supposed to keep me from being violent to anyone—"

"Except other slaves. We have little value, in the end. The bands cancel each other out in altercations between slaves. Mine still recognizes yours in spite of its dysfunction. Both bands are in perfect working order with one exception: a chip is burned out that measures rising aggression hormones and body signs. If it never redlines, it never instigates the pain deterrent."

Najir lowered his voice further, knowing Jhon's keen hearing could catch it easily. "The purpose is to make it look like accidental malfunction should you ever be caught, Jhon. So that blame cannot be placed on your Master."

"She would sacrifice us to protect herself?" Jhon asked in a hiss.

"She would sacrifice us to protect her House, but never to protect herself. Especially not you, Jhon. You are too important to her."

"I'm sure." Jhon responded with a frown. He knew Hanna wanted him to learn to shift to the Otherside and then to make love with her in that form because it would set her brother free from the Otherside. And then what was his next use? To breed kits with her? What else was there for him to do? He couldn't take charge of her protection or security forces. He couldn't stand beside her openly as she led her House. He was like a dirty little secret being quietly kept.

Had he agreed to this? What was the point of all this change when Najir had done just as well, except to serve the needs of a brother seeking a new life and the ability to breed? The thought infuriated him, hot and fast and without any chance to control it. He knew in an instant that she'd heard it because her entire body jerked taut and she stopped speaking mid-sentence.

"Master Drakoulous?" Master Harner asked politely. "Is everything all right?"

"Quite," she assured after taking a small breath. She couldn't help looking over Harner's shoulder and into the bellcat eyes of her lover. His thoughts of anger stung her hard, her throat closing up and forcing her to clear it before trying to speak again. "I just realized that . . . I hadn't told you Asha is back in town for a brief visit and I know you and your daughter enjoy having her."

"Indeed we do!"

Hanna let her peer express his fondness for her sister as her mind sought further thoughts from Vejhon. Her first instinct was to be defensive and hurt, and she was, but being so close to him now she knew his temper was a mighty force inside of him and she needed to give it respectful attention when it was guiding his emotions. Did he honestly think that was all he was to her? A means to a few ends? Had she been treating him as such?

She prayed not. It had never been her intention to devalue him in any way. Her intentions had been very much the opposite! He was vital to her for . . . for many reasons. Wasn't he?

Her spirit deep within cried yes. She couldn't name why or reason it out in her mind, but he was not so utilitarian to her as he thought. His companionship over these past two weeks had come to mean a great deal to her. At the first opportunity she would seek his advice because she knew as a former commander he had much to offer her.

But you require more than just me, she thought with a painful swallow, realizing how selfish it was to expect to be the center of his world. Najir took great pleasure in doing so, but Jhon was very different.

Vejhon heard the whispered thought of pained understanding in response to his unchecked anger and he instantly regretted allowing it free rein in this setting. Too much time to think was the problem. He needed better occupation. Would he ever be able to achieve that as a slave, pretend or not? In any event, it was something they should be discussing in private, not in emotional snatches across a chamber full of her peers.

He softened his expression and messaged his regrets with the strength of his eyes alone. She smiled softly at him, then wider when he winked at her. She turned back to her conversation, and it pleased Jhon when she couldn't resist sliding glances at him when she had the opportunity.

Baron Majum watched these little exchanges closely, his fingers tapping out a steady, annoyed rhythm on his knee. She had trained the supposed barbarian much more quickly than he would have been able to credit anyone with. How did she do it? Was her cunt really that miraculous? It was clear she was using it to keep her gorgeous team content because they both watched her with completely devoted attention. Jhon had kept his temper well concealed, years of practice serving him, so Majum had missed that aspect of the exchange between him and Hanna.

Why would she bring both of her toys to the COM if she wasn't trying to flaunt them in his face? Majum thought angrily. He'd suffered the insult for days now and he had reached his limit. He knew for a fact Drakoulous was heading to the marketplace after COM was dismissed, and he had a little surprise planned for her. The best thing he could say about the High City was that it was very close to the Low City and it was wide open to such nefarious types. Types that would do anything for a little bit of money. He wasn't expecting to excise the bitch as smoothly as he had her mother, a play he was infinitely proud of to this very day, but he was hoping to deprive her of at least one of her toys. Najir followed her everywhere, like a puppy completely devoted, and he was certain to be available for an unfortunate encounter with a few cutpurses. She also made the ridiculous error of sending the new one home alone every day. It made a terrific opportunity for him to "run away."

Really, it had taken him forever to make up his mind between them.

15

"**I** think you will enjoy the bazaar," Hanna said to Vejhon as they walked along one of the clay-colored walkways with its white lined markings to differentiate it from the matching road. He was a respectful number of steps behind her, but he heard her easily.

He didn't care for the procession much, but he did find some benefits in it. He liked to watch her backside as she walked, the rope of her hair sweeping from side to side across it with every step because she had that natural slink to her walk that she just couldn't shut off. Today she was wearing trousers, the pants as white as the buildings around her and as snug as her skin. Her blouse was more what he was used to on her, floating, feminine and shimmering silkiness in a splash of deep purple, and if she turned just right the sweet shape of her breast was formed perfectly in it.

"I am sure I will. I enjoy seeing the city. The genetics for your skin and the dark hair among your people is quite dominant, but I have seen some intriguing people who are out of the mold and obviously not slaves."

"Those people are often coveted for marriages," she noted. "Breeding with slaves is what is necessary, not what is generally wanted. Those with fewer PAN traits tend to be more fertile."

He noted her discomfort speaking of her people's cavalier treatment of fertile slaves and understood it was his earlier flash of temper that made her sensitive to it. But the truth was that it was a part of his purpose in her life. There was no denying that.

"Why do you suppose so many of you have become infertile?"

"The Apocalypse. The entire world was destroyed by war, famine, and disease. Those few who survived had suffered sterilizing illnesses in many cases, and the genetic pool of this country started from only forty-four families, Jhon. Forty-three if you take into account that my family wouldn't breed with outsiders. From those families sprang all of this." She swept her arms out to indicate the city. Since the entire city was on a mountain, all the streets were graded on a slope, and it allowed for a view to suit her point.

"The introduction of slaves is not so old a practice as you may think," she continued softly. "We were desperate. To go through all of that survival after the Apocalypse, only to be taken down again because our men were mostly sterile and our women little better? Have you any idea how horrifying it is to a society to be in a city this vast and have a zero-birth year?"

She had stopped and faced him, looking up into his eyes with a plea for understanding in hers. "New genetics was our only choice. Unfortunately, fear made the COM choose their methods badly. Slavery had been ignored until then; we weren't even part of the trade routes. Then we opened our doors to the flesh peddlers and it just went . . ."

"Out of control?"

"Yes. The corruption of owning others is amazingly powerful. People quickly become addicted to their power over a slave. Then it is only a matter of time before economy becomes dependent on it."

"Regardless of how it grew and evolved, Hanna, it still started as the intent to buy intelligent beings for the purpose of rape and forced procreation. Isn't that horror enough?"

"Yes," she agreed, visible tears wetting her blue eyes in tandem with the hoarse catch of her voice. "It is. And I am afraid you think I am doing that to you."

Vejhon sucked a sharp breath in through his teeth. He reached out for her, ignoring protocol and catching her arms so he could pull her close to his body where their joint heat provided mutual comfort for them.

"Hanna, I agreed to the terms you set and I don't mind them. I thrill in being your lover. I will one day take great joy in fathering your children when we are ready for that. My trouble is that it isn't all I can be. I need to be more. I need the right to be more."

"But appearances," she whispered. "I fear for your safety if you try to . . ."

"Fuck appearances," he snapped irritably. "I know all about them. I know all about your fears, too, Hanna. And if you ask me you have far too many of them. For a woman of such power, you are amazingly submissive."

Hanna felt as if she had been slapped in the face and she jerked back from his hold.

"Greetings, my Lady. May I be of assistance?"

Jhon and Hanna both jerked in surprise at the politely officious voice. They turned to see a stern-faced street sentry eyeing Jhon critically.

"Is this slave out of line, my Lady? I saw him grab you and thought to come to your assistance."

Hanna turned to the sentry and did what she did best; she smiled and slid with perfect charm into the space between Jhon and the sentry. "Of course you did. So attentive to your duty!" she praised, making the man turn lilac around his neck. "But you needn't worry. I am Master Drakoulous, and this is my slave. He is new, you see"—she offered with a broad wink—"and sometimes he craves my affections quite strongly. I'm afraid I encourage it. It is so . . . manly." This last statement was delivered with a sensuous shivering of her body for emphasis.

"I see," the soldier said, his pale blue eyes tracking down her body with obvious lasciviousness.

Jhon had to wrap a fist around the surge of fury that welled up inside of him. It was amazing how brightly it burned in his belly, almost as if he would radiate green light out of his mouth if he but opened it. Instead, he kept perfectly still and molded his expression out of the hardest stone.

"My Lady should discipline her slave better and perhaps pursue some of the after-hours social clubs that would cater to your needs for men like that," he suggested with a chuckle.

"I will take that under advisement. Thank you so much," she laughed. "Come Vejhon, we are late for the marketplace."

"Enjoy the bazaar, my Lady," the sentry said as he touched his hat in respectful farewell.

They walked on quietly for a long minute, Jhon swallowing back his impotent anger and Hanna cringing from how he was feeling. She had warned him how difficult it would be. It was only fair she gave him time to adjust, but another part of her couldn't bear the idea of him ever adapting to the role of a subservient. It simply did not suit his soul.

Had she done him a terrible injustice binding him to her and this world? Oh, she knew that taking him off this world was impossible. He could only accompany his owner offworld, and no Masters were ever allowed offworld, as it was deemed both too dangerous and too inconvenient for the needs of the Chamber. What could she have done differently that would have made his existence more bearable?

Her guilty emotions were radiating back to her mate in waves and snatches, but he understood enough to know she was wracking her conscience over her choices, forgetting that he had made choices as well. She always took too much responsibility onto herself, he was realizing. She had enough to do, beginning with caring for her family, taming her sister, and being responsible for the entire future of her House. This hardly touched on the responsibilities she was weighted down with because she felt everything she had to do for the people she represented.

There had to be a middle ground in all of this, and Jhon realized it would be his responsibility to think of it. In fact, it needed to be his own solution, rather than one laid in place by her for him. She had already handed him enough. What he needed was to figure out a way to contribute to her House and her society . . .

. . . while playing the role of a slave.

That was the part that made him gag almost every time. He needed to reconcile it. He had sworn to her that he was a mature and well-practiced man who could comport himself with perfect control.

Realizing he was letting himself be too distracted with inner thoughts, Jhon focused on the road that was leading into the bazaar. It was a dark day, everything like deep night around them, except everything was brilliantly lighted around the colorful tents. The difference between the average streetlamps and those in the market was momentarily blinding, but Jhon adjusted quickly enough to catch up with Hanna as she began to browse tables, racks, and displays on rugs on the ground right from the moment she saw them. He stood close to her back, watching her as she touched and examined all sorts of things.

What she liked, of course, were things of unique art or art forms, handmade and painstakingly creative. She enjoyed praising the artists, many of whom knew her as a frequent patron. What was more, she remembered their names, the names of their families, and little personal details. Watching her make her way through the bazaar with people calling out, smiling at her and waving, some giving her free trinkets or flowers filled him with a sense of awe. She was by far the best politician Jhon had ever known. Regardless of her fears and flaws, she was always sincere and she worked in her world with her heart behind her actions. Vejhon realized that all of these people understood that. If her office had needed an election to obtain it, she would easily have earned her place.

He was back to taking pleasure in simply watching her walk. She took him on a wild ride through his own emotions, definitely in a way he had never experienced before, but she was proving to be worth the ride. When she beckoned him forward to a table he was already smiling at her because of the shine of excitement radiating from her vivid eyes.

"Look," she said.

He did. He felt his entire body tense with . . . he had no idea what he was feeling as he stared down at the beautiful display of weaponry. Blades, blasters, and more, things he had no idea what they were but he quickly began to figure out how they were used. He reached to touch a slim stiletto in its hard, black lacquer sheath. The bejeweled stuff was ridiculous to him, but this blade was black and silver, slim and simple. He drew the knife and found the blade to be the thinnest metal he had ever seen. So thin it looked like it would snap at the slightest pressure. He glanced up at the merchant, who was chuckling.

"That is *frizzon* metal. It is the strongest metal in all the worlds. Also, easy to work with. You will be amazed. Go ahead, try to bend the blade on the table."

Jhon did exactly that, expecting easy flexibility from something so thin. Instead, the unbending blade slid into the wood a half inch before he stopped to pull it out.

"Gods," he swore, "this thin and strong, sharp besides? You could take it across a throat and leave your enemy talking for a minute before he realized it!"

"My Lady, your slave has a fine eye for weaponry. Would you care to purchase this for yourself now that you have his recommendation?"

Of course. A slave couldn't be armed.

"Yes, my Lady," he said quietly. "It is a perfect blade for a woman. Slim and easy to conceal. Excellent for your protection."

Hanna watched him perform his part and felt her heart shattering. What had she been thinking, bringing him to a treasure of things he loved . . . that he could not have? Her impulse had been to please him, to give him the pleasure of seeing the fine weaponcraft on her planet.

"Excuse me," she said softly.

Jhon watched her suddenly turn away and hurry away from him. He reset the blade in its sheath and handed it to the merchant. "It is truly a work of art, my Lord."

"Thank you for saying so," the merchant said with sincerity, even though he did not have to acknowledge a slave with such respect.

Vejhon turned to look for Hanna quickly, hurrying in the direction she had moved. He sought her clothing, but the place was crowded and the lights as they hit the verandas and tents threw just as many in shadow as they disclosed. He resisted calling her name and forced himself to pause and calm himself. He could track her anywhere. Her scent was imbedded in him bone deep. Even with such a mass of odors and trails of scent, he would be able to find her.

It struck him like a starburst, that familiar concoction of sex and chocolate, and it made him smile. She was moving quickly, in a ragged pattern because she was pushing through so many others. He followed at top walking speed, not quite running because he didn't wish to attract attention. Stronger and stronger her trail grew, then dipped into one of the tent alleys. These were the rare partings of the fabric in a row of merchants. They opened into long strips of space between the back-to-back rows of tents in the bazaar street that the merchants used to travel behind the stalls and to store surplus inventory. Why she would travel such a route was completely beyond him, but he followed in spite of all of Najir's warnings never to do so alone. He wasn't going to let her stay out of his sight like this.

She actually leaped into his sight quite easily a minute later. He saw the flash of her white clothing first, and then the whip of her hair in the deep shadows cast by the two heavy tents she stood between.

Stop!

Vejhon obeyed simply because the command racing through his brain was like a shock. Then he saw the larger, darker forms closing in on Hanna. He honestly tried to remember everything Najir had tried to tell him, about how Hanna could defend herself, a fact he had seen firsthand. But the simple truth was that he didn't have it in him to hold back, and the agony ripping through his chest and guts told him that he could never forgive himself if she got so much as a hair out of place because he hesitated to act.

He was, however, aware of the need for stealth. He could draw no attention to them or he would be risking his life and possibly Hanna's. He moved with a speed that was part of the gifts she had given him to reach her, and he knew from that instant he would never bitch about the sacrifices he had been forced to make ever again. It was worth it. The instant his fight instinct was agitated the darkness seemed to lighten up, shapes and movement becoming much clearer. He was able to count quickly what the odds were.

Six to two.

Hmm.

Good odds.

The irreverent thought was pushed at Hanna and she turned to see him coming, ignoring her command to stop. He didn't realize that these thugs weren't after her. They were after him. Sure enough, as soon as they caught sight of him, they stopped the delaying taunting they had been using to keep her corralled among them and burst into instant action.

On the plus side, they were completely ignoring Hanna. They would regret that. On the negative? These guys knew nothing about stealth. And not too much about fighting either, Jhon learned quickly as the first one reached for him with a roundhouse. Idiot. Jhon dodged and let him overshoot his balance from his missed momentum, then grabbed hold of his head, kicked his feet back out from under him, and let him land face first in the questionable stickiness of the tent alley ground.

Someone grabbed him from behind.

Someones. One wrangled him around his neck, hanging down his back like a monkey and two others grabbed his arms and pulled back until Jhon felt straining on his shoulder sockets. He tried to brace his feet, but the simian around his throat was swinging back and forth like crazy, shifting his weight and bending him back.

Until a fist shot past Jhon's cheek, missing him completely and landing soundly in someone else's face. That was when he realized it was Hanna standing that close to him, her arm extended past his cheek.

"Excuse me, lover," she said with a playful purr and a wink, coming just shy of kissing him as she gripped hold of the simian and hauled him right over Jhon's head.

"Thanks, babe," he shot back, able to plant his weight now and plan his escape. He almost wanted to stay there a minute and watch the beauty of that sleek sexy body kicking the shit out of the guy she had hold of.

But . . .

Two other bodies came crashing into the melee. One struck Hanna in the back, sending her sprawling onto the ground in a tackle with her foe lurking large on her back. The second rammed Jhon in his exposed belly, knocking the heartbeat right out of his body.

"Can't fight back, slave boy, or you go night-night and we have fun with the lady after we tie you up so you can watch."

The taunt was . . . unwise.

Between the threat and seeing Hanna go down, Jhon reached a point where a little something clicked over in his brain. All cautions, all acts, and everything not connected to his immediate survival shut down and became nonconsiderations. The warrior burst forward and on the way it melded with that new part of him: the predator, the protector, and the ruthless animal instinct that was pure cat.

Jhon's fingers opened and flexed, his nails growing in wicked curves. He vocalized as his body crouched inside of itself, a low growl of threat and imminent attack.

"Jhon," he heard Hanna whisper, her fear a palpable thing. He could taste it on his tongue and it infuriated him. She was his mate! She was cat! She should not fear what they were.

His strength and speed, cat and warrior combined, could not be matched. Hanna watched in a stunned sort of horror and pride as his huge body contorted to free itself, throwing off one man and turning viciously on the other. She saw him grab the man by the neck, heard the little pops as his claws punctured the soft flesh they found. By the time he had ripped out the man's larynx, she was growling in excited support.

Blood was on the air.

Hanna reached back and raked her pointed nails down her attacker's face. He drew breath for a scream as he fell away from her, but she never forgot that silence was their only savior at this point. She seized his throat and cut off his air single-handedly, hissing with low fury as she rolled him beneath her body. His eyes were wide with terror at what he saw, the woman upon him whose face flickered between person and vicious cat. He bore witness to her secret . . . for all of twenty seconds. Then she grabbed hold of his head and broke his neck with a powerful double snap of bone.

She rose into a crouch, her hair whipping hard as she turned her head sharply to find her mate. Hanna wanted to scream when she saw the mass of men beating on him and trying to tear him down, but she knew she had to resist. Instead she satisfied herself with a chilling growl as she rushed into the mix of men. She entered the fight just as Jhon was plowing a fist up under the rib cage of one of the bigger men. Unable to tell his race or the location of organs, he had no specific target. He just grabbed and pulled and used his free hand to punch the guy in the throat so he wouldn't scream.

His friends were grasping the direness of their situation, however. They were no longer trying to fight, but trying to escape. Hanna and Jhon exchanged looks and they agreed. There could be no survivors. No witnesses. Three were dead, and three would join them. Hanna took the next kill, putting her fist hard enough into his spine to silence him for good. The two remaining started to keen and wail, screeching about monsters and trying to scrabble away on the ground like the rodents they were.

The mated couple pounced on them as one, dispatching them with a slit throat and a broken neck. Hanna then looked at Jhon. Both were breathing hard and splattered with blood. She realized her mate preferred to make his prey bleed, when she could give or take it. He was new to the cat, feeling the fever of it for the first time, so she understood. He was staring at her hard, his eyes shifting over her restlessly, and she knew why. His adrenaline was high; the beast made demands. He smelled the excitement on her through the rusty tang of blood.

But they had six bodies around them, and she had to think of consequences.

Jhon saw her looking around at the carnage, and the haze of his bestial self lifted slightly. He knew her fear. Her worry. He had to make this right for her.

"Hanna," he said, his voice little more than a rough cough. "Go home."

"No!" she hissed. "If you get caught you need me to defend you!"

He didn't want to argue with her. He stripped off his shirt, wiping himself free of as much of the violet-colored blood as he could. Her pants were obviously stained, and his were even worse.

"I have an idea." She ran two steps and leapt into the Otherside, the cat landing with a graceful soundlessness. Her clothing fell to the ground along with her hair ornaments. He looked into her eyes and immediately knew what she was planning to do.

"Hanna, no! If you get captured or . . . you could get killed!"

In this crowd?

She had a point. The stampede of people alone would protect her if she was careful. The bodies would be explained away as victims of the wild bellcat that came into town inexplicably . . . or it would be blamed on Hanna's House and her collection of cats.

Acceptable risk.

A tactician's term. It was the only choice. He quickly gathered up all clothing and evidence of their presence, and found a spare piece of canvas to wrap it up in, tucking it under his arm. They needed to hurry out of there before they were discovered. Jhon moved to one of the splits between the tents and crouched low, waiting as Hanna prepared to run out into the crowd and start a panic that would allow him to run undetected as he blended in with the stampeding people.

She shook herself hard, fluffing out her dark coat to make herself look bigger, then bared her fangs in a wicked smile as she leapt free of the alley. He watched her jump bold as hell onto a display table, a massive roar shuddering out of her. There was total shocked silence for all of a heartbeat, and then pandemonium broke. He waited for a minute, and then bolted into the crowd of runners. Troublemaker that she was, Hanna chased after him and the crowd, getting close enough that he felt her nip playfully at his ankle. Then she reeled and tore off in another direction.

The streets were full of screaming shoppers pouring out of the bazaar. Sentries came hurrying to the source of the panic, leaving the way clear for a bare-chested, blood-smattered slave to sneak his way home from shadow to shadow with no one the wiser.

When Jhon ran into the house looking the way he did, he thought Najir was going to have a medical fit right on the spot. He rapidly explained what had happened and they both rushed to aid in the deception. Jhon burned everything they had worn.

Najir dropped a dress over the wall of the enclosure where no guards walked. There wasn't a need for guards by the enclosure when nine wild bellcats made their home there. Hanna would smell the dress easily then change and put it on so she could simply walk into her home.

16

Vejhon paced for a good hour, his stomach in knots for leaving her, his eye on her brother. If anything happened to her, her brother would shift out of the Otherside. When the door opened and she stepped into the large foyer, Vejhon tackled her right off of her feet, his body nailing hers back against the door and his mouth fastening to hers with ferocity.

I thought the worst. I need you. We are safe.

The jumble of thoughts had no discernable origin. They were as melded together as their mouths and just as emotional. Jhon was breathing so hard from relief of fear that his breath heated her face. She slid her fingers through the white waves of his hair and held him to the passion of his kiss.

The dress she wore was short skirted and both his hands ran up her legs beneath it until he had a firm hold of her ass and was pulling her forward into the press of his hips. They devoured each other's mouths, the heat and intensity blinding them with the sensuality and need of the moment. She lifted her leg and hooked it over his hip, her calf crossing over his tight backside as she pulled him between her legs.

Vejhon could feel the heat of her radiating through his clothing and he reached to shove her skirt out of the way and to release his penis from its cruel cloth prison. He needed her. He would always need her. But now, now he needed her around him pulsing and alive. Safe. His. He guided himself between her moist folds, following the increasing wetness as he rubbed over first one clit, then the other, making her gasp into his mouth both times.

"Yes," she cried when he hovered right at her entrance. "Now. Now!"

He agreed. Now was not the time for pause or patience. This was a time for heat and raw need. He plunged into her, gritting his teeth when she thwarted his thrust yet again in that pleasurable, frustrating clench of muscles.

"Relax," he murmured against her mouth. "When you do, I'm going to fuck you until your juices run down your legs. I'm going to make you scream, Hanna."

She couldn't possibly relax after a promise like that, and his evil little chuckle told her he knew damn well she wouldn't. But luckily the vice inside her body worked on different commands than the rest of her and he was sliding up hard with a bump into her cervix.

"Oh . . . I felt that," he notified her with a grin.

"Feel this," she whispered against his cheek. She consciously put every ounce of focus on reclamping her vaginal walls around him. He jerked and let out a gruff groan. She smiled sweetly and relaxed. "Now you can fuck me," she instructed.

Jhon laughed and did exactly as ordered. He rammed up into her again and again, putting all the power of his legs into each thrust as the door held her in place. He freed a breast from her neckline and bent to suck the rigid nipple. Hanna squealed loudly as the voracious sucking shot up along those same nerves being stimulated by his constant rhythm across her clit and over her G-spot. She grew dizzy, pleasure swimming over her until all focus and control faded completely away. She began a cadence of low husky moans, timed to his thrusts into her. They grew in volume, spurring him on, turning him on. Jhon was nowhere near done with her, though, so he just reveled in her sexy cries.

Hanna came with a low-register scream that turned into pleasured grunts as her head fell back and her nails bit into his shoulders. Jhon felt heat and wetness rushing down over his pumping cock, the sensation maddeningly divine.

"I know what you like," he whispered against her throat between hard breaths. "I know what makes you come."

He shifted, drawing her leg off his hip and tilting her hips back toward the wall. He was thrusting into her a little shallower than before, but he was also stroking over both of her clits now. She gasped wildly again and again, already too sensitive from barely finishing her first orgasm. He tore her dress, ripping the neckline open so he had better access to both breasts. Now he bit and licked and sucked at them both, feeling her body jolt every time he sent those bolts of pleasure down the same group of nerves.

She opened her eyes and stared into his as tears flooded her vision. They were triggered by the overload of the orgasm that tore through her, shredding every nerve she had into little pieces. She felt him jerk her leg back to his hip, felt him deepen his stroke and quicken it. He was close. She sensed it. Even as overwhelming darkness tried to steal her away from savoring his release, she held on with everything she had as she listened to him rasp out her name over and over again, her name becoming his moan of pleasure. He slammed up into her and froze like time standing still. She loved this part, where the recoil of pleasure was too much for his body to handle so everything just paused for an instant. Then it released in a blinding rush that made him shout and swear because he felt himself turning inside out for her.

Hanna let go.

Vejhon had barely caught his first breath when he felt Hanna fall in a dead weight against the wall. He held on to her a moment, giving himself time to gather his senses. He leaned forward and kissed the side of her neck, and then her shoulder, little worshipping touches that she wouldn't know about, but would be left on her just the same. He eased away from her just far enough to repair his state of dress with one hand while holding her against his side with the other. He tried to tidy her up a little, but he'd done too much damage. He scooped her up in his arms, turning her close to his chest, and moved toward the stairs.

At the foot of the steps he suddenly stopped, his senses refocusing and picking up the fresh familiar scent of someone else in the room. Jhon clenched his teeth together, blaming himself for his haste and need that had had him taking his mate in so public a venue. But he would deal with the watcher later. Now his only care was Hanna. Jhon wasn't satisfied until she was safe and comfortable in her own bed, with himself tucked up tightly behind her.

It was many hours later when Hanna flew lightly down the stairs, her bare feet hardly touching the cool mosaic tiles. She hurried to the door and activated the scanner. It opened to reveal a group of official-looking persons.

There were two sentries, their uniforms a distinctive white. A City Official, one of those in charge of investigating crimes. And two Masters. Or rather, one Master and one Baron. Just by the makeup of the group and the grimness in their eyes, it was obvious to Hanna immediately that their purpose in being there was to oversee the examination of one of their own.

Hanna instantly bristled, unable to hold back the reaction when she saw Majum on her doorstep. She realized that she must allow the group in to appear as guiltless as possible, but she would be damned if that murderer would cross her threshold.

"Gentlemen, what may I do for you today?"

"Master Drakoulous," Master Fusut began, "you may or may not have heard, but a large jungle cat was seen loose and wild in the bazaar yesterday. It mauled six men to death and caused a panic that destroyed a fortune in goods, not to mention those who were injured running away from the thing."

"How terrible," she said with total honesty. She had not intended to harm so many and it pricked at her conscience to think anyone would suffer from what she had had to do in order to save herself and Jhon.

"In point of fact, Master Drakoulous, you are the only one with a collection of wild cats in her gardens," the Baron spoke up, his dark eyes studying her intently. "You will be held responsible for all deaths and damages, my Lady."

"If it should be proven it was one of your cats," the other Master hastened to add. "We will need to come and inspect your enclosure."

"Gentlemen, as you are well aware, that enclosure has housed a great many cats over a great many generations, and never once have they escaped. I treat my cats like family and would never see them set loose on society where they could harm or be harmed."

"Let us in, my Lady," the Baron said, stepping forward to crowd her, "or forfeit all of your animals to the city at once."

Hanna's nostrils flared as she picked up all the vile little scents clinging to the Baron, from his obnoxious cologne to the remnants of another male's ejaculate. She could even smell blood. And why not? The man was stained to his soul in the stuff.

"Baron Majum, I advise you to step back," she said coldly.

"That's it then, gentlemen, you see she refuses!" Majum was

just shy of gleeful as he became excited at the prospect of seeing her strong-armed.

"On the contrary," she broke in smoothly. "You gentlemen are most enthusiastically welcome," she said with a smile to charm the others before turning frozen eyes on Majum. "But you, my Lord, will never step foot in the house of my mother. The house of my father. The house of so many who fell beneath your boot heel. I will not desecrate their memories by allowing it." She snapped her eyes to the other Master who was gaping at her. "And how thoughtless of the COM to send the murderer of my parents to my home to question me! I am insulted and wounded that you would be so heartless! Back away, Majum, or I promise you I will risk fifty years of banishment to see you brought to justice for the crimes you still owe in my book."

"You dare to threaten me?" he hissed, fury shuddering visibly through his frame as she stood to bar his way. "You threaten me in front of these venerable witnesses? You all heard her!" He turned to the witnesses who were paling to the fairest of blues. "You can stand in judgment against her!"

"Threats mean nothing, Baron," Master Fusut said dismissively. "If they did then you would have been jailed countless times by now." The Master paused only long enough to wait for the muffled snicker of the Official to pass. "And she is right. You are only here to cause damage where you can whilst still remaining in the guidelines of the Feudal sanctions. I ought to have realized it myself when you so eagerly volunteered for this duty. Take yourself away, Baron."

"The investigation requires two Masters for authority! To prove there is no favoritism!" Majum was so furious now at being thwarted yet again from a victory that he shoved himself up into the Master's face physically. "You favor her and we will never gain an unbiased investigation into what has happened here! People are dead, Master Fusut. Something must be done about that!"

"I can easily call on another Master. Any number of them will be happy to stand for this investigation. You are simply inflaming the situation, Baron."

"I believe you heard the gentleman when he said to take yourself away, my Lord?"

The prompt brought everyone around in surprise, especially the Baron. He wasn't used to a male voice speaking for the House of Drakoulous. Women had been heirs for two generations now. When Majum saw the stoic figure of a beautiful and familiar male standing at Hanna's back, he stood in total shock for the longest moment. His surprise broke when Hanna turned slightly to lay a quelling hand on the brute's chest. A warning. That was what it took for him to snap to the awareness that a slave had just given him a command. Instantly his mind raced with the advantage he could turn this into. He had wanted to deprive his enemy of one of her two precious jewels, and he had failed so far. He didn't care how she was deprived; only that it happened. There might be the added delight of obtaining him for his own purposes, the Baron thought with a rush of excitement running down his chest and into his belly.

"You dare to address me as an equal, slave?" He hissed out the sentence with a huge measure of affront, making certain everyone there felt the depth of his insult. Inside he was so delighted he could hardly think. The slave had made the critical error in front of witnesses of the highest order. If he could not use them against Hanna, he would use them against her slave.

"No, my Lord. I was merely reminding his lordship of the request already put forward by the esteemed Master Fusut."

The heavy-handed respect and following bow made Fusut smile in pleasure and effectively beat the wind out of the sails of Majum's advantage. He felt it wash away with a receding pull like water swirling down a drain. Worse, he knew he had been purposely thwarted. The clever bastard had done the dance on purpose and with perfectly plotted steps. And Majum had left himself open for it. For all of it.

Vejhon couldn't resist pushing his luck and smiling. He felt Hanna's nails pushing into his skin through the material of his shirt. He reached up and caught up her hand in his, smiling as he pressed an affectionate kiss in its palm. Her brilliant eyes slid over to him and the sly look that she shot him out of the corner of her eyes was a mixture of humor, affection, and warning.

Hanna looked back at Majum, knowing full well what he had been gearing up to do. It was as if the man had made a career of plotting against her at any and all opportunities. She had never quite understood what her family had done to earn such bone-deep wrath and hatred, but she wished it would end. She had her preferences of how she wished it would end, but any end would do at this point. She merely wanted her family to live in peace.

Unable to justify any further protests, the Baron had no choice but to turn sharply on his heel and march off in an obvious fury. The group at the door watched his progress down the drive for a long minute before Hanna cleared her throat to get everyone's attention.

"Gentlemen, please come in. I will have Jhon gather the cats in a safe place so you may inspect the enclosure at your leisure. Master Fusut, you may use my communication system to contact a second impartial witness. Please choose someone who contests me frequently in the COM. I would not wish to be accused of any further acts of avoidance or favoritism."

"I know just the one," Master Fusut said with a wink and a chuckle.

"It was a terrible risk," Hanna sighed after she had closed the door on the final visitor to her House.

"We have come through the entire incident unscathed,

Hanna. It serves no purpose to rehash what might have happened."

"And you should not have baited Majum, Jhon. I fear for your safety. For your life."

"I don't," he retorted. "I think there's entirely too much fear in this House already. It's suffocating your entire family. Don't you see that?"

"That's easy for you to say. You made a living putting your life and those of others on the line. My family is not an army about to volunteer for you while you play the god with us!"

"Hanna," he said, his eyes darkening with simmering emotion. "I take nothing about you so cavalierly. I want nothing to harm you or your family, least of all me. I am only saying that you need to realize that you're not living a full life so long as you suppress the needs and the potentials of your . . . of *our* other half. It's bad enough you ask me to suppress my independence and strength when in public; now you give me this other power, all this potential and capability, and you want me to suppress that as well? You also need to consider what happened yesterday, and what Ashanna has done. Why do you think the cat took us over like that? Why do you think Asha instigates trouble? She is suppressing something not meant to be suppressed and it bursts out in uncontrolled behaviors.

"I'm not saying you should come out of the closet and show off what you can become, merely that there's something to be said for embracing the bellcat within you and letting it feel everyday freedoms. You are already cunning and quick witted in the COM, but why not be sensual and dominant as well? Maybe a little forcefulness is called for. Maybe it will keep those like Majum in check, keep him from thinking you are an easy target. I guarantee you he's stewing over that knowledge right about now."

"Very likely," she agreed, not able to hide her smile of pleasure over that fact. "But I know Majum well. His anger will fuel him into action. It will not bode well for this House. I . . . I have a brother out there whom I have not heard from in some time. Majum continually implies he is the reason for that . . . as if . . . as if he has him locked away in his dungeons somewhere. I dread the very idea of it. The only reason I know my brother is still alive is because the next eldest in his litter remains trapped in the Otherside."

"He's probably lying to you. Somehow he found out that you were worried about not hearing from your brother and he is using it to mess with your mind. It's an old tactician's trick."

"I don't doubt that it's a possibility, Jhon, but you do not know this man the way that I do. You don't know the lengths he is willing to go to just to get back at this House."

"Just what is he getting back at this House for?" Jhon wanted to know. "What offense have you committed against him?"

"I offend him by not being afraid of him. By standing up to him and his cutthroat ways, and by reminding him that very shortly his nephew will be the Master of his House and Majum will be nothing of importance afterward. I remind him of how little power he truly has. I make certain he knows that there is at least one family in this city that he will never intimidate and never win against."

Her passion struck him like a bell. "And what has he done to you, Hanna, that has made you hate him with such a passion?"

"He killed my parents," she told him. "He knows he killed my mother, but until just now what he didn't know was that the slave he cut down to get to her was my beloved father. And mere hours after doing so he was pardoned of the crime by the Feud sanctions. I was . . ." Her fingers curled into fists and Jhon could feel her shaking. "I was never so angry in all my life. I felt so cheated of my right to avenge them. I have all of this power at my fingertips and yet can do nothing to see him answer for his crimes. Anything I did would make them look at this house much too closely. As you know, we cannot afford that."

"And yet as long as Majum lives, you will continue to be at risk. Think, Hanna. Who do you think was responsible for what happened in the bazaar? We were targeted on purpose, that much was very clear to me. Now tell me if you have another enemy I've not heard of; otherwise, I have to believe that it was Majum coming after me."

"Perhaps," she agreed grimly. "But you weren't supposed to be with me. It was supposed to be Najir. I changed my mind in the COM. No one else would have known there would be a switch."

"True," he said, looking puzzled as she dodged his logic. "But tell me, do you suspect otherwise? Do you believe it was anyone else but Majum who sent those men after us? And don't say you think it was a random attack," he argued quickly with an upraised hand. "They were dressed too well and fought too much like mercenaries to be common street thugs. The entire event was a hit, plain and simple. The only reason they weren't more successful was because they thought this band would make me an easy target." He flicked a finger against his armlet, making it ring softly. "That and they didn't realize you're a vicious little thing when you get riled up." He said it with a low growl in his voice, making her smile when he jostled her for good measure.

"You have way too much testosterone for your own good," she chided him.

"Not my fault. You did this to me, remember?"

"Oh, really?" She made a snort of disbelief, a delicate, sniffy sort of defiance. "Seems to me you came that way. Ready-made."

"Perhaps," he relented. "I'm not adjusted to this new way of being entirely yet, though. I feel . . ." He hesitated, not wanting to upset her but feeling he had to make himself clear. "I feel not entirely right in my own skin. Sort of like being armed with a weapon you've never used before and being thrust into battle. It's awkward and you feel insecure."

"I see," she said softly, a frown tugging at her scarlet lips.

"And I haven't explored the Otherside yet. It's like a ticking bomb waiting to go off . . . and I don't know how to work the detonator."

Hanna got up from the divan they'd been seated on together, moving out of his embrace pointedly as his words disturbed her. "You're right, of course. But there's really no way to explain how to go to the Otherside. It just sort of happens. Once it does, it's like accessing it automatically from then on." She turned to cast him a look. "You came very close in the marketplace. I could feel it on you; I could see it. And afterward . . ." A lavender blush crept over her cheeks as she recalled how fiercely they had taken from each other right there against the front door.

"I know Majum's type," he said carefully, changing the topic on her so he could get back to making his point. "I saw enough of it on both sides of the war at home. The man thrives on the pain and suffering of others. He'll need to be taken care of eventually, Hanna, or you risk him prying open this can of secrets you have here. You should let me do what I do best."

"You mean sink to his level?" she demanded. "Absolutely not!"

"And meanwhile as you adhere to these precious principles of yours he gets farther and farther under your skin, picking off your family members one by one! You just told me you wouldn't put it past the man to have your brother imprisoned for months! You think you're being moral by letting him live? Who knows how many lives he's ruining with every poisoned breath he takes! Is that morally right?" he demanded.

"Stop it!" She covered her ears, as if it could drown out the conflict of conscience churning through her. "What I speak of is the law! Morality remains ambiguous and open to interpretation, but the law does not!" She turned on him, beautiful fury radiating out of every pore. "I am Master of this House, a lawmaker and respected member of this society! I will not resort to back-alley feuding and hypocrisy, no matter how justified!"

"Then you put this whole House at risk, Master Drakoulos," he railed back at her, lurching to his feet as he whipped her with her title. "You already are a hypocrite! Your entire heritage, your entire House is hypocrisy! Everything you hide is nothing but a lifelong game of cloak and dagger! Men died in that marketplace simply because they saw what we were! Where's the justice in that?"

"Don't you dare try and make me feel guilty for protecting myself and my family!"

"I'll dare that and much more, sweetheart," he growled at her as the hackles on the back of his neck rose in aggression. "You use that excuse much too easily and much too often for convenience's sake, but when I suggest something meant to protect your precious family you get all holier than thou on me and act as if you are above it! You mark my words, Hanna, that man is gunning for you and yours and one of these days this balance you try and maintain is going to crack right down the middle! You'll be exposed for what you really are, which is nothing more than a clever little liar! You justify what you've done to me with games of conscience and worded tricks to absolve yourself of guilt, but what it comes down to is I never asked for this! You tricked me and goaded me and connived until you felt your conscience was clear! Well, it's not! You could have been straight with me, asked me if I wanted to die and be reborn. Taken the risk and been aboveboard, but you didn't. You didn't because you wanted what you wanted and fuck everyone else and what they want!"

"No!"

"Yes! Hanna, *yes!* You think about what you've done here as if you gave me choices, but you didn't give me one real goddamn choice in any of this. I was a slave. I still am! I have no rights, no freedom, no power to even so much as express an opinion counter to your own! Just listen to you! Even now I can feel the thoughts washing off of you in waves! You want to yell at me and say I dare too much. Tell me to shut my mouth and watch my step! Your 'freedom' within a prison is a joke, sister. I'm nothing here. Nothing but a means to an end and a stud for the gene pool."

Jhon growled savagely before turning on his heel to leave her presence. He was so furious, everything inside of him so suddenly coming to the surface, he was afraid for what he'd do in his temper. He left her there, stormed out of the room and into the hallway, nearly tripping over her sister.

"Lover's quarrel?" she asked archly, raising one of her pointed little brows.

Jhon wasn't in the mood for her cheek. He turned on her, his face right up in hers with a vicious snarling roar. She jerked back in surprise, banging into the wall behind her.

"You," he hissed. "You are going to mind your manners with me, you spoiled fucking brat! I don't care who or what you are, I will beat your ass if I ever catch you disrespecting me or your sister again. That includes your smart mouth and your indiscriminate voyeurism. You think I don't know you stood there watching us the whole time? I have the exact same senses as you do and while you have the advantage of experience on your side, I have the advantage of knowing how to use all my skills, old or new, to aid me in any and every battle. You will not get under my radar, little girl, so stop trying. And you better keep your smart little ass in line or I will force it there. Do I make myself clear?"

"How dare—!"

"I dare!" he roared again, the utter savagery in the retort

shutting her up and forcing her to turn her head aside in submission. "Don't test me! Do you hear me? I've had about all I
am going to take from you and from your sister. Both of you
are going to get it through your heads that I am no slave and I
will not be pushed around! Do I make myself clear?" he demanded.

"Yes," was all she could whisper. She didn't even nod her
head for fear of his taking the movement the wrong way. She
kept her neck exposed to him, making sure he believed her sincerity.

"Good." Jhon pushed away from her and stormed off to go
deeper into the house. Ashanna exhaled in sudden relief and
slid down the wall until her butt hit the floor.

She wondered if her sister realized exactly what she had gotten herself into.

17

Captain Sozo was dallying with one of the treasures in Majum's vaults when the Baron came storming in. It was obvious he was in an unparalleled rage when he drew a short dagger and plunged it into the Drakoulous guard's eldest brother's heart. The prison became an uproar of screams and wails, the younger siblings bursting apart at the seams as the brother died in front of them.

Hyde sighed, withdrawing from his victim of the moment and quickly redressing himself. When the Baron wasted valuable resources on a whim like that, it meant things were bad and fun would have to wait.

"What happened?" he asked his companion.

"That rotten whore!" Majum snarled, his eyes livid with fury and his skin mottled violet because of it.

"Her again?" Sozo asked dryly.

"Again and for the last time! I don't care what it takes! I'm going to get her and both those fucking treats of hers if it's the last thing I do! That whole family! First I'll kill off everything around her, watch her suffer as they die one by one! Then she'll be the last to go! Killing her is too good for her. I'm going to mutilate her! Cut her up bit by bit over the span of a year!"

By that point every word Majum spoke was being punctuated by rising wails and sobs from those trapped around them. But Hyde couldn't even take the time to enjoy their distress. The Baron had to be calmed down or he'd take to killing all their remaining leverage.

"So how do you want to start?" Sozo coaxed him, redirecting him from his rage to the cold calculation he knew he would excel at.

"Najir! No, wait, the sister. She is constantly running around in the dark corners of this city. She'll be easiest to get to."

"People have tried that," the Captain reminded his friend carefully. "She's not as delicate as she looks. The last fight she was in she was the only one left standing. Remember, House Drakoulous trains their family well."

"Then you do it! Personally. No lackeys, no hires. You're the only one I can trust to get it right. So you do it, Hyde. You understand? I want that brat hanging on my wall, dead or alive, by the end of this week. Am I clear?"

"Perfectly."

Hanna couldn't understand where all of Jhon's sudden fury had come from. Or maybe it wasn't really all that sudden. They'd been running on a high of a sort for the past few days, discovering each other and indulging in the passions their inner natures made them crave. Between that and introducing Jhon to the culture he would now call his own, they really hadn't had a chance to slow things down and take stock. It was a lot of change all at once for him, a lot of sacrifice and adaptation he was being forced into. Clearly, it was taking a toll on him. One that, perhaps, he'd hardly realized himself. He hadn't yelled at her like that since a day or two after he'd gotten there. She couldn't remember them arguing once since he'd gone through his metamorphosis. But now he'd more than made up for it all in one shot.

Was he right? Was she being selfish and manipulative? She could easily see how he would think so. She'd orchestrated everything that had happened to him since he'd arrived in her home. And yes, her methods of getting him to agree to going through the change to join her family had not been as aboveboard as she would have liked. In fact, they hadn't been aboveboard at all.

Hanna bit down on a dark nail as she stared out at the panoramic view of the city. She came to this room to clear her mind, but now it seemed it was difficult for her to think of anything else but the passion she had shared there with Jhon not too long ago. But his passion, it seemed, could run very independent of the rest of his emotions.

Of course, she was quite similar, she acknowledged to herself. She compartmentalized her life all of the time. Her work. Her family. Her relationship with Jhon. Each moved independently of the other. She didn't see how Jhon had a right to tell her what to do with her family. Couldn't he see that his bloodthirsty ways could only cause them trouble? As it was, the sighting of the bellcat in the marketplace was bringing undue attention onto their House. They couldn't afford any more scrutiny! She had taken a terrible risk doing what she had done. Only fortune had kept them safe this far. If he was right and there was someone seeking to harm him or Najir, she would have to keep them both confined to the house. She simply couldn't take any more risks. And Asha had to return to the country. The farther she was from this mess the better off she would be. She could only add to the trouble.

"My Lady."

Hanna turned at the familiar address to face her long-trusted servant.

"Najir, what am I doing wrong?" she asked him. "I thought he was growing happy here. Why has he suddenly turned on me like this?"

"He isn't turning on you," Najir chided gently.

"He says I forced this on him. He's chafing at the constraints he has agreed to already!"

"I'm sorry, my Lady, but I don't think Jhon has ever really agreed to any of this." Najir paused thoughtfully. "You mistake him for me, I think. While we are both of warrior stock, Jhon is a leader. It is in his blood to take charge of things and to fight his way through them until he achieves his objective. You expect him to act and react as submissively as I have done, but he and I are very different. You cannot forget that. He chafes at being subordinate, Hanna. It is not in his nature."

"Every soldier is a subordinate in some way," she argued.

"He can take orders, but in the end he is used to directing how those orders are carried out. You cannot manipulate him like a game piece telling him to do this and that, yet expect him to be silent in return. He's a tactician, experienced and with much to offer. Did it ever occur to you to listen to what he has to say?"

She snorted. "No more or less than I would listen to you, Najir. The difference is you are familiar with this world. He is here but days and thinks he knows enough to overrule what I say and do!"

"And yet you know him only days and think to overrule what he says and does without knowing more about him." Najir shook his head. "You've taken total command of a weapon and yet know nothing about it. Its balance, its power, its limits . . . none of it."

"Uh! What is it with you men and your weapon analogies!" she demanded in disgust. "Why must it always be about war and death and fights!"

"You live in this society and have the nerve to ask that?" Najir queried gently. "You know full well this peaceful surface the Houses show to the cities is a farce! Ours is not the only House that has secret enemies trying to undermine it. The Feuds are too deep running. A law made only eight years ago doesn't change things as instantly as it is made. If anyone can appreciate how slow change is to come, I would think it would be you."

"Slow and interminable!"

"And you think you suffer for it? There is no law against slavery, Hanna. It is still legal and allowed socially—in fact it is an economic constant—yet when was the last time people like you, people who don't believe in it, stood up and said so? You are a voice of great power in our society; you could initiate remarkable change, yet you have never once spoken of it in Chambers. Why is that? Are you afraid you would then have to sign away all your rights to me and, now, to Vejhon? If not for the slave trade, you and your family could never hope to find those who are like Jhon to come and free your siblings. Is that why you have never made a single stride at abolishing the trade?" Najir held up a silencing hand when she tried to choke out a reply. "You see, Hanna? Neither one of us can stand here toe-to-toe with you and point out the flaws in your thinking without you taking offense and thinking you are above the reproach of mere slaves."

"Najir!" she gasped, horrified he thought these things of her. They had been the best of friends for so long! How could he think such terrible things of her?

Because they were true.

The touch of icy cold realization that flowed through Hanna made her shiver with terrible chills. They were right! They were both telling the truth of it! With all the power she had at her fingertips, both in and out of the COM, what was she doing with it? Oh, she did her part in ending the Feuds and making very important laws; she couldn't undersell herself on that point. But on such a critical issue that touched the hearts and lives of two men she professed to care about? In all of this time as she had tried to use them both to make life better for herself and for her family, had she ever once done anything to try to make life better for them? Giving them a home, clothing, food, and comfort was not enough. In fact, it was a right that all people deserved. The right to walk free, the right to defend their lives, the right to have opinions of their own: they had none of it and she, for all she was a prisoner of her own genetics, had more freedom than any slave on the planet could even dream of. It wasn't enough to simply refuse to attend auctions. She had still kept an ear out, always hoping for that special slave, for a slave like Jhon.

Tears welled in her eyes as she realized that desire in and of itself had created the market for a man like Jhon to be stolen away from everything that had mattered most to him. It had created the situation he now found himself in against his will. Even one was one too many.

"Oh no," she squeaked out in horror, her entire face ravaged with the realization of what she had done . . . and what she hadn't done.

"Easy," Najir soothed her softly, instantly hating to see the pain and obliteration in her eyes. Instantly knowing that a heart as well meaning as hers would suffer great pain at such harsh realizations. And for all he wanted her to see the light of her own wrongdoings, he would not ever wish her any pain.

"Don't coddle me!" she snapped at him as tears dropped onto her cheeks in little rushing rivulets. "Don't tell me it's okay!"

No wonder Jhon had yelled at her as if she were the most hateful of creatures! She was all that and more. She was everything he had accused her of.

Pushing away from Najir, unable to stand the compassion and tolerance in his eyes, Hanna ran away to find the one man she knew would always tell her the truth of the matter and not comfort her when she clearly didn't deserve it.

Jhon was fighting his way through his anger, literally. He had gone out to the training grounds to round up a few of the guards. One of the beauties of the armlet that was supposedly keeping him in check was that it would allow him to train and keep fully practiced, so long as he meant no ill will toward his opponent. So, those who were fighting against him saw nothing out of the ordinary in his ability to beat them into the ground. They just assumed his intentions were well meant and that his band would keep him from doing any real harm whether he was armed or not.

The staff he held in his hands was the most rudimentary of weapons, nothing outwardly lethal about it. But in the right hands it was just as deadly as anything bladed might be, and his hands were definitely the right hands. The benefit of using just the staff was that it made him work twice as hard for victory, therefore working all of his muscles to the fullest extent and calling on every ounce of skill he could muster.

Jhon cracked the staff hard against the shins of his opponent and in a swift movement he hooked the thing back around to the rear of the knees and swept him fully off of his feet. His adversary landed on his back, a cloud of dirt coughing up around him and blinding him to the swift securing of the end of the staff against his throat. It brought with it a full defeat and the understanding that he was well outmatched even when Jhon wasn't in a bad mood. .

Jhon stepped away from his opponent and looked at the ring of guards standing there staring at the swift annihilation of their comrade.

"Next?" he asked.

After dusting the ground with three men successively in under fifteen minutes, volunteers were hard to come by. They all knew they were outmatched. The only one on the entire property who might have a hope of taking the big brute of a slave was the only other slave among them. And Najir was nowhere to be found at the moment.

Jhon looked them over with a frown, needing someone to give him a good run. That was when he spied the blue-skinned beauty at the heart of his fury running toward them, her long, black hair flying like a kite behind her. Jhon felt his heart lurch with sudden anxiety to see her so obviously distressed. He didn't want to feel the compassion he felt, but he felt it just the same. It only served to make him angrier. How had she gotten so thoroughly under his skin so damn quickly? The power she had over him was becoming frustrating and so intense he hardly knew what to do with himself. All she had to do was shed one little tear and it was tying him up in knots!

He had never been the sort to fall under the spell of a woman's wiles, so he couldn't understand why he would do so now. Why did he make it so easy for her to work on him?

"Jhon!"

The way she called his name made his throat tighten with concern and worry . . . and frustration. Something terrible was upsetting her, turning the strong and confident Hanna he knew into this distressed, weakly panicking little thing. He had to force himself to remember that there wasn't a single weak thing about the tall, proud beauty he had come to know. He forced himself to remember the marketplace and how she had been able to rip violently through full-grown men, tough men, with barely a thought.

Then Hanna broke through the ring of men surrounding him and ran to him, throwing herself against his sweat-dampened body, her elegant hands desperate as she clung to him. She didn't even seem to notice that he had not dropped his weapon and he was not hugging her or touching her back. She didn't seem to care.

"Jhon. I'm so sorry!" She cried it out without care or concern for the curious eyes that were on her. "I was so wrong and you were right. I've asked you to do the impossible and for all the wrong reasons, for reasons that are all my own and all so selfishly motivated!"

Her words began to sink in past the armor of resistance he was struggling to hold up against her. What she was saying, in full witness of her household, was finally sinking into his head. She was groveling for his forgiveness. Her. The Master of a great House. She was begging a slave for his good graces and his attentions.

Unable to stand it any longer and feeling a sudden creeping shame, Jhon held his weapon in a single hand so he might wrap the other around her. He hugged her to him strongly, closing his eyes briefly as he took in the scent of her hair beneath his nose and absorbed the trembling warmth of her body. She had never been shy about showing him affection or sexual interest in front of the household, but this was something very different. And suddenly, despite all of his earlier righteous anger, Jhon could see her behavior for the danger that it was. She was displaying a weakness for all to see. She was showing them all that her emotions could be affected at the whims of a slave. And if any one of those witnesses were to find themselves exploited for their knowledge of her, if Baron Majum were to get ahold of any one of them, then he would know without a shadow of a doubt that all of Hanna's weakness lay in the person of a slave.

"Hanna, easy," he tried to soothe her, trying not to feel the tumult of emotions that washed first one way and then another within him. First he wanted to tell her to control herself, then he wanted her to explain what she meant, what it was she thought she saw. Did she truly see? Did she see how damn untenable this whole situation was? He was a fighter rendered utterly powerless in this society, and more so under the simple touch of one woman's tears.

Dropping the staff to the ground, Jhon turned all of his attention to Hanna. He wrapped her up tightly and protectively against him, lifting his head to glare at the curious eyes that yet gazed at them. Instantly they all began to pretend to look elsewhere, to inspect the weapons they held, to study the dirt at their feet. He knew it meant nothing. The only thing that mattered right then was Hanna.

Jhon bent to scoop her from the ground, her body flying up high against his chest even as she wrapped her arms like a tight vice around his neck. Her face pressed wetly against his throat and she simply sobbed. He could all but taste the depth of her regret and self-flagellation. He had no doubt whatsoever that she was feeling her mistakes with him just as deeply as he had wanted her to, and now he would wish for anything but. He wished he had not been so blunt and harsh with her. He wished that he were a better man who knew how to use words more diplomatically to slowly gain his way. Had he been a more patient man she would not now be so exposed. So raw.

Jhon carried her into the house, using his foot to shut the door behind them. He quickly brought her upstairs and into his room. As soon as he had her laid in his bed, he took both of his hands and smoothed them over her face, wiping away her tears before he leaned forward and kissed her on her forehead.

"I'm so sorry," she said, her voice so high-pitched it was like facing a child who had done something bad. It clawed at Vejhon's heart to see her so low. "I have done so many things wrong. I've wronged you in so many ways and I don't know how to make it up to you. I don't know how I can change what I've done. How will you ever be able to stand me?"

"Ah, Hanna," he sighed, wrapping her up tight and hugging her as closely as he dared. As strong and vital and powerful a woman as she was, she felt fragile just then in a way he had never thought possible. "You think I hate you, but I don't. And it's unfair of me to lay all the blame at your door. I did make choices here. Maybe they weren't fully informed choices, but it was my choice to go ahead recklessly into them without seeing I knew everything there was to know. I am a powerful and independent man and I could have said no to you at any given moment, slave or no slave; you gave me that choice at almost every turn."

Jhon pulled back until they were no more than a nose's tip apart, looking fiercely into one another's eyes. "But I need you to know that I cannot live my life with all these secrets. One I can manage, but a shipload? You ask too much of anyone to ask that of them. I can keep the secret of the bellcat, and I agree and understand why it must be kept. I know people, whether they are here or on my world or anywhere in the universe. People destroy what they don't understand because it frightens them. You think I don't see the danger here? I do. I see it all too well.

"But you can't also ask me to be a slave but not a slave. It's a lie and an illusion on both of our parts. A pretend slave is still a slave. Still a man with no rights. I'm not even allowed the freedom to choose to defend my own life. Armlet or no, if I defend you or myself I still have to face the antiquated laws of your people that say I am lower than even the lowest murderer and must die if I take his life. Where in anyone's mind is that sane? Where does it make sense?"

"It doesn't make sense. None of it does. And I have been wrong for being quiet about this in the COM. You'll see," she sniffled. "Tomorrow you'll see. I'll be better. I don't care what it takes . . . what it costs me. I'm going to change this. I'm going to fix it. I won't rest until it's no longer another secret for you. Do you believe me?"

She was so earnest, so eager for him to believe what she was saying. He also knew as well as she did that it wasn't going to be an easy road. It wasn't going to be as simple as flipping a switch and saying it.

Hanna reached with a stretch of her neck to kiss his mouth, her soft, full lips trembling with her emotion, but still lush with the ever-present sensuality she had always exhibited. Jhon found himself instantly taken in, the amazing aroma of her suddenly penetrating his senses. It was a real task to let her pull away relatively unmolested, but he knew she needed more than just the lusty bellcat within him.

In fact, he needed more than that lusty cat as well. He wanted to ease her hurting heart, make her understand that he trusted her. He wanted her to know how he felt. But it had never been easy for Jhon to be familiar with emotions outside of anger or righteousness. He had spent so much of his life as a fighter, he had no idea how to truly be a lover. But for the first time in his life he felt close to it. He felt something more than just sexual intimacy with a woman. Something more than just the hunger of attraction. Damn it, he wished he knew how to put it into words. He wanted to know the right way to speak the things he was feeling.

"Hanna, you know I care for you." It was weak. A lame expression of the things he felt for her, but it was the only thing he could offer her just then. He needed time to sort it all out and figure the right way to connect with her.

"I care for you as well," she said. "A very great deal."

He realized he already knew that. He had known it the moment she had come running out to him begging for his forgiveness. If she hadn't cared for him, it wouldn't have mattered to her the things he said or thought. The understanding made him smile down at her, the grin irrepressible in the face of his understanding. He reached to brush back her hair, his fingertips gliding over the exotic contours of her cheek.

"You may not think that I do, but I count myself very lucky for the turn my life took in order to come to this. To come to you. I was made a slave long before you ever came into the picture, my fate scaled by enemies I will never lay eyes on again. But I know you were a one in a million stroke of pure luck. Had it been only a matter of minutes later, had Najir not stopped by that auction, I know I would be dead. Had Majum bought me . . ."

Hanna shuddered, shaking her head in an attempt to negate the thought that hung between them. He didn't need to speak it out loud. They both know he would have rather killed himself than ever submitted to the likes of the Baron. He would have found a way. It was a terrible thought and one that Hanna couldn't bear. She reached to kiss him again, her fingers diving into his hair and grasping onto the strands like a life preserver she refused to let go of. She opened her mouth to him, the flutter of her tongue against his lips enticing him to do the same. Before he knew it he was deep inside of her sweet mouth, savoring the luscious flavor of her.

And just like that the cats within them took over. Her nails scraped across his scalp, seeking out every nerve he had in his body. She made a low noise, a cross between a moan and a rumbling purr. Beneath him, her back arched and brought pressure to her breasts against his chest. He took in a breath through his nose and suddenly all he could smell was the divine scent of her needy little body. It made him growl low in his chest, made his hands streak to her sides and run hotly over her body. Suddenly the pronunciation of her ribs against his palms had him mad for the feel of her beneath him. But not this way.

No. He had another way in mind. And just like that he had her rolled over beneath him, face down on the bed. He lay over her, his cock nestling well at home in the space between her round cheeks. The instant he settled against her he was hard with wanting her, with needing her. As always, it felt exactly as it had that first time, all animalistic and uncontrolled. He rubbed against her fiercely, making his need known to her in no uncertain terms. As if he couldn't help himself he opened his mouth on the back of her neck and bit down hard, holding her still for the surge of his hard body all along the back of hers. The cry she let out was nothing near distress and everything about pleasure. It made him harder just to hear it. It was a sensation that rippled over him like a wave of chills, only ten times stronger. He slid his hands beneath her and filled them with the heavy weight of her breasts. His knees wedged between hers, spreading her thighs apart.

Then he rocked back up onto his knees, turning his hands to brace against the bedding as yet another powerful shudder ran through him. Lust was like a beautiful red haze in his head, but there was more to it than that. There was more to them. He wanted to describe the feeling to her, to explain just how gorgeous it was, but he found he couldn't speak. He was aware of her turning around beneath him, of her hands cradling his face.

"Don't fight it," she whispered to him. "It's like being born, Jhon. You have to push your way into the world. You have to follow the will of each contraction and then slide free." She ran her hands over his head and down his neck, stroking him over his shoulders and back until he thought he would purr with pure pleasure. He felt what she was talking about, as if he were hovering on the cusp of two different worlds. One was familiar, with Hanna, full of his overwhelming need for her, and the other . . . the other was vastly different. So much sharper. So keen in its way. His vision changed, color washing out to black and white at first and then slowly the monochrome changed so that the blue of her fabulous skin was the only thing to stand out for him.

His tongue seemed to grow too large for his mouth, so he opened it and began to pant in rough coughs of air. Every muscle in his body went tight and tense, almost to the breaking point and then . . .

Like birth, he slid into the Otherside.

He had thought such an enormous transformation would have to be painful in some way. He had thought he would need to be in motion, concentrating on it or somehow willing it to happen, and that might be true of the future, but like the bellcat instincts that had taken him over during the fight in the bazaar, this just overtook him and was in control before he even knew it. It was strange because at first he felt like a man trapped in a big cat's body, and that it was a bad fit for him, like it was not meant to be. But then, like the aligning of planets to make a perfect horoscope, he settled into his new form as if they'd been the oldest of friends for the longest of times. He was aware of having all of his thoughts and logic firmly intact, but they immediately took a backseat to the call of his instincts, and his instincts were saying he had his mate beneath him.

As if she had read his mind, she rolled back over onto her stomach, settled squarely between his massive paws. He thought then of how fragile her skin was, how easily any one of his claws could puncture her in a deadly manner. She was his mate . . . but only almost.

With one large paw he swiped claws down her back, shredding the back of the gown she wore and exposing the rosettes along her spine. He only had a moment to look at them before they began to spread across her skin and ripple into black fur with barely discernable brown spots. Then she was bucking up against his deep chest, her spine writhing with a soft stroke of fur along his chest, belly, and groin.

That was when he was made to remember the true depth of his lust and need. He desired her more than anything, more than food or warmth or air. She, above all else, was the one thing he needed. He backed away from her slightly, his muzzle skimming her sides and then her rump. He could smell the heat on her, the depth of the musk scent on her making his head spin with need. He nosed his way beneath her tail and then used his rough tongue to lap at her several times, taking her wet taste like the aphrodisiac that it was.

It was all he needed. That and the receptive purr that rolled out of her. Before he could gather his thoughts he was dragging her beneath the huge press of his body, biting her once again on the back of her neck and holding her still. He nudged his way past her tail and in all of an instant was sinking himself deep inside of her.

Here there was no trick to her body, no trap. In this form it was nothing but pure connection done absolutely perfectly. Jhon didn't even think about what he was doing. He had her pinned beneath him and he wasn't going to let her go until he had put his seed into her . . . possibly even his children. The man that he was knew that it was all right, that Hanna would do everything in her power to see that those children were born free. Free of slavery, free of the curse that hung over her family. The mating between them then turned savage and frantic. It wasn't meant to be lovemaking or tenderness, although it was all of that within their minds; it was meant to be a claiming. He was taking her as his mate, for now . . . forever. She would be his and no one else's. He would protect her, care for her, and carry her through good and bad times the best as he was able.

They would face the future together.

And as he felt orgasm racing up on him, he shook her in her place between his jaws to make certain she was well aware of it. She agreed to the message by raising her rump high in the air and making it as easy as possible for him to thrust inside of her. It was an act of total submission.

She was his.

18

When the couple broke apart, they fell aside and out of the Otherside as if they had synchronized the act between them. Changed from their cat selves to man and woman once more, they were left lying on their backs and trying to catch their breath. Hanna had no idea where his sudden change had come from, but she had recognized the struggle the instant she had seen it. She had known the minute he had changed what it was he would demand of her and she was more than willing to give it. Her heart was racing so hard in her chest she felt as if it would explode, but never had she felt so overwhelmingly satisfied. Never had she thought a mating could feel this way. She had never mated while in her bellcat form before, so how would she have known?

It was extraordinary. Purely extraordinary.

Then, suddenly, Hanna sat up with a gasp of shock.

"Lukan!"

Before Jhon could question the outburst she was flying off the bed, trying to redress her tattered clothing onto her body as she ran for the door. Jhon realized she was acting in haste and not thinking and he leaped up to stop her.

"Stop! Hanna, you can't leave the room like this!" He grabbed hold of her arm and pulled her to a halt.

"No! Let me go! I have to see!"

"And everyone in the house will see you naked? I think not." He turned her against her straining body movements and hustled her over to the wardrobe.

"Let me go! You don't understand!"

"I understand that if you run out there baring a spine full of spots your servants are going to ask questions I know for a fact you don't want them to ask. Calm yourself down and put something on!"

"Oh. Yes. You're right," she said, hurrying to grab one of his tunics from the closet. She threw it on over her head and was racing back to the door before he could clothe himself to follow her. She was halfway down the stairs before he caught up with her.

"What is so damn important all of a sudden?"

"Don't you see?" she demanded as she raced for the doors to the family den. She passed her hand over the lock and cursed the mechanism roundly when she did it too fast for it to read. She slowed down almost indiscernibly to do it again, but luckily it was enough to make it work. The doors clicked open and she shoved her way into the room.

There, on his hands and knees and naked among the milling cats, was a grown man.

"Lukan!" Hanna cried again, racing into the thick of the rustling family to throw her arms around him. "It worked! You're here! I was so afraid . . . . I wasn't sure it would really happen!"

That was when Jhon realized he was looking at Hanna's brother, the second oldest of her litter. He remembered then what she had told him, about how he would only shift out of the Otherside if and when the elder sibling mated while in bell-cat form.

He had forgotten all about it. And so had Hanna, in the moment. He didn't doubt that. He had seen the very instant the realization had struck her. Jhon had known it was somewhere on her agenda, but neither of them had even been trying to make it happen. It just had. Now Lukan was there, able to walk on two legs for the first time in his life. Fascinated, Jhon wondered if he would know how to talk, how to walk. Did he even understand what had happened to him?

Of course he did. All he had to do was listen to Hanna speak to him and he knew that Lukan understood. Also, he remembered what it had been like to be the cat. It had been no different for him than it was being the man he now was.

Less emotional about the transformation than Hanna was, Jhon moved through the family to offer a hand to Hanna's newly reborn brother. He was a handsome man, with rugged, angular features and vivid green eyes that were set off in stark relief by his pitch-black hair. Lukan looked up at the hand Jhon offered and then, with a decent case of the shakes running through him, he took the proffered assistance. Jhon braced his feet as Hanna wedged herself against her brother and together they got him to his feet. Then Lukan turned those startling green eyes onto Jhon and spoke his first words.

"Thank you," he said. And it was understood just how deeply that thanks was meant to go. He wasn't just thanking him for his help in standing, but for his help in bringing him fully into a life that had long been denied him.

"Any time," Jhon said with a grin.

Hanna meanwhile was doing less to help him stand and was doing more in the way of hugging him to death. Realizing how overwhelmed the other man clearly was, Jhon pulled her away from Lukan and turned her tearstained face against his chest as he held her close. He watched carefully as Lukan got his balance and Jhon realized all the skills of bipedal life were going to come easily to him, but would still take a bit of doing.

"I should get you some clothes," Hanna said, finally starting to think like the clearheaded woman of logic Jhon knew her to be. She pushed away from Jhon and hurried to do so, leaving Lukan alone with Jhon and the family. But it was immediately clear that Lukan had little interest in his sister's mate. Instead he bent over, risking unbalancing himself, and began to systematically butt his head affectionately against his brothers' and sisters' heads. He scratched them all lovingly between their ears as Jhon had often seen Hanna do. He buried his fingers in their fur and rubbed them fiercely between their hipbones. The reception he got for his loving attentions was dramatic. Every cat in the room and in the gardens came to take part of Lukan's new forms of affection. To Jhon's eye, however, he still acted more like a cat than he did a man. It was clearly going to take some time for him to make the adjustment.

Hanna returned right away, instantly fawning over her brother as if she had never seen him before and, Jhon supposed, she really hadn't. Oh, they had known each other well enough in cat-to-cat form and on cat-to-humanoid levels, but to Hanna this must be like welcoming home a long-lost brother . . . or even a brother gone off to war for all of his life. They were siblings and strangers all at once. Jhon could easily see how Lukan would be a stranger even to himself in this situation.

They helped Lukan figure out clothing and how to dress himself, and then, as if she were taking a member of royalty through her house for the first time, Hanna led Lukan from the room and showed him around the house he had probably never seen before. It made Jhon wonder if she had ever let them out of the enclosure at all. Even when there were no servants around. But, he realized, there were always guards posted on duty and she could never have done anything that would open her up to questions.

No. Lukan had never once been outside of the enclosure.

Suddenly, the chains of slavery paled in comparison. They were prisoners, all of them, of the curse of being locked in the Otherside. It came very sharply to Jhon just then how very hard it must have been on Hanna to stay out of the auction parlors and away from the only resource her family had for freedom. He had judged her so harshly, but the truth was she had to bear the responsibility of more freedoms than just his own. For her to have taken a stand against slave auctions had no doubt cost her very dearly. He also had a suspicion that Najir had attended that auction without his mistress bidding him to. In fact, he would bet that the loyal servant had been haunting auction houses quite diligently on her behalf without ever letting her know.

And how like Hanna to not question him about the hows and whys of how Najir had happened to be there. She just accepted it on faith. It gave Jhon a whole new level of respect for his homeworld companion. Najir, on the surface, was easy to figure out. He was heavily motivated by whatever saw to Hanna's happiness, but Jhon knew there was more depth to him than that. Najir kept quiet about himself and his origins in every other respect. Perhaps one day Jhon would be allowed the opportunity to figure his new friend out, but he had a suspicion it wouldn't be anytime soon.

The remainder of the afternoon was spent showing Lukan the finer points of being a person, like how to manage eating utensils and food that was cooked instead of raw. Eventually the day wore him out and Hanna found him a room he could call his own in the family suites. When Jhon closed the door on Hanna and himself at last, Hanna immediately turned to him and threw her arms around his neck. She hugged him so tightly and for so long that she was in danger of strangling him. Jhon had little choice after a while but to pick her up and carry her to her nearby room, eventually settling them both down on a divan together with her in his lap and his hand stroking down the length of her spine.

"Oh Jhon, I cannot tell you how happy I am," she breathed against his ear after a while. "You will never know how grateful I am to you. You have been the sole reason for this. You have given my brother new life."

"I think you had more than an equal part in these matters," he corrected her. "And Najir as well. A great many drops of fate made this particular waterfall possible."

Hanna moved suddenly to face him, her warm thighs straddling his lap and her hands clutching insistently at his shoulders as she looked him in the eyes. That pretty blue color of hers and the intensity he found within them had the power to take his breath away.

"I feel the most spectacular joy, Jhon. To have my brother here with me as he was always meant to be is something I long ago lost hope of ever expecting to experience. And yet I don't want you to think for a minute that I have forgotten what price you had to pay in order for it to come about. I will never forget that again."

"I didn't think you would," he assured her, reaching forward to kiss her dark little mouth gently. "Enjoy Lukan free of guilt, Hanna," he said. "You do deserve the right to do that. Your family has been heavily weighed down by this curse of the Otherside. I only spent the briefest of times there, but it was long enough to know just how aware I was of who and what I am. I cannot imagine being trapped in a place where all of your life must be spent outside of your true potential."

"I had always thought that it was hard for them to miss what they had never known," she pointed out, "but at the same time they are confined to that room and the enclosure and are not free to see and do whatever it is they want to do. I often thought of taking them to the country place, freeing them to run the range of the vast property we have there and at least give them the illusion of freedom."

"But that would mean giving away your seat of power, Hanna. And I think we all understand that you cannot afford to do that. Not with enemies at your heels and so many dishonest Masters in the COM. The people of this city and those in your family are best served with your voice of truth and reason in the COM."

"That is what I tell myself," she sighed. "But some days it is harder to swallow than others. Today is one of those days where I am torn right down the middle about it. Just earlier I was so grateful I had the power to do something to help you and other slaves like you, and now I see Lukan shakily making his way through the last few hours and realize what an injustice I have done him by not letting him taste freedom until just now. Here he is a full-grown man and he knows little or nothing of the world that he hasn't heard from my two lips."

"Tell me, how do you plan to explain a new brother to those who know this household so well? Even the Baron seems to know exactly who every member of your family is. Something of a disadvantage to living in the public life."

"It will be yet another sacrifice. I can never publicly proclaim him to be my brother. He will have to be introduced as a cousin. We are known to have family in the country places, so it will be easily believed. It will also explain how he will seem so uncomfortable with city life and the ways of the things around him as he learns to live in his new form. But if history tells me anything, it's that learning how to emulate being a person will be the easy part. The hard part is going to be wanting to remain a person. Living a life of an animal is very uncomplicated. I cannot say the same for life as a person."

"Agreed," Jhon said grimly. "He did look a little like a man in shock. It will be a hard transition for him. It is even possible that he may not want to be the person he now is. He may wish to be the bellcat instead."

"At first, perhaps," she agreed, "it is natural to prefer to stick with what you know. But a part of Lukan has long wanted to know the freedom of shifting in and out of the Otherside. It is his birthright."

"And what of Ashanna's reaction to all this when she finally finds out?"

"What of it?" Hanna asked curiously.

"You don't think there will be a problem? Everything she does is to gain attention for herself and standing in this family. With another person to compete against, I don't see her swallowing it well at all."

"Do you really think so?" She pondered it for a long moment. "All of this time I thought she was merely being spoiled and selfish."

"Perhaps there is some of that, but trust me, she does what she does for the sake of gaining attention. And though you think her behavior proves otherwise, she is eager for your approval. Why wouldn't she be? You do not give it lightly. Especially not to her."

"She does nothing to deserve it," Hanna said with a frown. "She goes out of her way to get into trouble. She knows how I hate anything that draws attention to this family."

"Yes, but you never give her leeway for mistakes of youth and always having lived in the shadow of a very impressive older sister. Hell, your parents even named her after you. Everything she does is a cross between striving for an identity of her own that will get the same recognition you get, or she does it out of impulsiveness from her youth. She is at that age where one of two things will come of it. She will either find a way to make her own mark and learn to be satisfied with her own place in the world, or . . ."

"Or?"

"Or she will turn on you, Hanna, and try and take what you have from you. It's the laws of your own people that could aid her, just as they have aided Majum in his bid for power. All he had to do was kill everyone in his own family until it got to a point where he could step into power. Now, I am assuming he has no direct birthright to being Master of the House of Majum, or he would have done away with his nephew as well. He may yet still do so. You yourself said time was growing short. The boy will come of age soon and either he will be a perfect puppet for Majum, letting the Baron rule by pulling his nephew's strings, or he will kill who he has to until he is in power once again. Power is all that man cares about. It's hardwired into him to get it by any means necessary."

"I am afraid for Kell, then. Majum's nephew. He does not strike me as a stupid boy without a mind of his own, nor does he seem as perverse as his uncle is. Oh, I have no doubt that the Baron can dupe him as he has duped many others in the COM for many years, but it will not last for long with Kell. One day he will catch the Baron in his deceit, and if he is not careful Majum will have him killed as he seeks a more biddable marionette. Unfortunately there is a long, strong line of family on Kell's branch of the tree. I wouldn't put it past Majum to cut through every last one of them if that was what it took for him to one day assume the real power of Majum House."

"Just as he is determined to cut through every one of this House to destroy the power of yours."

"Well, it will not work. There are 'cousins' galore to take up the mantle of this House. When he strikes one of us down, another will always appear."

"True, but the pain you will all suffer in the meantime." His hands tightened around her arms. "And regardless of the endless train of brothers and sisters you may have, there is only

one Hanna Drakoulous, and I don't want anything to happen
to her."

The sentiment visibly touched her and he saw her eyes and
features soften toward him. It was a look that had a peculiar
and powerful effect on him. Jhon reached up to brush a thumb
over the rise of her cheek and she turned her face into his entire
palm with a kittenish nuzzle. He smiled at the affection, then
pulled her to the kiss of his lips.

"Ah, Hanna," he breathed into her mouth, "you have the
most unusual power over me."

"Really?" She quirked up a brow. "I think I like the idea of
that," she said smugly.

"That's all right," Jhon chuckled, reaching around to catch
one shapely buttock in his palm, "because I know I have a great
deal of power over you as well."

"Mmm," she purred. "That you do."

Ashanna sat in the dark tavern wearing men's clothing and
with her feet propped up on the table before her. It wasn't that
women weren't allowed in such establishments, it was just that
advertising the fact to the kinds of patrons that attended a dark
corner place like this was likely to get her into trouble. As it
was, the servers were women and they wore very brief and
provocative outfits, clearly as a way of luring in customers. But
Asha could easily see the bruises they sported at the edges of
their clothing from the hard pinches and rude grabs of the
rowdy patrons; apparently the owner didn't care enough about
them to do anything about it.

But that was often the way of things in the Low City. Since
Asha had spent most of her life in the High City, she had never
really been exposed to this level of callousness until about two
years ago when she had started hanging out with her new group
of friends. They were all highborn like she was, second and
third siblings of High Houses, who just happened to find a

thrill in walking around the more dangerous streets of the Low City. They would frequent the taverns, gamble in the odds houses, and party with less sterling types down at the docks. It was actually kind of exciting to see the short flyers come in with their cargo, sitting there wondering where they had just come from, and wondering how they might one day sneak aboard one of them and stow away to the coasts where they could pay for passage off that miserable planet of their birth.

Asha was not trapped there by law like her sister was. She was free to come and go as she pleased, actually. By law, anyway. But then there was the law of Hanna to contend with. Even her brother had been allowed to leave the city, but Hanna had put her foot down at leaving the planet. And all because of the nature of who and what they were. Hanna was afraid that somehow, somewhere, their secret would get out. Hanna was always afraid.

Well, maybe it was okay for Hanna to live a life throttled by fear, but Asha refused to do so. One of these days she was going to find a way to get off this miserable planet and away from suffocating family secrets. She was going to explore the vast unknown of space and other planets. She didn't know how exactly it would all come about, but every step she took was one step closer to the inevitable. She didn't just come out to the Low City to go slumming and to get herself in trouble. She came out here to gamble. She was going to take her allowances and multiply them again and again until she was certain she had what she needed to get out from under her sister's thumb. That was why she had needed to get out of the godforsaken country sooner than her sister had planned. She couldn't earn as much money as quickly as she could here and couldn't do it with as much anonymity and secrecy.

Hanna's new lover was a stroke of pure luck and pure danger all wrapped up in one. On the one hand, Hanna was so preoccupied with her new mate that she was barely paying any attention to Asha. Had he not been there, Hanna probably would have sent her back to the country long ago.

But Jhon was no one to trifle with either. Asha had realized that today when she had faced his full rage. He was far too smart for her own good and he meant what he said when he threatened to keep her in line. She had no doubt about it. So now she was here taking bigger risks to try to earn the jewels she needed to get out of there as soon as possible. She was working on borrowed time and she knew it.

That was why she was taking chances being surrounded by men in a dark corner of this seedy place, playing a card game with them for high stakes. There was always a chance she could lose, she supposed, but she had her keen bellcat senses in her favor. She could smell the ways their bodies told her what kinds of hands they had, when they were winners and when they were bluffing. Their adrenaline would spike, the smell of sweat would grow strong on them, or their excitement would be overpowering. Add that to the fact that she was a hell of a cardplayer, and she had the edge she needed to walk off a winner almost every time.

"I've got six cycles," the man across from her said triumphantly as he laid out his cards for her to see. It was a damn good hand, she had to admit. But this time that good hand was not going to be good enough. Her luck had been running really high tonight and she had drawn a hand that would be almost unbelievable.

"Seven ropes beats that," she said, tossing the cards out for him to see. She reached for the huge pot in the middle of the table, keeping an eye on the rage that was working its way through the loser's body.

"That's impossible," he ground out. "No one has that kind of luck."

"I was just as surprised as you are," she drawled. "Besides, I didn't deal. Your friend to the left did. Are you saying he's a cheater, too?"

Her logic was hard to beat. The two men were, indeed, really good friends. It would take a two-person team to cheat at the game they were playing. Still, the man was not happy to see his jewels sliding away from him and into her significant pile. Asha knew right then that it was time for her to go. She was drawing too much attention to herself and she could see her friends were getting nervous.

"Well, that's enough for me," she said. She reached up a hand and snapped her fingers for the attention of one of the serving girls. The server came up to her quickly, knowing a good tip when she saw one.

"Yes, miss?"

"Bank these for me, will you, sweetie? And take two for yourself. I know exactly how much is there, so don't try to cheat me," she warned the girl as she dumped the pile of jewels on the girl's tray. There was a banking machine behind the bar. It was standard equipment when it came to places like this. No one wanted to walk the dark streets of the Low City with jewels streaming out of their pockets. It was asking for trouble. Especially when there were pissed-off losers at your back. Asha dropped a single-use deposit card on top of the tray as well so they would go straight into her account. "Then I want you to bring these boys each a bottle of whatever they are drinking." She looked at the men she had been playing. "Consider it a peace offering. I'll be back in a day or two and you'll have your chance to break even with me if you think you can."

That seemed to mollify them a little and the tension began to ease away from the group. Asha stood up and shrugged into her jacket. She wore clothes made of lower-grade fabrics, clean and neat but not too rich looking. Nothing like what she wore at home. She didn't want these people knowing who she was and where she came from. It just made for too many risks. Anyone who knew she was the highborn daughter of one of the most powerful houses in the High City wouldn't hesitate to try to find a way to take advantage of it, and the last thing she wanted to do was draw attention to herself any more than she already did with her gambling skill.

Soon. She was almost there. Soon she would be out from under her sister's thumb forever. She would finally be able to come and go as freely as the wind. No one's rules but her own to be followed.

Asha left the bar with Gyro and Hex in tow. As usual, they barely waited until the door of the place shut behind them before they started to crow with laughter.

"Asha, I love how you do that! You fleece these lowborns as easily as you snap your fingers and then leave them wanting more of it!" Hex chuckled as they walked out onto the street.

"Hush up, Hex. Don't gloat too loudly. You never show any sense," she grumbled at him, shoving her hands in her pockets. "One day someone is going to hear you. Just like that last time. And I'm the one who ended up getting into trouble. I'd like to see how funny you would think it is if you got banished out of the cities. You'd just about die from boredom, believe me."

"Yes, that was very bad of your sister to do that. I never understood why she reacted so strongly. It wasn't as though you got hurt or lost the fight. My family would be mad if I got beat down, not if I managed to come out safe and alive and clearly on top," Gyro said.

"The problem was that I was somewhere I wasn't supposed to be, doing something I wasn't supposed to be doing. Hanna almost found out about everything that night. If you two want off this rock with me then you better keep it quiet. I need a team that's going to help me, not hurt me. I have to do this my way or she'll have me called back before we even make it out of dock. I just can't do it. I can't stay here anymore being the little sister of the most powerful woman on the damn planet. It makes me sick."

"We know. We'll keep it cool. Promise," Gyro said, giving Hex a dirty look. "We want out of here just as much as you do. You know that."

"I know. I just want—"

Asha was cut off with a loud grunt as big and powerful bodies came hurtling out of the darkness. She didn't have breath to react as she was taken straight to the ground. Her head smacked into the hard pavement and she saw brilliant stars as pain blossomed across her head and face. Through the sparkling curtain of her daze she saw other men hitting her friends. Hex was thrown against a nearby building and with a muffled blast was shot right in the chest. Gyro was struck in rapid, fierce blows and it wasn't until moonlight glinted off of it that she saw the knife that was stabbing into him. He dropped just as someone stabbed something into her.

She reacted instinctively, throwing the person off of her with a snarl. She rounded up onto her feet in a swift, lithe movement . . .

. . . and dropped right back down to her knees again as her head hazed over with numbing confusion. The bellcat inside of her screamed with a savage sound raging to come free of the Otherside, but the drug that had been injected into her trapped it inside of her and there was absolutely nothing she could do about it. She struggled to remain upright, trying to see the faces of the men who were attacking her, trying to see if it was the men she had just left in the bar.

But why and how would they have a paralytic drug on them? It was much too sophisticated a method of incapacitation for the likes of those who had been at the bar.

That was when she finally saw a face she thought she recognized. Because of the drug, it took a full minute for her to put a name to the face, and by then she had rolled onto the ground on her back.

"Ah," he said. "I see the light of recognition in your eyes." Hyde Sozo bent over her with a half-cocked grin. "I bet you are just now beginning to think, with no little amount of fear, that you are finding yourself in a great deal of trouble. I bet you are lying there hoping that your bitch of a sister can get you out of this mess. In fact, that is what my friend and I are hoping as well."

He didn't need to mention the friend's name. They both knew very well whom he meant.

And Asha was suddenly very afraid for her sister.

19

Hanna woke up to find herself wrapped in Jhon's embrace. It made her smile to know he held on to her so tightly in his sleep. She reached to give his cheek a kiss, but stopped just before touching his face when she realized someone was standing over them.

Staring at them.

"Lukan, what are you doing?" she demanded in a heated whisper. She and Jhon were both naked beneath their covers and she was barely covered herself. Lukan was also just as naked.

"I was watching you sleep," he said simply. "He is most possessive of you."

"And I believe he is also not going to be happy to find his privacy invaded," she warned him.

"Privacy?" Lukan tested the word out on his tongue, almost as if he were tasting it. "What is privacy?"

"It's . . . well, people like to keep things to themselves. Not share it with others. Jhon is not going to be happy to find you here like this. And Lukan, you really have to wear clothes."

"I don't like them," he said with a shrug. "They are tight and itchy. They are most confining." Lukan stepped up onto the bed and, without so much as shaking the mattress, walked over to her side, lowering himself into a crouch until he was balanced with a single hand on the bedding and his knees spread wide. He took a moment to groom back the cowlick at the front of his hair. "You shift so easily between our worlds, Hanna. I do not see how. The freedom is appealing, but the food and smells are strange and confusing. The clothes are unnecessary. There seems to be a lot of work involved in maintaining oneself in this form. Even speech is peculiar. If I had not heard you speak to us so much over the years, I would not know how."

"This is why we were so often tutored in the enclosure, so you would learn with us." Hanna eased herself from Jhon's embrace, but before she could sit up, Lukan turned around and lay down, resting his head and shoulders in her lap. He was so used to sleeping among a pile of big cats, she realized. She wondered if he'd been able to sleep at all.

"Sleep was difficult so I went downstairs and slept with the family," he answered her unspoken question. "You should do that more often. The family misses you a great deal and you have neglected us too often."

Hanna felt instantly guilty, knowing immediately that it was the truth. The older she had gotten the less she had treated them as family and the more she had treated them like big pets. Not that she felt differently for them, because she loved them just as any sibling would, but she would let herself get caught up in her life outside of the enclosure and spending time with them had earned a lower level of importance on her list of many things to manage. It had been wrong of her, and hearing Lukan state his discontent made her feel that extraordinarily so.

"Lukan, I have a mate now. I need to spend my time with him. Alone," she added pointedly.

But the stressor in her voice was lost on him . . . or at least he pretended that it was. "We like your mate. You chose well. Now that he can travel to the Otherside you ought to have him spend more time with the family as well."

"I will do that," she assured him, reaching down to stroke her fingers through his hair, petting him until he smiled and began to purr low in his throat.

"Hanna, do you want to explain why your brother is in our bed? And without his clothes on?" Jhon asked, making her suddenly aware that he had woken up, most likely because of their discussion.

"Jhon, be patient," she begged him softly. "He has been a cat all of his life. He doesn't understand."

Jhon seemed to take that in for a moment, and then he nodded. He sat up and peered at Lukan and his relaxed state in Hanna's lap. The brother and sister made a matched set, both of them having strong and athletic bodies, the same even blue skin except in those darker cobalt areas of intimacy. They both had full dark lips and hair the exact same color. But Lukan's rosette pattern down his spine was far more pronounced and more thickly populated. Jhon wondered if the difference was normal or if it was somehow indicative of the amount of time Lukan had spent in his catlike existence.

"You can't let Lukan go out into the city until he's had time to learn some of the basics," he told her sagely. "The first and most important being the issue of clothing."

"Why are you both so obsessed with all of that fabric? It is most uncomfortable."

"It is also the social norm. If you want to fit in as a normal humanoid, you are going to have to get used to it." Jhon wasn't being harsh when he said it, merely matter of fact.

"I know." He sighed and nudged his sister's hand, which had gone absently still, reminding her to pet him. "We often talk about how we long to be able to leave the Otherside, but I don't think the family realizes just how difficult this is. I am going to have to tell them. Perhaps it will help them to be more content." He paused and looked up at Hanna. "They see you come and go and I think what they want most is freedom. It can be boring to be stuck in the enclosure all of the time." He yawned and his thick lashes began to drift closed.

"You look very tired, Lukan. Why don't you go downstairs and sleep with the family?"

He immediately perked up, liking the idea. He got up off the bed, his big body unfolding into long, lithe limbs much like his sister's. At the edge of the bed he paused a moment, then looked back at Jhon.

"May I ask you a question?"

Jhon was leery, but said, "Of course."

"Do you not find it inconvenient to have your sexual organs hanging out in so vulnerable a place?" Lukan picked up his penis between two fingers and held it in askance, turning it to and fro to view it from all sides.

"Uh . . . yes, sometimes it is very inconvenient," Jhon said as seriously as he could manage when Hanna was biting her lip in an attempt at not giggling. "However, it is also very convenient when it comes to mating."

"I see." Lukan thought about it for a moment.

"Sex was very different for me before I was changed," Jhon said candidly. "It was still pleasurable and intense," he said, "but normal humanoids don't have that sense of smell that your family does. Nor do they give off that distinctly powerful aroma of arousal."

Clearly Jhon was thinking of the last time he had experienced all of those things with Hanna because his tone roughened up and his eyes went dark when he turned them to her.

"I would not know. I have never mated. This, perhaps, is one of the other reasons why we wish to come out from the Otherside. We are all lonely adults with only our brothers and sisters nearby and available to us, and that, of course, is not an acceptable outlet. Because of the level of inbreeding we must even refrain from our cousins."

"Well, Lukan," Jhon said with a grin spreading across his features. "I can tell you right now that clothing is going to seem well worth its weight in discomfort as soon as you manage to get a girl to take hers off."

"Jhon!" Hanna gasped with a laugh.

"Well, it's the truth," he said unrepentantly, chuckling as he dodged her swipe at his head.

"I look forward to that, then," Lukan said eagerly. "Thank you, Jhon."

"You're both terrible." Hanna said, throwing off her covers and getting out of bed. She grabbed her gown up from off the floor where it had ended up at some point last night while Jhon was making love to her. Dropping it over her head with a wriggle to get it into place, she heard the sound of the front door chime being sounded. "Hmm. It's a bit early for visitors. Boys, I am going to bathe and get ready for my session in the COM. Behave yourselves."

Some time later, Jhon and Hanna emerged from their bedroom. Lukan had still been quite tired, so he had gone down to the enclosure to take a nap with the family. Jhon saw Najir at the foot of the stairs as he held Hanna's hand and guided her down. It was their usual routine for them to all go to the COM together. But just as they reached the landing, Najir held out a folded white note card with a blue ribbon wound around it.

"This arrived for you a little while ago. There's no House seal on it and no outside marking as to who sent it. The messenger was most unforthcoming. I am sorry I could not make him tell me who sent it. I don't think he really knew."

"Perhaps the answer lies within the message," Hanna mused, pulling at the ribbon and flipping open the card. If a blue-skinned beauty could go pale, that was exactly what Hanna looked like she was doing. All but the lightest of color drained out of her face, her lips even draining to a fair lavender color.

"Hanna, what is it?" Jhon demanded.

Clearly she couldn't speak, so she just handed over the note with trembling fingers, her hand shaking so hard she nearly dropped it to the floor. Jhon snatched it up and read the lines within.

If you don't want your sister to end up like your mother, you will meet me while COM is in session. And while you are at it, bring one or both of your pretty little toys with you. But alert no one else or she will come back to you worse than dead. I promise you that and you know I am good for my word.

"It's him. It's Majum," Hanna whispered hoarsely. She reached out to steady herself against Jhon's arm. "He has Ashanna. Oh . . ." She clutched her stomach as if she were going to be sick, and indeed she looked deathly ill. And deathly afraid. "How long?" she wondered. "How long has that sick bastard had hold of her?"

"She went out late last night. After you had already retired, my Lady," Najir said gently. "The message came in the breaking of dawn. He hasn't wasted time to play with her. He's not interested in her."

"It's you he wants. You and me," Jhon pointed out.

"Then let's give him what he wants," she said with sudden ferocity, her fist coming up to scrub furiously at the tears skimming down her cheeks. "Let's give him so much of us he will choke on it!"

"That's my girl," Jhon said with fierce pride as he drew her in for the tightest embrace he dared. He meant it as a show of strength and support, and she took it as such. By the time he had stepped back away from her the color had returned to her face and was rising high in her cheeks.

"We cannot go after him in a full frontal assault and he will be expecting us to try and sneak in. What should we do? Why can we not go to the COM with this proof?" Najir asked.

"What proof? The note isn't signed and there is nothing to say it is from Majum."

"The accusation could be enough to get city guards to search his holdings," Najir said.

"She'd be dead and disappeared long before they got to where he's keeping her," Hanna said. She frowned. "There's only one way to do this. I have to go in alone."

"What? No!" Jhon barked. "I won't let you face him alone!"

"I have no intention of facing him alone. I don't have a death wish. What I also do not have is any idea as to where they are holding Ashanna. Majum not only has his main residence but he has a country residence. He could also have many more that I don't even know of. Perhaps somewhere secret where he carries out all his perverse little games. What I do have is two fine warriors on my side, and one of them can track my scent with all ease and be able to find me relatively quickly."

"So you mean to go ahead of us, let him lead you to Ashanna and then have us follow and surprise him. But what if he doesn't bring you to Asha? What if he is lying to you? You know you cannot trust him."

"I know. But I can trust my knowledge of him. Majum thrives on the pain and anguish of others. He knows he will get no reaction out of me by having me alone. The best way to hurt me is by hurting my family . . . and doing so right before my eyes is the only way to make it effective enough for him. He will bring me to her because I will see to it he has no choice. Then, once we are in the same room together, you can come and find me, you and Najir . . . and I think one other person."

"Who else?"

"Lukan. With all of us trapped in a room with him, Majum will have nowhere to go. He will be very surprised to find himself host to four spitting-mad bellcats."

"I don't like it," Jhon said, his anxiety clearly written on his features. "It leaves you alone with him and vulnerable to him for much too long."

Hanna turned to rest comforting hands over his chest. She leaned in to give him a small kiss on his chin. "We don't have any other choice. I know that you see that. You are a tactician, Jhon. If you can see some way of doing this that I am not thinking of, some way that will spare my sister pain and humiliation, please let me know what it is. Believe me when I tell you I loathe the idea of letting him have the opportunity to put so much as a finger on me, but I will do anything to rescue Asha and see that she is safe. Please. Tell me how else I am supposed to do that. And tell me quickly, because every minute we waste is a minute more she is in his power."

Jhon tried to think, wanting so badly to come up with another plan, but he could hardly see straight because of the fear he felt as he looked down into her frank and expectant gaze. The idea of that monster having her in his power was too much for him to bear. He knew men like Majum all too well. He wouldn't be alone, would use his borrowed power to make certain no one could get close to his captive. He would be expecting something like what they were planning.

"Can't we at least do some recon at his home here in the High City and see if we can scent any traces of Asha?" he asked. But he already knew what her answer was going to be.

"It's probably been much too long for us to find and trace a trail of her. And I can't take the chance, the risk of us skulking around his property and possibly being caught. You know he is going to have his guard on high alert, and his security system is every bit as complex as mine. The only way we are going to be able to defeat it is that it's set up to keep people out, not cats. Even so, there's no guarantee you won't be shot or somehow wounded." Her hands clutched tightly around his biceps. "I should be more worried for you than you for me. I can keep him off of us long enough for you to get to us, but there's no telling what you and Lukan are going to run into as you clear the way for Najir."

"Shh." He hushed her gently when he felt her tremble. "This is the type of mission I have trained for all of my life. I will lead them well and easily and I will not let any of us be harmed. Do you trust me to do that?"

"Of course I do," she breathed. "You are the one thing I trust most in this world. I have complete faith in you, Jhon." She turned to look at Najir. "Just as I have complete faith and trust in you, Najir. I know you will not let me down."

"I cannot let you down," he noted grimly, tension wrapped tightly throughout his big body. "I never have before and I am not about to start now." He reached out to briefly touch her cheek, the petting stroke a little too intimate for Jhon's liking, but considering the circumstances he let it slide. Despite what he had promised her, Jhon knew there was a good chance that they would not all make it back in one piece.

"Hanna, you'd best change into something easier to fight in. I know clothing becomes a nonissue once you change into the bellcat, but you may not want to make the change unless you absolutely have no choice. You do not know what kind of witnesses there may end up being," Jhon pointed out.

"I know. I will go do that now. Then we'd better hurry off. I don't want him to have any more time to touch her." She shuddered when she thought of it, then she pushed away from Jhon and ran up the stairs to her room.

That left Najir and Jhon at the foot of the stairs alone together. Jhon turned to Najir with a grim set to his lips. "It's as

THE BID / 273

good a plan as we can come up with in such a short amount of time."

"True, but there is one detail I wish to add," Najir said carefully.

Hanna walked up to the gates of Majum's household, her heart racing in her chest and the snarling bellcat roaring angrily in her mind. No one threatened the family. No one. Majum was going to regret the maneuver if it was the last thing she ever did. And if he had laid so much as a fingertip on her sister, he was going to pay for it in ways even his sadistic mind could never conceive of.

She moved up to the guard at the gate carefully, making sure Majum's cameras could see her approach and that she held her obviously empty arms out to her sides. The leggings and snug shirt she wore clung tightly to her every curve, very obviously showing off that there was no possible way for her to conceal a weapon. What he wouldn't understand until it was much too late was that she herself was a weapon concealed.

"Tell the Baron that Master Drakoulous is here at his bidding," she said softly to the guard, working very hard at keeping the emotions of anger and outrage from being apparent in anything she did. She might be feeling all of those things, but she refused to give him even an ounce of satisfaction by showing it.

The guard didn't even have to call in to check. Apparently they had been told to expect her. The gate opened and the guard walked her up to the main house, letting her through a second locked gate and the front door besides. When she entered the main foyer, she could see straight into the hall and on to the parlor. There her target stood, leaning back against a desk with his arms folded across his chest and his booted feet crossed at the ankles.

Without hesitation, she crossed to him, noticing out of the corner of her eye that his right-hand man, Hyde Sozo, was just out of the line of direct sight, a little deeper into the room, but he came fully into view the minute she crossed the hall. Majum's partner in crime was sitting in a wing chair, one ankle hooked over a knee as he gave the impression of lazing back in the chair. But he wasn't fooling her. She could smell the tension on his body, like a tightly coiled spring that was oh so eager to be released. Sozo wanted to be a part of what was to come every bit as much as his master did. So, not only would she have to manipulate Majum, but she'd have to work through the cooler head that Sozo represented in this little setup. She could easily trick Majum into losing his temper. Sozo, however, was going to be a strong obstacle working against her.

"Well, well," the Baron said. "I was beginning to wonder if you were going to take me up on my invitation. But, of course, Hyde knew you would. He knew you wouldn't leave your poor, defenseless sister here under our tender auspices."

"Where is she? I want to see her and I mean right now. This will go no further if you've harmed her in any way," Hanna warned.

This made Majum laugh. He looked over her head at Sozo. "She says that as if she has a choice now." His cold eyes then turned to her. "You are in my House now. This is my property. These are my guards. What makes you think you are ever going to leave here at all? What happens to you and your sister now are my decision."

"Mmm, except for the part where if I don't call off Najir in the next hour you will find the city guard jumping over your lawns and a delegation of the COM at your door. You really don't think I would be that stupid, do you?"

"That stupid and more," Majum hissed. "If you don't call

off your dog I will see to it that this next hour will live wretchedly in your little sister's memory for the rest of her days. So far she's only gotten to watch us do to others what we will do to her. And believe you me, she is quite thoroughly shaken."

"Where is she?" Hanna demanded through her teeth, her hands curling into fists she could not help. She wanted to claw his throat open right then and there and be done with it, but she knew she had to wait. She had to see Asha first. "Or do I need to call on Kell to ask him where it is you do your dirty deeds?"

"As much as I would have liked to have him round us out into a nice trio"—Majum indicated Sozo—"Kell doesn't have what it takes to understand and enjoy the darker tastes of life. Oh, he certainly has the Majum blood in his bones, his passions running deeply and, I suppose in their own way, darkly, but he simply wouldn't understand our enjoyments. No, Kell will remain ignorant of my pastimes. And you can tattle all you want. The boy trusts me. Thinks I'm a saint, to be perfectly blunt about it. I may have to hand over power of this House to him very soon, as you so kindly pointed out, but with me as his sole and most entrusted adviser, he will make for a very pretty puppet. And if he should grow too independent . . . well, as you also pointed out, I have my ways of dealing with that as well.

"No, Hanna," he continued, "I will always have guardianship over this House in one form or another. And with Kell as the leader of it, it will be no different than it is today. He will vote the way I wish him to vote and he will always resent House Drakoulous for all its committed atrocities during the Feuds."

"Lies. More and more lies until you are living in a house built of them!" Hanna stepped up to him, her blue eyes snapping with fierce determination. "One day Kell will know what a monster you really are, and on that day I will feel nothing but pity for him. He will be crushed by the understanding that he has been holding a viper to his breast all this time. That he has been so sorely manipulated. Yes. That day I will feel very, very sorry for him. But I will also be there for him. One day, Majum, you are going to fall hard and fast, and House Drakoulous will come to Kell's aid, burying all ill will between us once and for all."

"It must be nice," the Baron speculated, "to live in such a dreamy world of pure fantasy. The day you speak of will never come. And even if it does, I assure you that Kell despises your House more than enough to keep this Feud going for generations to come. Now, let us stop talking about the future and focus on the here and now. You have a call to make. Although, I must say I am very surprised to see you here alone. Either it means all that beautiful muscle you were so keen to have houses the soul of a coward who would let you face this trial alone; or you denied him access and he obeyed, making him far more subservient to you than I would have ever given him credit for; or he is waiting in the wings with Najir for this call you are supposed to make in the hopes that you will be able to get a message across to him and let him know where you are."

Baron Majum stood up straight and began to walk casually around her as he posited Jhon's reasons for not being there. "But you underestimate me if you think I am going to allow you to have a chance to let that happen. When you make your call you are going to speak only what I tell you to speak and my friend Sozo will hold your sister's life in his hands for every single second of it. One wrong word and she will die before your eyes."

"Bring her to me. I want to see her and I am not going to breathe so much as a word to Najir of anything if I do not see her here before me. I will never make that call. I can promise you that."

"Such defiance from someone in such a weak position," he

mused. "It's absolutely nauseating. Very well then, I will take you to see your sister and you will make that call."

Before she could even think to react, Majum suddenly punched Hanna right in her face. The single belt was like being hit face on with a sledgehammer; a stunned Hanna could do nothing but fall flat on her back. Dazed with pain and a jostled brain, Hanna couldn't put up a fight as Sozo and Majum dragged her up from the floor and hauled her between them out of the rear exit of the main house. She couldn't even get her feet under her, they moved so swiftly, taking her to one of the many back buildings.

"How do you know she wasn't followed? That they aren't trying to breech the grounds?" Sozo asked his partner.

"Because they can't. I've doubled the guard and you know the alarms going off will give us plenty of time to kill them both and dispose of them. She thinks she still has the upper hand but we are about to show her just how wrong she is."

Leave it to Majum to be so cocky that he did all of his dirty work right there in the main Majum residence in the High City. It was as though he wasn't even afraid of being caught or being seen. Then again, she had a feeling that it was very rare for any of his victims to survive to a point where they could ever accuse him. He was a cold bastard through and through, Hanna thought, but this one time was all it was going to take for him to make a mistake.

Hanna had her senses back in place by the time they were dragging her down several flights of treacherous stairs. At the bottom of the stairs was a door; and they opened it and threw her to the floor inside the room beyond it. This time her reflexes served her well and she caught herself against her hands, her body flying lightly around and up onto her feet. She came up with her fists held up defensively to protect herself while at the same time letting her eyes scan the dungeon they had dragged her to.

To her dismay, there was far more to see than just her sister chained up and banded tightly to the wall, much in the way Jhon had been when he had first come, and just as naked. But she was able to shake off her initial reaction of fury with the utter shock she felt at seeing young children, two in cages and two chained up so tightly they were nearly suspended by their wrists. They were practically *babies*, she realized with horror. The youngest couldn't be a day over thirteen, although she couldn't be certain because he was gaunt with obvious hunger and his face was turned away against the wall. There was a fifth child, a young girl about sixteen, strapped to one of the tables in a spread-eagle fashion. She was there in body, but it only took moments of looking at the glassy vacancy in her eyes to know her mind had left her quite some time ago. And if the bruising on her thin body was anything to go by, Hanna could easily imagine why. They must have been doing horrible things to her for a very long time to have broken her spirit in such a way.

Her throat went tight with impotent rage, and it was all she could do to swallow it down. She could not show how much this all affected her. Not until she was ready to do so. She would not give them that power over her. If she did, then they would do all of that and worse to her own sister.

"This is unbearable," Jhon growled at Najir as he paced around the room for the hundredth time since Hanna had left them. "I want to go after her now! What if he doesn't let her call here?"

"We said we would give her an hour before you tracked her scent and that is what we are going to do. We need to stick to this plan if it is going to work. We both know he isn't going to allow her to say anything to us, and he is counting on that to keep her location a secret. He doesn't know that as soon as that phone rings we can be on his trail." Najir was pacing as well, doing no better than Jhon was at being patient. But they knew they had to give Hanna time to be taken where Asha was or it would all be for nothing. The only one in the room who was calm, it seemed, was Lukan. He was in his bellcat form, sitting perfectly still with only the turn and twitch of his ears showing that he was following the men's movements and their conversation. His tail slowly switched back and forth, the muted gold of his fur broken only by the black rosettes spotted over him.

For the first time Lukan was in his cat form without being in the enclosure. They figured that since they were in Hanna's office no one would be the wiser for it as long as the door was closed. No one ever disturbed her when she was in there anyway.

As if he had no worries for his littermate, Lukan leaped up onto a large chaise and stretched his big muscular body out along the length of it, his natural coloring blending curiously well with the gold and black pattern to the fabric. Now, with lazy half-mast eyes, he could watch the agitated pacing of the other two men.

It wasn't that he wasn't worried for his sister. With a great deal of explanation and with what emotional thoughts he felt bursting from her and these two men, he had come to understand the kind of man this Baron was and what a real danger he might pose.

To anyone else.

But this was Hanna they were speaking of. She was a strong and fit female and Lukan knew that, after having run their House for so long, she was as cunning as the day was long. She would not fall as easy prey to these men who now had her. He just didn't understand why these males did not trust her as Lukan did. Hanna had been in charge of the family for some time now. Did they really think she couldn't take care of herself? Did they think this was the worst challenge she had ever met?

Jhon was yet new to Hanna and did not know her as well, so he could be excused, but Najir should know better. He had been by her side the day she had had to swallow the brutal deaths of their parents. She had had to overcome it all and take charge of all their futures. She would do so again. As far as Lukan was concerned, Asha was as safe as a newborn babe.

A knock sounded at the door. The men were so surprised by it that they halted their steps across the room and looked at one another. Irritated with the interruption, Najir stormed up to the door and pulled it open to give words to the intruder. No one was allowed on these floors from the household staff. Whoever it was had overstepped himself.

That was Najir's last thought before a gun was fired at his chest.

20

Najir fell back under the power of the blast, the big man crashing to the floor. Jhon reacted instantly to the sound of gunfire by dropping down and rolling behind a piece of furniture. It did him little good as the arm of the chair exploded under the second blast of the gun, raining debris down on him. Without a weapon he was trapped and there was nothing he could do about it.

But he realized an instant later that he was thinking like a man. He realized it because a man who did not have that problem used his cat form to launch himself at the attacker. Twice the man's weight and strength, the huge bellcat male wrenched the guard to the ground and clamped his jaws on his shoulder. Within a second there was a bloodcurdling scream from the victim and Jhon poked up his head carefully just in time to see Lukan shaking the man vigorously between his teeth like some kind of giant chew toy. Then with one toss of his head he sent the body of the guard flying into a nearby wall.

"Lukan!" Jhon was on his feet and hurrying forward, his call preventing the cat from leaping for the man's exposed jugular. "Don't kill him! We need him alive!" Jhon scooped up the weapon the guard had helplessly discarded under Lukan's overwhelming attack. He pointed it at the heavily bleeding guard. One of his arms was torn nearly off from the rest of his body, the other hand was raised weakly as if to fend off both man and cat.

"Th-they have m-my family! P-please, if I d-die there will be n-no one to save them!"

"You expect us to show you compassion and leniency when, instead of coming to us, you try and kill us? All but securing the torture and death of your Master? Do you think she would have done such a thing to you? Didn't you even once think of coming to her and telling her this? No. You acted like a coward and betrayed her trust!" Jhon knelt as he spoke, touching the gaping blast wound in Najir's chest. The other man was gasping for breath, proving that the integrity of his lung had been compromised.

"There's nothing she can do! She's never been able to do anything against Majum in all of these years! She even swallowed the death of her own mother for the sake of obeying the law! Even when retribution was deserved!"

"She lives by the law because she knows it is the only way she can make this city better for it," Najir gasped. "She fought with every breath for the end to the Feuds; she was not going to be the first to break the sanctions!"

"Now she has put herself in Majum's hands to save her sister's life and if you had succeeded here—!" Jhon had to stop speaking for fear he would inflame himself to a rash action. His finger was already squeezing the trigger too tightly. "So this was Majum's plan. He isn't afraid in the least to have her there because he planned for all of her support to be annihilated. He may even be planning to let her and Asha go, just so they could come here to find us dead. And it might have worked if not for Lukan."

"Jhon, you and Lukan must go find her now. We cannot afford to wait. I'll stay here." Najir struggled to sit up and Jhon quickly reached to help him, leaving Lukan to snarl at their prisoner to keep him well under control. "I'll be here if she calls." Najir had to pause to suck in several short breaths.

"Her call isn't going to matter. It's his call that will make the difference." Jhon pointed to the wounded guard. "If he tells them he succeeded, then Majum will take his time. If he doesn't tell them we are dead . . ."

"There is no telling what he will do," Najir finished for him.

"Isn't that right?" Jhon demanded. "You are supposed to call him, aren't you?"

A weak nod was the guard's only reply. The traitor was losing blood far too fast. If he didn't make that call for them, if he died first, then all hope might be lost. Jhon moved quickly to Hanna's desk, yanking a cord free from her supplies on her bench. The material was more stiff than pliable, but it would have to do. Stripping off his tunic he knelt beside the guard and very quickly fashioned a cross between a tourniquet and a pressure bandage. He cared nothing for the other man's screams. It was bad enough he was forced to give aid to him above Najir, but if this man died without making his call there was every chance he was going to lose his Hanna.

The very thought of it sickened him. For the first time in a very long time Jhon felt a fear unlike any other. For the first time he wasn't able to grit through the idea of a loss like any good soldier should. Somewhere in the middle of all of this, Hanna had come to mean more to him than anyone else in his whole lifetime. Then, the terrible idea that he might not get the chance to tell her that entered his thoughts and he had to grit his teeth against the nausea that overwhelmed him. Gods, how she had gotten under his skin! Why didn't he think that was a bad thing? He had lived his entire life thinking that attachments would only slow him down, that they were a poison that could only weaken a man against the things he had to face. Even now it felt like poison as it pulsed through his veins, but it didn't matter. It would never matter. All that mattered was Hanna. Somehow she had done to him exactly what she always seemed to do to everyone: she had won his unquestioning loyalty and devotion.

He loved her. More than even Najir could lay claim to, because unlike Najir he would never let her go. He would never willingly turn her into someone else's hands. Never. He would rather die first. And that was what had felt wrong about this entire situation. He had willingly turned her into Majum's hands.

Well, that was a mistake he was going to correct with all due haste.

"Najir." He turned to the other man, roughly shucking off his tunic and then pressing it to the gaping and bleeding wound on Najir's chest. He picked up the other man's hands and forced him to put pressure on his own wound. "I'll get you help as soon as he makes this call. Then Lukan and I will go after her."

He went to get up but Najir grabbed him by his wrist to stay him. Jhon looked at him with impatient questioning. "Tell Hanna . . ."

It was apparently all he had the strength to say, but just the same Jhon nodded. "I know," he said. "I will tell her. But I think she knew the minute you came home and told her about me, Najir. But you made that choice and she's mine now. I'll tell her if something happens to you, but if you survive this . . . and I think you will survive . . . you need to look elsewhere. I'll let you love her like a sister, but I won't stand for anything else. Not in the same house that we are in. You understand?"

Najir nodded and it was clear by his expression that he didn't blame Jhon in the least. Perhaps, if he had it to do all over again, maybe Najir would do it differently, but he was never going to have that chance. Jhon would see to it. He was her mate. He had come together with her on the Otherside and had rebirthed her brother. There was no going back and there would be no getting between them now. Jhon would see to that as well.

He would see to everything.

"So, I see I underestimated the true depths of your depravity," Hanna observed as she indicated the helpless and battered youngsters in the room. "And your cowardice. You couldn't be satisfied with adult slaves, could you? You had to take advantage of the young and helpless creatures I see here, those who can't even defend themselves. Or was it that way with your adult conquests, too? Did you keep them drugged so they couldn't put up a fight? Was their helplessness the only way you could get off, Majum?"

The Baron chuckled, seemingly unfazed by her assumptions. But Hanna's senses were keener than the average woman's. She could smell the surge of anger that pulsed through him. He may not want to show it, but she had struck a chord with that blow.

"Conquests. What a charming word," he mused instead. "Do you like that, Hyde? Conquests?"

"I like it very much," Sozo said as he walked over to the girl who lay in a near comatose state on the table. He smacked her lightly a couple of times, then sighed as if he'd just lost his best friend. "This one's broken," he complained. "She'll be no fun anymore." He eyed Ashanna. "And this one's too old for my usual tastes."

"Never fear, Hyde. If you help me tame the older one I'll be happy to get you something young and unused," Majum assured him. "But first we wait."

"You have less than forty minutes," Hanna warned him. "I wouldn't wait too long if I were you."

No sooner had she finished speaking then the com panel on

the far wall let off a tone indicating an incoming call. "Aha!" the Baron exclaimed. "There we go. Not a very long wait after all."

Hanna's eyes narrowed suspiciously as the Baron brought the call in, keeping one eye on her the entire time. "Go ahead," he greeted the party on the line as if he fully knew what to expect them to say. It was only an instant later before she realized he had put the call on projection so she could hear it. She had a sudden and terrible sinking feeling in her belly to go with the sickly sweet scent of Majum's spiking excitement.

"The two slaves are dead, as ordered," the male on the line said. "I shot them both. Now will you let my family go?"

Cold, untenable fear dropped down the center of Hanna's body. Her head whipped around to take in the chained-up children and she suddenly realized exactly what had happened. "No," she whispered, shock radiating out in her every limb.

Najir. Jhon. She had left them behind thinking they were somewhere safe, but they hadn't been. They'd been exactly where Majum had wanted them to be. Had needed them to be.

"I believe 'yes' is the more appropriate term," the Baron said to her, a devious chuckle filling the room. He was positively in his glory, so she knew it wasn't an act for her benefit. He wholeheartedly believed what the other person was saying and it was giving him a great deal of pleasure to hear it.

"No!" Hanna lurched forward, nails crooked outward as she lunged for Majum. She leaped into the air, her body stretching out at the peak of its arc, and with a brilliant wink of light she crossed into the Otherside. The rippling gold of her fur shuddered as she landed on the Baron, his shocked screams meaning nothing to her.

Najir.

Jhon.

Jhon. Not Jhon! Not Jhon and not her family. Not anyone

else's family either! Never again! No more! She was done with it! Done with playing by the rules and playing fair! Done!

Her claws sank deep and true, the gleaming ivory fangs in her maw as long as Majum's own face. She wished she could burn the image of his expression into her brain, but all she could see was Jhon dead. All the beautiful life ripped out of him. He was dead. He had died a slave.

Because of her. All because of her! Now she would never have a chance to fix it! She would never be able to free him from the confines of the life he'd been sold into. Someone else had done it for her. And now he would never know.

He would never know how deeply, so very deeply, he had embedded himself within her. Deeper than words or lovemaking could ever reach. He was invaluable. Irreplacable. For all he and Najir looked alike, she had never known two men more different. Jhon was so much stronger. So much more powerful!

Was.

She cried out, the scream of the cat echoing in the underground room. She heard Sozo shouting, the shock and terror in his voice something she wanted to bathe in. And then she wanted to bathe in his blood. She wanted them both as dead as her beloved men were dead. Worse. Much worse.

She pinned Majum down beneath her huge paws, her mouth snapping at his throat as he tried to hold her off.

Just long enough.

Suddenly a dark light shimmered over Majum, and to her shock fur now rippled over where skin used to be. Before she could realize it, another muzzle was snapping into the fray, equally long fangs gnashing for her face. But this was no bellcat. It was a firewolf. The reddish brown gleam of his fur marked him as such, and as a full-grown male he easily had weight and power over her. Her only advantage came in her position on top, but she wouldn't keep it long if she allowed herself the time to be shocked by Majum's transformation.

Firewolf! How was this possible? Had they not died out with all the rest in the Apocalypse?

But how could she question it? It stood to reason that if her family could keep its secrets this long, then so could Majum's.

Firewolf.

A vicious lupine scrapper, the firewolf fought best in packs, multiple members taking down prey of all strengths and sizes. They were not meant to fight one on one, but they could if pressed to the point. The bellcat lunged for the wolf's throat, locking down its puncturing teeth with an iron jaw. Even when the only free humanoid left in the room threw a blade deep into her side, she did not let go. She kept locked on and shook her head with all of the strength in her body. Snarls of fury filled the air, half cat and half wolf, but the fact was she had all of the advantage as long as she had his throat.

Thick claws tore into her chest and belly as he grappled her with his front paws and rent her with his back paws. Still she did not let go, and she shook him again as she clamped down harder and harder. The wolf cried out with a high-pitched whine as she pulled her paws into the fray and mauled him in savage, wrestling tussles. Wounded or no, she would kill him and be done with him. She would. And when she was done . . .

The wolf exhaled once, blood spraying into her mouth as the critical arteries in his neck were fully compromised. Air was now bubbling out of a gaping wound in the throat and burst in bloody tattoos against her tongue. The wolf's body went suddenly limp, but still she could not make herself let him go. It had been too quick for him. Too easy. He should have suffered more! He should have felt her pain!

The bellcat felt a heavy weight ramming its side, and she finally let go of her victim to turn on Sozo, who had grabbed the hilt of the blade sunk into her body and was grinding it into her. But he was nothing. A fragile humanoid man who was tossed away with the broad swipe of a single paw.

He was nothing. He had made these children into nothing. Shells without souls, the life and spirit long since burned out of them. And so she treated him like the insignificant creature that he was. She raked him down his spine with one massive paw, yanking him and the knife free of her body. Then she listened to him scream as she batted him to and fro between her paws like a stuffed doll. She threw him up against the wall again and again, his skull and bones cracking sickly over and over. Soon the screaming stopped and she knew he, too, was dead.

She stood over her kills, panting hard for breath, blood dripping from her side. They were useless now. Gone. A poison to no one any longer. As the bloodlust of her rage wore off, she heard weeping in the dark, dismal room. She could hear chains rattling as the children shook in fear of her.

"It's okay. It's okay," Asha kept calling to them. "She won't hurt you. She would never hurt anyone. They had to die or you would never be free!"

Worried now for the fragile minds of those who could still comprehend the world around them, Hanna rolled over and came out of the Otherside. She fell onto the floor on her side, naked and bleeding from the wound in her side and the rending down her front. She panted hard for breath, the pain of her wounds finally being felt now that she was PAN again. She was exhausted, the brief but violent fight having taken everything she had. Still, she was badly wounded and if she took the time to collapse now she might never get another chance to free the children. Without Najir and Jhon to come after her, she was their only hope.

She staggered to her feet after several tries, then fell over the com panel. She realized it was mostly voice commands that controlled everything in the room, but she had to at least try to override it and free her sister so she could free the others. The equipment in the room was pretty old considering, the chains themselves outfitted with key locks. She changed her plans mid thought and reached down for Majum's clothing. Feeling around the pockets and all the seams, she finally came up with an old metal key. Making her way shakily over to the nearest child, she had to hush him gently before she could reach for his shackled wrists.

"Shh. I will not hurt you," she assured him in gasping breaths of pain. She fitted the key to the lock and in two turns freed the boy. Then she pressed the key into his hands. "Free your family. And then, please, my sister. Find a way. If you can't . . ." She collapsed against the wall, sliding down to the floor. "Get help. I have saved your lives. So now, I beg you, say nothing of the cat. Spare my family. I beg you."

Then she passed out.

Jhon knew he made a terrible sight to see as he raced up the steps of the COM, still covered in the blood of two badly wounded men, but he didn't have time to bother with niceties like cleaning himself up. He hurried past the outside guards, but he was aware immediately that he had caught their attention in passing. He put on speed, running for the inner chamber where the Masters were holding session. The doors were open, as traditionally they were, and he could hear the voice of a speaker echoing into the hallways. There was also a second set of guards who were already drawing to an alert state; there was no way in hell they were going to let a wild and bloody slave charge past them and into the inner chambers.

But he had to try. Hanna's life depended on it. There was only one way to safely get onto Majum's property without setting off alarms and alerting guards.

"Master!" Jhon shouted, surging forward past the guards and shouting into the chamber, his voice booming over the present speaker and making the Chamber of Masters break out into startled, rapid whispers.

"Hold!" the guards commanded him, throwing their weight

against him and seizing him by his arms. But still he fought forward, putting brute power into every step until he had lurched over the threshold of the door.

"Master Fusut!" he shouted, making it very clear to them all who he wanted. The man in question got to his feet quickly.

"What is the meaning of this? Why does a slave address me so? Where is your Master?"

"She is in danger. Deadly danger," Jhon said, keeping his voice loud and bold so everyone would hear him. "I come to you because you have proven to be wise and fair. I beg you, my Lord, to hear the plight of my Lady and take action before it is too late!"

"What danger?" he asked, hushing the room fiercely when their speculation threatened to drown out Jhon's reply.

"The Baron Majum kidnapped her young sister." Gasps rang through the room before he could rush to continue. "He sent her a note, taunting her with this fact. My Lady then went to his residence here in the city and put herself into his power in an effort to win her sister's freedom. He then sent an assassin to kill myself and Najir so that no one would be the wiser and he could then keep her for his twisted pleasure."

"You have proof of this? I cannot invade the Baron's privacy on the word of a slave," Fusut said, even as he moved forward toward Jhon and eyed his bloodied state.

"I have the note, which is not signed, and I have the assassin."

"Will the assassin name Majum?"

"No, my Lord. He was very careful to keep his name untouchable. But the assassin was to make a call and tell the person on the other end that we were dead. I forced him to make that call and to do exactly that. I know you see me only as a slave, and that I have very little value in your eyes, but take me at my word, my Lord, when I tell you the voice on the other end of that call was none other than the Baron Majum himself.

He speaks with a very distinct cadence, as you have no doubt noticed for yourself, and there was no mistaking this."

Jhon had to pause to draw in several deep breaths, trying to soothe the racing of his heart and the pure panic that was threatening to pump through him in an endless cycle.

"Even if you do not believe me, let me take you to the side of my Lady and if I be wrong you may do with my life what you will."

That seemed to give the Master significant pause. He walked up to Jhon, searching his eyes carefully.

"You would stake your life on this claim? Because believe me, for a slave to call a Master into question like this only to have the accusation be false, it will lead to your death. There will be no question of it."

"I am staking my life on my Lady, my Lord. She is all that matters. So long as she is well, nothing else will matter to me."

It seemed to be enough for Master Fusut. He turned to the rest of the COM. "I will need four Masters to come with us to bear witness. If what he says is true, Majum must be brought to justice by his peers." He turned back to Jhon and said more softly. "And I pray you know what you are doing."

Jhon could care less about what may or may not become of him. He was soon following Hanna's scent trail straight to Majum House with five Masters and a contingent of city guards in tow. All he wanted was to get onto that property as quickly as possible and free Hanna. Going to the COM and exposing Majum for what he was had been Najir's idea. A good idea. They were a force not to be contested as they stormed the property. They started with the main house but Jhon knew they were no longer there.

"What is the meaning of this?"

The demand was deep and authoritative, despite coming from such a young man. Jhon did not recognize him, but Fusut did and stepped up to where he was rapidly descending the stairs. Jhon felt a sick sinking feeling of dread. Was this going to be an opposition that could sway the Masters to halt their search before it even began?

"Young Master Kell," Fusut greeted him. "I am sorry for the intrusion, but your uncle has been accused of committing a high crime by this slave."

Kell looked up to meet Jhon's eyes. He seemed wary and defensive, but did not act as though he had something specific to hide.

"And what does this slave say about my good uncle? I am certain he is mistaken."

"He says your uncle holds Master Drakoulous and her sister captive here on this property. His proof is somewhat compelling. You understand that we cannot ignore the accusation when their lives might be in immediate danger."

"Drakoulous." The young man frowned darkly, clearly biased against the House. "I confess our Houses have never been friends, but this accusation cannot be true. My uncle would not dare endanger this House by disobeying the Feudal sanctions."

"Then you have no objections to our continuing the search?"

Jhon held his breath. Kell could protest the invasion of his privacy and it could ruin the momentum he had earned so far. He knew Hanna's trail led back behind the house, but he couldn't explain how he knew exactly where to go. He could not tell them that his senses were ten times keener than theirs.

"I welcome your search. Just as I will welcome the justice you will deliver to this slave for his lies against my uncle."

Good enough. It was good enough. Jhon hurried out of the back of the house, picking up her trail so easily he knew just how fresh it was. He was aware of Kell following close behind him. Since he was trying to lead the search in that direction, he welcomed the other man's presence. The Masters would be drawn to follow him more than they would be to a slave.

To his surprise, Kell started to walk in the direction of Hanna's trail. It was almost as if he, too, could sense it.

"My uncle's workrooms are in this house back here. He is probably there even now. He will want to face these charges," Kell announced.

Ah, so that was where they were! And Kell was leading them right to her! Jhon had the urge to grab the boy and hug him, but knew it had to be resisted. He was more interested in finding Hanna anyway. He and Kell hurried to the smaller house together. When they entered, it looked like a craftsman's workshop, with benches and tools lining the walls and a partially carved wooden creature, like some kind of wolf, had been scraped out of a huge chunk of wood. It was almost surreal to see the beauty of the piece, to see an artistic side to a creature so rotted with corruption.

But there was no visible sign of Hanna.

However, he wasn't following his eyesight. He was following her scent trail and she had definitely been in this room. Searching carefully, he came to the end of the trail just as Master Fusut was saying, "He's not here." And then to Jhon, "And neither is your mistress."

"Wait," he said, forgetting to add proper address as he stared at the workbench where her scent seemed to have gone right through it. What was more, he thought he could smell the sharper tang of blood now. They were close! So close! But the smell of blood made his stomach sicken. Were they too late?

"Behind here," he said with all confidence, trying to pull at the bench. There had to be some kind of trick to it. Some kind of lever.

"How do you know that?" Kell asked, his eyes narrowing as he seemed to study the bench carefully. Then, after a moment, Jhon could swear he saw the boy pale under his dark blue skin coloring. "He's right. There's something back there." He looked up and seemed to realize what he had said. "I can feel a draft."

Plausible explanation, but Jhon was starting to get just as suspicious of Kell as Kell was becoming of him. He put it aside and started pulling at tools. It didn't take long to find the lever, making the bench swing away from the wall. The Masters behind them gasped, but Kell grabbed a working light from the bench and wasted no time pushing ahead into the stairwell.

Jhon had overtaken him and run ahead of him by the time they hit the second flight. With his extraordinary eyesight he could see just fine in the dark, and he wasn't about to waste a single second getting to Hanna.

He burst into the room, the surprise in his barreling action causing several frightened screams from within. Then he just stood there a moment, trying to take in the horror of what he was seeing. The children. Asha. Blood everywhere. A dead man and a mauled beast of some kind.

And Hanna.

"Hanna!"

Jhon was on his knees by her side in a heartbeat. He ignored everything else, Asha's cries for help where she was lashed to the wall, the shocked gasps of the Masters and even Kell's heartfelt curse. All he could see, all he could feel was Hanna. She lay naked in a pool of blood, most of which was her own. She was slumped forward over herself and the floor, her long hair barely concealing the speckling along her spine. He saw her dress on the floor and scooped it up, pulling it over her as carefully and as swiftly as he could. Let them think he did it for the sake of her modesty. Let them think whatever they wanted. Let them know the truth of it. Jhon did not care. All he cared about was that her skin was cold to the touch and her breathing was hardly discernable. She had a vicious wound in her side and something had raked her down the front. He held her close as tears of fear and impotence burned in his eyes. He had to get her home. She needed to be safe and cared for. He needed to get her out of this disgusting pit Majum had brought her to. It enraged him to think that Majum wasn't there . . . but only for a moment because as he gathered Hanna close to his chest he realized he could smell Majum all over the place. Most specifically, where the dead wolf lay.

Understanding dawned and he looked to meet the eyes of the young man Kell, who had taken a knee beside the thing's mutilated carcass. By the expression on Kell's face, Jhon could see that he knew it was his uncle.

So. It appeared Hanna's House was not the only one with secrets.

Kell met Jhon's starkly knowing eyes and gave him a little nod before saying aloud, "It appears this slave's accusations are all too true. This is a sad day for my House. Masters, I assure you that as soon as I find my uncle he will be delivered to you for justice. You may search the entire property until you find him." Kell rose to full height and looked down into Jhon's eyes from above. "Bring her to the house. I will see she gets the very best of care. I . . . I thought I knew my uncle. I do not know how I could have been so very wrong."

Jhon heard the bitterness and anger in his young voice and felt compelled to say, "Men such as this have always had their ways of keeping their depraved secrets. Even from those closest to them."

Kell nodded, and then turned to the communications panel. "Release the restraints," he told it.

On command, the computer released Asha's restraints, exposing how raw she was at all contact points. Despite obvious weakness, she managed to keep her back against the wall, hiding the spots down her spine until she requested one of the Master's robes to wear and had herself safely concealed. Then she hurried to Jhon, who was carrying her sister out.

"Is she alive?"

"Barely," he replied.

"Young man, can you tell us who did this to you? Can you tell us what happened here?" one of the Masters was asking one of the male children. Jhon stopped and turned, looking at how the boy cowered away from anyone trying to touch him. He hesitated, knowing by the look of the place what the children must have seen. He could only hope that if the child started ranting about a woman who could become a bellcat, they would put it down to the ravings of a damaged and fragile mind.

But the boy did speak up.

"The man came in with the firewolf. It attacked her."

And that was all. He wasn't willing to say more, and probably wouldn't for some time . . . if ever. But his gesture had been clear even before his dark, haunted eyes looked up to unsteadily look at Jhon's.

They would keep her secret.

21

Hanna's eyes fluttered open, her lashes sticking together at first. Long enough for her to realize her mouth was equally gluey and she was very thirsty. Then, she felt two large hands swallow the whole of her face between them and, as if pouring water on a desert, a wondrous sensation of lips pressing to hers. She'd know those lips anywhere, and those hands as well. She unstuck her lashes by opening her eyes wide and then cringed when the light seemed suddenly too bright.

"Shh, shh, shh," Jhon soothed her softly when she tried to move. It was a good thing, too. Just gearing up to make movement had tensed her muscles enough to send alarming pain rocketing up and down her body. Her entire torso lit up as if it were on fire and she groaned against his mouth.

"Jhon, w-what—?"

"Easy. You're home and both you and Asha are safe."

Her eyes widened at the mention of Asha's name. Instantly she tried to sit up, but he was having none of that and blocked her with the low bridge of his body over hers.

"Asha?" She looked around her bed to see if her sister was there.

"She's been here for two days, right by your side, waiting for you to wake up," he told her just as her eyes fell on her sister, who lay curled up in bed beside her, fast asleep. She had both of her hands clasped around one of Hanna's, and the purplish coloring under her eyes spoke of the truth in Jhon's words. She had not had much in the way of rest recently. Her young face looked strained in a way Hanna had never seen before. She wore no makeup, her hair was left to simply fall where it would, and she wore such a plain little dress that Hanna hardly recognized her. She looked younger than usual, and vulnerable in a way she wasn't used to seeing.

"Did he hurt her?" she blurted out, squeezing her sister's hand where it rested in hers. "Jhon, did he hurt her?"

"Not that I know of," he said, gently stroking his fingers over her cheek. "But I am not certain I am the one she would tell."

"I'm not certain I'm the one she would tell either," Hanna said, her voice tight with emotion all of a sudden. "To be honest, I know very little about her. It used to be different. We used to be closer. But then . . . then our parents died."

"Trauma like that changes people," he noted, reaching for her free hand so he could bring it up to the press of his lips. "Trauma like this changes people."

"Then I want her to be just as stubborn and willful as ever. I want there to be no trauma. I want to take it back for her." She swallowed as tears swam over her eyes, blurring the image of her sister.

"We can't do that. No more than we can change the damage that was done to you."

That got her attention and she looked at him. "Is it bad? Am I badly hurt?"

"If you were anyone else, you'd probably be dead, Hanna," he said, his voice very stark as he did so. "I just thank the gods for those very special genetics of yours. The doctor is completely baffled by you, I'll have you know. He has no idea how you managed to pull through. Don't worry," he assured her as she geared up to say what he knew she was going to ask. "I made certain I was with you every moment. No one saw anything about you that you wouldn't want them to see. They stitched you up right here in the house and I made a big stink about being the only one to take care of you. To bathe away the blood on you. To change the bandages. With Asha's help, they had to listen."

"Thank you," she breathed. "But did the children say anything? Oh Jhon, are they all right? I saw them locked away down there and all I could think about was that someone was probably as worried sick for them as I was for Ashanna."

"Someone was. That someone was one of your guards. He tried to kill Najir and myself as a way of getting them back." She gasped and immediately tried to look him over, to check him for injury. "No, no. Not me," he said softly.

Her eyes shot up to his and he saw them widen with fear. She bit her bottom lip so hard she was sure to puncture it. He knew what she would ask him, if she could only find the courage to do so, so he took the initiative for her.

"He's badly injured. He was shot. And unlike you and I, he doesn't have the benefit of an advanced immune system. An infection has set in. His fever has been pretty high and the doctors are worried. But," he tendered, "they do not know Najir like you and I do. He is far too strong and much too loyal to you to simply let you go so easily."

"Oh Jhon. If he dies it will be all my—"

"All Majum's fault," he interjected. "Do not take responsibility for the acts of that madman. I won't have it, Hanna."

"Jhon, Majum was like me," she said. But she hastily corrected herself when she saw the glare he gave her. "I mean, he was from the Otherside. One of the other breeds. I couldn't believe it when I saw it. And that means his whole family is from the Otherside. Kell . . . all his cousins and more. They are the firewolf. It's a fierce fighter, a pack animal. Very different from the bellcat."

"And yet very much the same," Jhon noted. "It makes me wonder if there are other families who were able to survive the Apocalypse who could travel to the Otherside."

"Believe me, it is shocking that even one has survived this long, and highly improbable that there are two. I do not have those types of illusions."

"Perhaps it is at the root of this feud between your families," Jhon speculated. "You said yourself that you don't know what started it all. It seems to me that the lupine and the feline would be very natural enemies."

"More than you know. In the wild they prey on one another. You are not at all wrong about the possibility." Hanna pushed him back a little so she could feel the bandages wrapped around her chest and belly. "The scars may fade," she said hesitantly, peeking up at him through her lashes.

"Don't make me turn you over my knee," he warned her darkly.

"I only meant—"

"I know what you meant. You think it will matter to me if all this perfection suddenly has a blemish or two?" He indicated down the length of her body. "Do you really think I am so shallow a man?"

"No. No, not at all. Maybe I'm just that shallow a woman. I'm sorry," she said sincerely, reaching to stroke her finger over his stubbly chin and jaw. "I say such stupid things sometimes. You'd never know I am a great public speaker."

"This isn't public," he relented, "and you've been through a great deal. I am very inclined to forgive you."

"Well, thank you." Her small smile faded. "I should get up and see Najir. Are you certain he will be all right?"

"I said he would be, didn't I?" The look that stole over him was pure suspicion. "Why are you so hot to see Najir?"

"Because he is my friend and a loyal companion, that's why. Jhon, don't be this way. You know it's you that I . . . that I care about the most."

"Is that true or are you just saying it to appease me?" He sounded almost petulant.

"Jhon! Of course it's true! Don't you know what it did to me to hear that you were dead? It tore me up inside! I went crazy! Jhon, I love you. More than anything, except my family. I went to pieces when I thought he had hurt y—"

She was cut off by a strong and fervent kiss. He ate at her mouth like a starving man, trying hard not to crush her in his passion. He couldn't help himself. Hearing her say those words meant as much to him as hearing she was going to survive her ordeal. He was projecting very tellingly with his sudden actions, so she laughed and told him again.

"I love you, Jhon. Not just because you came from the right place and looked the right way. I just can't help myself. You're so strong and stubborn and you have such a righteous soul. You make me so much better than I was before. I hope you know that."

"I know it well," he replied hotly as he kissed her again. "I know it because I feel the same way. I love more about you than just the fact that I depend on you to show me around this world of being the bellcat. Your caution and the way you care about this family, the way you take on all of the PAN to see your ideas and what is right come to fruition. You'd risk everything for anyone, family or no, just because you know it is the right thing to do. I love you because you make me crazy!"

She laughed at that, trying not to cry and failing miserably. The sobs made her side ache, but she wasn't about to complain. She was in between the huge, loving hands of a man who loved her. A true mate. No longer just a convenient one. Now she would know what it had been like for her parents. For her uncle and his mate. Now she would know what it felt like to have a perfectly reciprocal love.

"Can I ask you something?" Jhon said, clearly reading her thought. "Why is it you and Najir never ... why me and not him? Not that I am wishing it be any other way, but ... why wasn't he good enough?"

"Didn't I tell you? They had doctored his eyes at the auction. Once I realized they weren't really bellcat green, I was afraid to try to bring him over to the Otherside. I was afraid to do even the littlest thing different."

"But he loves you, Hanna. What kept you from him for ten years? What is so different about us?"

"I wish I could tell you. Even if he had been right, had the right eyes ... I would love him, I would be his mate but it wouldn't feel like this. I don't know. Maybe it's because you would never have accepted your fate as a slave. Maybe the fact that you would always fight rather than be so easily won over. Maybe that is what I needed to love you." She sighed. "Najir is a good man. A strong man. But he's not the one for me. Perhaps one day he will find what we have found with each other. But it will never be with me."

"You're damn right it won't be with you," he said fiercely.

"No. There will never be anyone for me but you. And I am going to prove it to you."

Epilogue

"Hanna, you shouldn't be doing this. You should be at home and resting. It's too soon," Asha fretted as she stood on one side of her sister. Jhon stood on the other, and together they were helping her to ascend the long flight of stairs leading up to the Chamber of Masters. It frustrated Asha that she couldn't get her sister to see reason. It had only been three days since Hanna had woken up from her ordeal. The power of the bellcat at her command or not, it did her no good at all to be climbing all those stairs and then spending the day arguing with a bunch of politicians.

"You know, I think I liked it better when you didn't give a damn what happened to me," Hanna joked. "Stop mothering me. I'll be fine."

But the remark made Asha draw to a halt, making Hanna stop and look at her questioningly.

"I always gave a damn," she said with a very deep frown. "I know I didn't show it, but I do care what happens to you. I always have. You're more important to me than I led you to believe. I'm sorry you think so poorly of me."

"I don't think poorly of you at all. I think you are young with a great deal of ambition, and that you felt overshadowed by your elder sister." At Asha's look of surprise she said, "You see. I do know you better than you think I do. For instance, I know that you have been working very hard at saving enough money to do something. Perhaps leave the planet?"

"Hanna! How do you know that?" she gasped in shock.

It said something for the change in their relationship that Asha didn't spin off into a long chain of denials. It made Hanna smile, as did the gape-mouthed surprise of her sister. "Darling, you are saving money in the very same banks that I use. Though you suppose them to be beholden to your privacy, you forget that they work on the principle of earning money. And since our House is one of the richest in this city, it was only a matter of time before it came to my attention in one form or another. As for where you are trying to go, it was the only thing that made sense. I have a great deal of power and prestige here. The only way to get out from underneath that is to leave it all behind.

"It's a daring and brave choice," she continued. "Am I happy about it? No. It's dangerous out there and you have a secret that needs to be kept. I don't want my sister in danger. I don't want our secret in danger. But," she said when she saw the deep and obstinate frown that began to crease her sister's features, "I also understand your motivations and I know you are more than capable of taking care of yourself. I know that you know just how important it is to keep this secret of ours. I also know that you are long since an adult with the right to make her own choices in things like this."

The surprise on Asha's face was clear. The last thing she had ever expected was that Hanna would actually approve of this venture she wanted to go on.

"Why wouldn't I endorse it?" Hanna asked. "It's no different than our brother wanting to go off on a voyage of discovery. He chose to remain on this planet, but it's still a dangerous expedition. I wouldn't think of hindering you any more or less than I tried to hinder him. In the end I realize it must be your choice. That I must give you my trust."

Asha honestly could not believe her ears, but at the same time she didn't know why she was so surprised. There was a reason Hanna was the head of their House, and it had very little to do with being the eldest. Hanna, she realized, was made to manage all the ins and outs of such a large and complex family. All of these years Asha had fought to compete with her sister, but the fact was, Hanna was in a league of her own. There was no way to compete. They were both cut too differently and meant to excel in different ways. Asha would prove that one day. One day soon.

"So you're saying I can leave? You won't oppose me?"

Hanna smiled and urged her forward toward the stairs again. They began to climb once more. "No. And what's more I will give you access to the remainder of the money that you need so you can do so right away if you wish."

Asha was stunned and didn't know what to say other than, "Thank you."

They finished the journey to the top of the COM in silence. Jhon and Asha brought her inside, all of them ignoring the murmers and glances of surprise and speculation. Obviously, everyone in the Chamber of Masters was privy to the dangers Hanna had faced at the Baron's hands, and they were all curious as to how she was faring. Most of all, though, they were curious as to why she was there. She had made a point of securing the podium for a speech. They wondered what it was she had to say.

They sat down, waiting through the preliminaries that were always done before the session was opened to the floor, and then at Master Fusut's nod, Jhon got up and helped Hanna to the lectern. Once she had her hands on the marble of it and could steady herself, he stepped back . . . yet he made certain he was no more than a single stride away from her. He wanted to be there to support her if she needed it in the matter of a second.

"My fellow Masters of the Chamber. My fellow Masters of the High Houses," she began. "I will keep this direct and brief since I know I will grow tired quickly and you, no doubt, will grow tired of listening to me." This earned her a ripple of chuckles, and Jhon smiled at her back. "You all know the ordeal my family has been made to face recently. Let me assure you that, while it has only driven this point home to me, I have long since had this issue on my mind. My friends, I am here to announce to you today that I have every intention of seeing slavery abolished on this planet. And"—she raised her voice at the immediate clamor that arose—"that I am going to start by setting much more of an example than I have been to date. You see, I thought it was enough to avoid auctions and to employ, for the most part, only free men and women in my household.

"But it was not enough. It was half measures, and lackadaisical ones at that. Well, my friends, I am not a lackadaisical woman. I do nothing in half measure. I intend to make these changes, to argue with you stubbornly until I have wrestled you to the ground and have made you see the errors of our ways. I intend to do that by setting the example. As of today, I am setting free all the slaves of my household."

The uproar was unbelievable. Most of it was, obviously, against her. Slaves were a matter of fear in their society. The citizens feared their own infertility. Feared not being able to bring new generations into their world. If slavery was abolished, how would they ever be able to defeat that fear?

Hanna had the answer to that.

"Instead of using slaves to assure our future generations, instead of perpetuating this cruel demeaning bondage, I suggest to you that we try a different method. One that may, in the end, be less costly to us, both financially and as a society. I suggest we lure free men and women here with bounties and rewards. That we pay for the surrogates we need—not forcefully, but freely. We ask their permission. We coax them to us. It will open the borders of our world to a massive influx of off-worlders, adding much needed and much varied DNA to our gene pool, and, just as important, an influx of economic opportunities. Instead of the single costly trade of slaves, we will open this world to trade, tourism, and more. People seeking these bounties will need places to stay, food to eat, and more of the luxuries that our businesses can provide."

The room went suddenly quiet. Jhon had not known she was going to do this today. He had not known she had thought it through so thoroughly. He had not realized, until then, what a truly powerful politician she was. He was so stunned and so damn proud of her that he could barely keep in one place. He realized that by solving all the issues the PAN may take against her, she had pre-empted their arguments. And, by solving their problems, she had also solved her own. Opening this world up to a massive influx of fortune seekers would open her family up to the possibility of future mates. Instead of waiting for just the right slave to come along every few years, now they could go directly to the source planet and advertise for the men and women they might need.

It was brilliant.

But he made no mistake about it; this was only the beginning of a long battle. It would take more than a single speech to convince those who were not only inured in their ways, but were afraid of what it might mean to let go of them.

"I realize that it will take an act of this body to actually be able to free slaves," she said, "since it has never been done before. But I am here today to begin by asking you to vote on the right of each household to independently set free whatever slaves they wish to. These precious men and women who have given us our children, defended our needs and"—she turned to indicate Jhon—"saved our very lives must be allowed to be recognized. They must be allowed to walk our world as free beings if we, the heads of those households, deem they should do so. They can then enjoy all of the same rights as any natural member of this society. Please. I beg of you to hold a vote today that will see these rights be put into power, for I know I am not the only one who has this much gratitude toward a bound person that they wish to give them the rights they deserve in return. Start with this one step, and then we will discuss the rest."

Jhon saw her bend forward and knew she'd had all she could take. He stepped up to support her and, unable to help himself in his joy and pride, he pressed a kiss to her temple.

"Thank you," he whispered in her ear.

"No. Thank you, Jhon. They will vote with me today, I think," she said softly, "and you will soon be free to come and go as you like." She looked up into his eyes. "You could leave me and this world if you liked."

"I could," he agreed. "But having the choice to do as I please in that matter was all I ever wanted. The actual leaving, however, will never happen. I will never leave you, and you are never allowed to leave me."

"Now you see," she murmured with a smile as she leaned into him. "You have been mistaken, Jhon. You are not the slave here. It is I who has a chained heart and soul. I am yours and always will be."

"Isn't it funny?" he asked. "For all this tying together and chaining of souls, I will never feel freer than I do in this moment."

She smiled at him and, in front of the entire Chamber, she

stood up on her toes and touched her mouth to his. Let them know what her true motivations were. Let them know she loved him.

It would let them know that she would not rest until she had her way.